Punky Brewster™

by
JOELLE SELLNER
and
LESLEY VAMOS

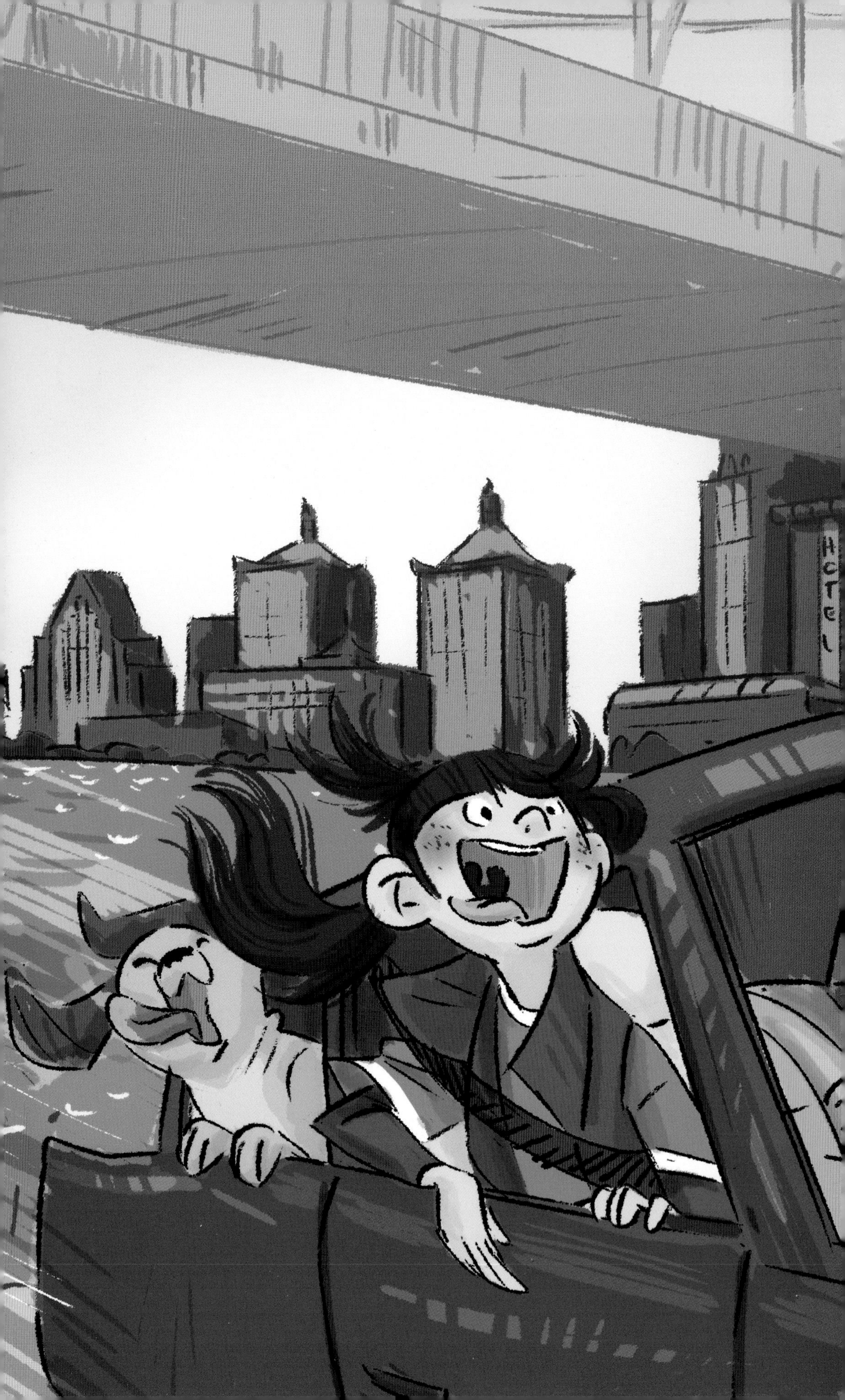
HOTEL

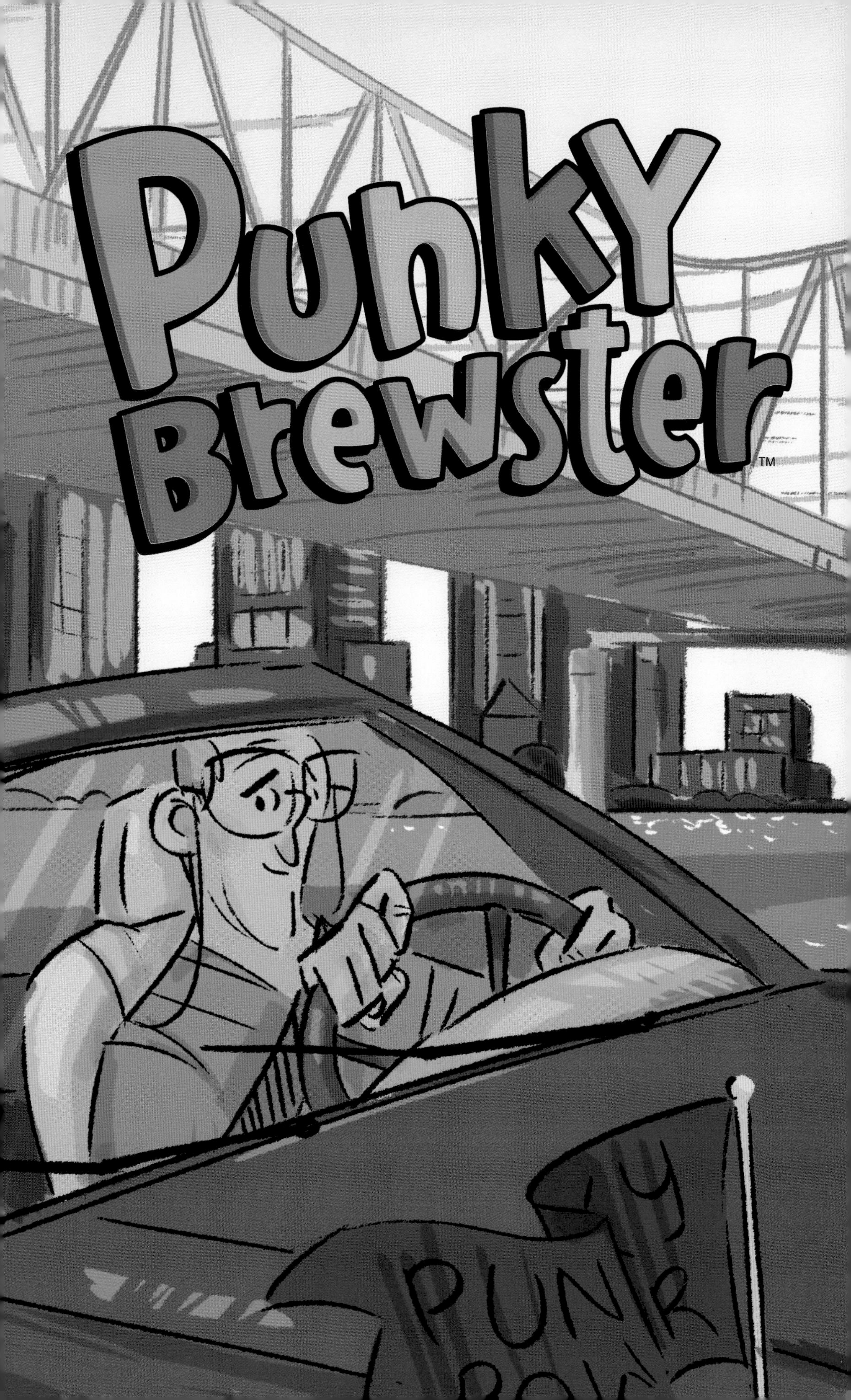
Punky
Brewster™

JOELLE SELLNER
WRITER

LESLEY VAMOS
ARTIST

STEVE WANDS
LETTERS

ANDREW ARNOLD
DESIGN

ADAM STAFFARONI
EDITOR

PUNKY BREWSTER CREATED BY
DAVID W. DUCLON

Publisher's Cataloging-In-Publication Data
(Prepared by The Donohue Group, Inc.)

Sellner, Joelle.
   Punky Brewster. [Vol. 1] / Joelle Sellner, writer ; Lesley Vamos, artist ; Steve Wands, letters ; Andrew Arnold, book design ; Adam Staffaroni, editor ; Punky Brewster created by David W. Duclon.

   pages : color illustrations ; cm

   Summary: Punky Brewster, a bright eight-year-old girl, has been abandoned by her mother and lives on the streets of Chicago with her puppy sidekick Brandon. Punky thinks she doesn't need help, but after getting picked up by the police, she enters a foster home and starts to search for a family. Punky meets Henry, a long-lost relative, and decides he's the adoptive dad for her. All she has to do is convince the foster home, adoption judges and lawyers, and possibly Henry himself.
   Based on the television series, Punky Brewster.
   Interest grade level: 006-010.
   Issued also as an ebook.
   ISBN: 978-1-63140-314-9

1. Brewster, Punky--Comic books, strips, etc. 2. Foster children--Comic books, strips, etc. 3. Abandoned children--Comic books, strips, etc. 4. Girls--Comic books, strips, etc. 5. Puppies--Comic books, strips, etc. 6. Graphic novels. 7. Domestic fiction, American. I. Vamos, Lesley. II. Wands, Steve. III. Arnold, Andrew (Artist) IV. Staffaroni, Adam. V. Duclon, David W., 1950- VI. Title. VII. Title: Based on (work) Punky Brewster (Television program)

PN6727.S45 P86 2015
813/.6 [Fic]

J-GN
PUNKY BREWSTER
62-8167

ROAR COMICS Brought to you by **ROAR COMICS**, an imprint of **LION FORGE COMICS**

ISBN: 978-1-63140-314-9   18 17 16 15   2 3 4 5

LION FORGE COMICS
LIONFORGE.COM

David Steward II, Chief Executive Officer
Carl Reed, Chief Creative Officer
Sanjiv Teelock, Chief Operating Officer
DeWayne Booker, Director of Licensing
Shannon Eric Denton, Senior Editor
Adam Staffaroni, Senior Editor
Jesse Post, Marketing Director
Ike Reed, Director of Digital Media

IDW PUBLISHING

Ted Adams, CEO & Publisher
Greg Goldstein, President & COO
Robbie Robbins, EVP/Sr. Graphic Artist
Chris Ryall, Chief Creative Officer/Editor-in-Chief
Matthew Ruzicka, CPA, Chief Financial Officer
Alan Payne, VP of Sales
Dirk Wood, VP of Marketing
Lorelei Bunjes, VP of Digital Services
Jeff Webber, VP of Digital Publishing & Business Development

TABLE OF CONTENTS

CHAPTER 1

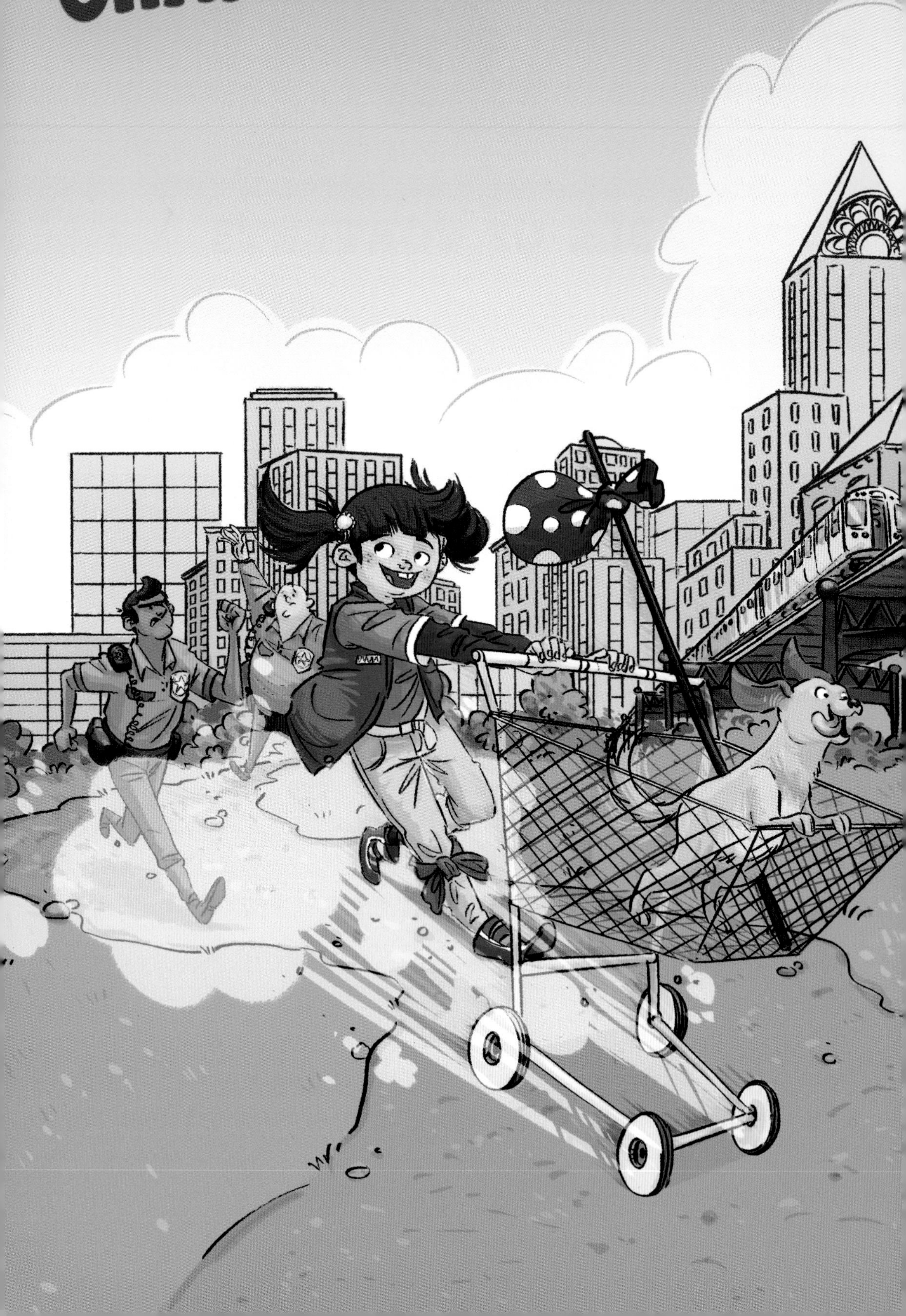

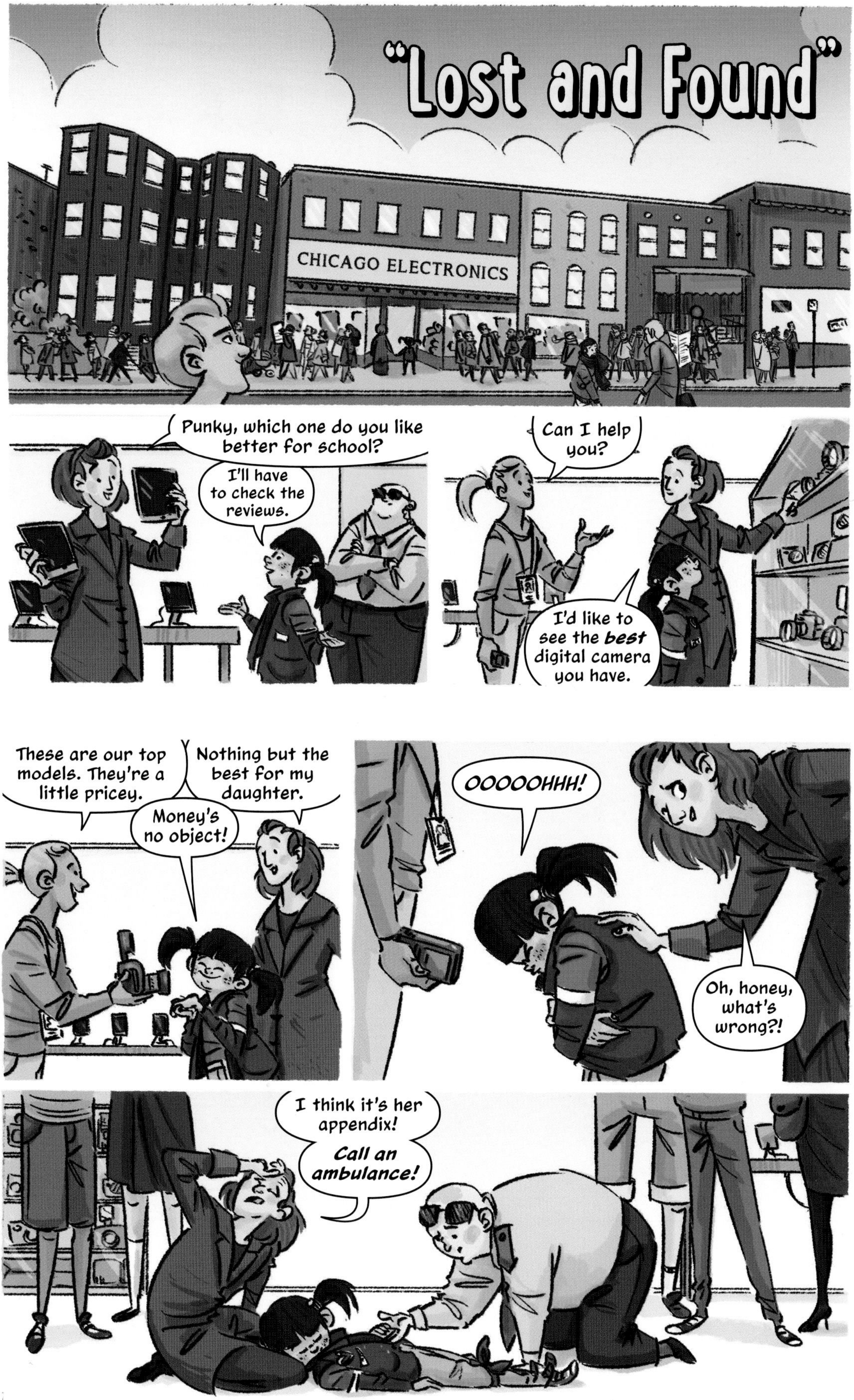
"Lost and Found"
CHICAGO ELECTRONICS
Punky, which one do you like better for school?
I'll have to check the reviews.
Can I help you?
I'd like to see the *best* digital camera you have.
These are our top models. They're a little pricey.
Nothing but the best for my daughter.
Money's no object!
OOOOOHHH!
Oh, honey, what's wrong?!
I think it's her appendix!
Call an ambulance!

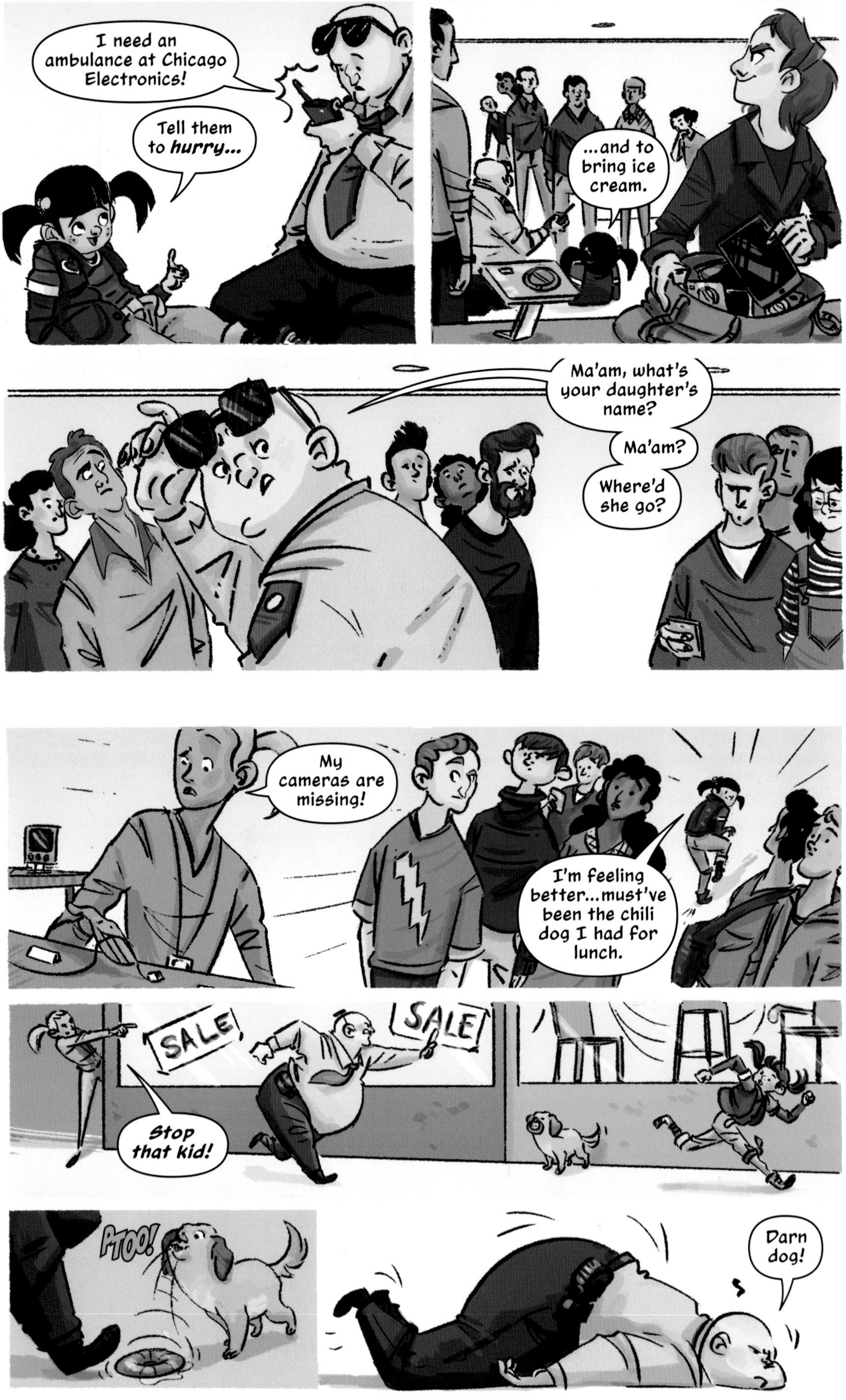
I need an ambulance at Chicago Electronics!
Tell them to *hurry...*
...and to bring ice cream.
Ma'am, what's your daughter's name?
Ma'am?
Where'd she go?
My cameras are missing!
I'm feeling better...must've been the chili dog I had for lunch.
SALE
SALE
Stop that kid!
PTOO!
Darn dog!

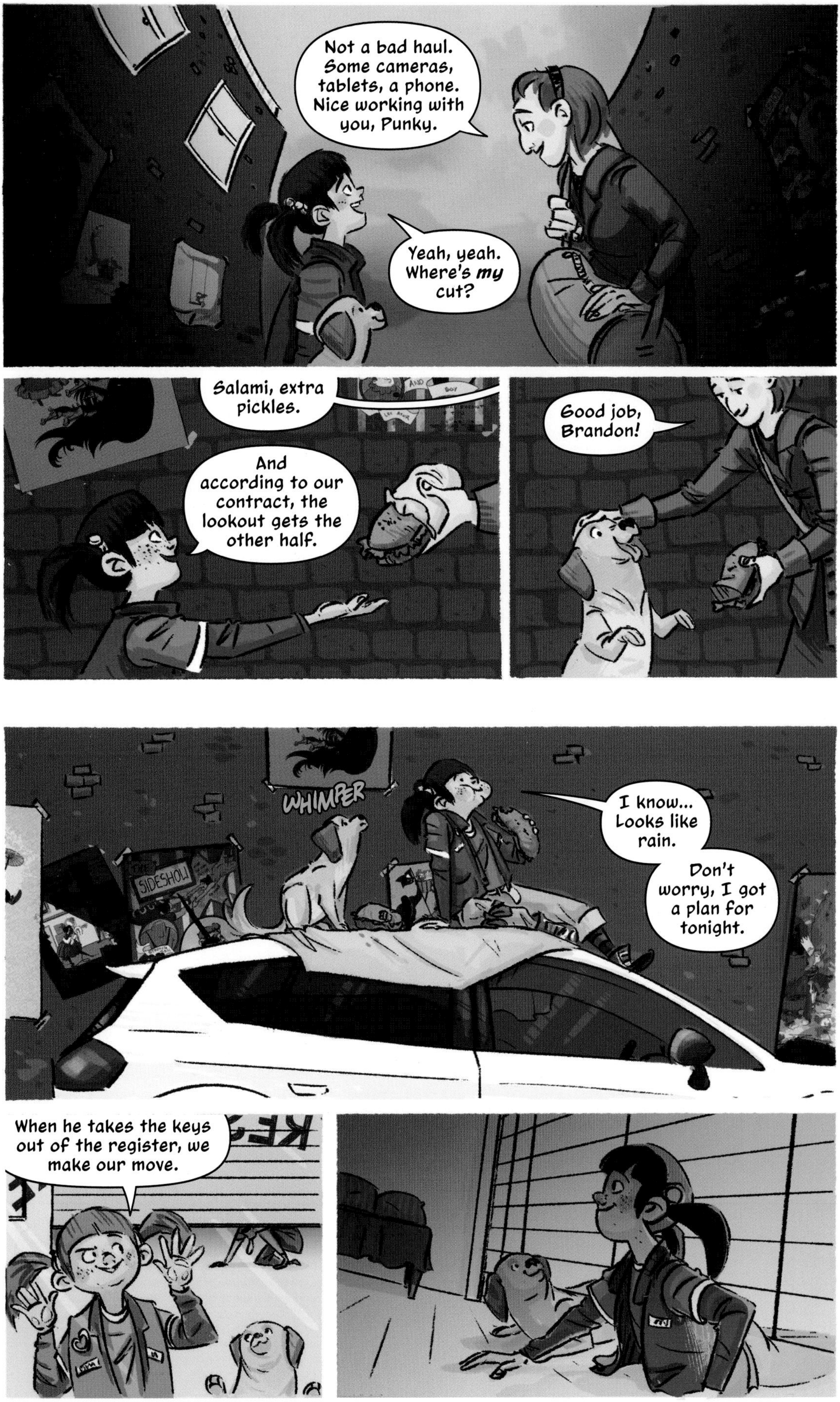
Not a bad haul. Some cameras, tablets, a phone. Nice working with you, Punky.
Yeah, yeah. Where's *my* cut?
Salami, extra pickles.
And according to our contract, the lookout gets the other half.
Good job, Brandon!
SIDESHOW
WHIMPER
I know... Looks like rain.
Don't worry, I got a plan for tonight.
When he takes the keys out of the register, we make our move.

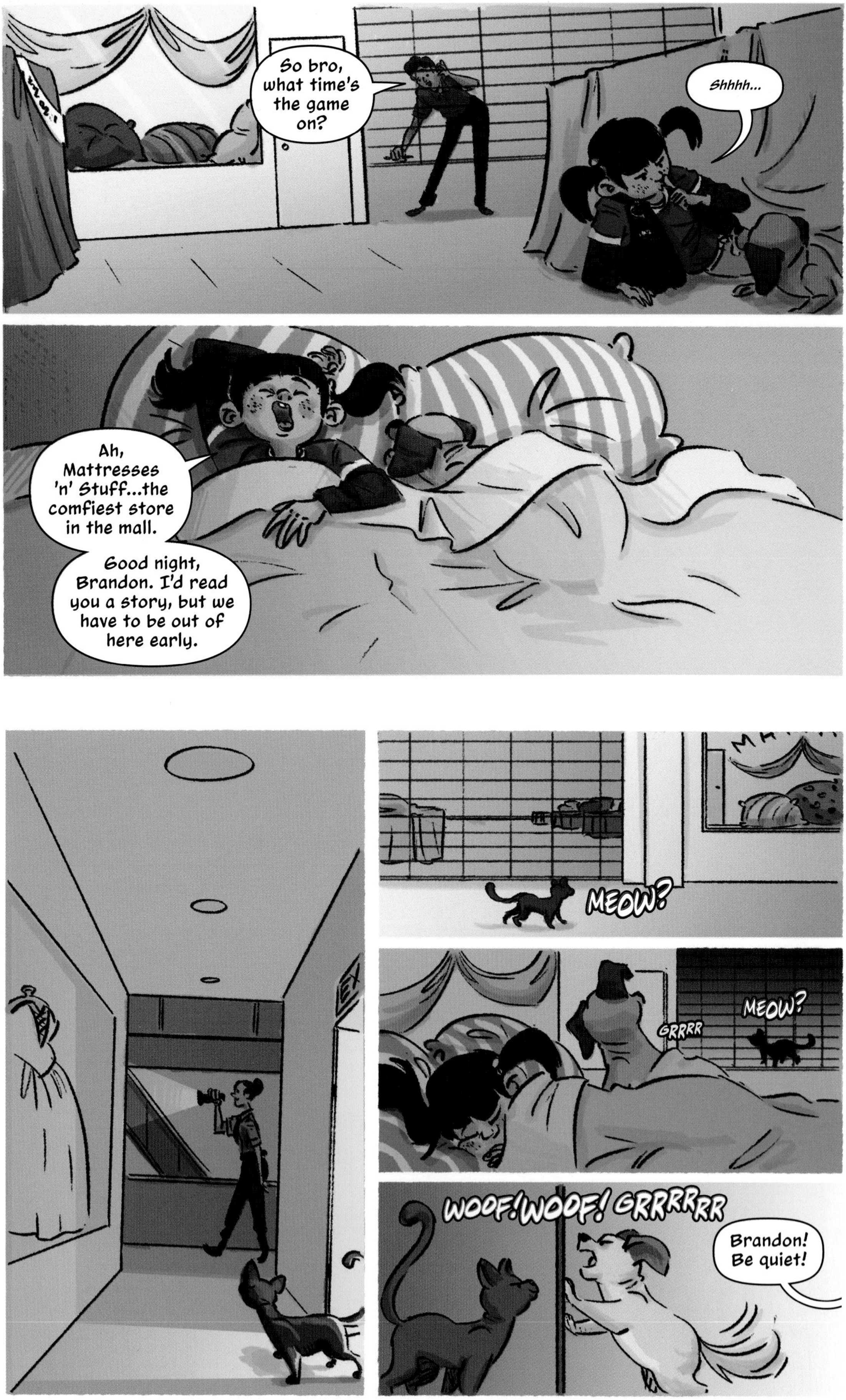
So bro, what time's the game on?
Shhhh...
Ah, Mattresses 'n' Stuff...the comfiest store in the mall.
Good night, Brandon. I'd read you a story, but we have to be out of here early.
MEOW?
GRRRR
MEOW?
WOOF! WOOF! GRRRRRR
Brandon! Be quiet!

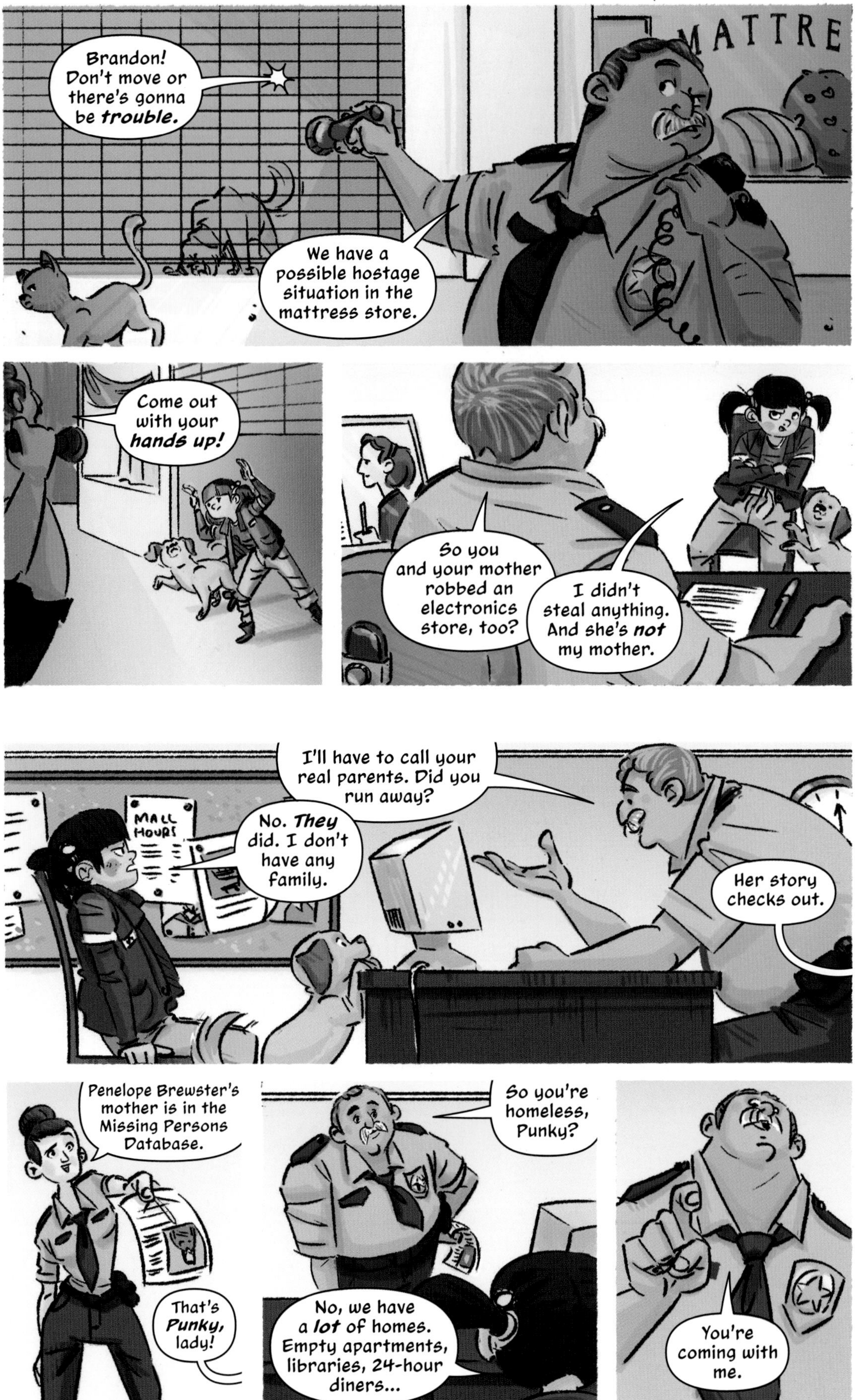
Brandon! Don't move or there's gonna be trouble.
We have a possible hostage situation in the mattress store.
Come out with your hands up!
So you and your mother robbed an electronics store, too?
I didn't steal anything. And she's not my mother.
I'll have to call your real parents. Did you run away?
No. They did. I don't have any family.
Her story checks out.
Penelope Brewster's mother is in the Missing Persons Database.
That's Punky, lady!
So you're homeless, Punky?
No, we have a lot of homes. Empty apartments, libraries, 24-hour diners...
You're coming with me.

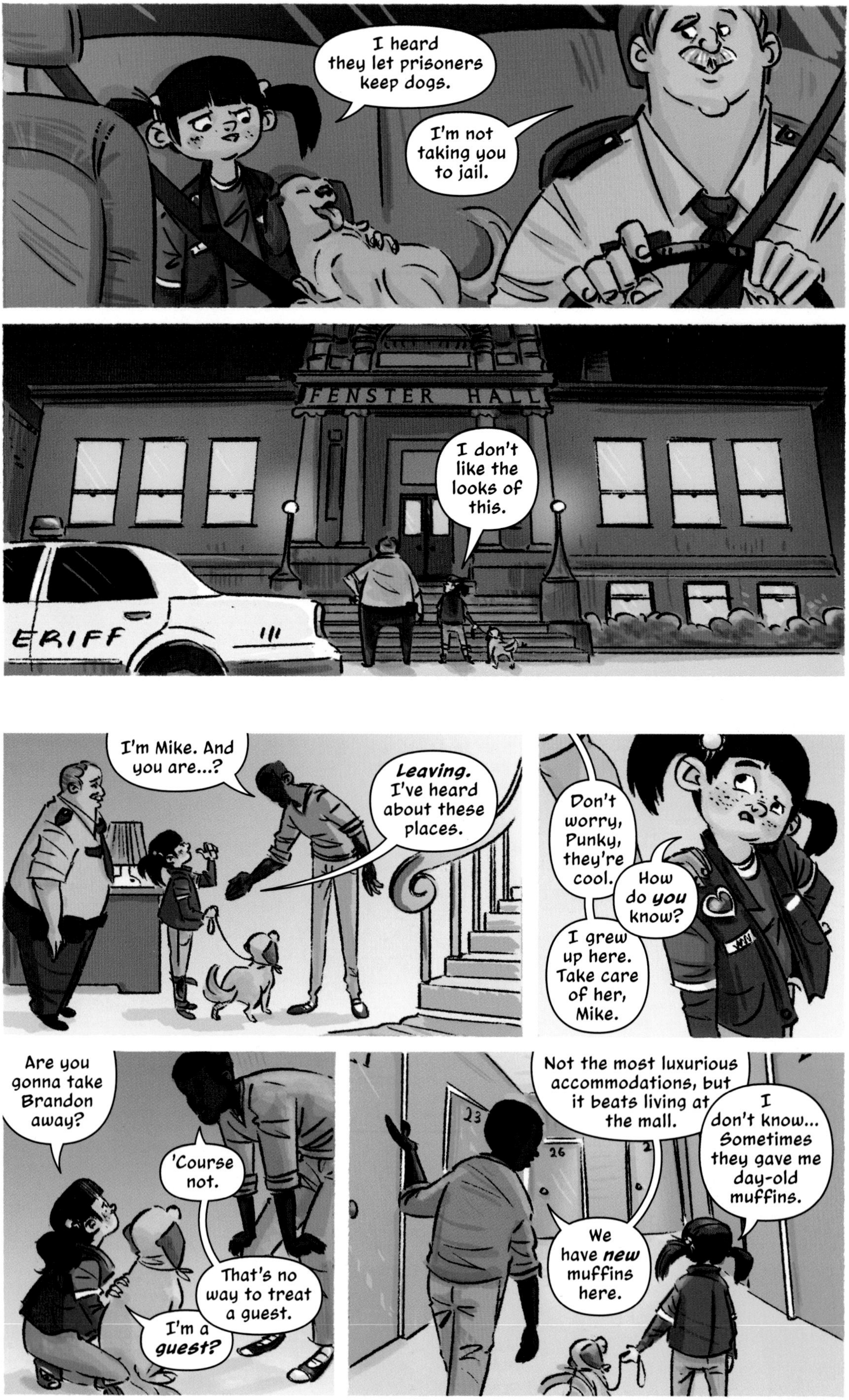
I heard they let prisoners keep dogs.
I'm not taking you to jail.
FENSTER HALL
I don't like the looks of this.
ERIFF
I'm Mike. And you are...?
Leaving. I've heard about these places.
Don't worry, Punky, they're cool.
How do *you* know?
I grew up here. Take care of her, Mike.
Are you gonna take Brandon away?
'Course not.
That's no way to treat a guest.
I'm a *guest?*
Not the most luxurious accommodations, but it beats living at the mall.
I don't know... Sometimes they gave me day-old muffins.
We have *new* muffins here.

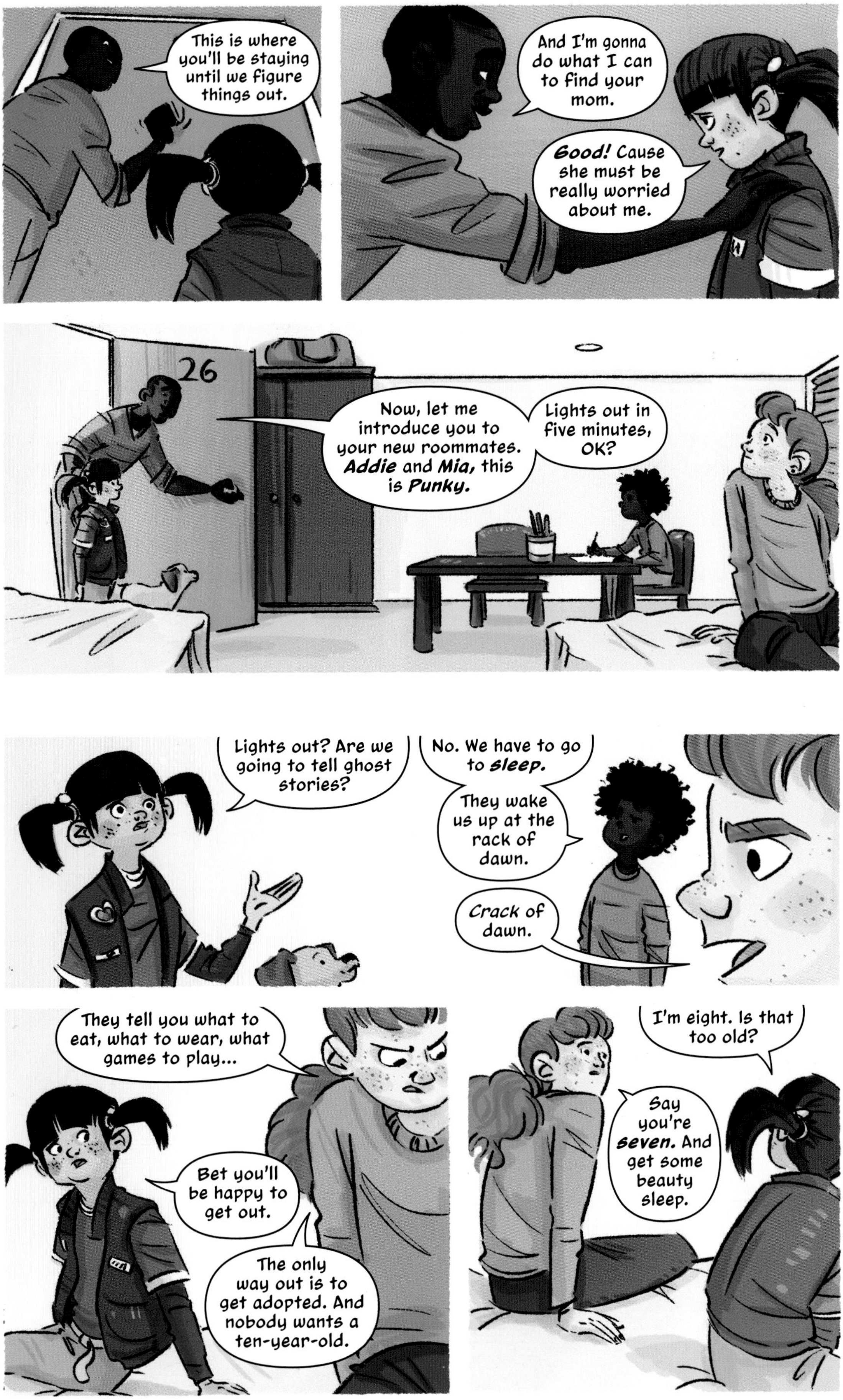
This is where you'll be staying until we figure things out.
And I'm gonna do what I can to find your mom.
Good! Cause she must be really worried about me.
26
Now, let me introduce you to your new roommates. Addie and Mia, this is Punky.
Lights out in five minutes, OK?
Lights out? Are we going to tell ghost stories?
No. We have to go to sleep.
They wake us up at the rack of dawn.
Crack of dawn.
They tell you what to eat, what to wear, what games to play...
Bet you'll be happy to get out.
The only way out is to get adopted. And nobody wants a ten-year-old.
I'm eight. Is that too old?
Say you're seven. And get some beauty sleep.

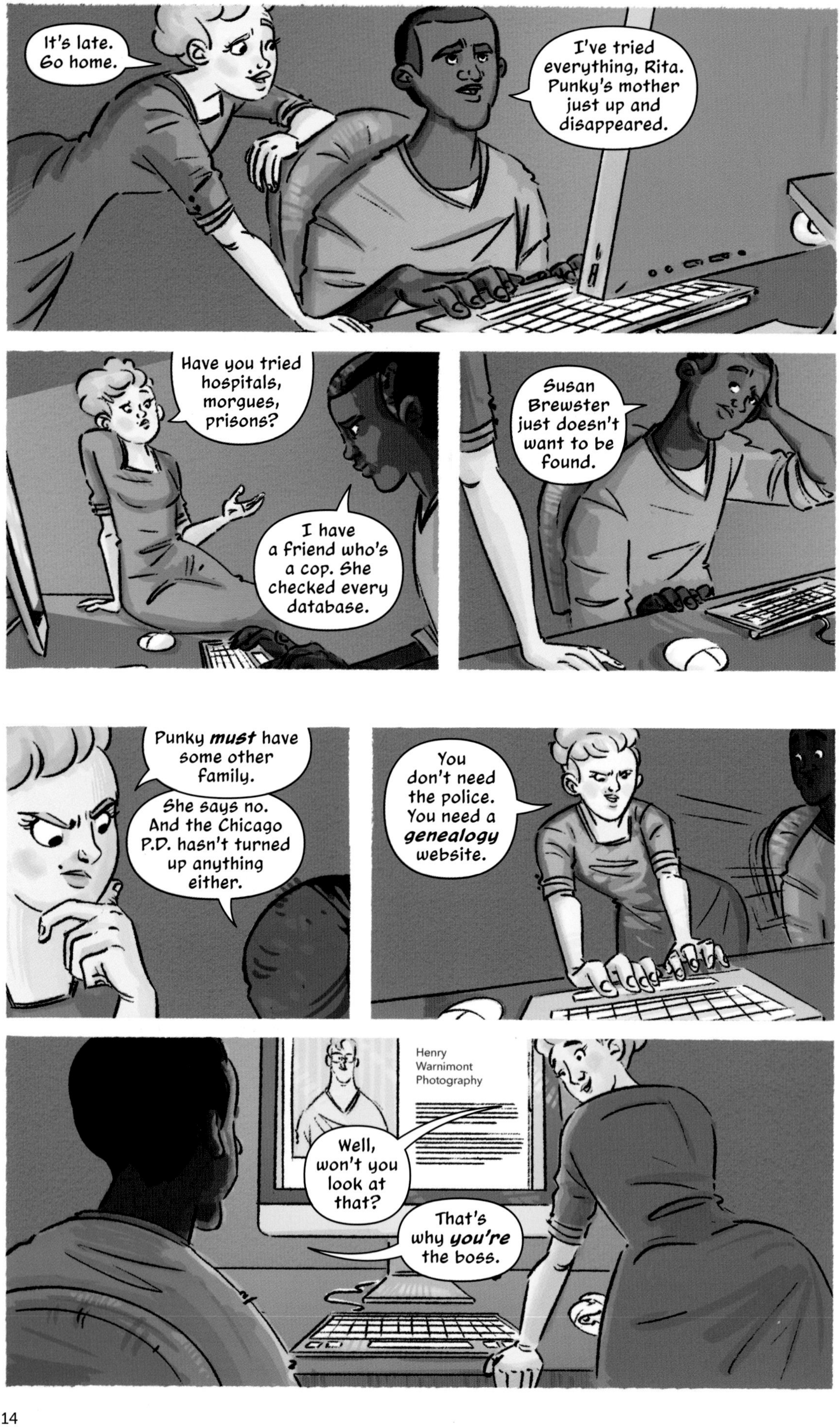
It's late. Go home.
I've tried everything, Rita. Punky's mother just up and disappeared.
Have you tried hospitals, morgues, prisons?
I have a friend who's a cop. She checked every database.
Susan Brewster just doesn't want to be found.
Punky must have some other family.
She says no. And the Chicago P.D. hasn't turned up anything either.
You don't need the police. You need a genealogy website.
Henry Warnimont Photography
Well, won't you look at that?
That's why you're the boss.

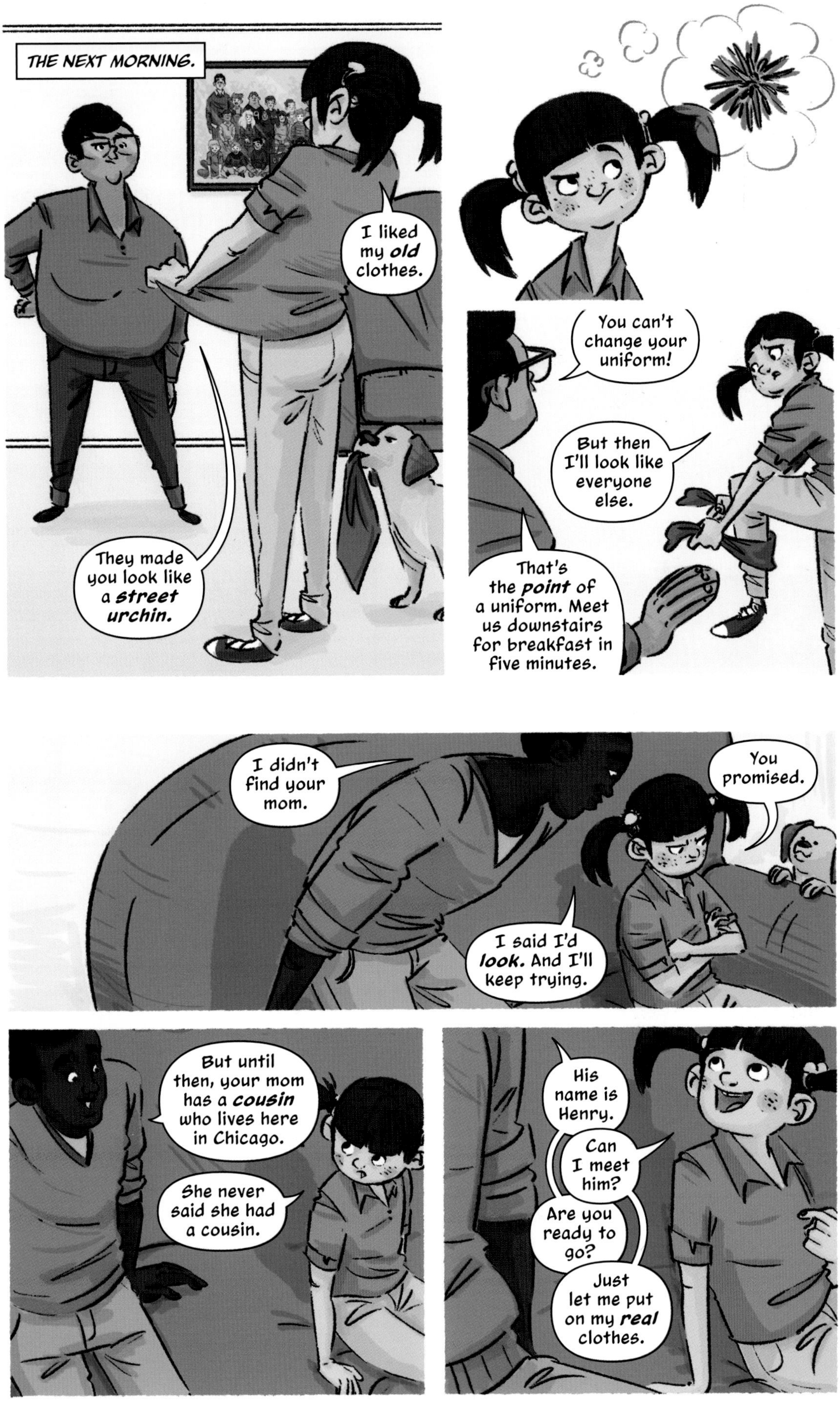

THE NEXT MORNING.
I liked my *old* clothes.
They made you look like a ***street urchin.***
You can't change your uniform!
But then I'll look like everyone else.
That's the ***point*** of a uniform. Meet us downstairs for breakfast in five minutes.
I didn't find your mom.
You promised.
I said I'd ***look.*** And I'll keep trying.
But until then, your mom has a ***cousin*** who lives here in Chicago.
She never said she had a cousin.
His name is Henry.
Can I meet him?
Are you ready to go?
Just let me put on my ***real*** clothes.

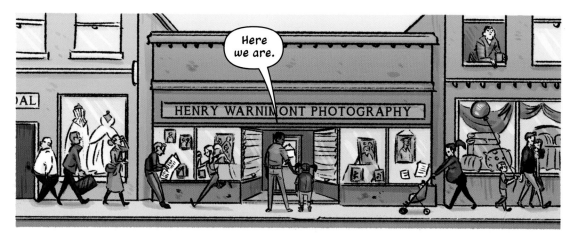

Here we are.

HENRY WARNIMONT PHOTOGRAPHY

Warnimont is *my* cousin. I want to ring it.

OK. And call him *Henry*.

BZZZZZZ

Somebody's coming!

open

RUFF

Henry must be super slow. How old is he again?

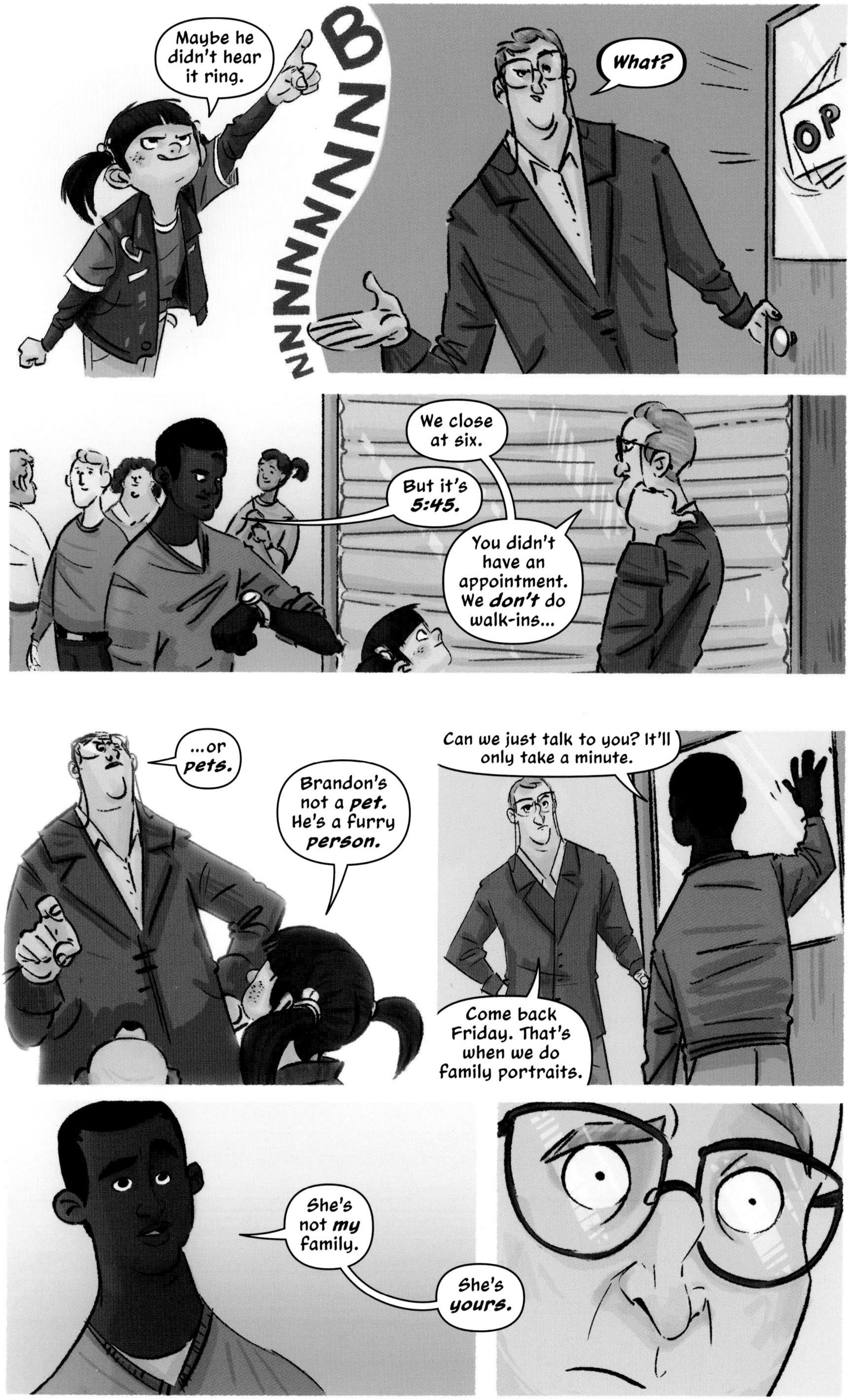
Maybe he didn't hear it ring.
BZZNNNNNNNN
What?
OP
We close at six.
But it's *5:45.*
You didn't have an appointment. We *don't* do walk-ins...
...or *pets.*
Brandon's not a *pet.* He's a furry *person.*
Can we just talk to you? It'll only take a minute.
Come back Friday. That's when we do family portraits.
She's not *my* family.
She's *yours.*

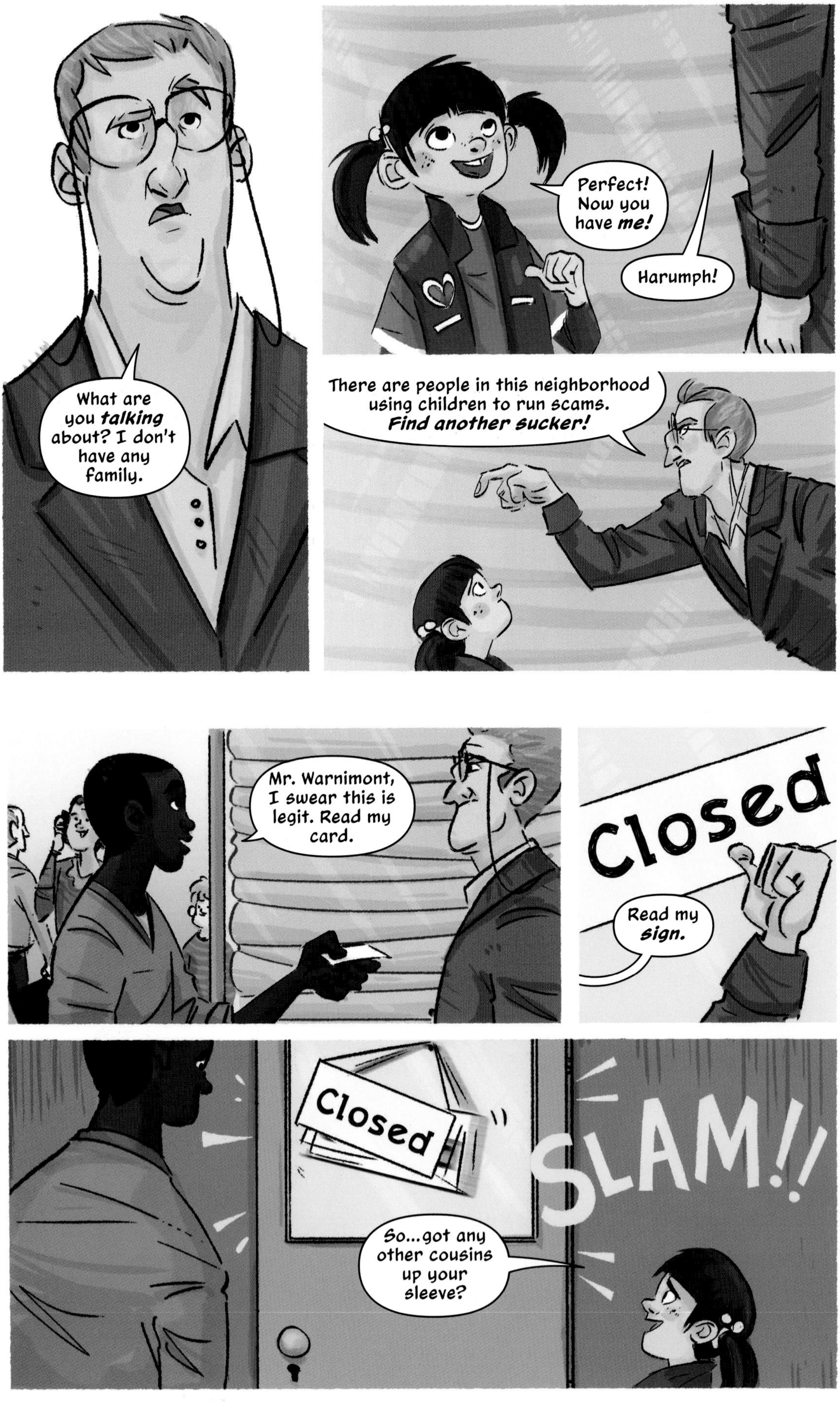
What are you *talking* about? I don't have any family.
Perfect! Now you have *me!*
Harumph!
There are people in this neighborhood using children to run scams. ***Find another sucker!***
Mr. Warnimont, I swear this is legit. Read my card.
Closed
Read my ***sign.***
Closed
SLAM!!
So...got any other cousins up your sleeve?

CHAPTER 2

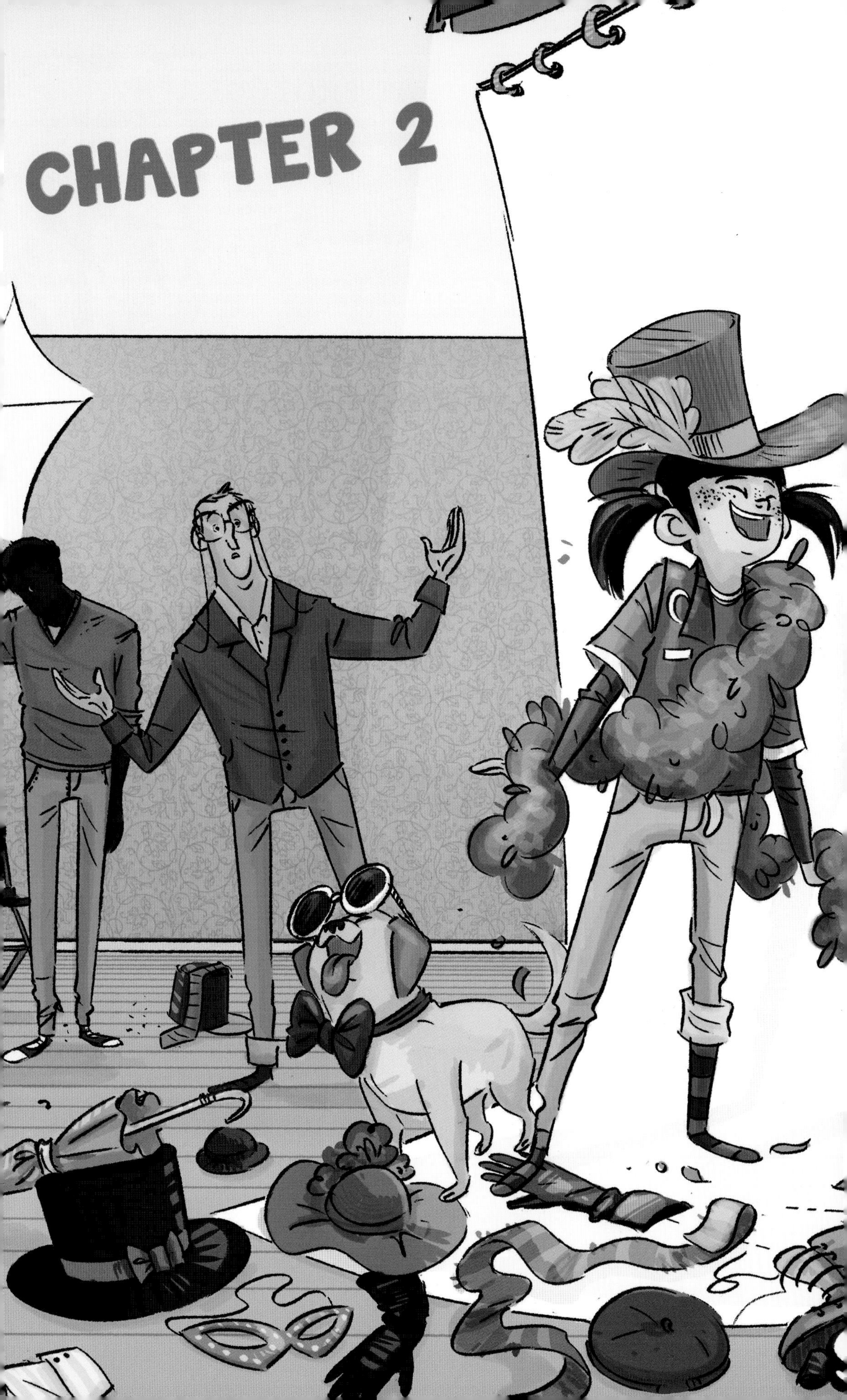

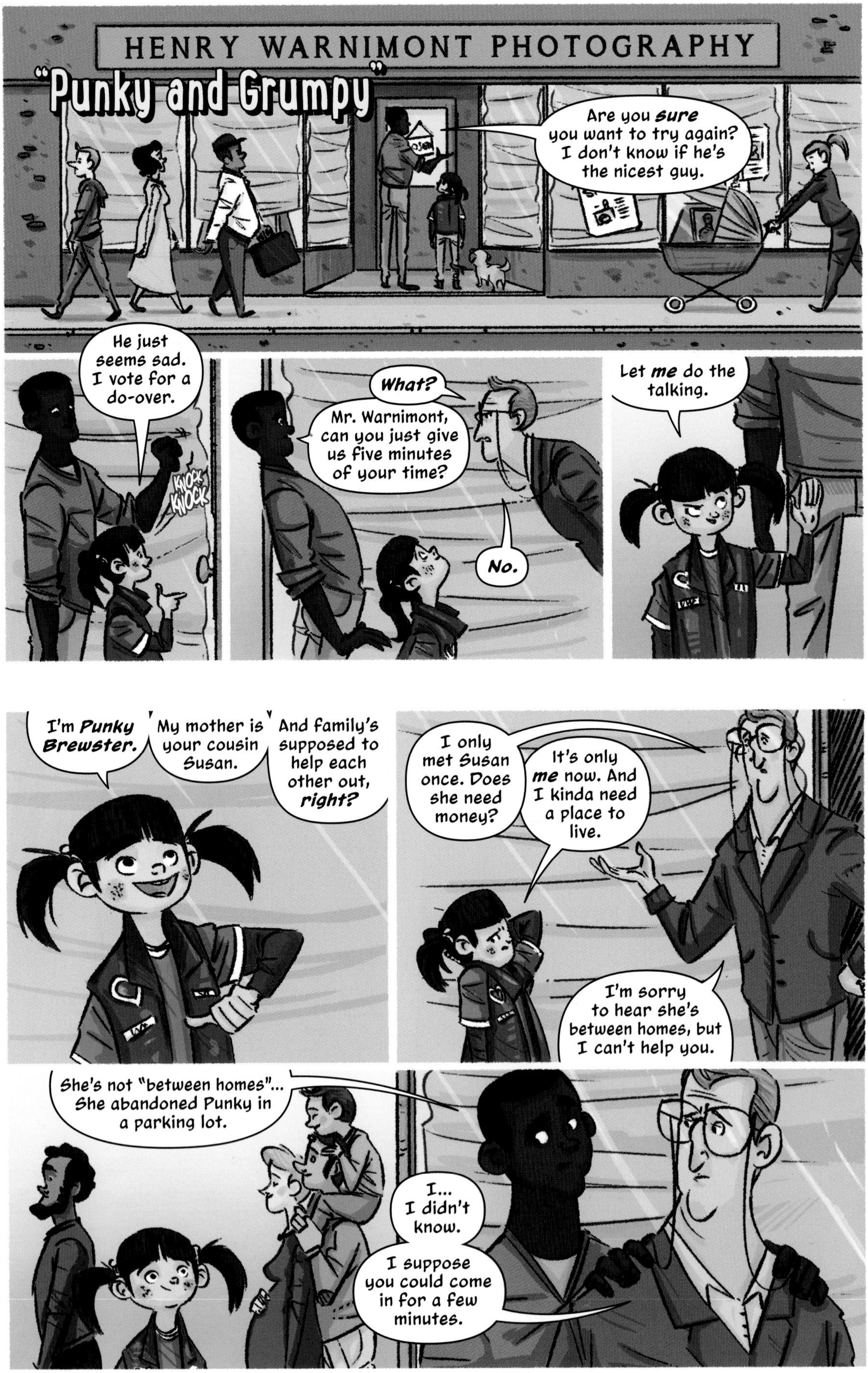
HENRY WARNIMONT PHOTOGRAPHY
"Punky and Grumpy"
Are you *sure* you want to try again? I don't know if he's the nicest guy.
He just seems sad. I vote for a do-over.
KNOCK KNOCK
Mr. Warnimont, can you just give us five minutes of your time?
What?
No.
Let *me* do the talking.
I'm *Punky Brewster.*
My mother is your cousin Susan.
And family's supposed to help each other out, *right?*
I only met Susan once. Does she need money?
It's only *me* now. And I kinda need a place to live.
I'm sorry to hear she's between homes, but I can't help you.
She's not "between homes"... She abandoned Punky in a parking lot.
I... I didn't know.
I suppose you could come in for a few minutes.

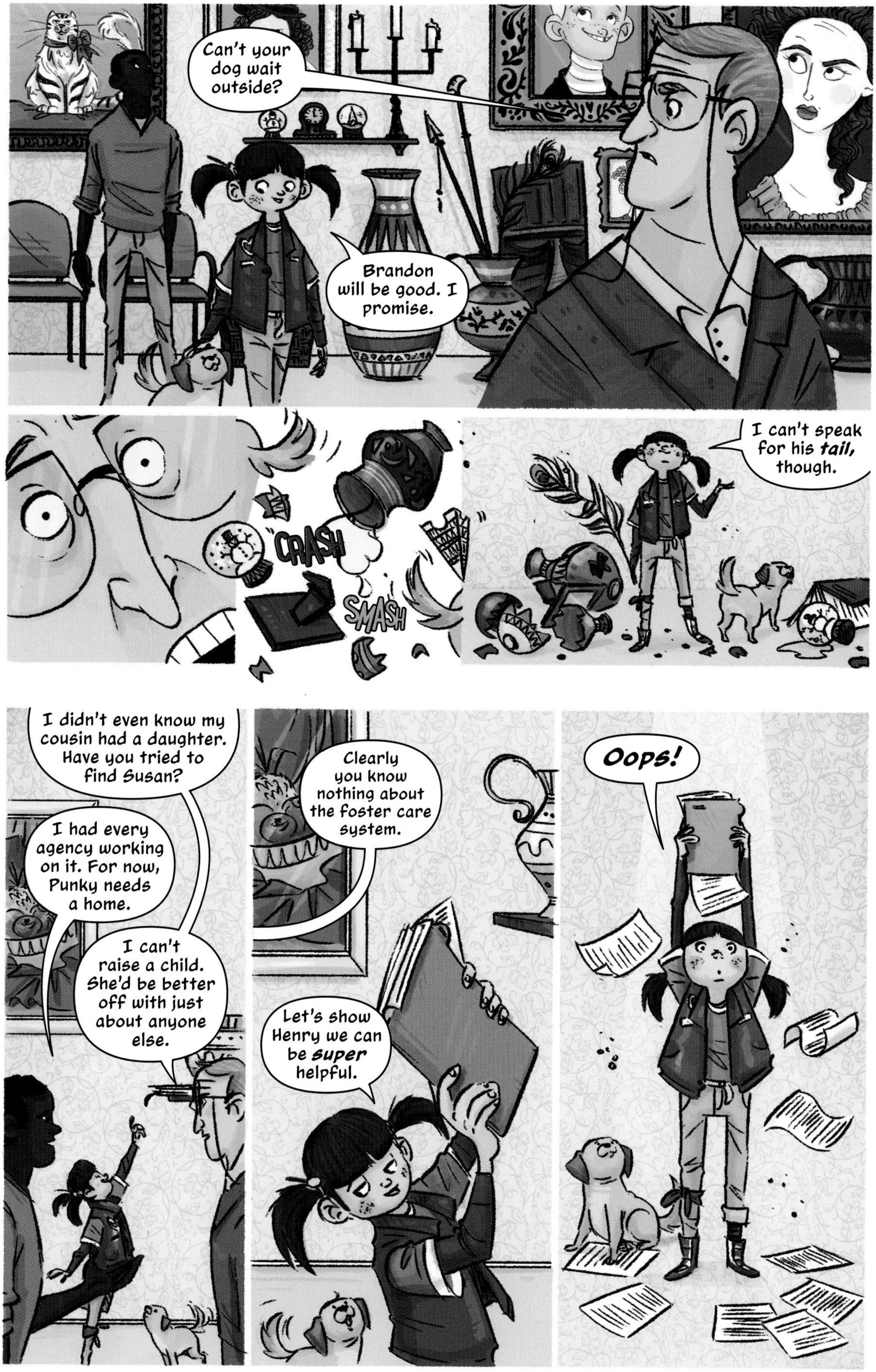
Can't your dog wait outside?
Brandon will be good. I promise.
CRASH
SMASH
I can't speak for his *tail,* though.
I didn't even know my cousin had a daughter. Have you tried to find Susan?
I had every agency working on it. For now, Punky needs a home.
I can't raise a child. She'd be better off with just about anyone else.
Clearly you know nothing about the foster care system.
Let's show Henry we can be *super* helpful.
Oops!

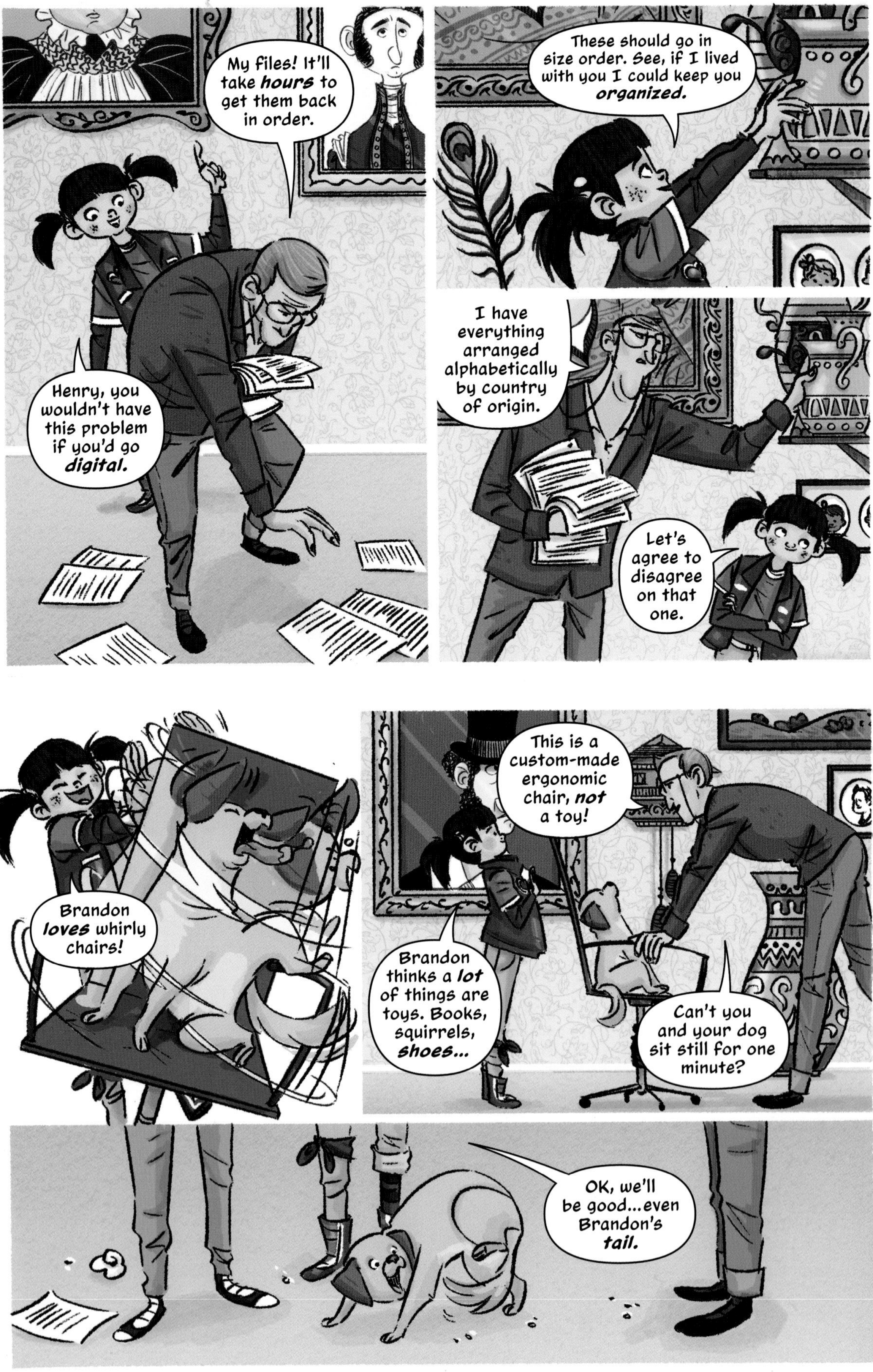
My files! It'll take **hours** to get them back in order.
Henry, you wouldn't have this problem if you'd go ***digital.***
These should go in size order. See, if I lived with you I could keep you ***organized.***
I have everything arranged alphabetically by country of origin.
Let's agree to disagree on that one.
Brandon ***loves*** whirly chairs!
This is a custom-made ergonomic chair, ***not*** a toy!
Brandon thinks a ***lot*** of things are toys. Books, squirrels, ***shoes...***
Can't you and your dog sit still for one minute?
OK, we'll be good...even Brandon's ***tail.***

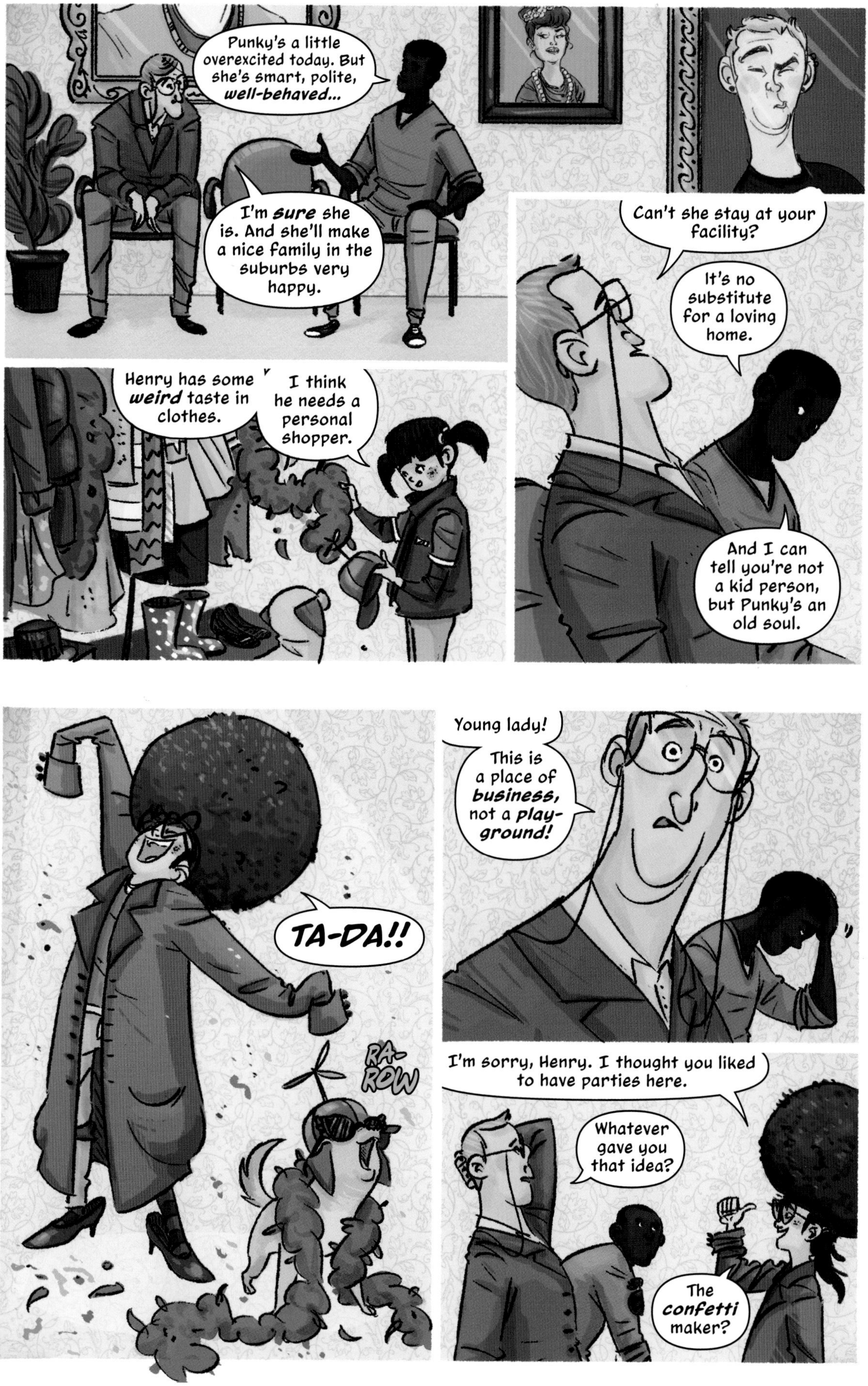
Punky's a little overexcited today. But she's smart, polite, *well-behaved...*
I'm *sure* she is. And she'll make a nice family in the suburbs very happy.
Can't she stay at your facility?
It's no substitute for a loving home.
Henry has some *weird* taste in clothes.
I think he needs a personal shopper.
And I can tell you're not a kid person, but Punky's an old soul.
TA-DA!!
RA-ROW
Young lady!
This is a place of *business,* not a *play-ground!*
I'm sorry, Henry. I thought you liked to have parties here.
Whatever gave you that idea?
The *confetti* maker?

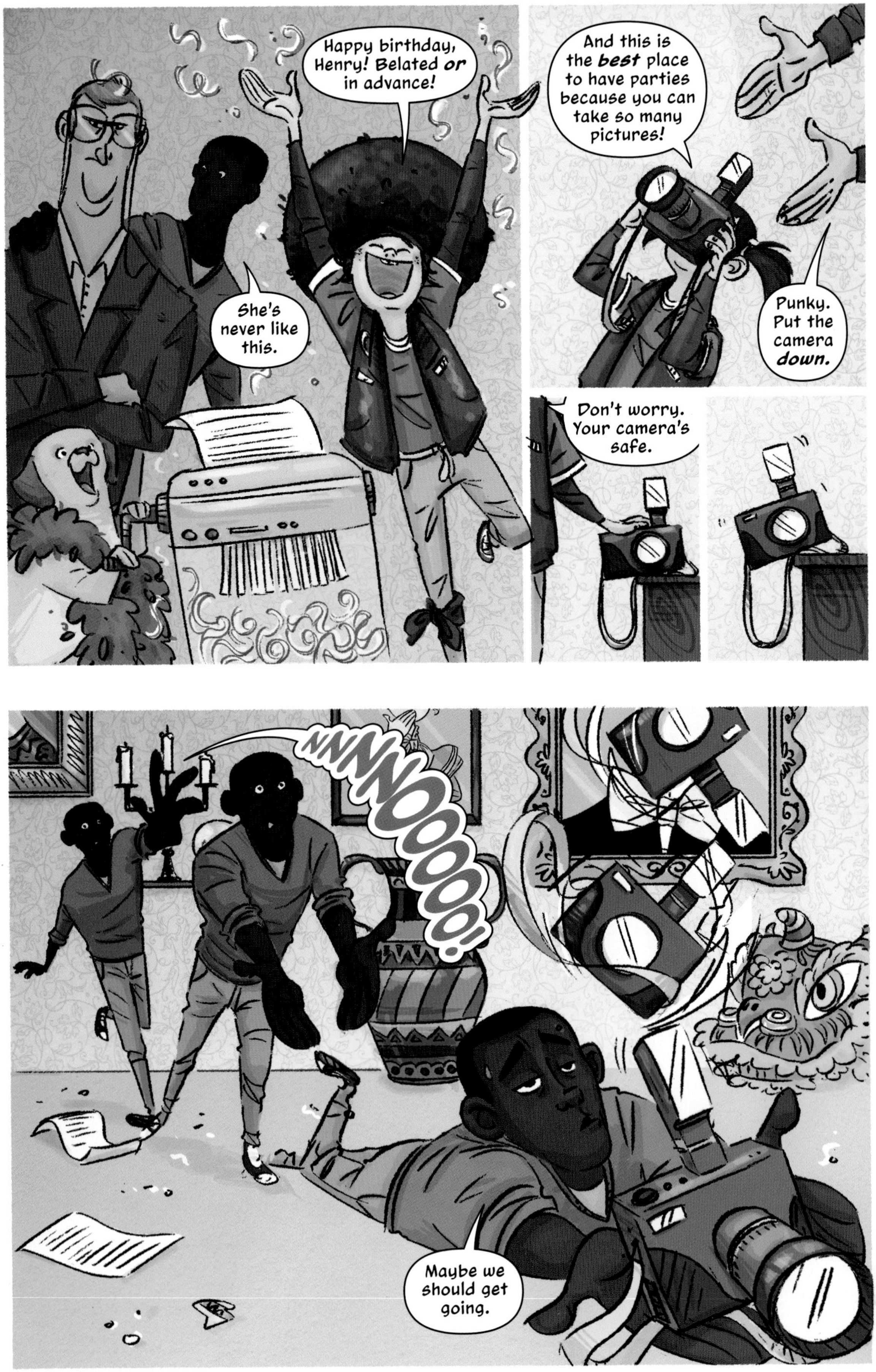
Happy birthday, Henry! Belated *or* in advance!
She's never like this.
And this is the *best* place to have parties because you can take so many pictures!
Punky. Put the camera *down.*
Don't worry. Your camera's safe.
NNNOOOOOO!
Maybe we should get going.

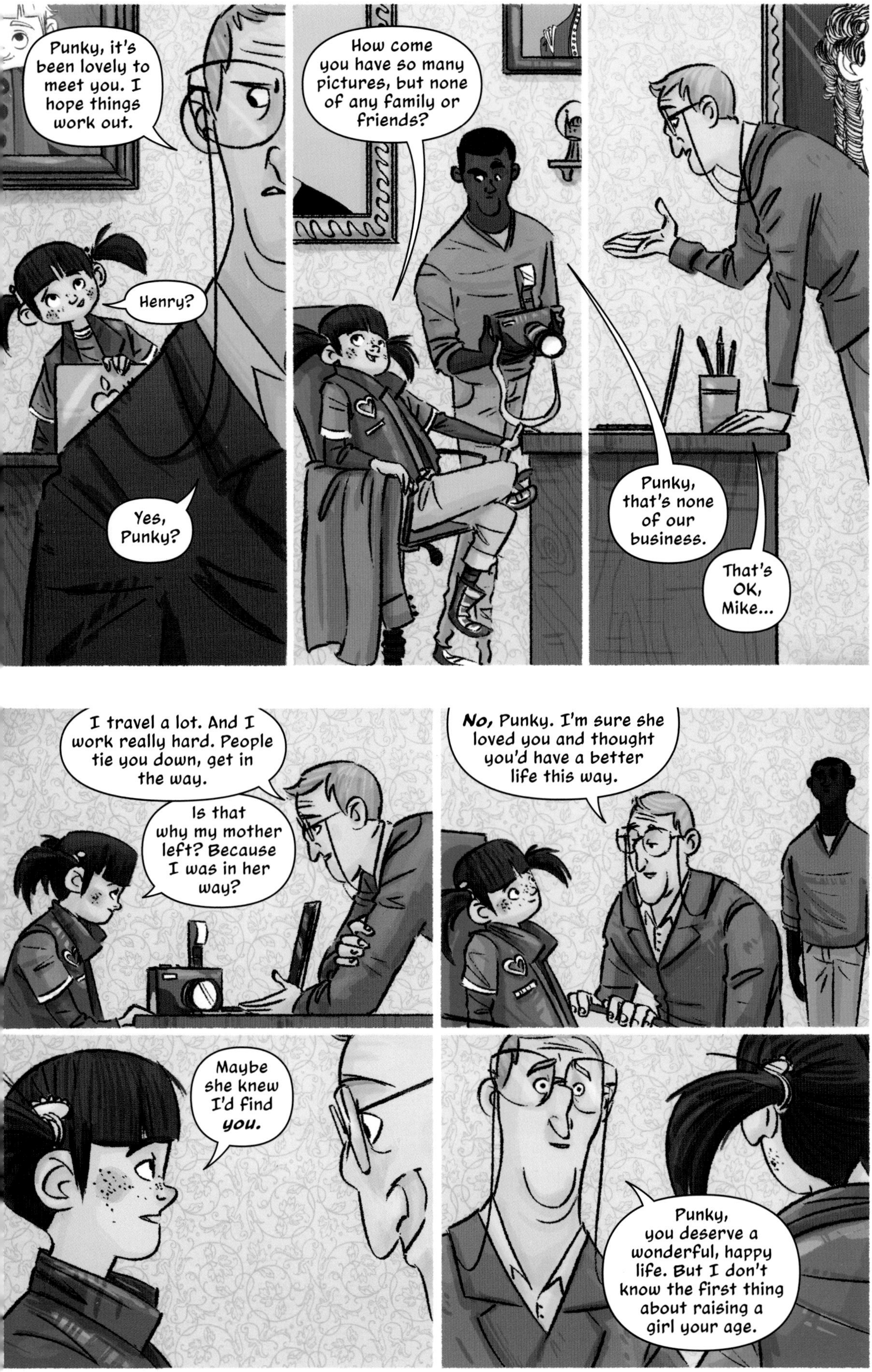

Punky, it's been lovely to meet you. I hope things work out.
Henry?
Yes, Punky?
How come you have so many pictures, but none of any family or friends?
Punky, that's none of our business.
That's OK, Mike...
I travel a lot. And I work really hard. People tie you down, get in the way.
Is that why my mother left? Because I was in her way?
No, Punky. I'm sure she loved you and thought you'd have a better life this way.
Maybe she knew I'd find you.
Punky, you deserve a wonderful, happy life. But I don't know the first thing about raising a girl your age.

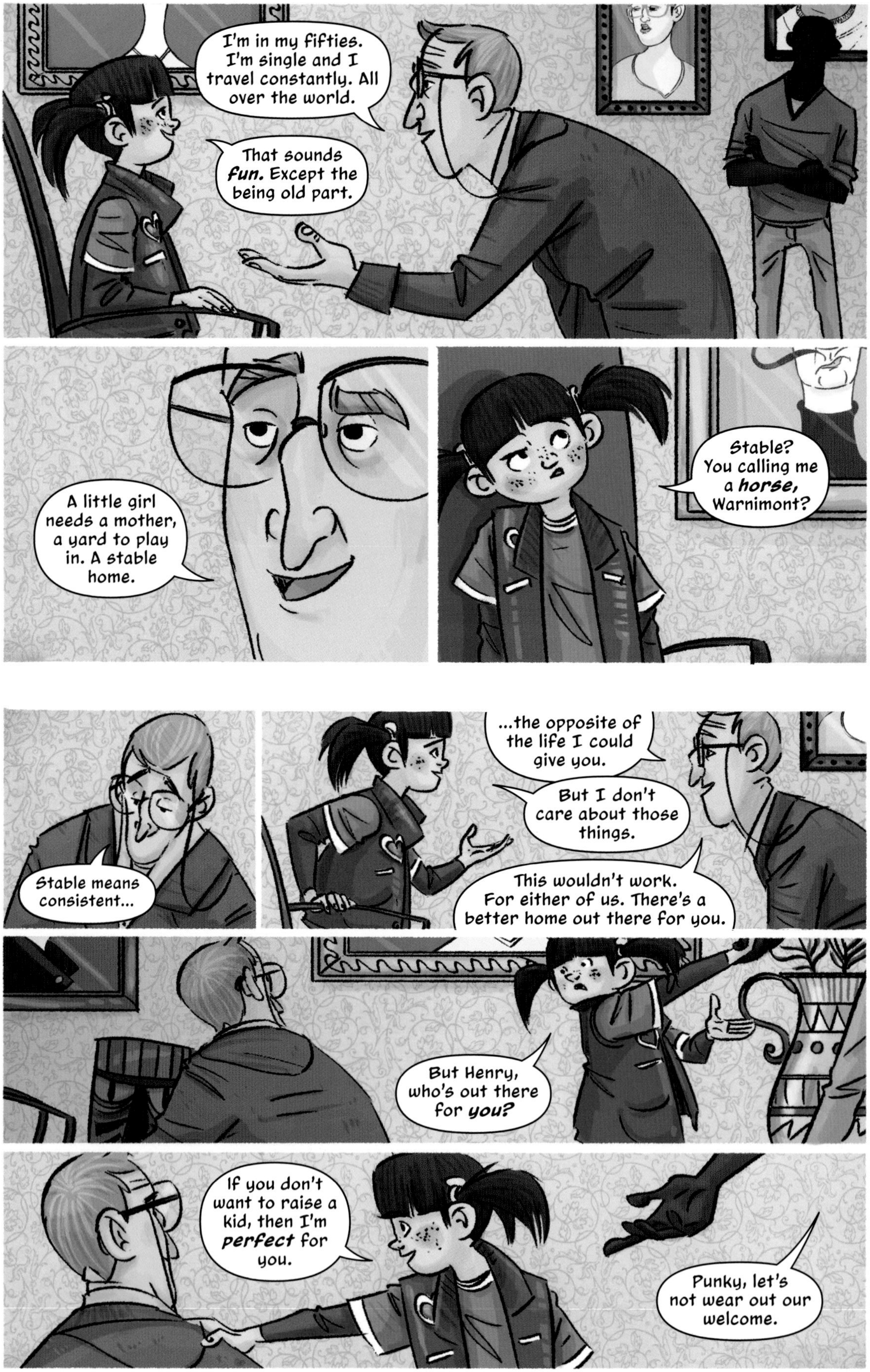
I'm in my fifties. I'm single and I travel constantly. All over the world.
That sounds *fun.* Except the being old part.
A little girl needs a mother, a yard to play in. A stable home.
Stable? You calling me a *horse,* Warnimont?
Stable means consistent...
...the opposite of the life I could give you.
But I don't care about those things.
This wouldn't work. For either of us. There's a better home out there for you.
But Henry, who's out there for *you?*
If you don't want to raise a kid, then I'm *perfect* for you.
Punky, let's not wear out our welcome.

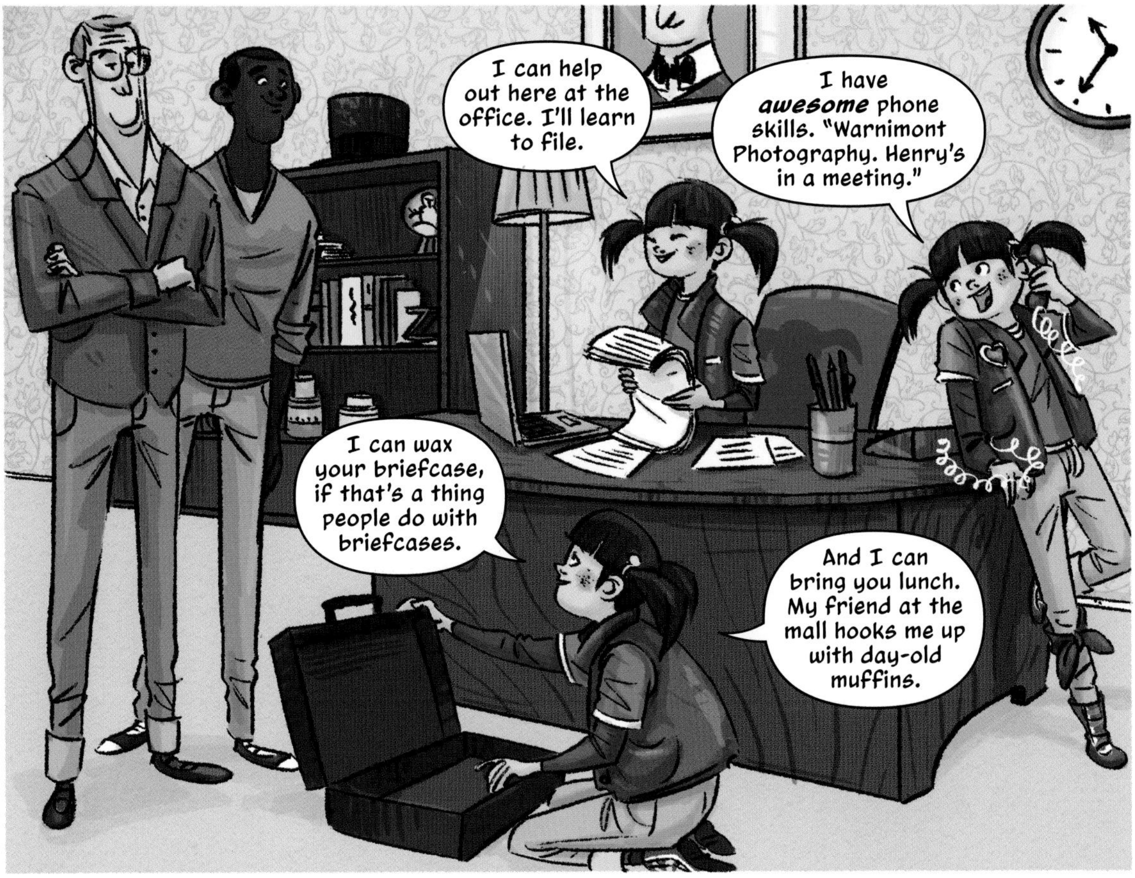
I can help out here at the office. I'll learn to file.
I have *awesome* phone skills. "Warnimont Photography. Henry's in a meeting."
I can wax your briefcase, if that's a thing people do with briefcases.
And I can bring you lunch. My friend at the mall hooks me up with day-old muffins.

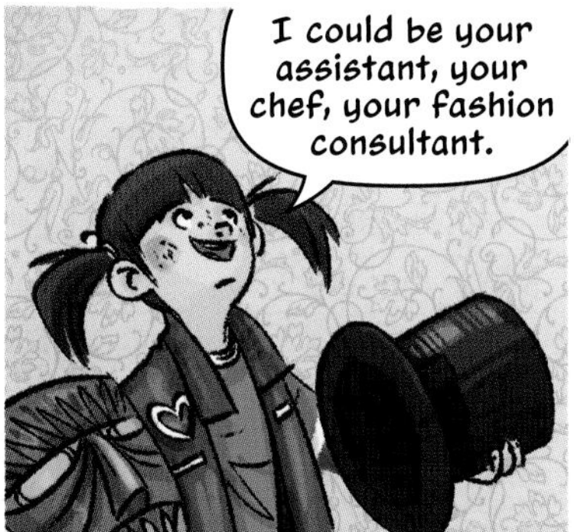
I could be your assistant, your chef, your fashion consultant.

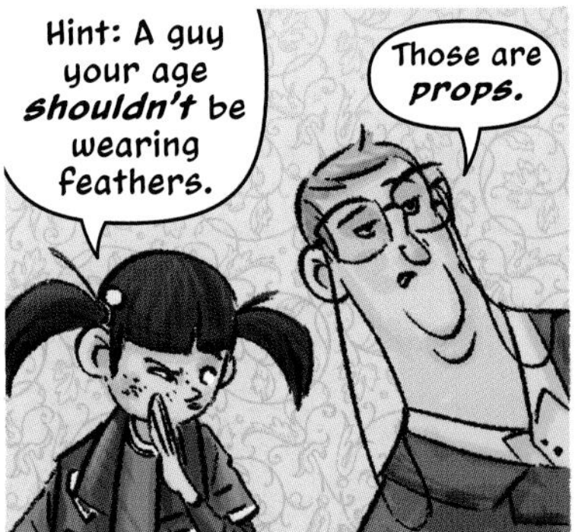
Hint: A guy your age *shouldn't* be wearing feathers.
Those are *props.*

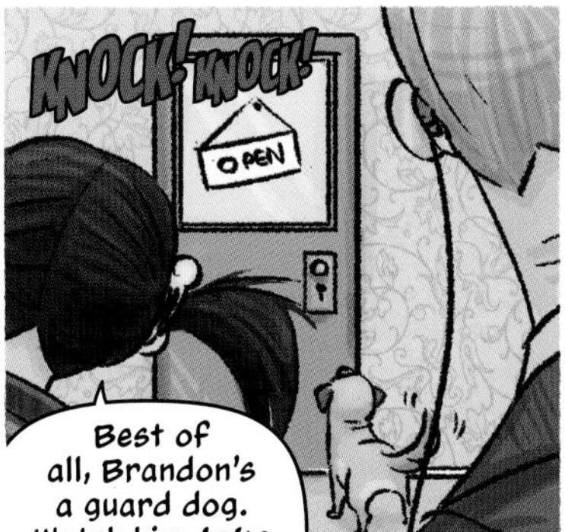
KNOCK! KNOCK!
OPEN
Best of all, Brandon's a guard dog. Watch him *take out* this intruder.

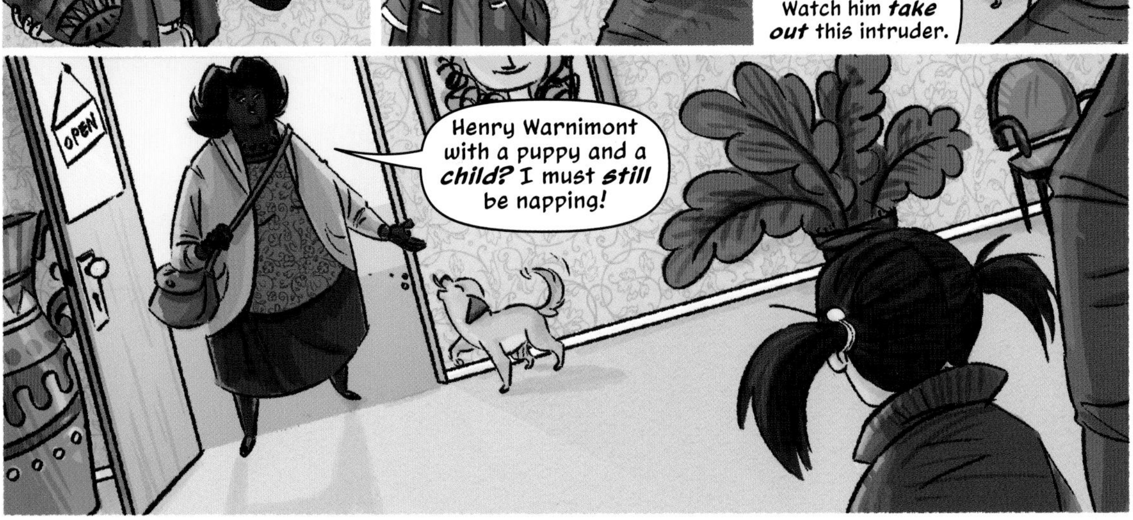
OPEN
Henry Warnimont with a puppy and a *child?* I must *still* be napping!

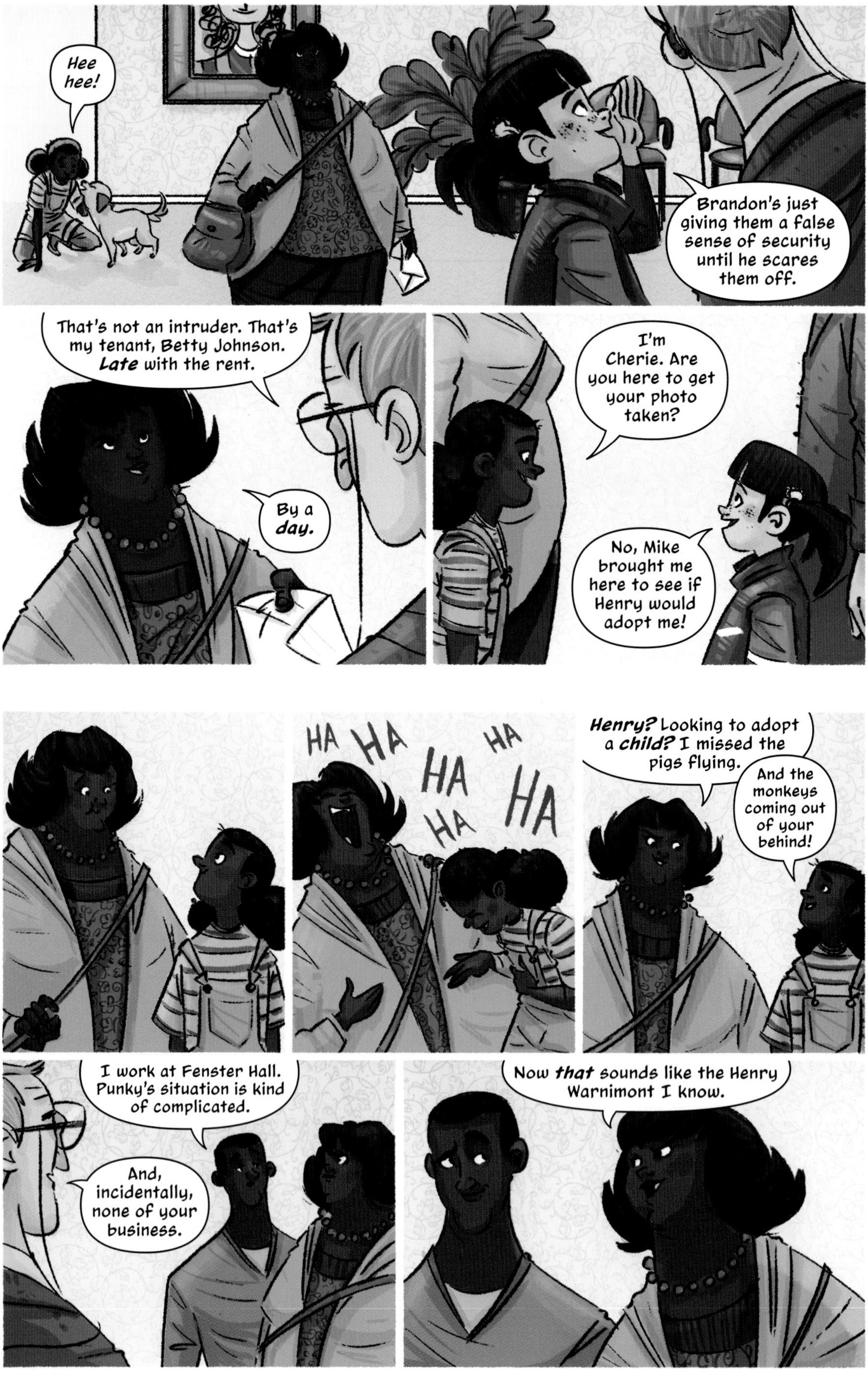
Hee hee!
Brandon's just giving them a false sense of security until he scares them off.
That's not an intruder. That's my tenant, Betty Johnson. *Late* with the rent.
By a *day.*
I'm Cherie. Are you here to get your photo taken?
No, Mike brought me here to see if Henry would adopt me!
HA HA HA HA HA HA
Henry? Looking to adopt a *child?* I missed the pigs flying.
And the monkeys coming out of your behind!
I work at Fenster Hall. Punky's situation is kind of complicated.
And, incidentally, none of your business.
Now *that* sounds like the Henry Warnimont I know.

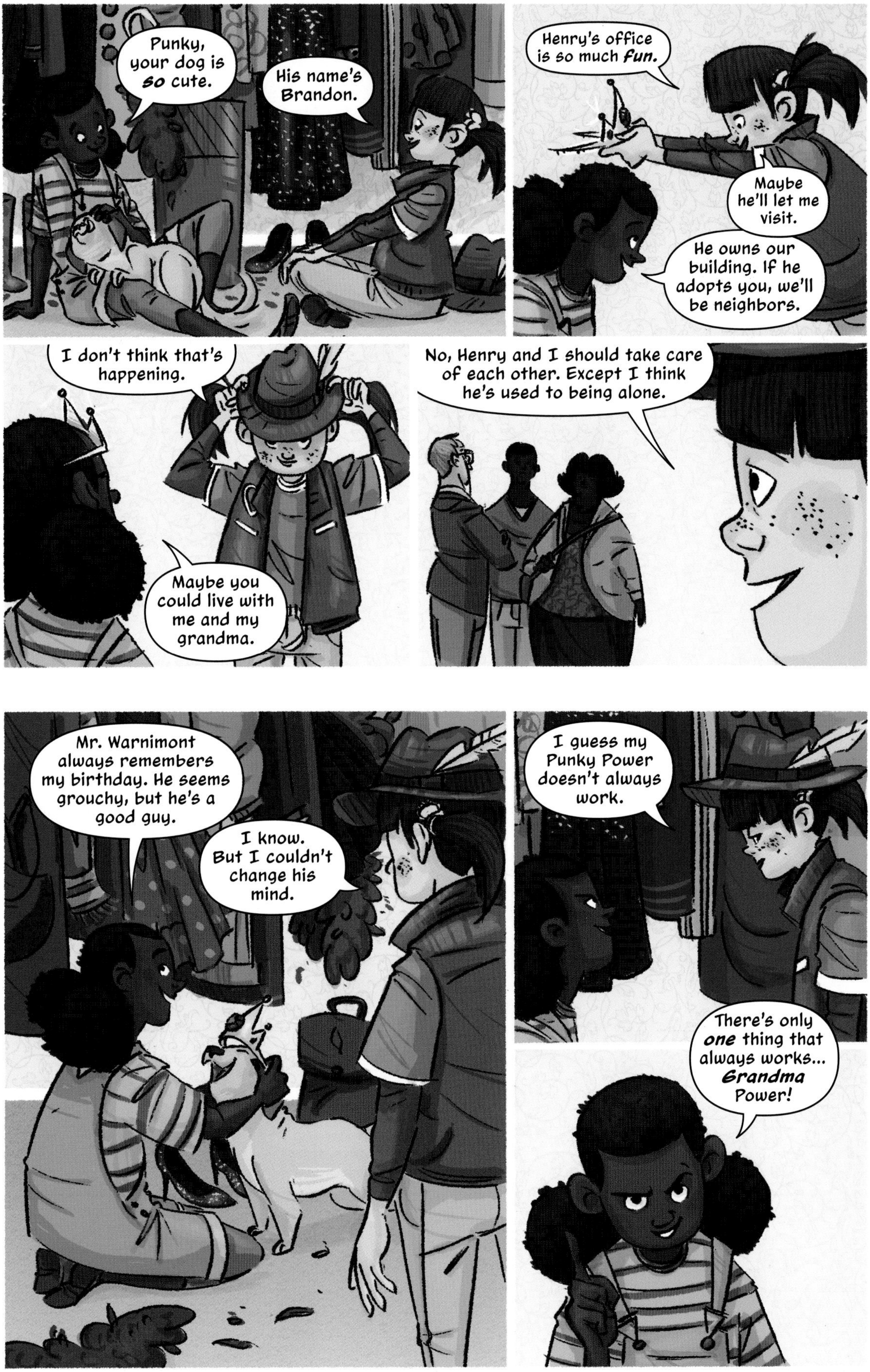
Punky, your dog is *so* cute.
His name's Brandon.
Henry's office is so much *fun.*
Maybe he'll let me visit.
He owns our building. If he adopts you, we'll be neighbors.
I don't think that's happening.
Maybe you could live with me and my grandma.
No, Henry and I should take care of each other. Except I think he's used to being alone.
Mr. Warnimont always remembers my birthday. He seems grouchy, but he's a good guy.
I know. But I couldn't change his mind.
I guess my Punky Power doesn't always work.
There's only *one* thing that always works... *Grandma* Power!

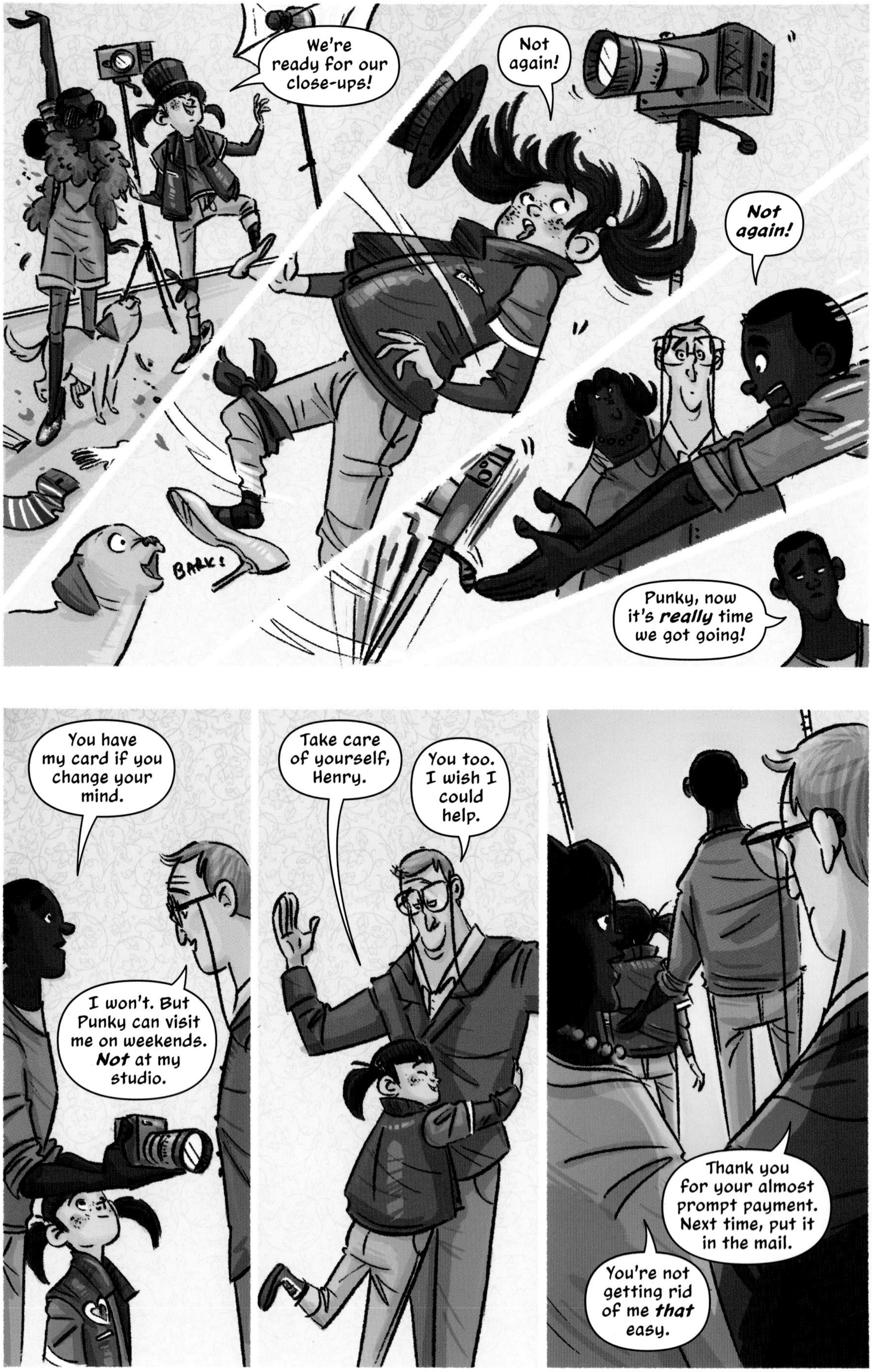
We're ready for our close-ups!
Not again!
Not again!
BARK!
Punky, now it's really time we got going!
You have my card if you change your mind.
I won't. But Punky can visit me on weekends. Not at my studio.
Take care of yourself, Henry.
You too. I wish I could help.
Thank you for your almost prompt payment. Next time, put it in the mail.
You're not getting rid of me that easy.

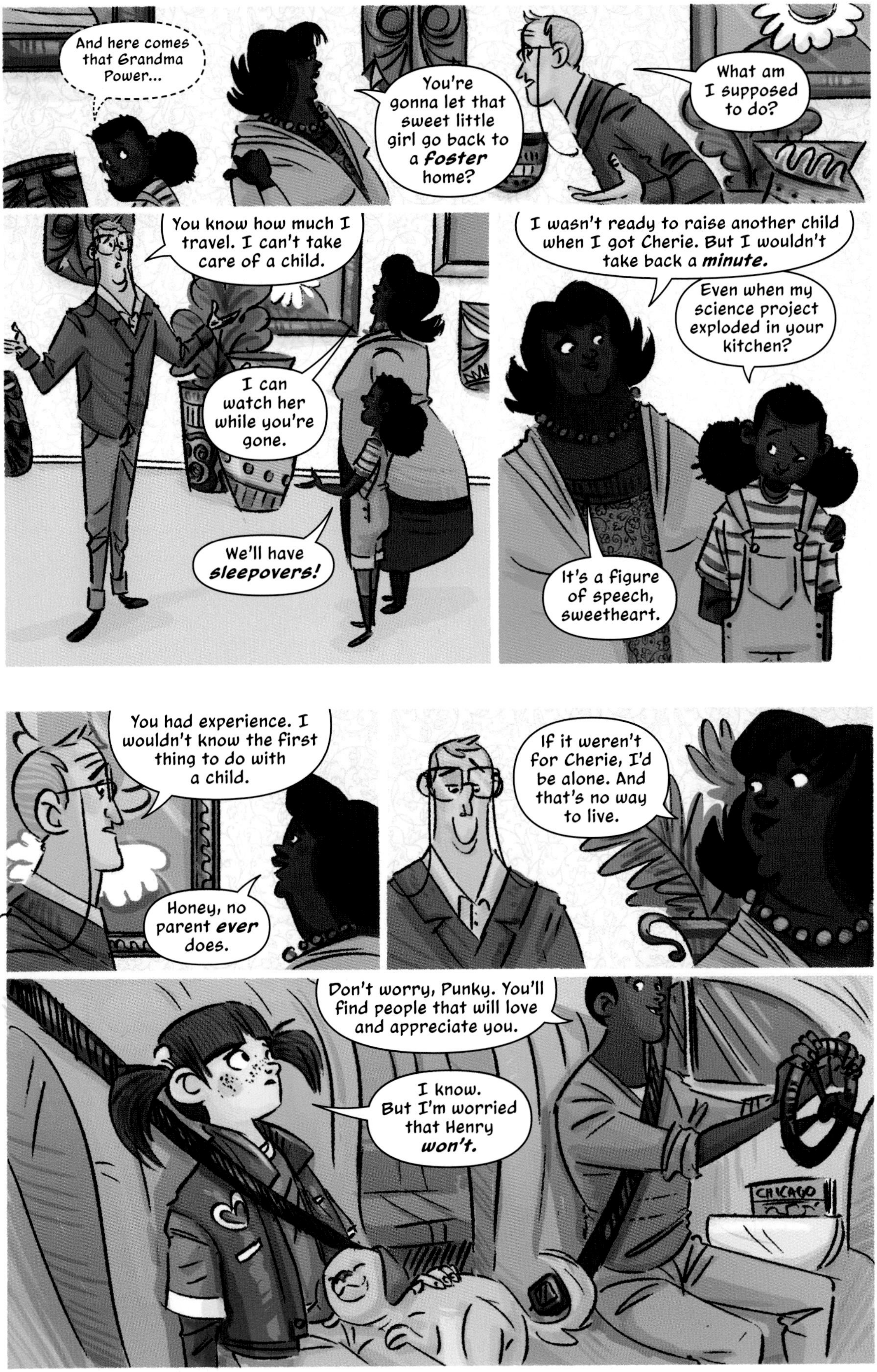
And here comes that Grandma Power...
You're gonna let that sweet little girl go back to a **foster** home?
What am I supposed to do?
You know how much I travel. I can't take care of a child.
I can watch her while you're gone.
We'll have **sleepovers!**
I wasn't ready to raise another child when I got Cherie. But I wouldn't take back a **minute.**
Even when my science project exploded in your kitchen?
It's a figure of speech, sweetheart.
You had experience. I wouldn't know the first thing to do with a child.
Honey, no parent **ever** does.
If it weren't for Cherie, I'd be alone. And that's no way to live.
Don't worry, Punky. You'll find people that will love and appreciate you.
I know. But I'm worried that Henry **won't.**
CHICAGO

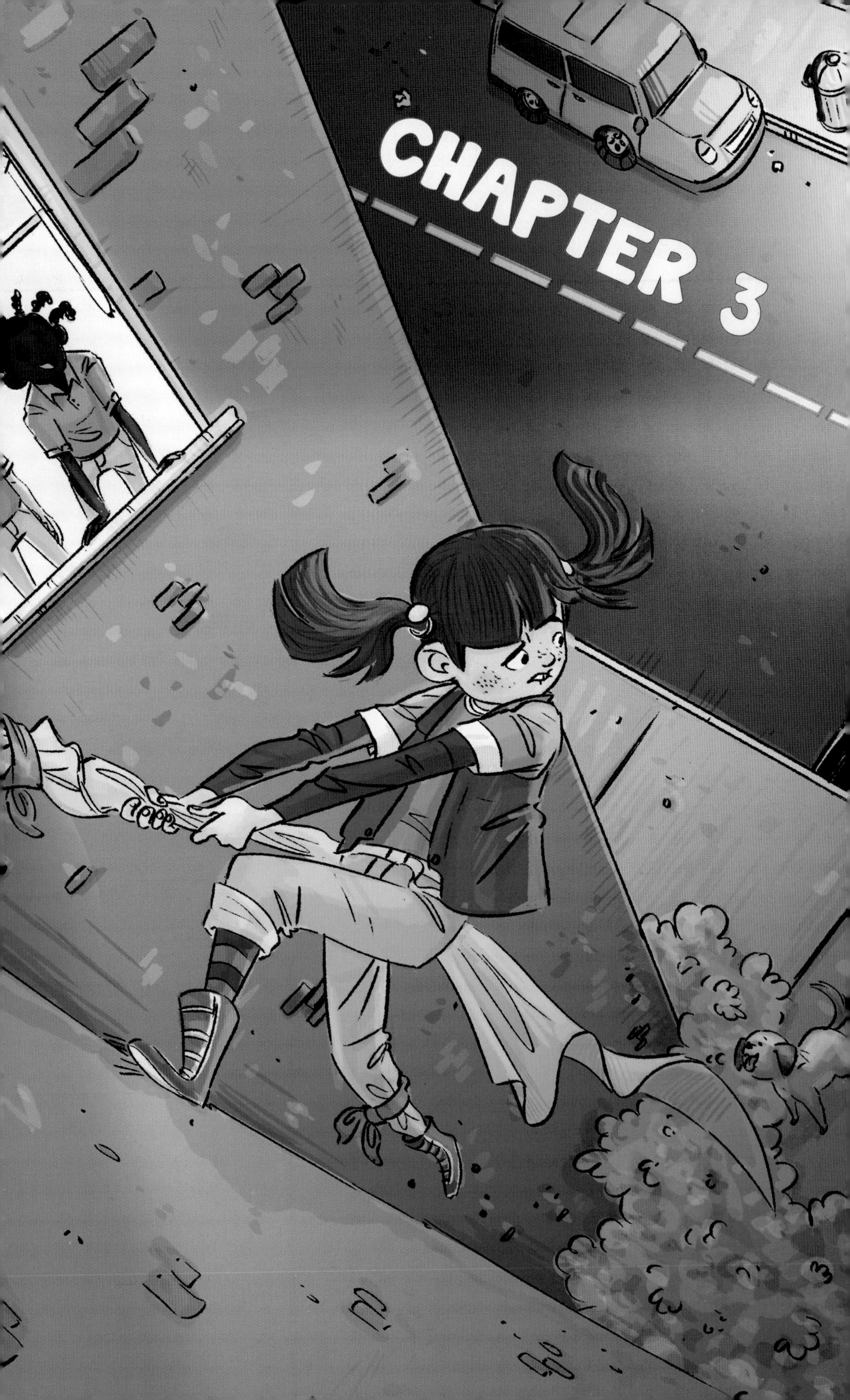
CHAPTER 3

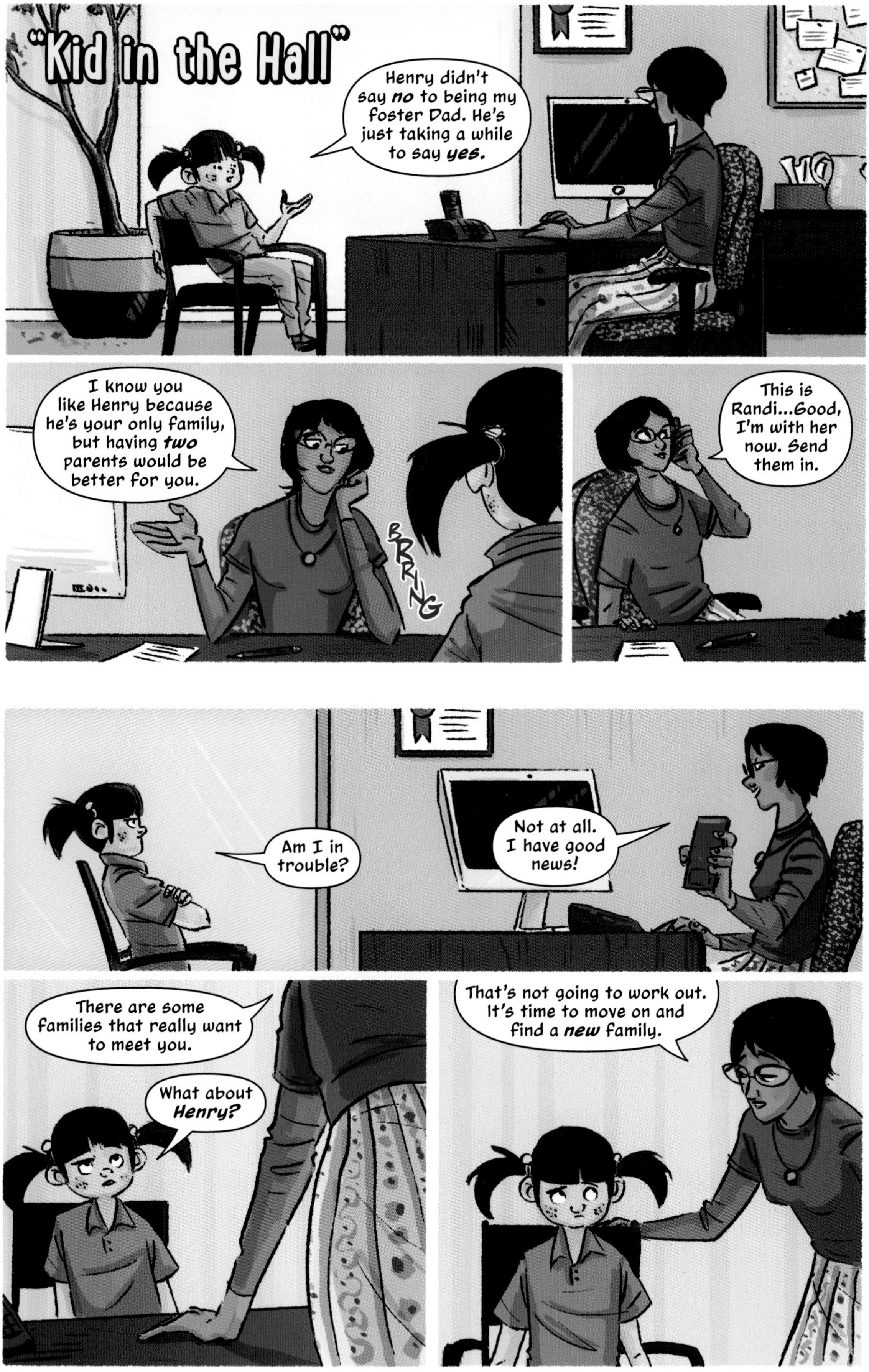
"Kid in the Hall"
Henry didn't say *no* to being my foster Dad. He's just taking a while to say *yes.*
I know you like Henry because he's your only family, but having *two* parents would be better for you.
BRRING
This is Randi...Good, I'm with her now. Send them in.
Am I in trouble?
Not at all. I have good news!
There are some families that really want to meet you.
What about *Henry?*
That's not going to work out. It's time to move on and find a *new* family.

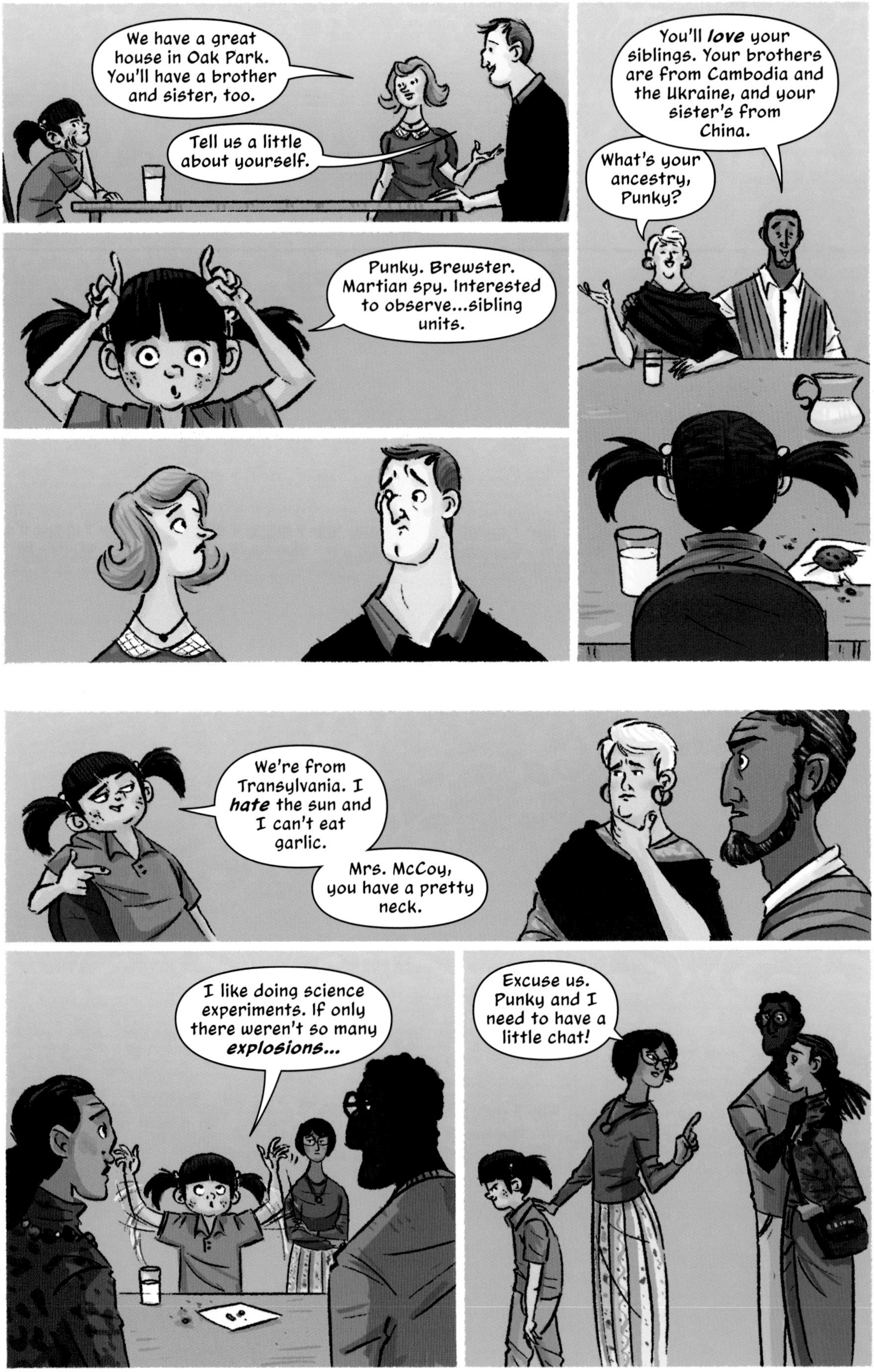
We have a great house in Oak Park. You'll have a brother and sister, too.
Tell us a little about yourself.
Punky. Brewster. Martian spy. Interested to observe...sibling units.
You'll *love* your siblings. Your brothers are from Cambodia and the Ukraine, and your sister's from China.
What's your ancestry, Punky?
We're from Transylvania. I *hate* the sun and I can't eat garlic.
Mrs. McCoy, you have a pretty neck.
I like doing science experiments. If only there weren't so many *explosions...*
Excuse us. Punky and I need to have a little chat!

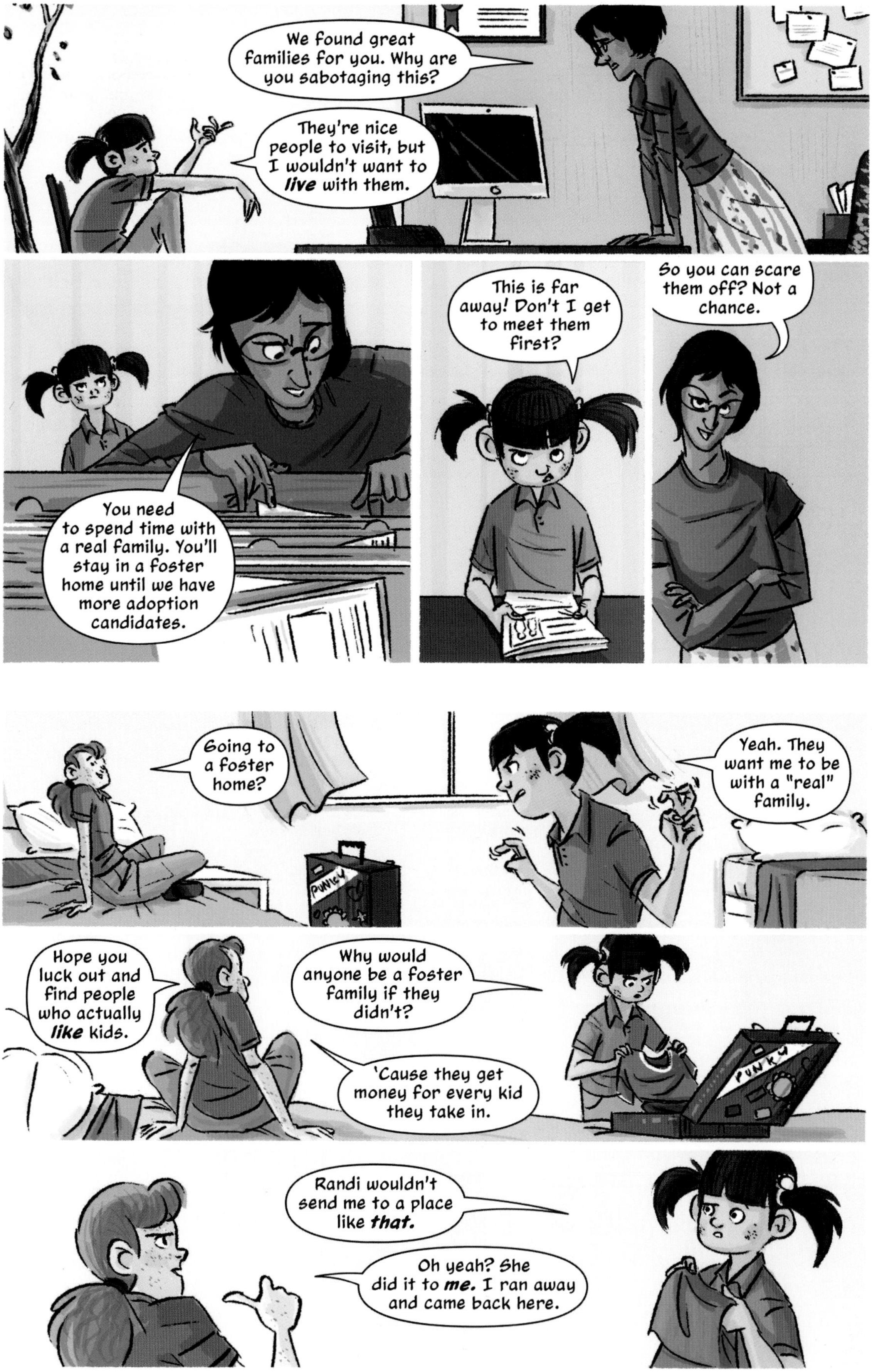
We found great families for you. Why are you sabotaging this?
They're nice people to visit, but I wouldn't want to *live* with them.
You need to spend time with a real family. You'll stay in a foster home until we have more adoption candidates.
This is far away! Don't I get to meet them first?
So you can scare them off? Not a chance.
PUNKY
Going to a foster home?
Yeah. They want me to be with a "real" family.
Hope you luck out and find people who actually *like* kids.
Why would anyone be a foster family if they didn't?
'Cause they get money for every kid they take in.
PUNKY
Randi wouldn't send me to a place like *that.*
Oh yeah? She did it to *me.* I ran away and came back here.

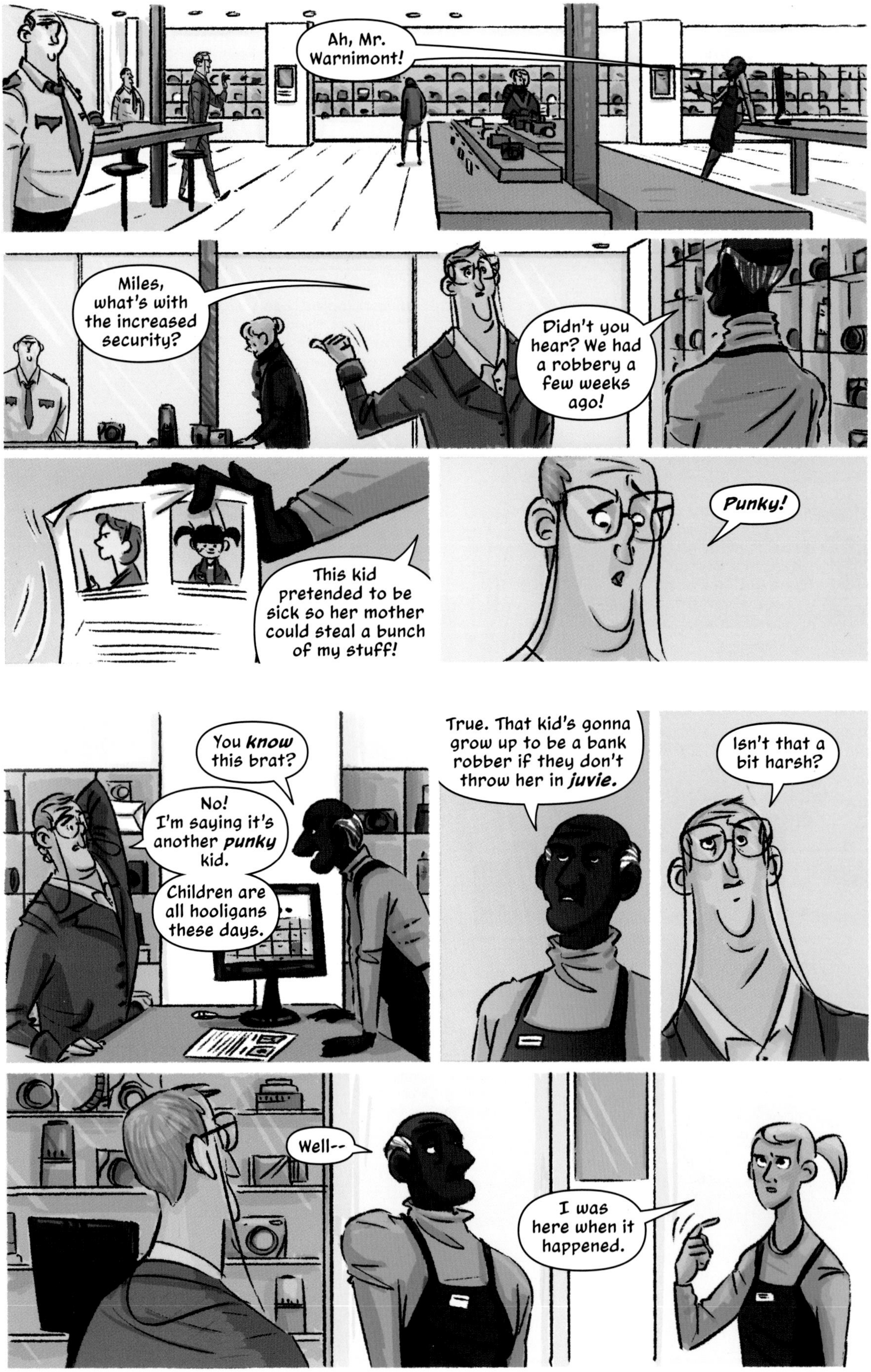
Ah, Mr. Warnimont!
Miles, what's with the increased security?
Didn't you hear? We had a robbery a few weeks ago!
This kid pretended to be sick so her mother could steal a bunch of my stuff!
Punky!
You know this brat?
No! I'm saying it's another punky kid.
Children are all hooligans these days.
True. That kid's gonna grow up to be a bank robber if they don't throw her in juvie.
Isn't that a bit harsh?
Well--
I was here when it happened.

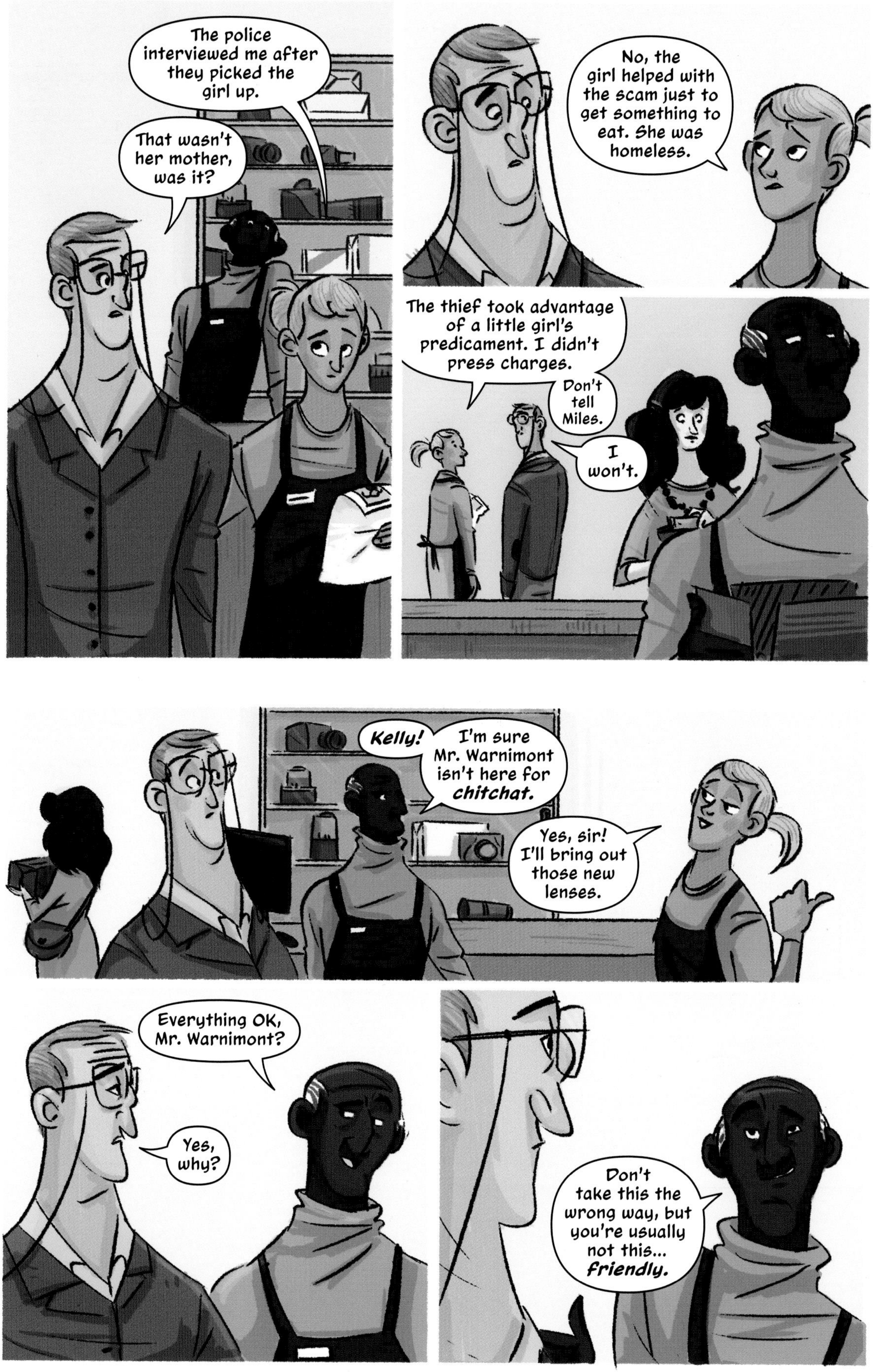
The police interviewed me after they picked the girl up.
That wasn't her mother, was it?
No, the girl helped with the scam just to get something to eat. She was homeless.
The thief took advantage of a little girl's predicament. I didn't press charges.
Don't tell Miles.
I won't.
Kelly!
I'm sure Mr. Warnimont isn't here for *chitchat.*
Yes, sir! I'll bring out those new lenses.
Everything OK, Mr. Warnimont?
Yes, why?
Don't take this the wrong way, but you're usually not this... *friendly.*

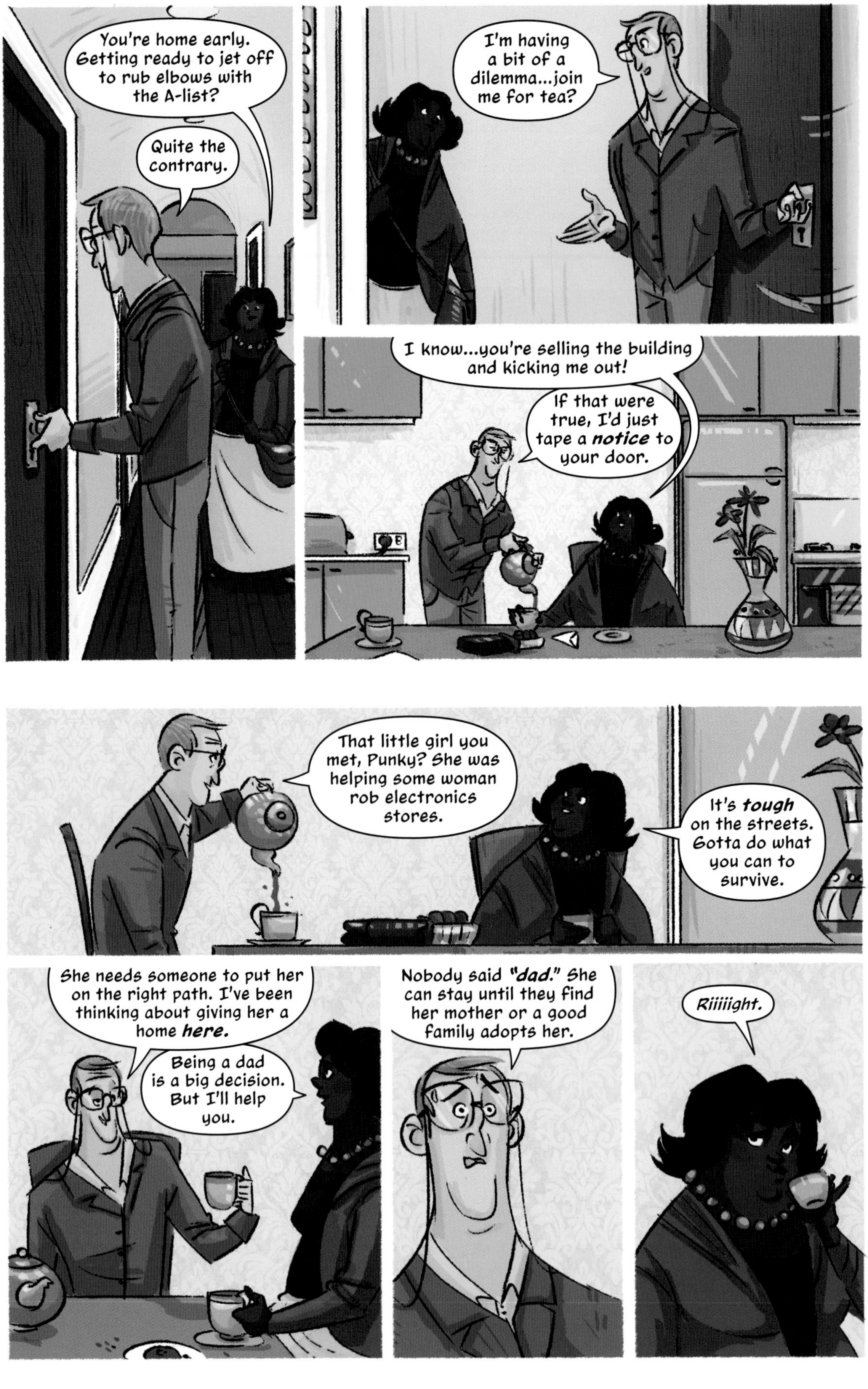
You're home early. Getting ready to jet off to rub elbows with the A-list?
Quite the contrary.
I'm having a bit of a dilemma...join me for tea?
I know...you're selling the building and kicking me out!
If that were true, I'd just tape a ***notice*** to your door.
That little girl you met, Punky? She was helping some woman rob electronics stores.
It's ***tough*** on the streets. Gotta do what you can to survive.
She needs someone to put her on the right path. I've been thinking about giving her a home ***here.***
Being a dad is a big decision. But I'll help you.
Nobody said ***"dad."*** She can stay until they find her mother or a good family adopts her.
Riiiiight.

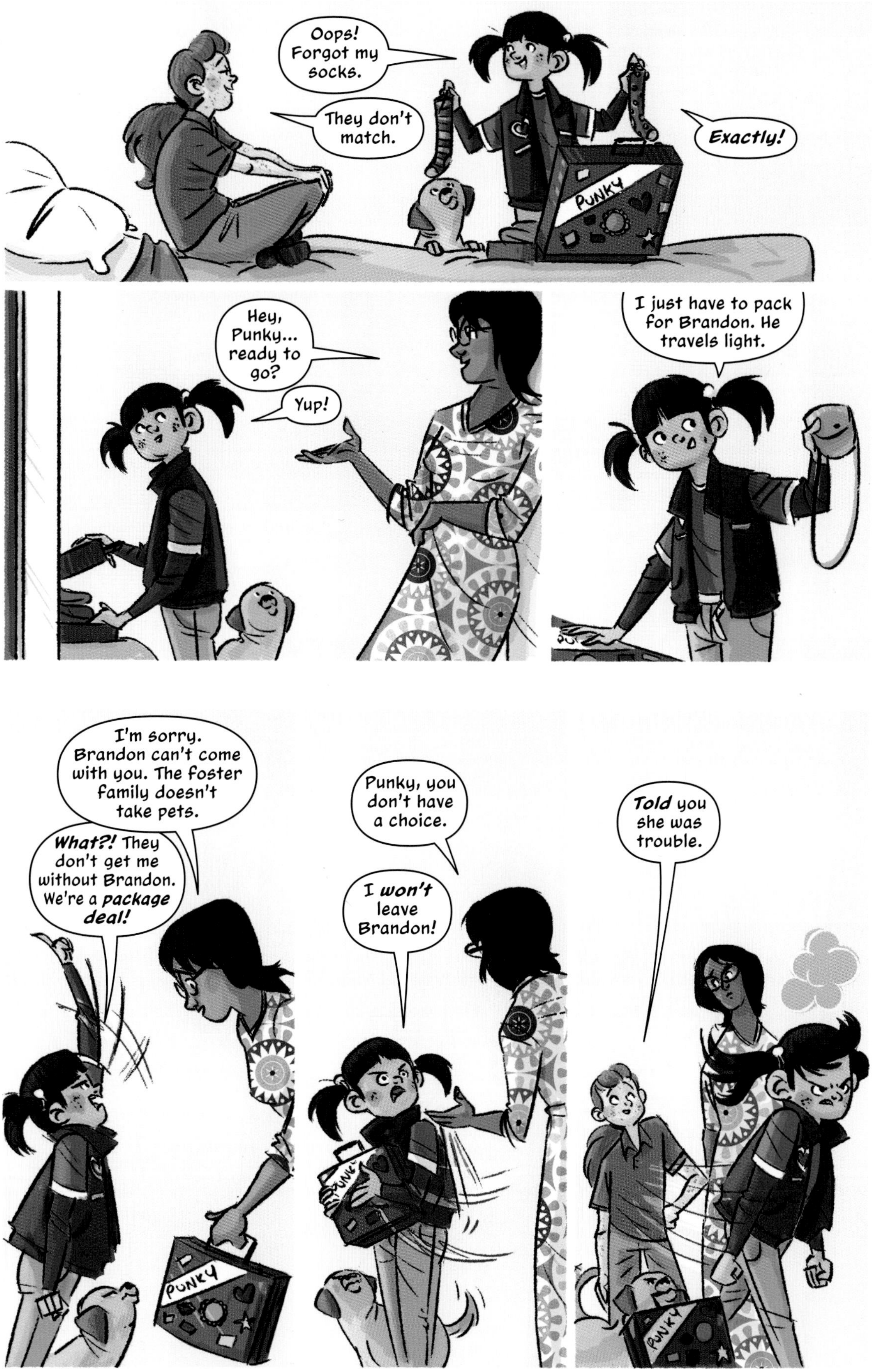
Oops! Forgot my socks.
They don't match.
Exactly!
PUNKY
Hey, Punky... ready to go?
Yup!
I just have to pack for Brandon. He travels light.
I'm sorry. Brandon can't come with you. The foster family doesn't take pets.
What?! They don't get me without Brandon. We're a package deal!
PUNKY
Punky, you don't have a choice.
I won't leave Brandon!
Told you she was trouble.
PUNKY

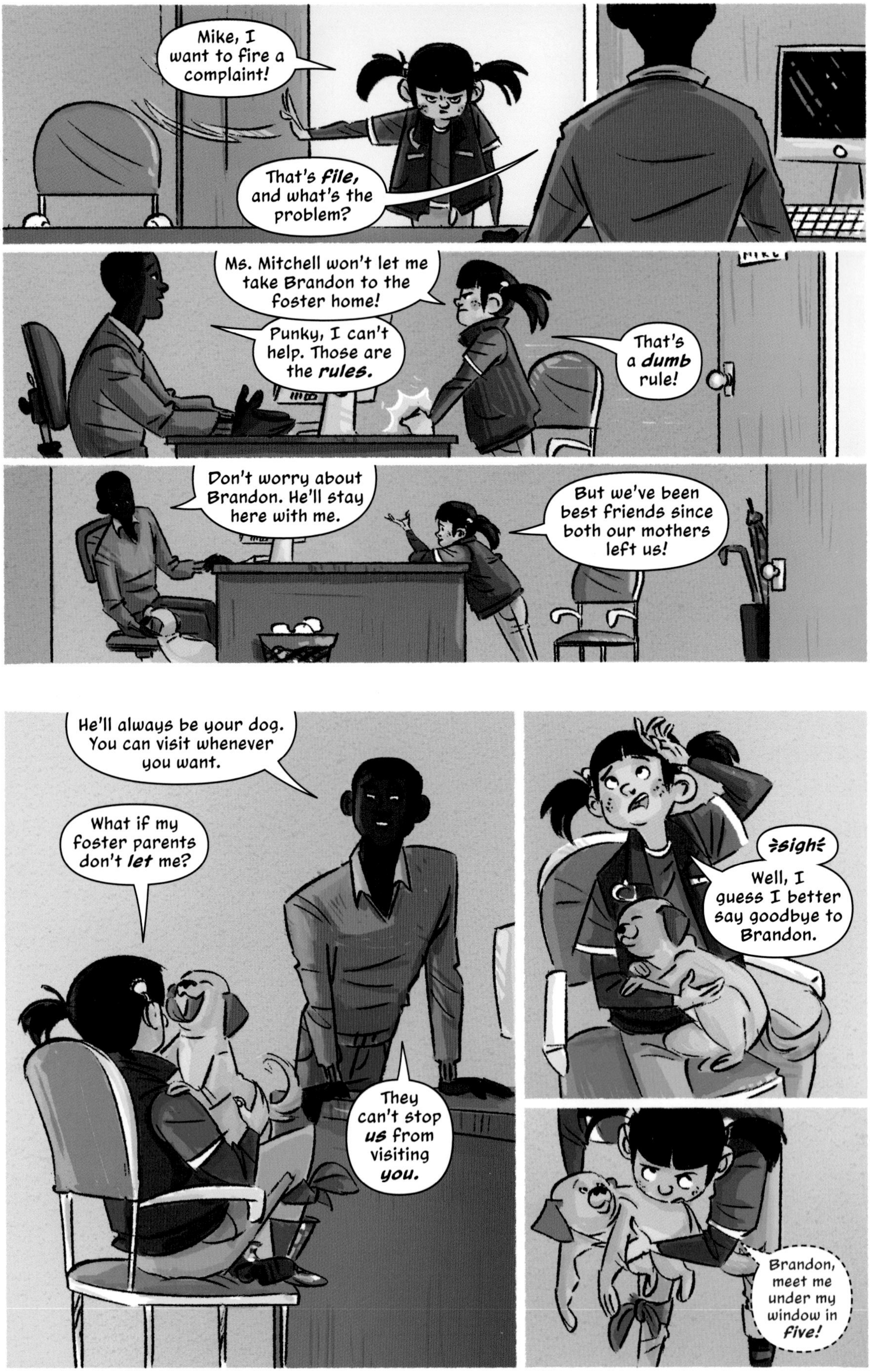
Mike, I want to fire a complaint!
That's *file,* and what's the problem?
Ms. Mitchell won't let me take Brandon to the foster home!
Punky, I can't help. Those are the *rules.*
That's a *dumb* rule!
Don't worry about Brandon. He'll stay here with me.
But we've been best friends since both our mothers left us!
He'll always be your dog. You can visit whenever you want.
What if my foster parents don't *let* me?
They can't stop *us* from visiting *you.*
sigh
Well, I guess I better say goodbye to Brandon.
Brandon, meet me under my window in *five!*

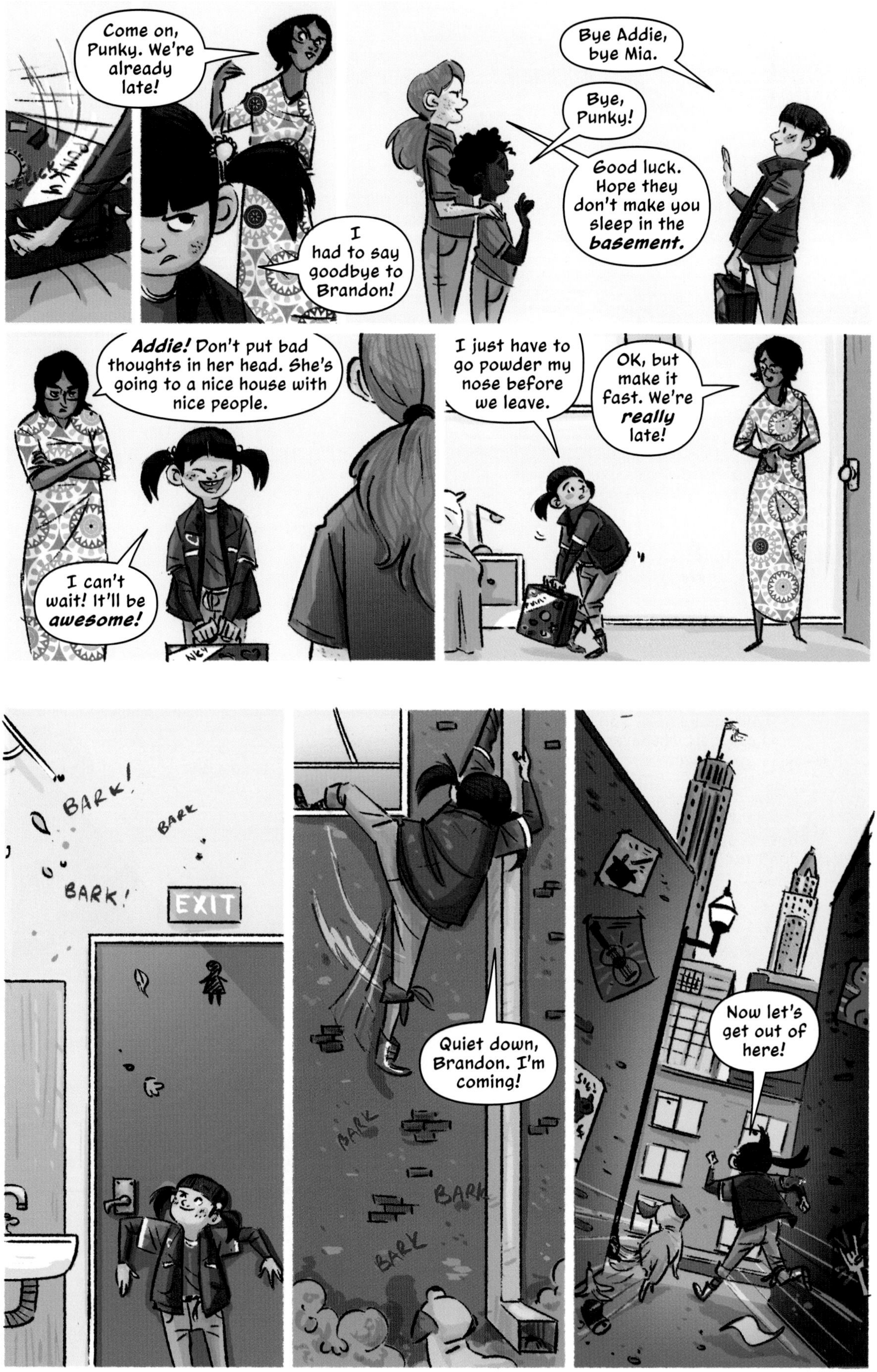
Come on, Punky. We're already late!
I had to say goodbye to Brandon!
Bye Addie, bye Mia.
Bye, Punky!
Good luck. Hope they don't make you sleep in the *basement.*
Addie! Don't put bad thoughts in her head. She's going to a nice house with nice people.
I can't wait! It'll be *awesome!*
I just have to go powder my nose before we leave.
OK, but make it fast. We're *really* late!
BARK!
BARK
BARK!
EXIT
Quiet down, Brandon. I'm coming!
BARK
BARK
BARK
Now let's get out of here!

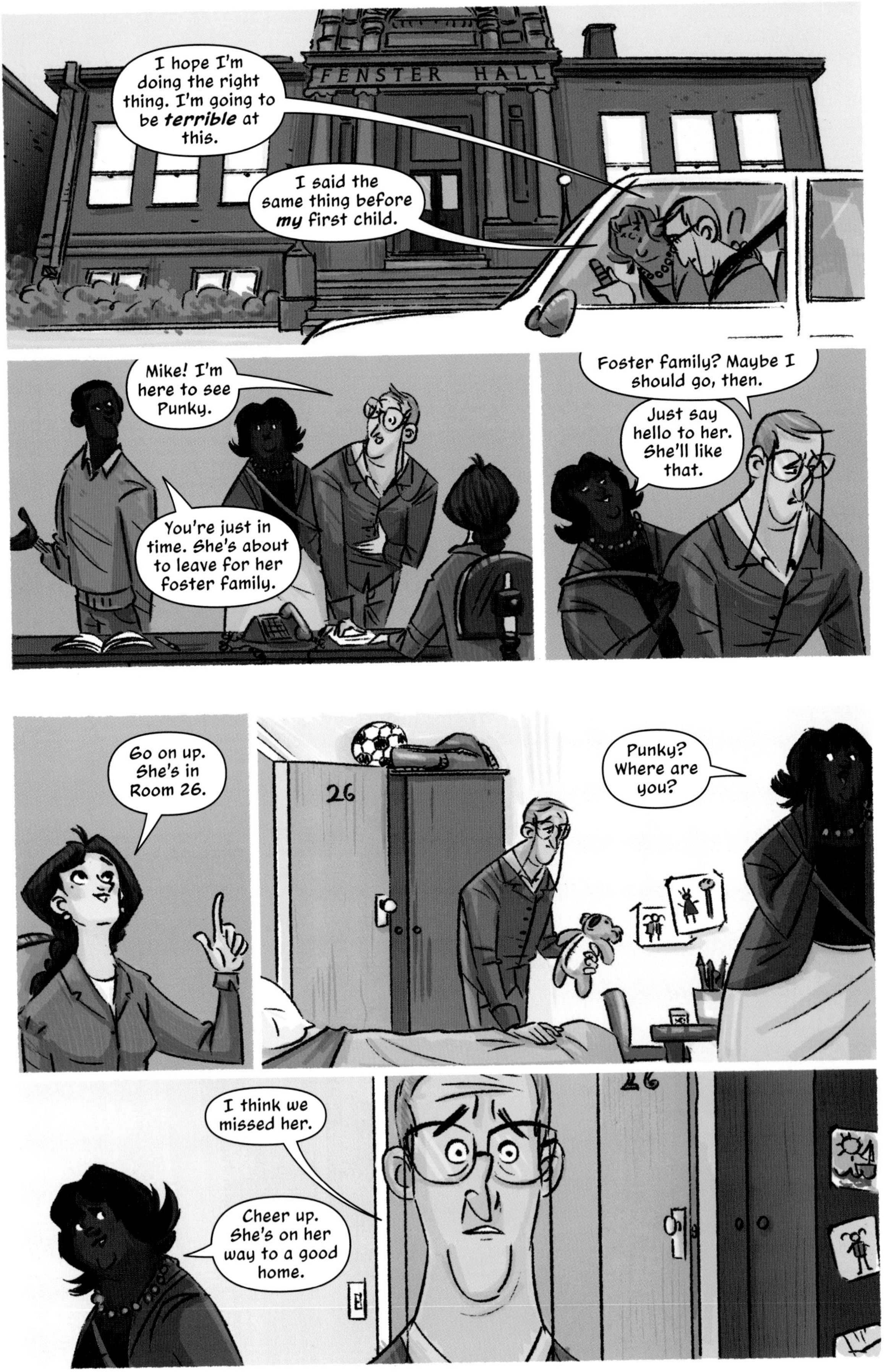
FENSTER HALL
I hope I'm doing the right thing. I'm going to be *terrible* at this.
I said the same thing before *my* first child.
Mike! I'm here to see Punky.
You're just in time. She's about to leave for her foster family.
Foster family? Maybe I should go, then.
Just say hello to her. She'll like that.
Go on up. She's in Room 26.
26
Punky? Where are you?
I think we missed her.
Cheer up. She's on her way to a good home.

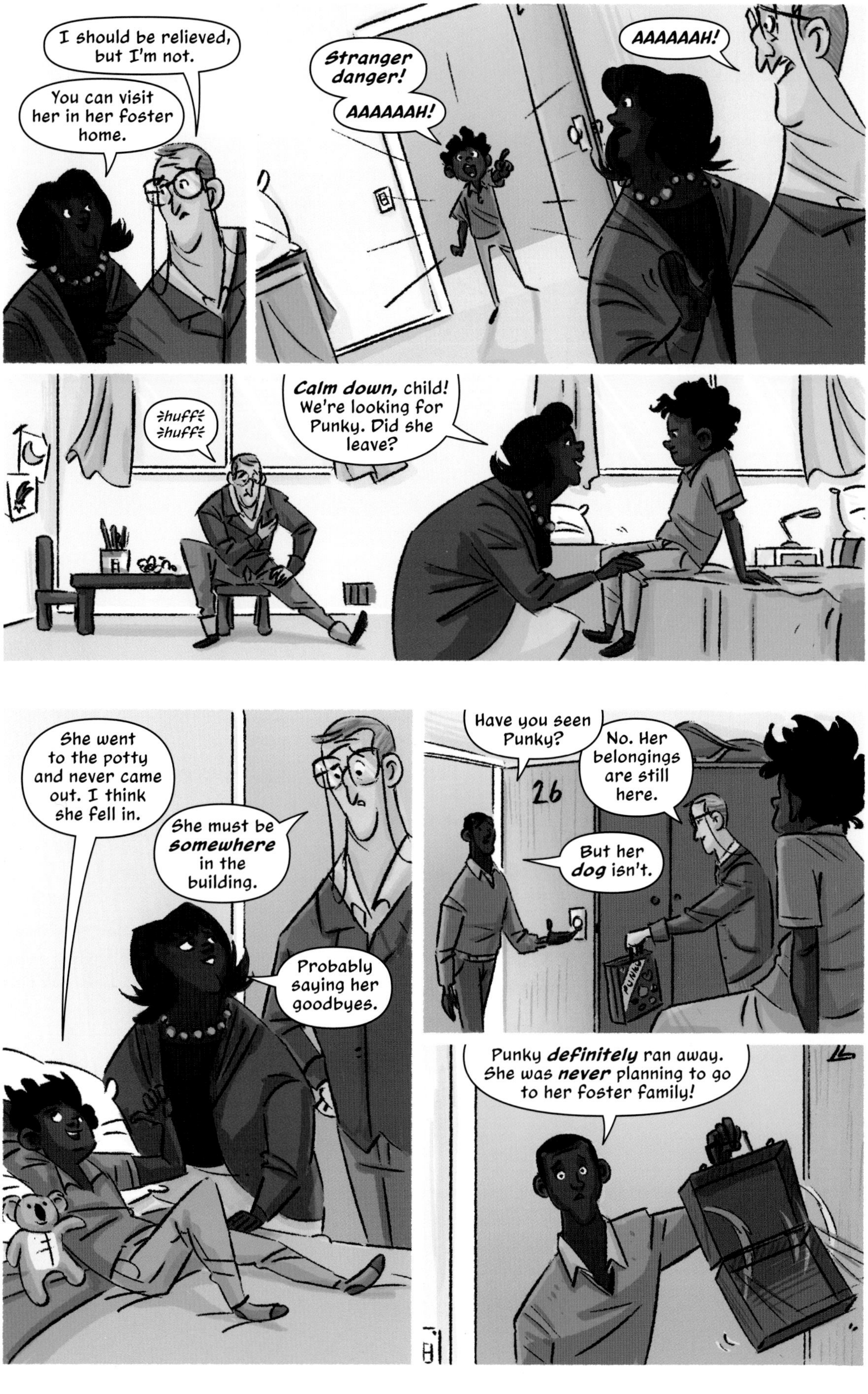
I should be relieved, but I'm not.
You can visit her in her foster home.
Stranger danger!
AAAAAAH!
AAAAAAH!
≑huff≑ ≑huff≑
Calm down, child! We're looking for Punky. Did she leave?
She went to the potty and never came out. I think she fell in.
She must be somewhere in the building.
Probably saying her goodbyes.
Have you seen Punky?
No. Her belongings are still here.
26
But her dog isn't.
Punky definitely ran away. She was never planning to go to her foster family!

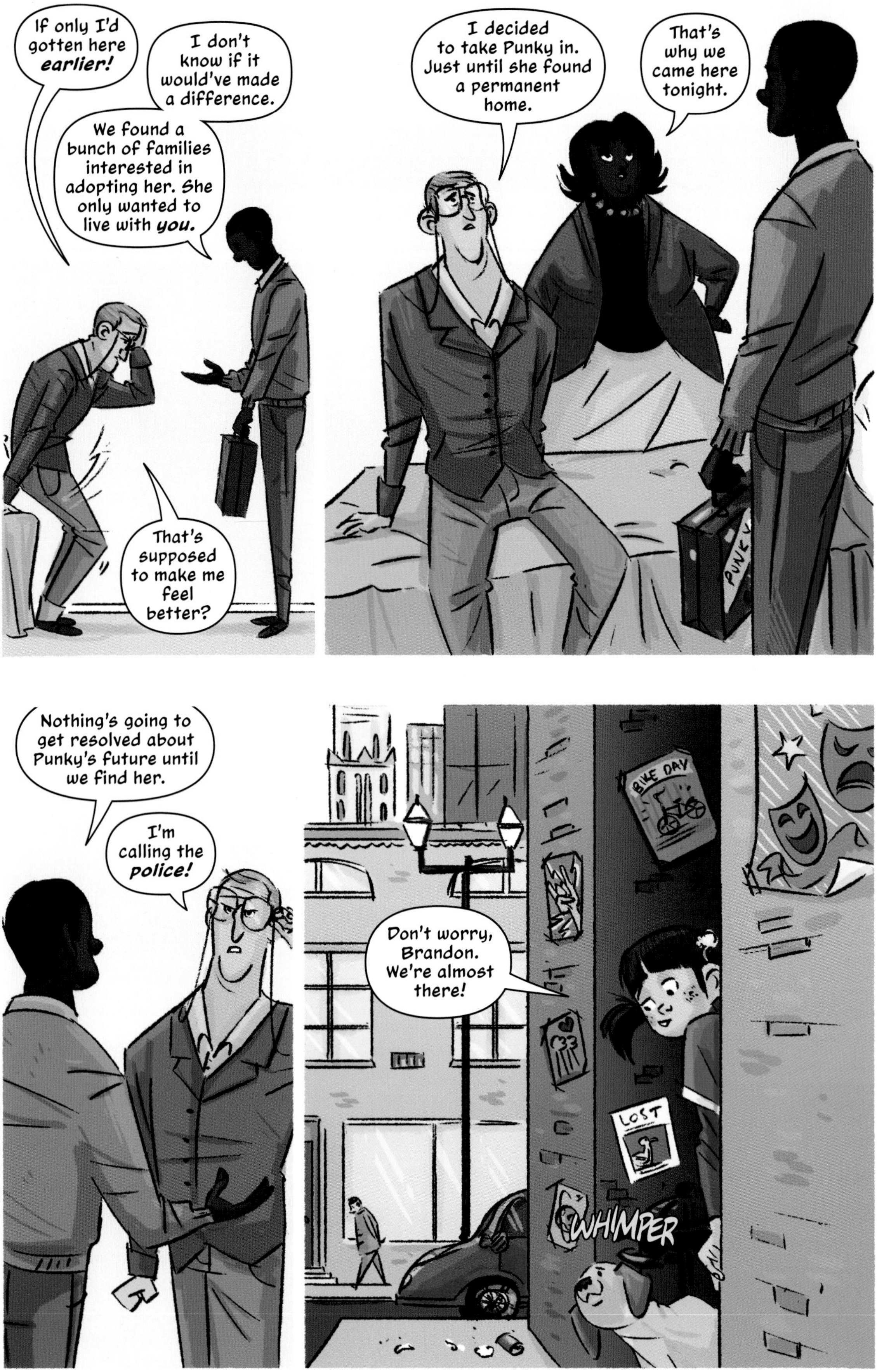
If only I'd gotten here *earlier!*
I don't know if it would've made a difference.
We found a bunch of families interested in adopting her. She only wanted to live with *you.*
That's supposed to make me feel better?
I decided to take Punky in. Just until she found a permanent home.
That's why we came here tonight.
PUNKY
Nothing's going to get resolved about Punky's future until we find her.
I'm calling the *police!*
BIKE DAY
Don't worry, Brandon. We're almost there!
LOST
WHIMPER

CHAPTER 4

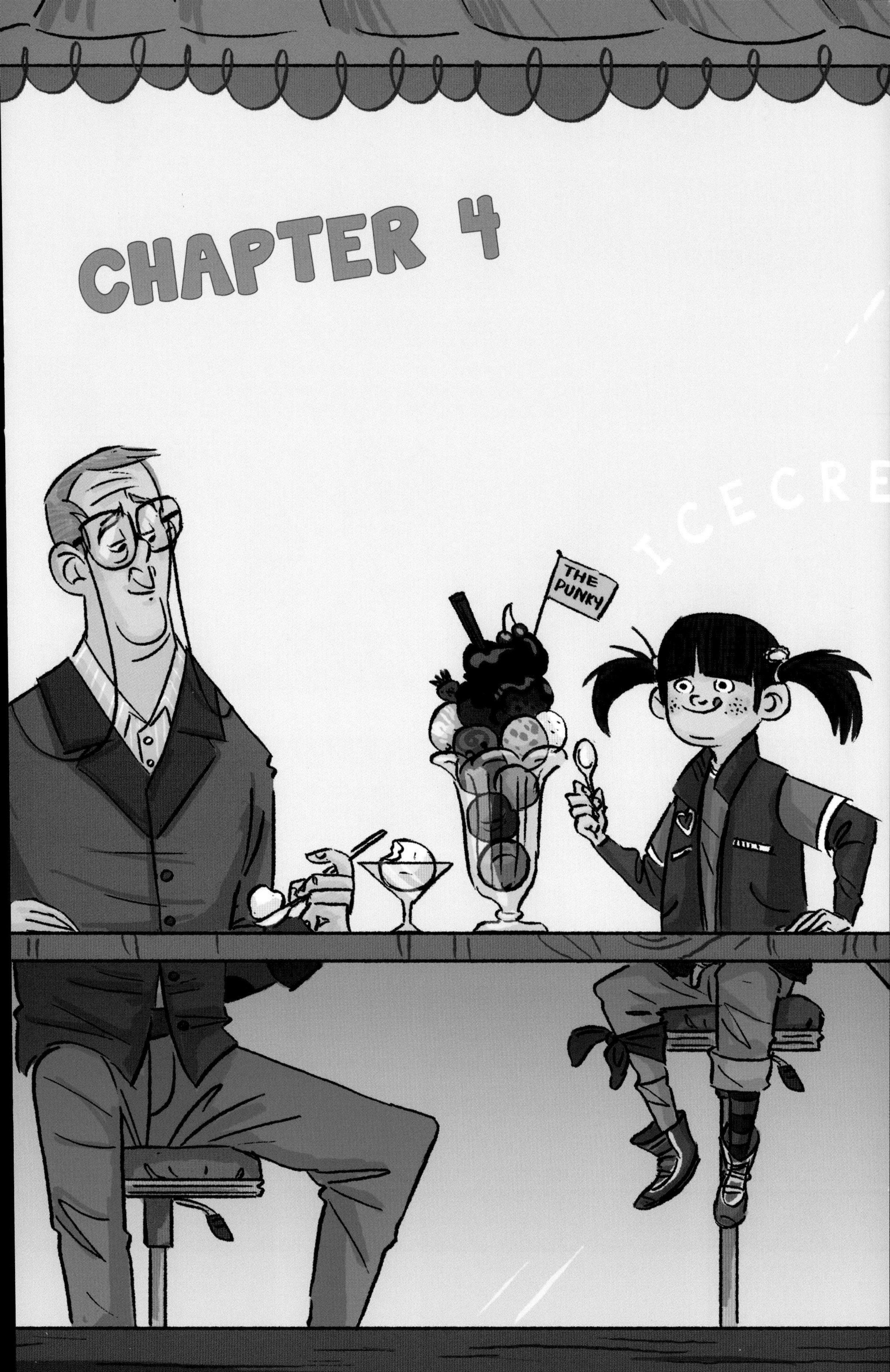
ICECRE
THE PUNKY

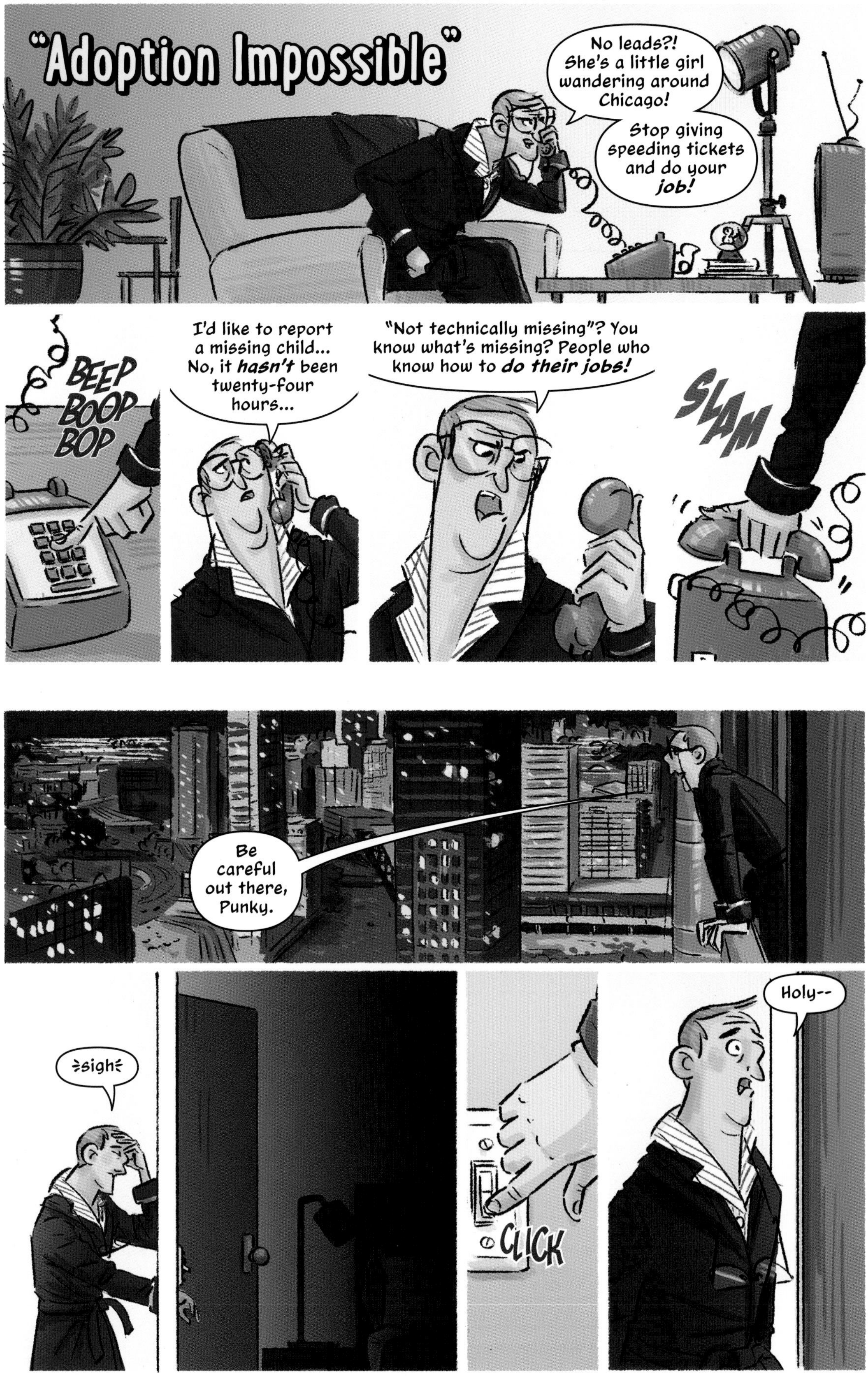
"Adoption Impossible"
No leads?! She's a little girl wandering around Chicago!
Stop giving speeding tickets and do your job!
BEEP BOOP BOP
I'd like to report a missing child... No, it hasn't been twenty-four hours...
"Not technically missing"? You know what's missing? People who know how to do their jobs!
SLAM
Be careful out there, Punky.
sigh
CLICK
Holy--

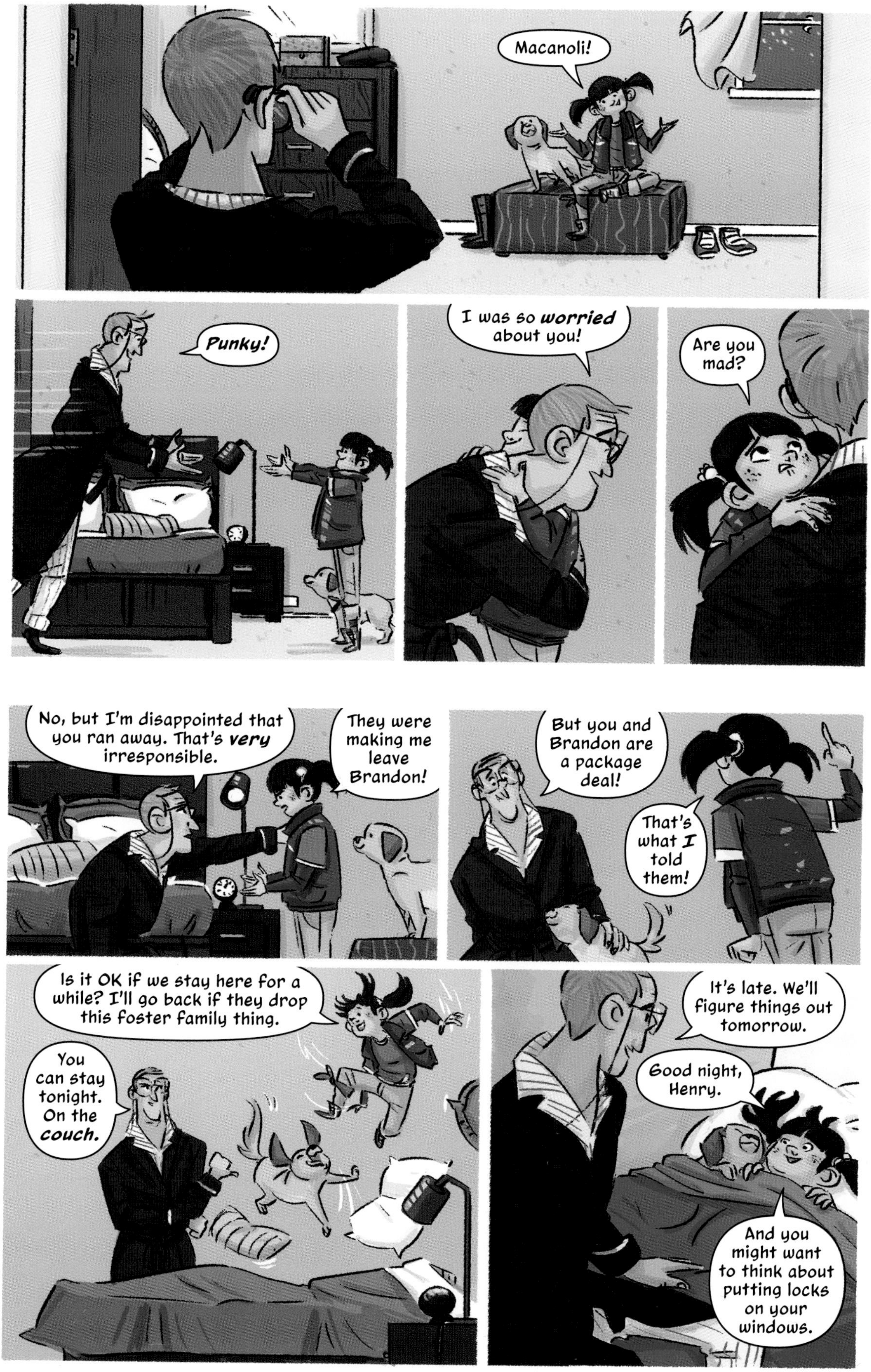
Macanoli!
Punky!
I was so worried about you!
Are you mad?
No, but I'm disappointed that you ran away. That's very irresponsible.
They were making me leave Brandon!
But you and Brandon are a package deal!
That's what I told them!
Is it OK if we stay here for a while? I'll go back if they drop this foster family thing.
You can stay tonight. On the couch.
It's late. We'll figure things out tomorrow.
Good night, Henry.
And you might want to think about putting locks on your windows.

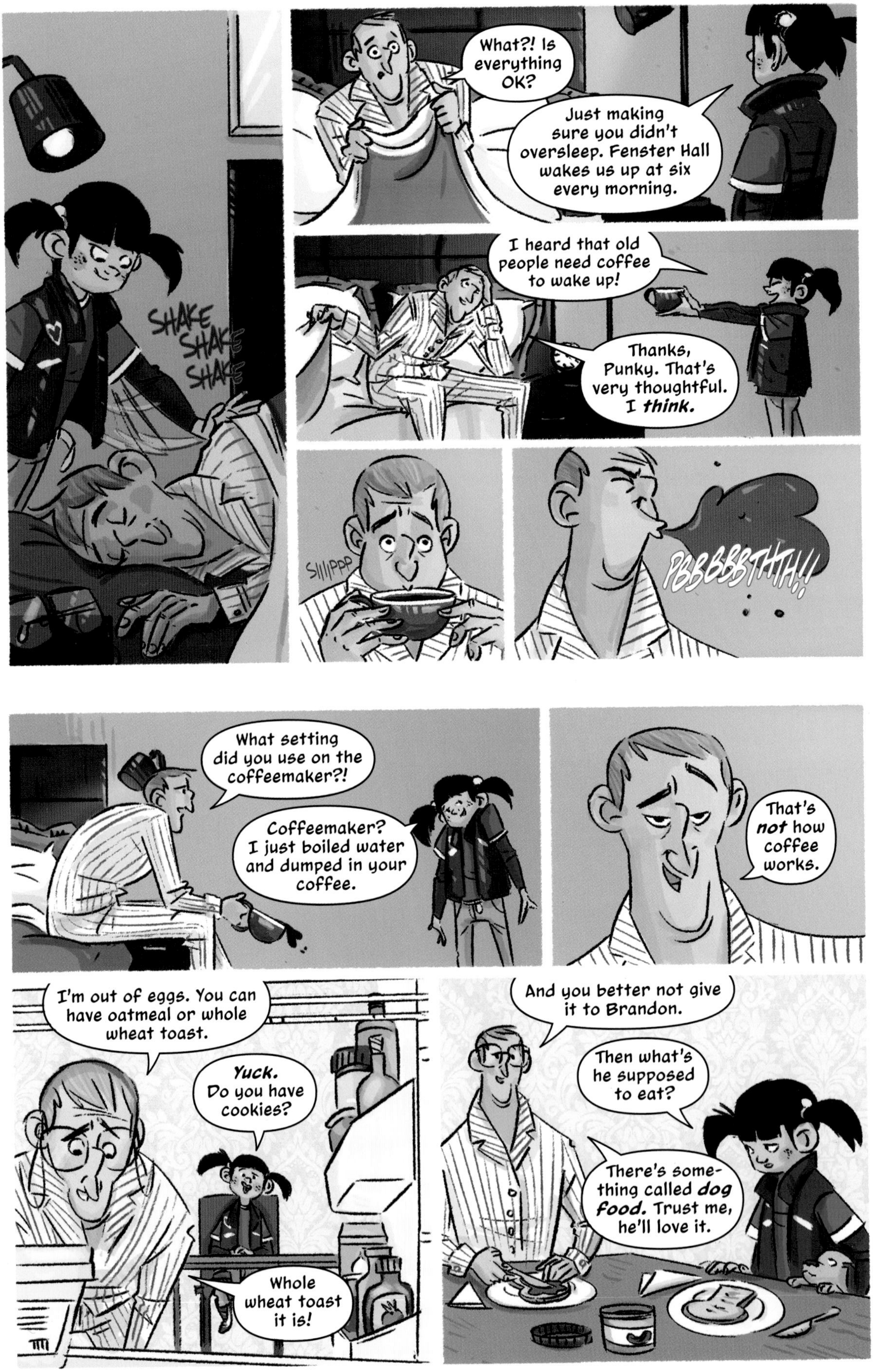
SHAKE
SHAKE
SHAKE
What?! Is everything OK?
Just making sure you didn't oversleep. Fenster Hall wakes us up at six every morning.
I heard that old people need coffee to wake up!
Thanks, Punky. That's very thoughtful. I *think.*
SIIIIPPP
PBBBBBTHTH!!
What setting did you use on the coffeemaker?!
Coffeemaker? I just boiled water and dumped in your coffee.
That's *not* how coffee works.
I'm out of eggs. You can have oatmeal or whole wheat toast.
Yuck. Do you have cookies?
Whole wheat toast it is!
And you better not give it to Brandon.
Then what's he supposed to eat?
There's something called *dog food.* Trust me, he'll love it.

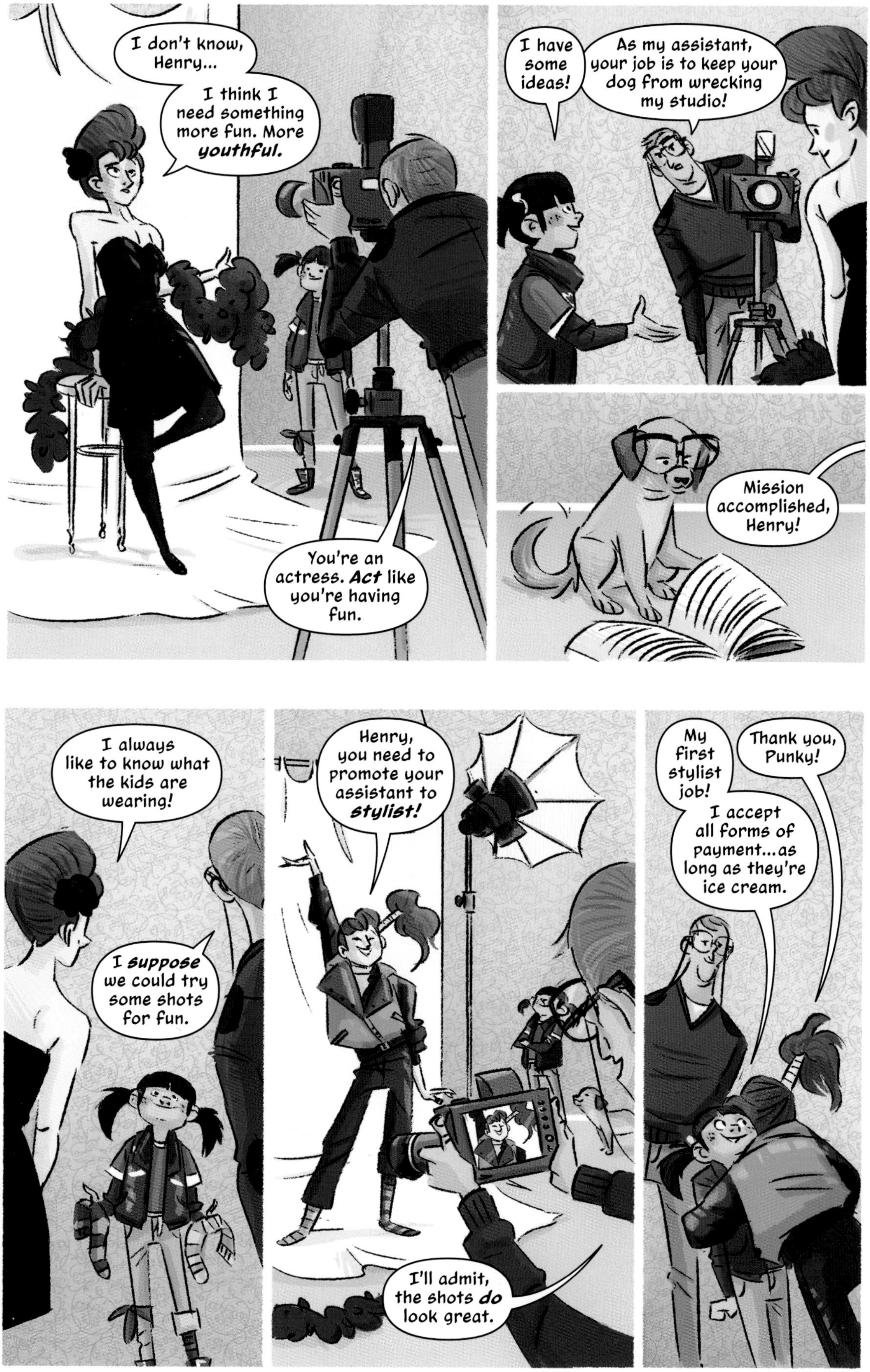

I don't know, Henry...
I think I need something more fun. More *youthful.*
You're an actress. ***Act*** like you're having fun.
I have some ideas!
As my assistant, your job is to keep your dog from wrecking my studio!
Mission accomplished, Henry!
I always like to know what the kids are wearing!
I ***suppose*** we could try some shots for fun.
Henry, you need to promote your assistant to ***stylist!***
I'll admit, the shots ***do*** look great.
My first stylist job!
I accept all forms of payment...as long as they're ice cream.
Thank you, Punky!

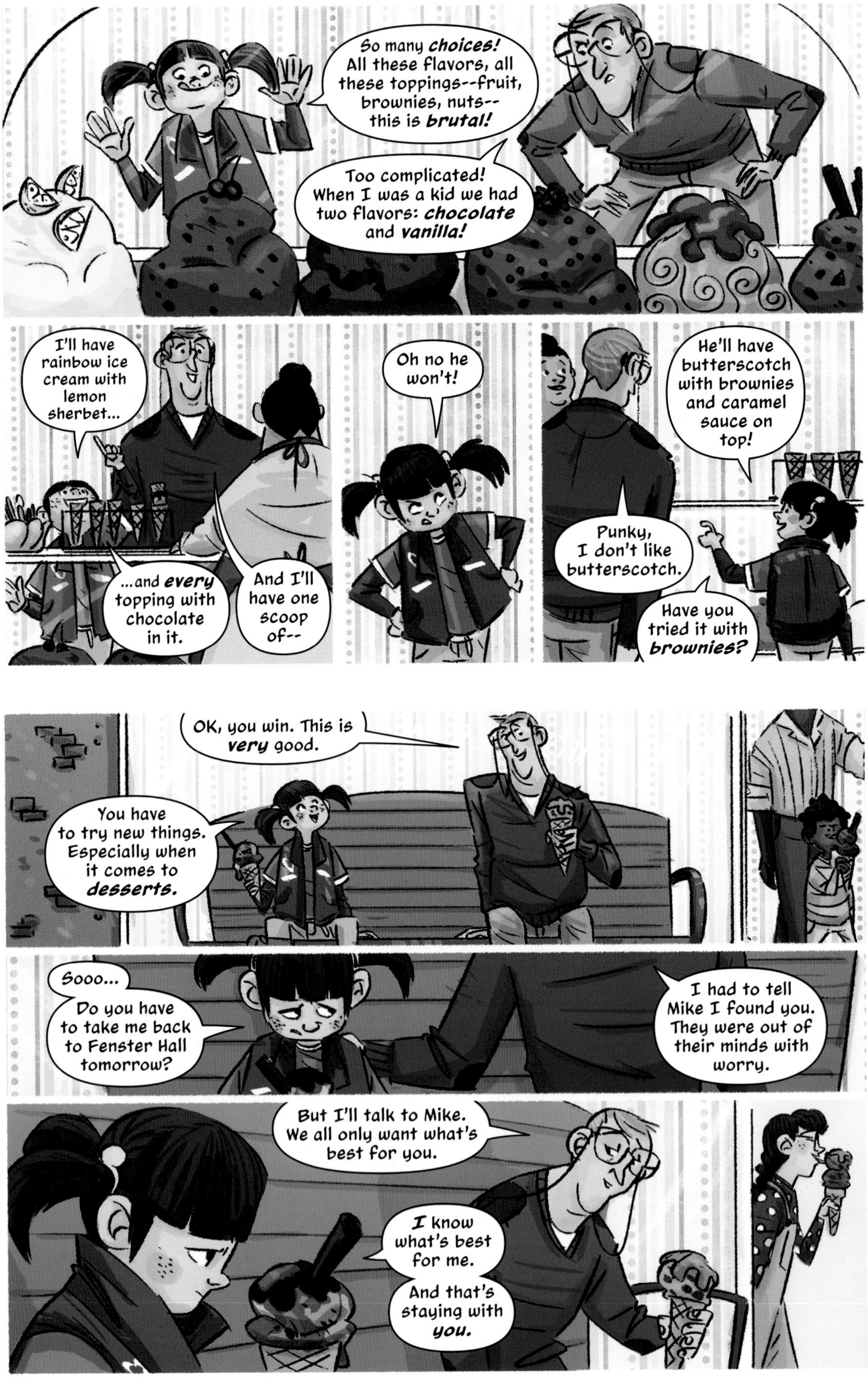
So many *choices!* All these flavors, all these toppings--fruit, brownies, nuts--this is *brutal!*
Too complicated! When I was a kid we had two flavors: *chocolate* and *vanilla!*
I'll have rainbow ice cream with lemon sherbet...
...and *every* topping with chocolate in it.
And I'll have one scoop of--
Oh no he won't!
He'll have butterscotch with brownies and caramel sauce on top!
Punky, I don't like butterscotch.
Have you tried it with *brownies?*
OK, you win. This is *very* good.
You have to try new things. Especially when it comes to *desserts.*
Sooo... Do you have to take me back to Fenster Hall tomorrow?
I had to tell Mike I found you. They were out of their minds with worry.
But I'll talk to Mike. We all only want what's best for you.
I know what's best for me.
And that's staying with *you.*

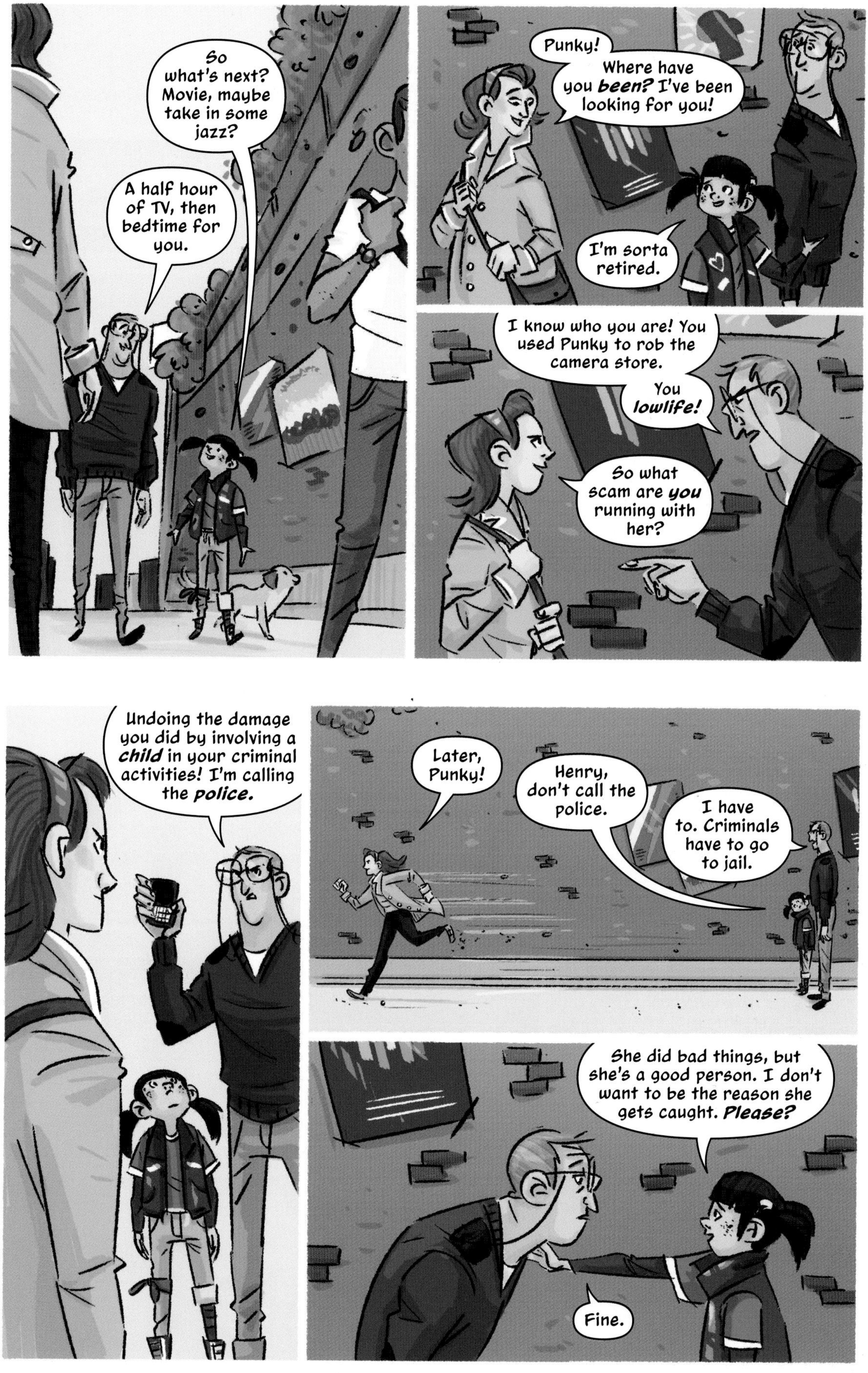
So what's next? Movie, maybe take in some jazz?
A half hour of TV, then bedtime for you.
Punky!
Where have you been? I've been looking for you!
I'm sorta retired.
I know who you are! You used Punky to rob the camera store.
You lowlife!
So what scam are you running with her?
Undoing the damage you did by involving a child in your criminal activities! I'm calling the police.
Later, Punky!
Henry, don't call the police.
I have to. Criminals have to go to jail.
She did bad things, but she's a good person. I don't want to be the reason she gets caught. Please?
Fine.

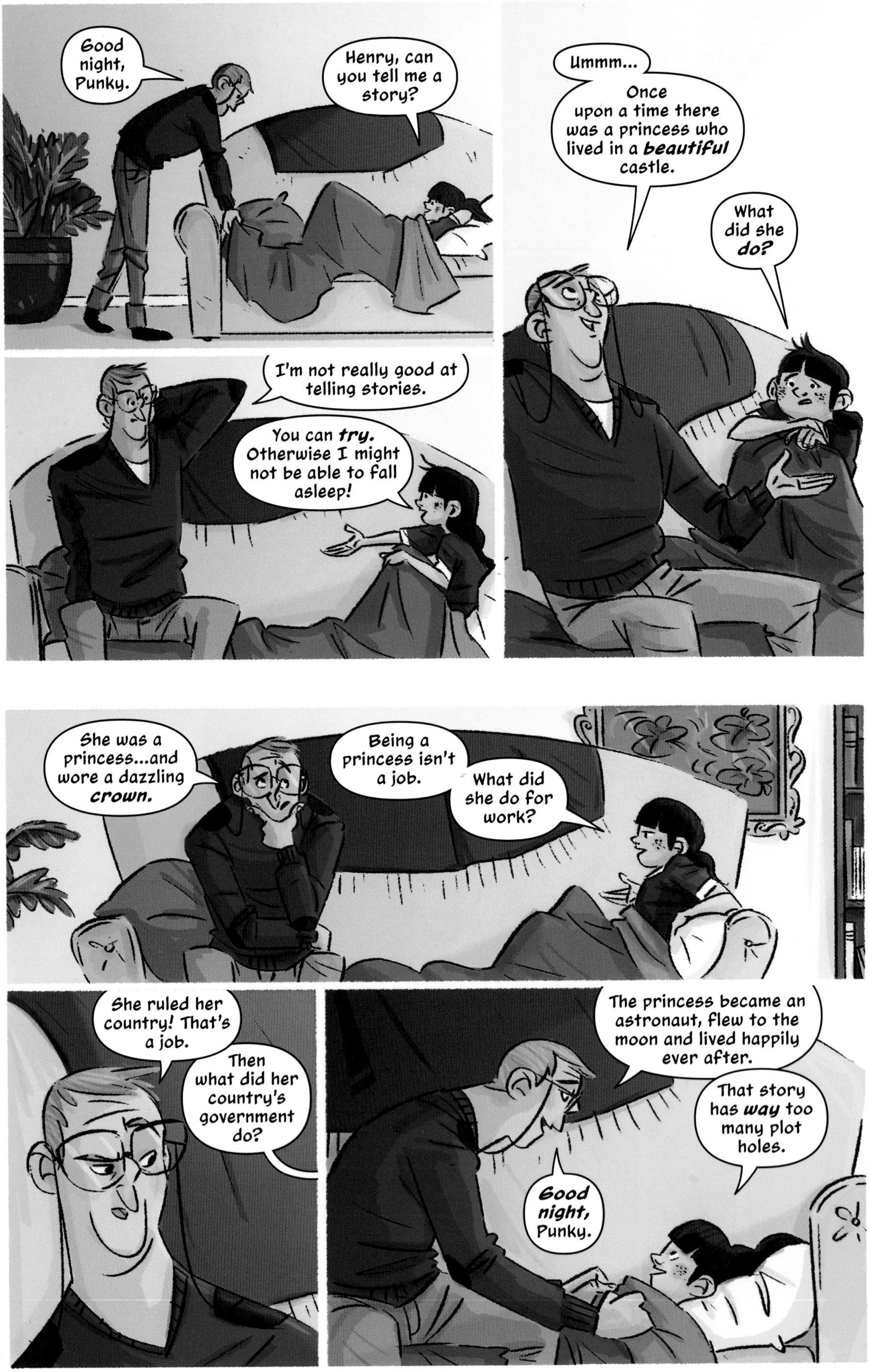
Good night, Punky.
Henry, can you tell me a story?
Ummm...
Once upon a time there was a princess who lived in a *beautiful* castle.
What did she *do?*
I'm not really good at telling stories.
You can *try.* Otherwise I might not be able to fall asleep!
She was a princess...and wore a dazzling *crown.*
Being a princess isn't a job.
What did she do for work?
She ruled her country! That's a job.
Then what did her country's government do?
The princess became an astronaut, flew to the moon and lived happily ever after.
That story has *way* too many plot holes.
Good night, Punky.

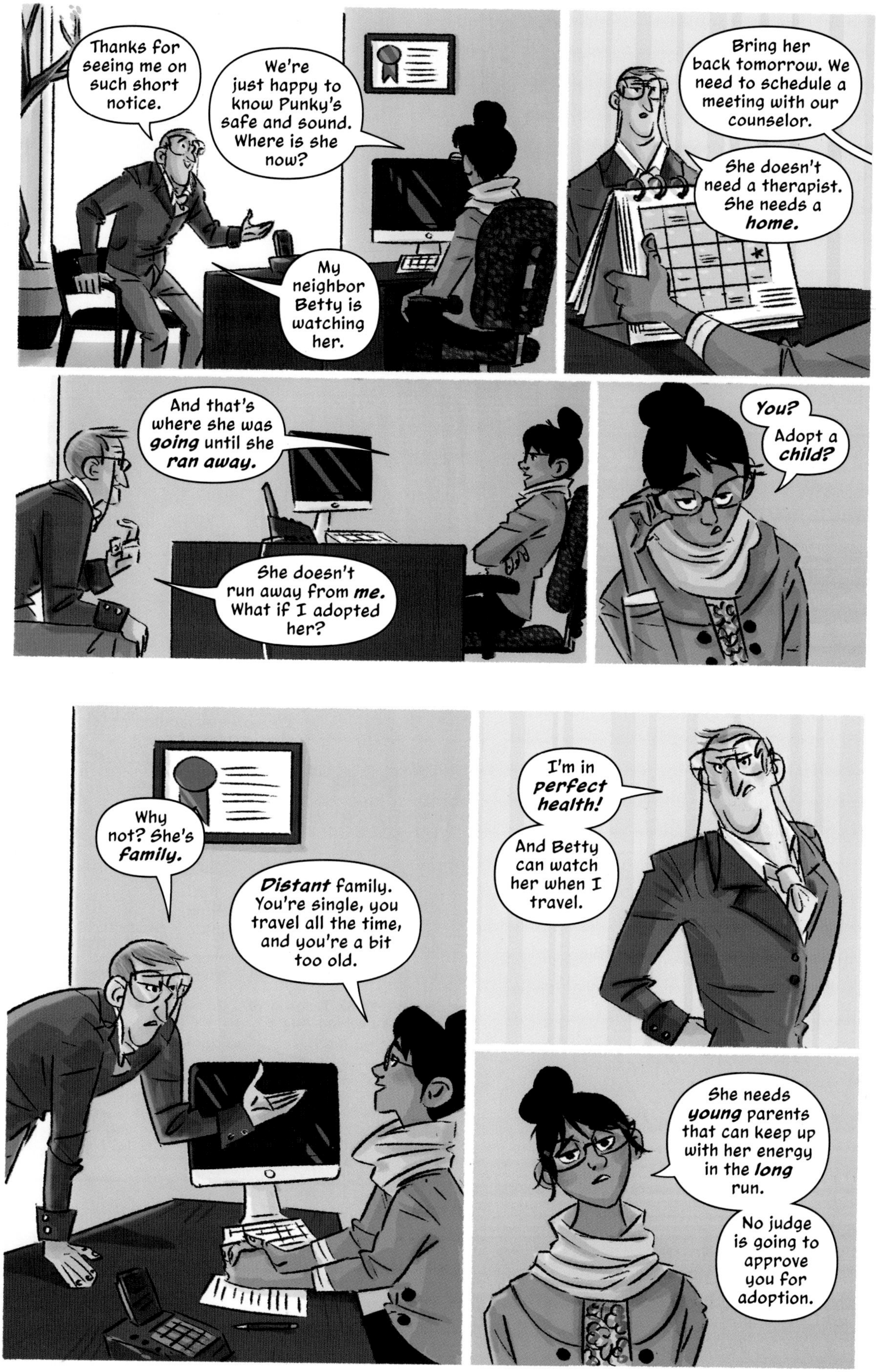
Thanks for seeing me on such short notice.
We're just happy to know Punky's safe and sound. Where is she now?
My neighbor Betty is watching her.
Bring her back tomorrow. We need to schedule a meeting with our counselor.
She doesn't need a therapist. She needs a *home.*
And that's where she was *going* until she *ran away.*
She doesn't run away from *me.* What if I adopted her?
You? Adopt a *child?*
Why not? She's *family.*
Distant family. You're single, you travel all the time, and you're a bit too old.
I'm in *perfect health!*
And Betty can watch her when I travel.
She needs *young* parents that can keep up with her energy in the *long* run.
No judge is going to approve you for adoption.

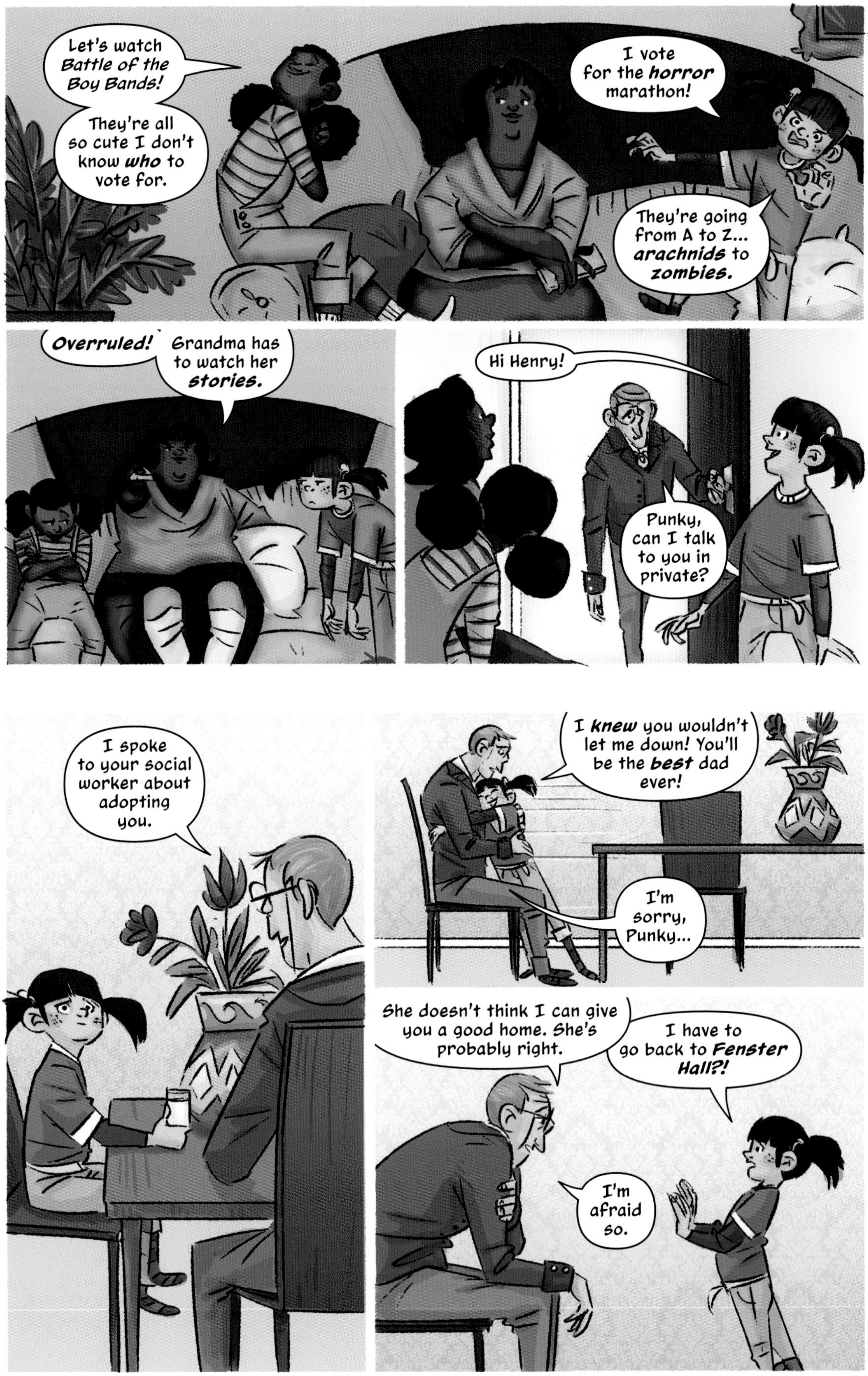

Let's watch *Battle of the Boy Bands!*
They're all so cute I don't know ***who*** to vote for.
I vote for the ***horror*** marathon!
They're going from A to Z... ***arachnids*** to ***zombies.***
Overruled!
Grandma has to watch her ***stories.***
Hi Henry!
Punky, can I talk to you in private?
I spoke to your social worker about adopting you.
I ***knew*** you wouldn't let me down! You'll be the ***best*** dad ever!
I'm sorry, Punky...
She doesn't think I can give you a good home. She's probably right.
I have to go back to ***Fenster Hall?!***
I'm afraid so.

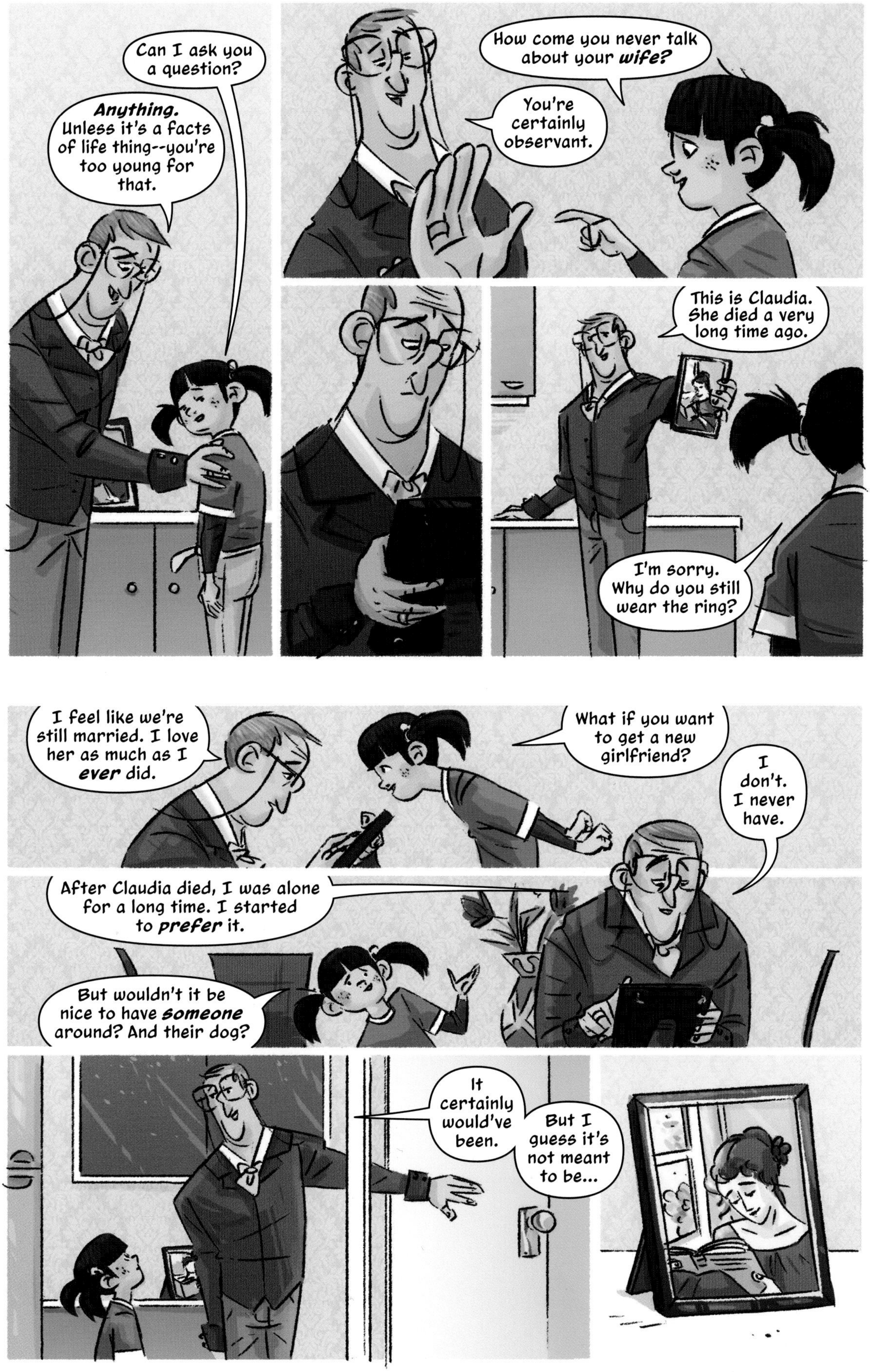
Can I ask you a question?
Anything. Unless it's a facts of life thing--you're too young for that.
How come you never talk about your wife?
You're certainly observant.
This is Claudia. She died a very long time ago.
I'm sorry. Why do you still wear the ring?
I feel like we're still married. I love her as much as I ever did.
What if you want to get a new girlfriend?
I don't. I never have.
After Claudia died, I was alone for a long time. I started to prefer it.
But wouldn't it be nice to have someone around? And their dog?
It certainly would've been.
But I guess it's not meant to be...

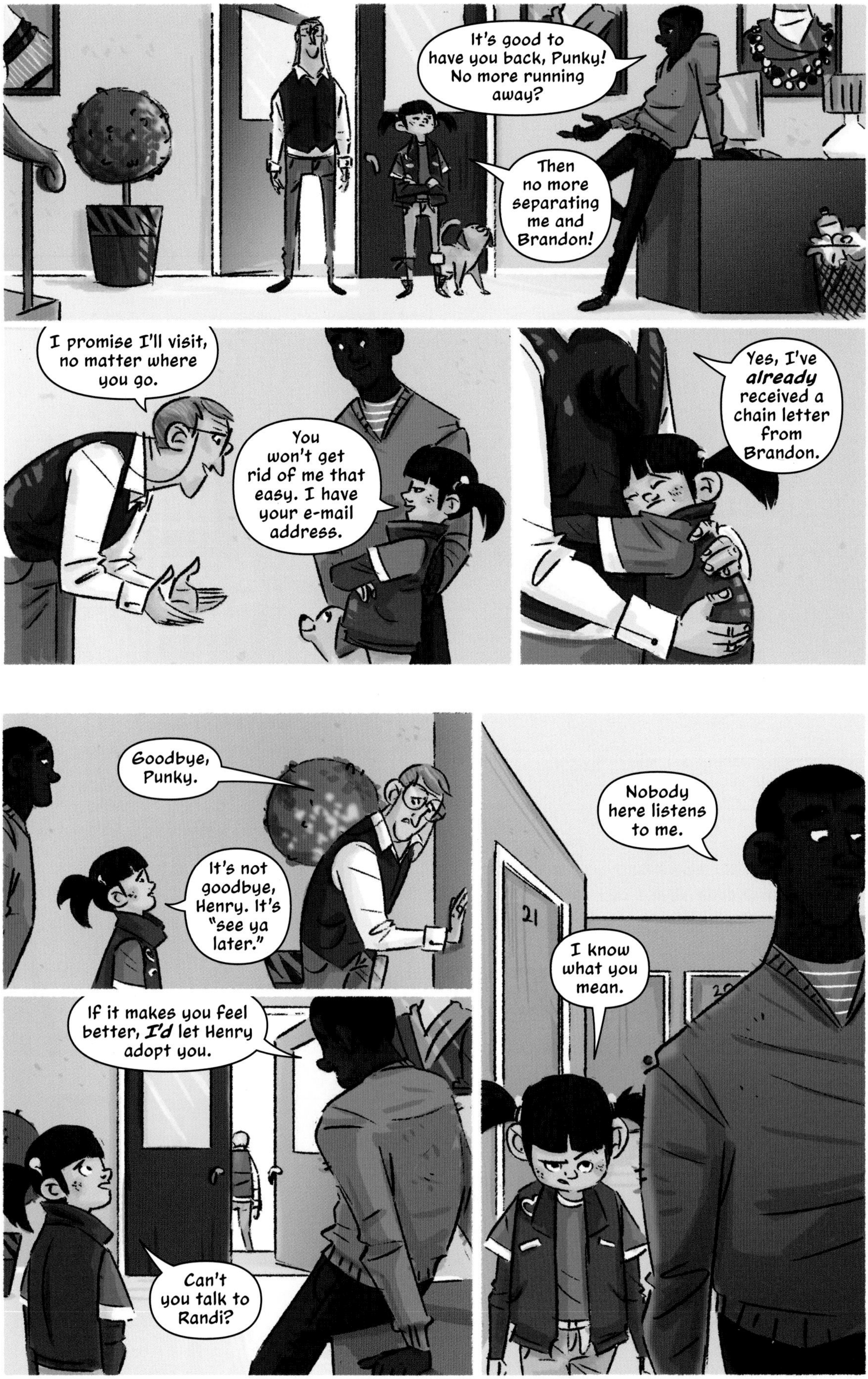
It's good to have you back, Punky! No more running away?
Then no more separating me and Brandon!
I promise I'll visit, no matter where you go.
You won't get rid of me that easy. I have your e-mail address.
Yes, I've *already* received a chain letter from Brandon.
Goodbye, Punky.
It's not goodbye, Henry. It's "see ya later."
If it makes you feel better, *I'd* let Henry adopt you.
Can't you talk to Randi?
Nobody here listens to me.
I know what you mean.
21

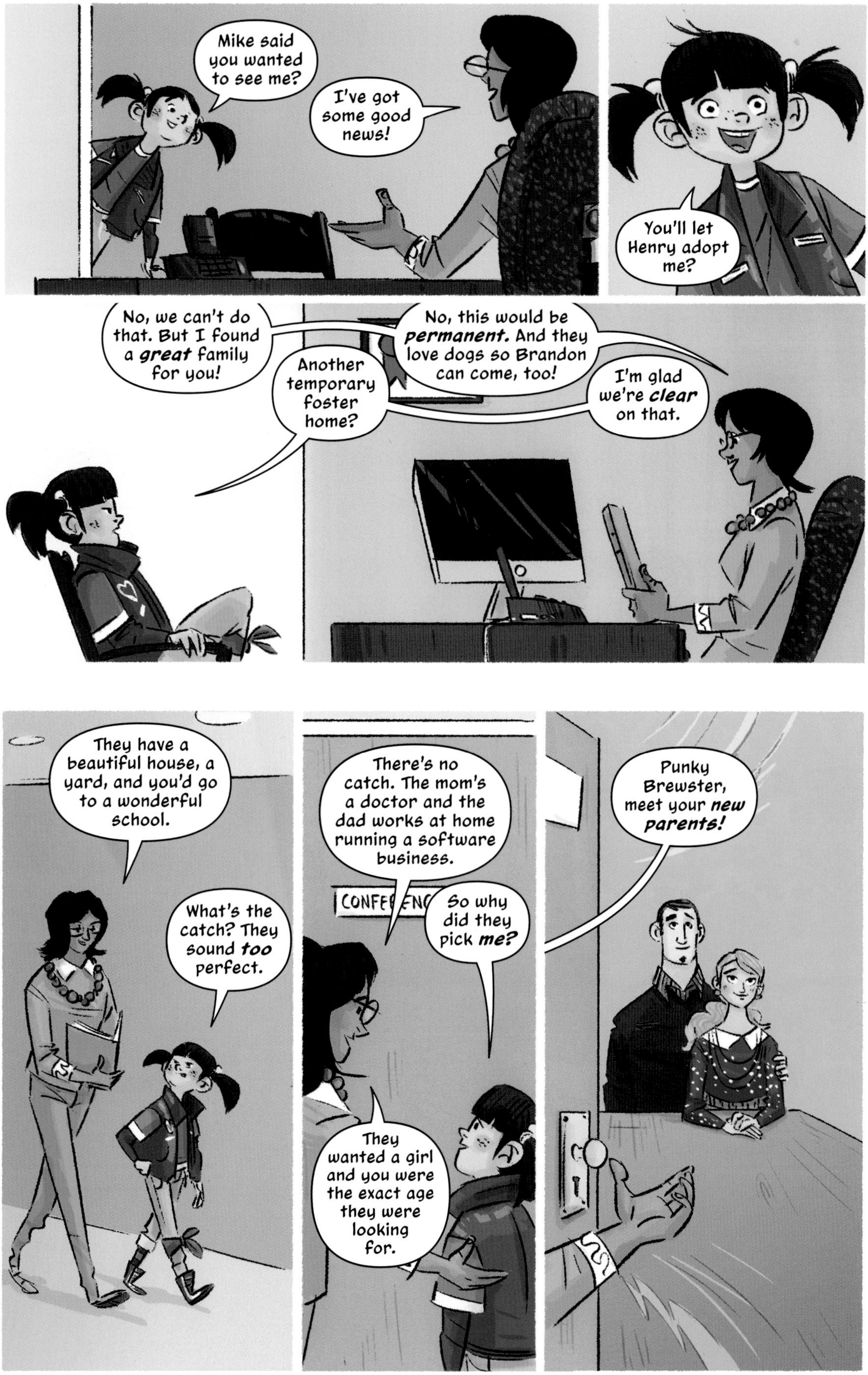
Mike said you wanted to see me?
I've got some good news!
You'll let Henry adopt me?
No, we can't do that. But I found a *great* family for you!
Another temporary foster home?
No, this would be *permanent.* And they love dogs so Brandon can come, too!
I'm glad we're *clear* on that.
They have a beautiful house, a yard, and you'd go to a wonderful school.
What's the catch? They sound *too* perfect.
There's no catch. The mom's a doctor and the dad works at home running a software business.
So why did they pick *me?*
They wanted a girl and you were the exact age they were looking for.
Punky Brewster, meet your *new parents!*

CHAPTER 5

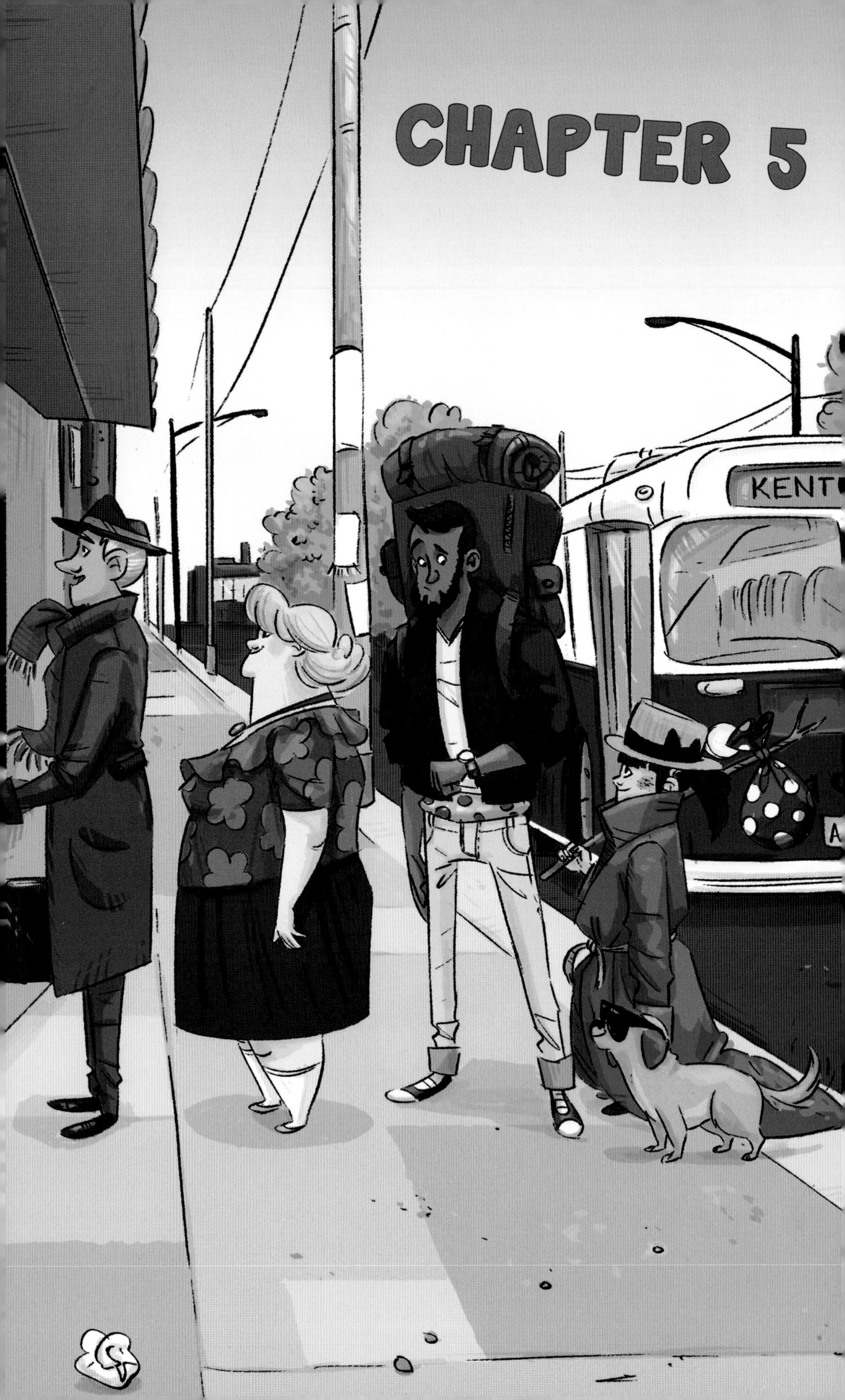
KENT

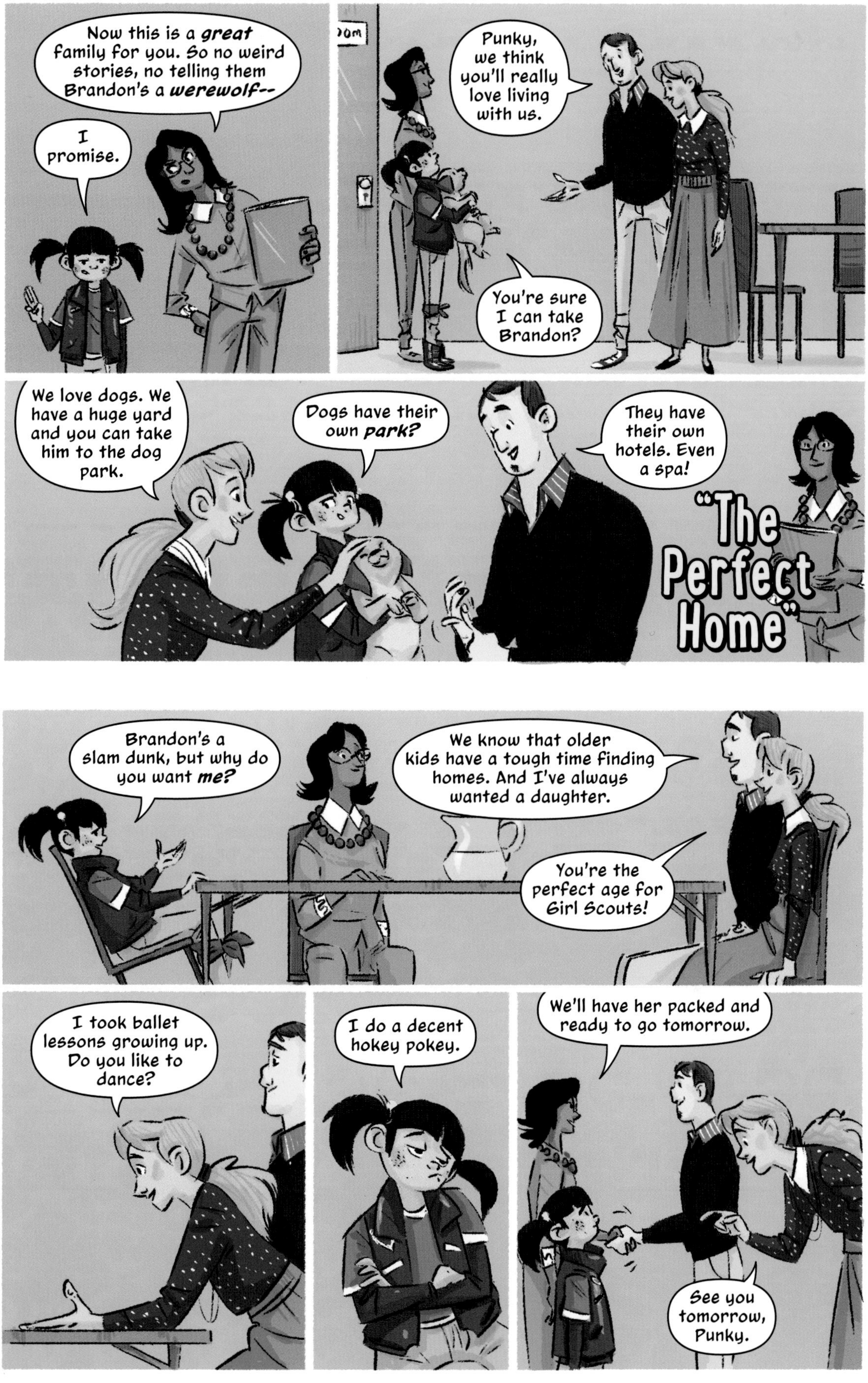
Now this is a great family for you. So no weird stories, no telling them Brandon's a werewolf--
I promise.
Punky, we think you'll really love living with us.
You're sure I can take Brandon?
We love dogs. We have a huge yard and you can take him to the dog park.
Dogs have their own park?
They have their own hotels. Even a spa!
"The Perfect Home"
Brandon's a slam dunk, but why do you want me?
We know that older kids have a tough time finding homes. And I've always wanted a daughter.
You're the perfect age for Girl Scouts!
I took ballet lessons growing up. Do you like to dance?
I do a decent hokey pokey.
We'll have her packed and ready to go tomorrow.
See you tomorrow, Punky.

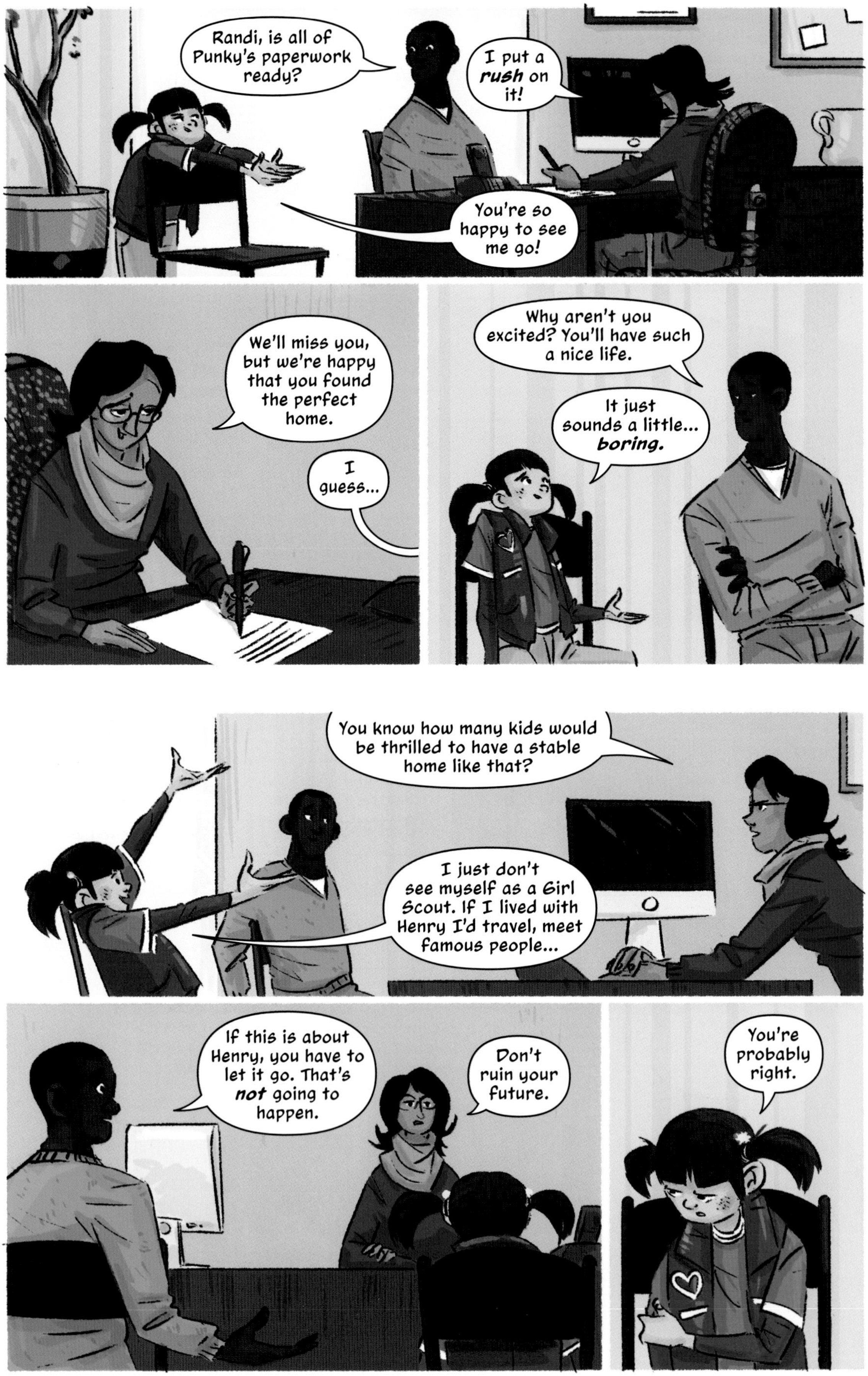

Randi, is all of Punky's paperwork ready?
I put a *rush* on it!
You're so happy to see me go!
We'll miss you, but we're happy that you found the perfect home.
I guess...
Why aren't you excited? You'll have such a nice life.
It just sounds a little... *boring.*
You know how many kids would be thrilled to have a stable home like that?
I just don't see myself as a Girl Scout. If I lived with Henry I'd travel, meet famous people...
If this is about Henry, you have to let it go. That's *not* going to happen.
Don't ruin your future.
You're probably right.

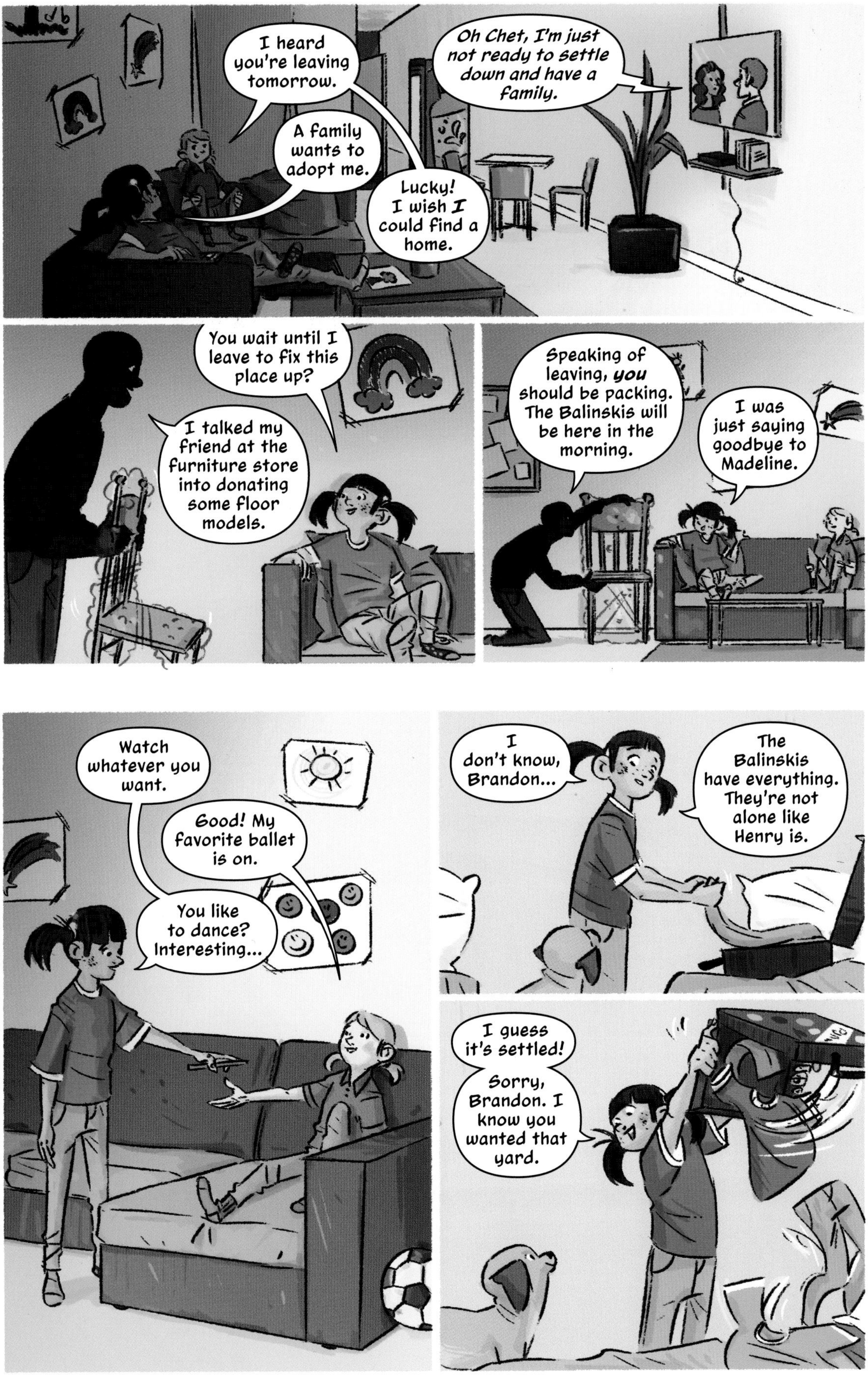
I heard you're leaving tomorrow.
A family wants to adopt me.
Lucky! I wish I could find a home.
Oh Chet, I'm just not ready to settle down and have a family.
You wait until I leave to fix this place up?
I talked my friend at the furniture store into donating some floor models.
Speaking of leaving, you should be packing. The Balinskis will be here in the morning.
I was just saying goodbye to Madeline.
Watch whatever you want.
Good! My favorite ballet is on.
You like to dance? Interesting...
I don't know, Brandon...
The Balinskis have everything. They're not alone like Henry is.
I guess it's settled!
Sorry, Brandon. I know you wanted that yard.

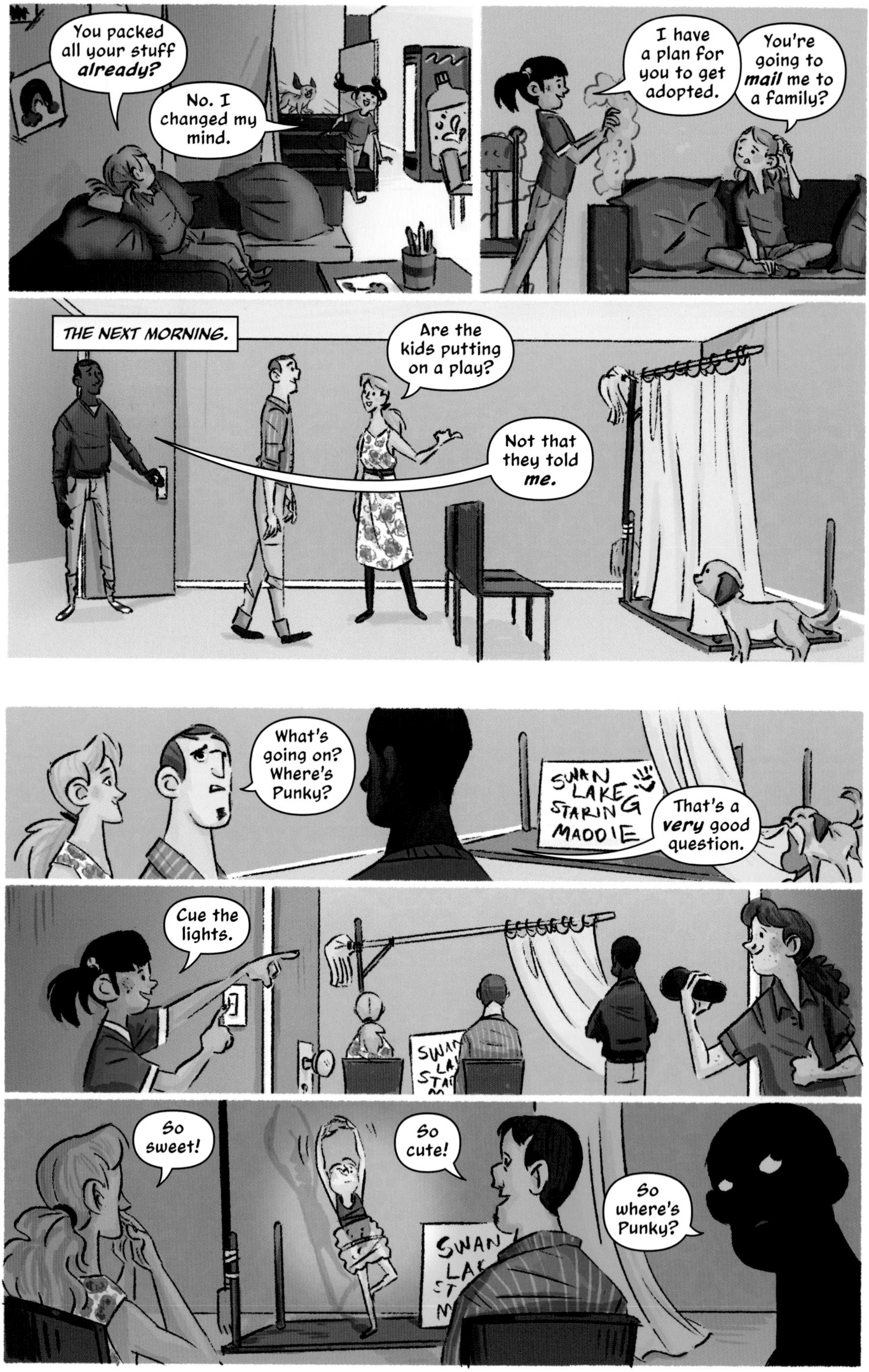
You packed all your stuff *already?*
No. I changed my mind.
I have a plan for you to get adopted.
You're going to *mail* me to a family?
THE NEXT MORNING.
Are the kids putting on a play?
Not that they told *me.*
What's going on? Where's Punky?
SWAN LAKE STARING MADDIE
That's a *very* good question.
Cue the lights.
So sweet!
So cute!
So where's Punky?

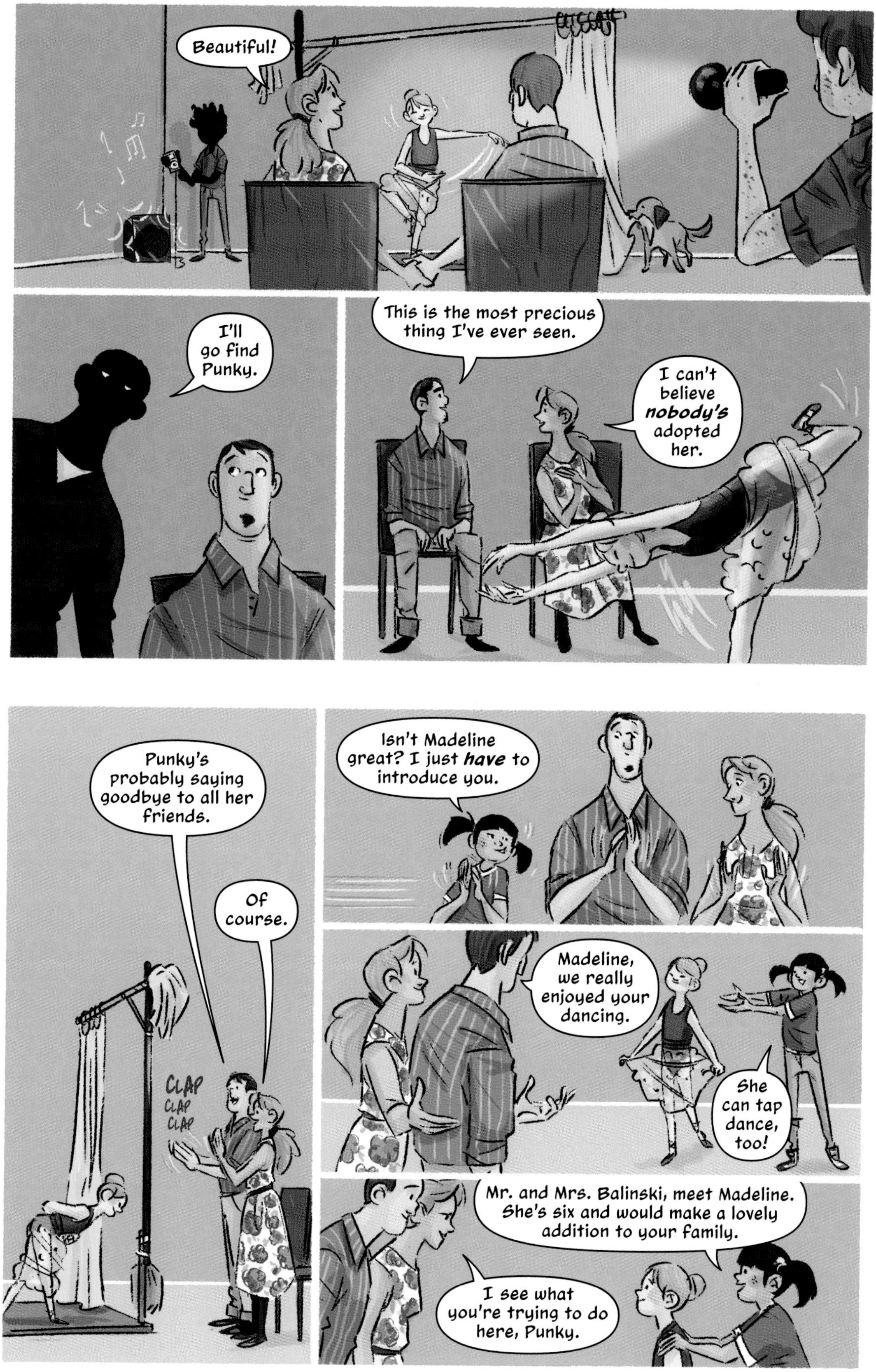
Beautiful!
I'll go find Punky.
This is the most precious thing I've ever seen.
I can't believe *nobody's* adopted her.
Punky's probably saying goodbye to all her friends.
Of course.
CLAP CLAP CLAP
Isn't Madeline great? I just *have* to introduce you.
Madeline, we really enjoyed your dancing.
She can tap dance, too!
Mr. and Mrs. Balinski, meet Madeline. She's six and would make a lovely addition to your family.
I see what you're trying to do here, Punky.

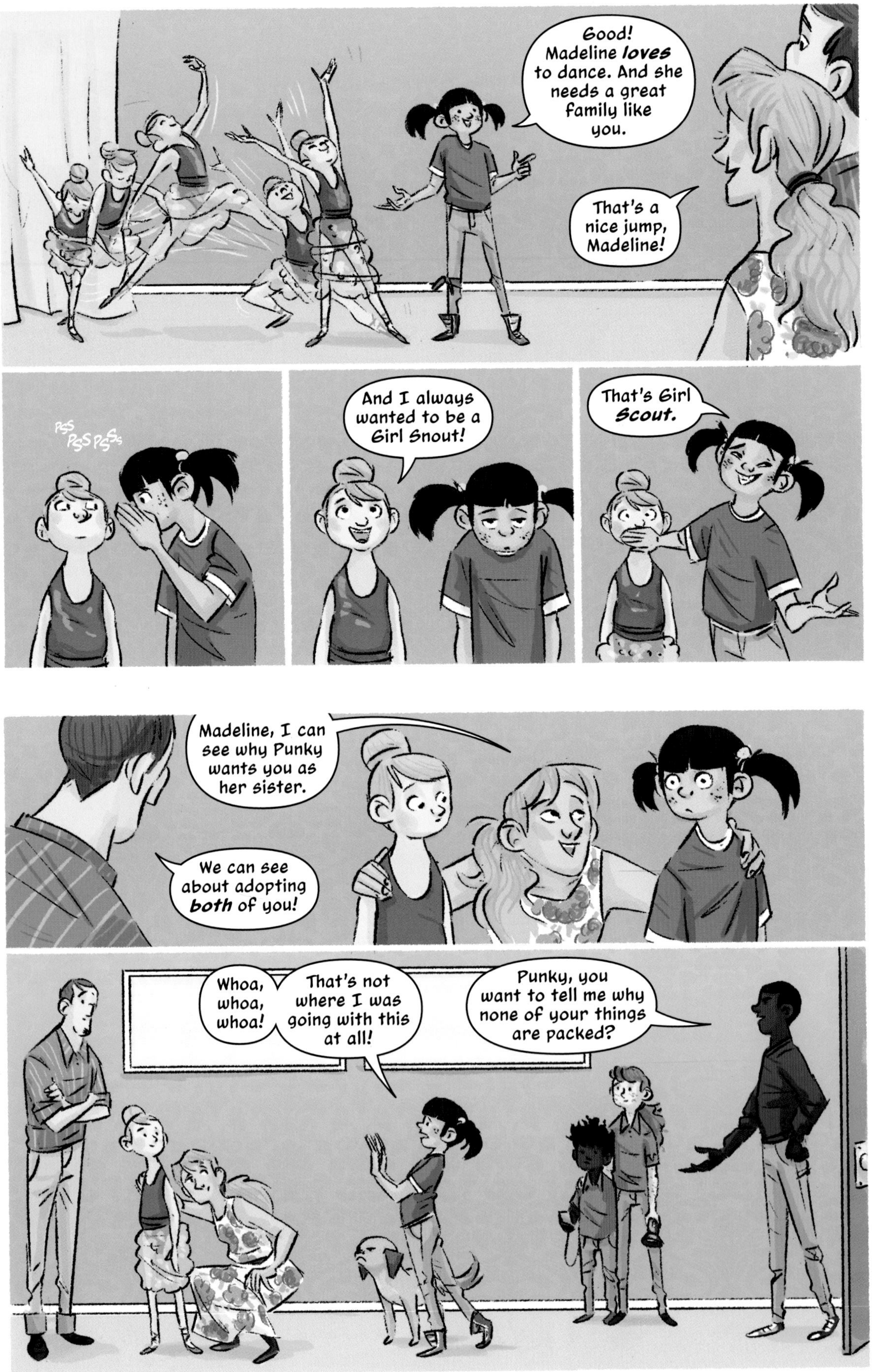

Good! Madeline *loves* to dance. And she needs a great family like you.
That's a nice jump, Madeline!
PSS PSS PSSSS
And I always wanted to be a Girl Snout!
That's Girl *Scout.*
Madeline, I can see why Punky wants you as her sister.
We can see about adopting *both* of you!
Whoa, whoa, whoa!
That's not where I was going with this at all!
Punky, you want to tell me why none of your things are packed?

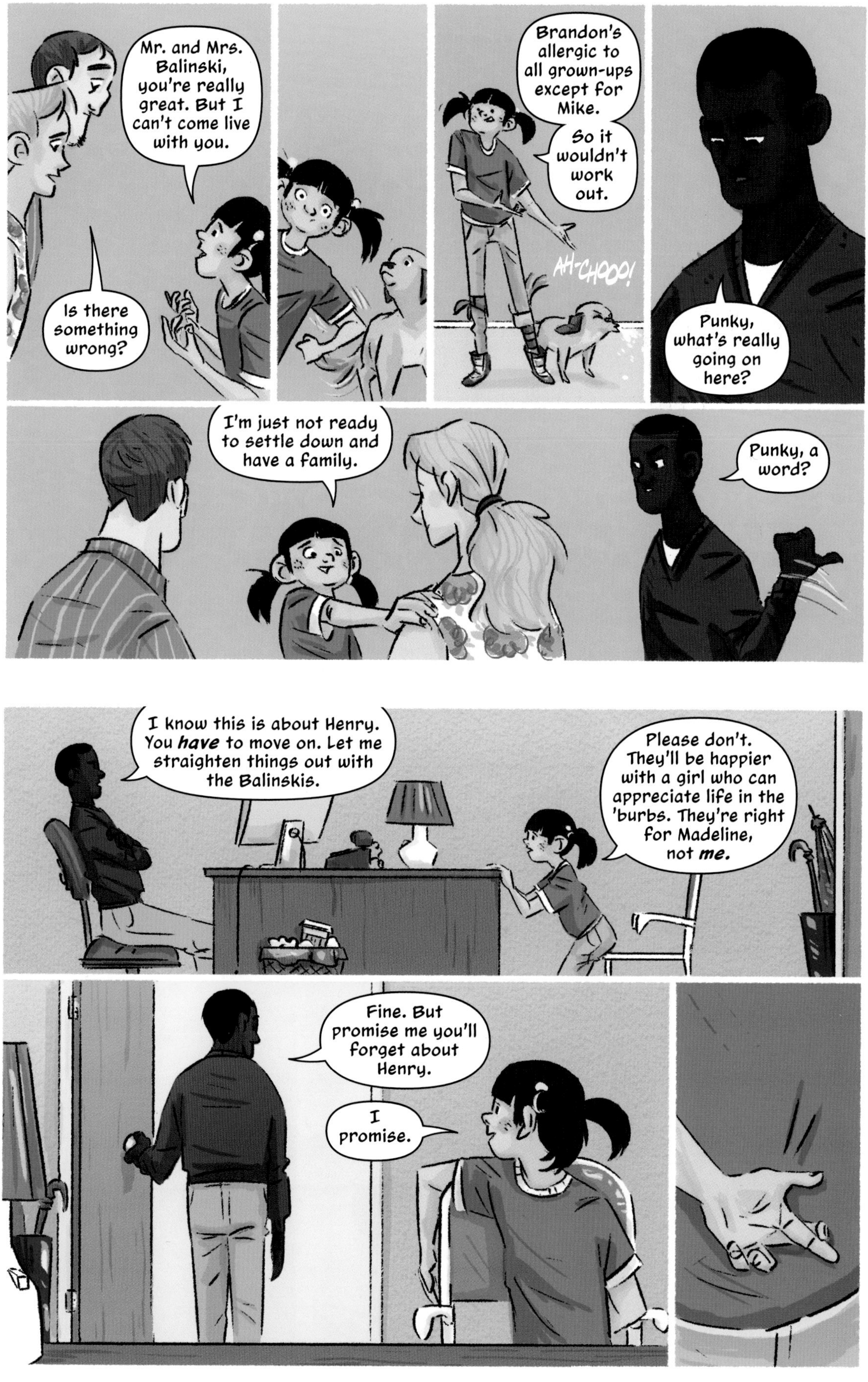
Mr. and Mrs. Balinski, you're really great. But I can't come live with you.
Is there something wrong?
Brandon's allergic to all grown-ups except for Mike.
So it wouldn't work out.
AH-CHOOO!
Punky, what's really going on here?
I'm just not ready to settle down and have a family.
Punky, a word?
I know this is about Henry. You *have* to move on. Let me straighten things out with the Balinskis.
Please don't. They'll be happier with a girl who can appreciate life in the 'burbs. They're right for Madeline, not *me.*
Fine. But promise me you'll forget about Henry.
I promise.

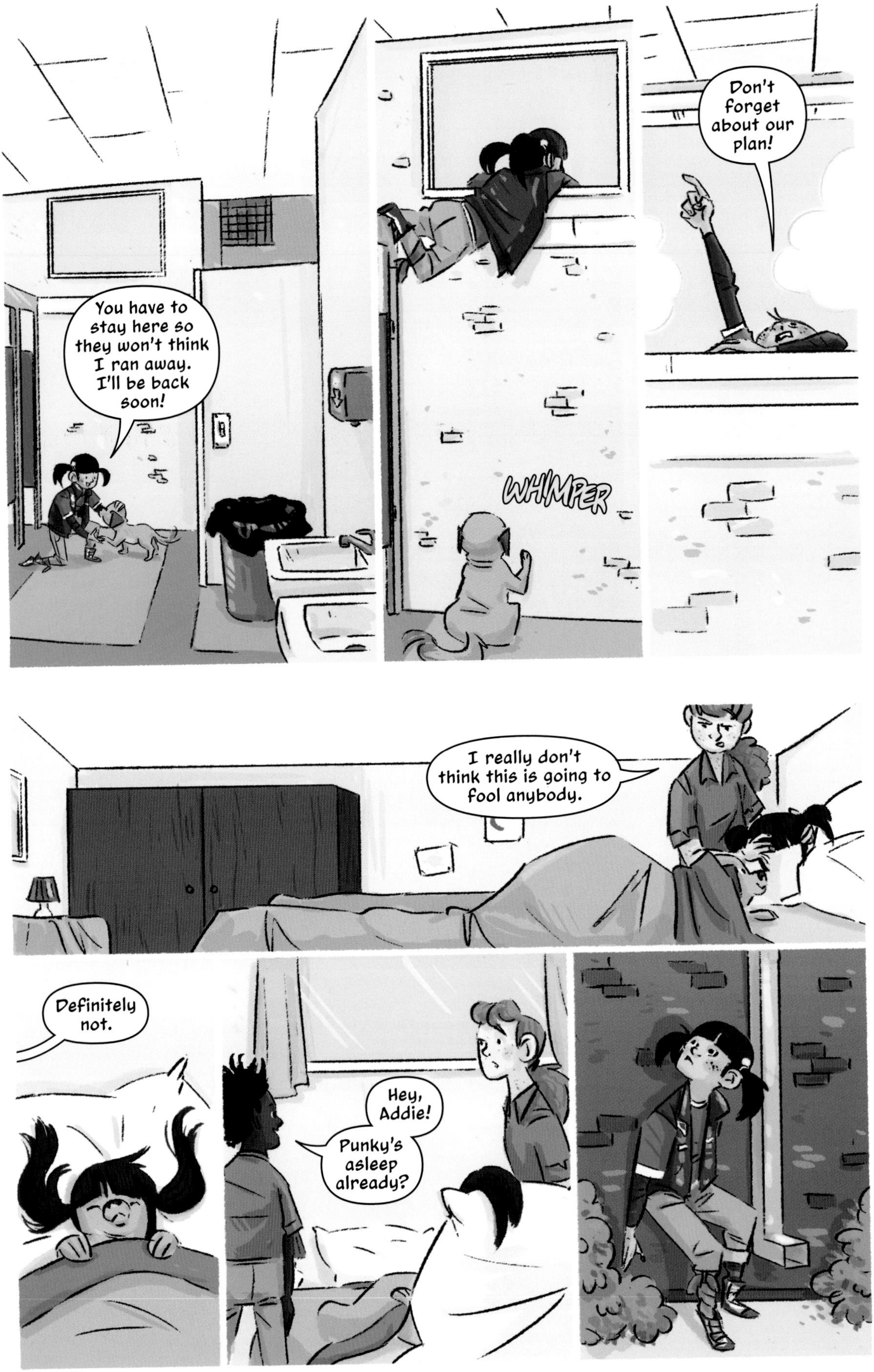
You have to stay here so they won't think I ran away. I'll be back soon!
Don't forget about our plan!
WHIMPER
I really don't think this is going to fool anybody.
Definitely not.
Hey, Addie!
Punky's asleep already?

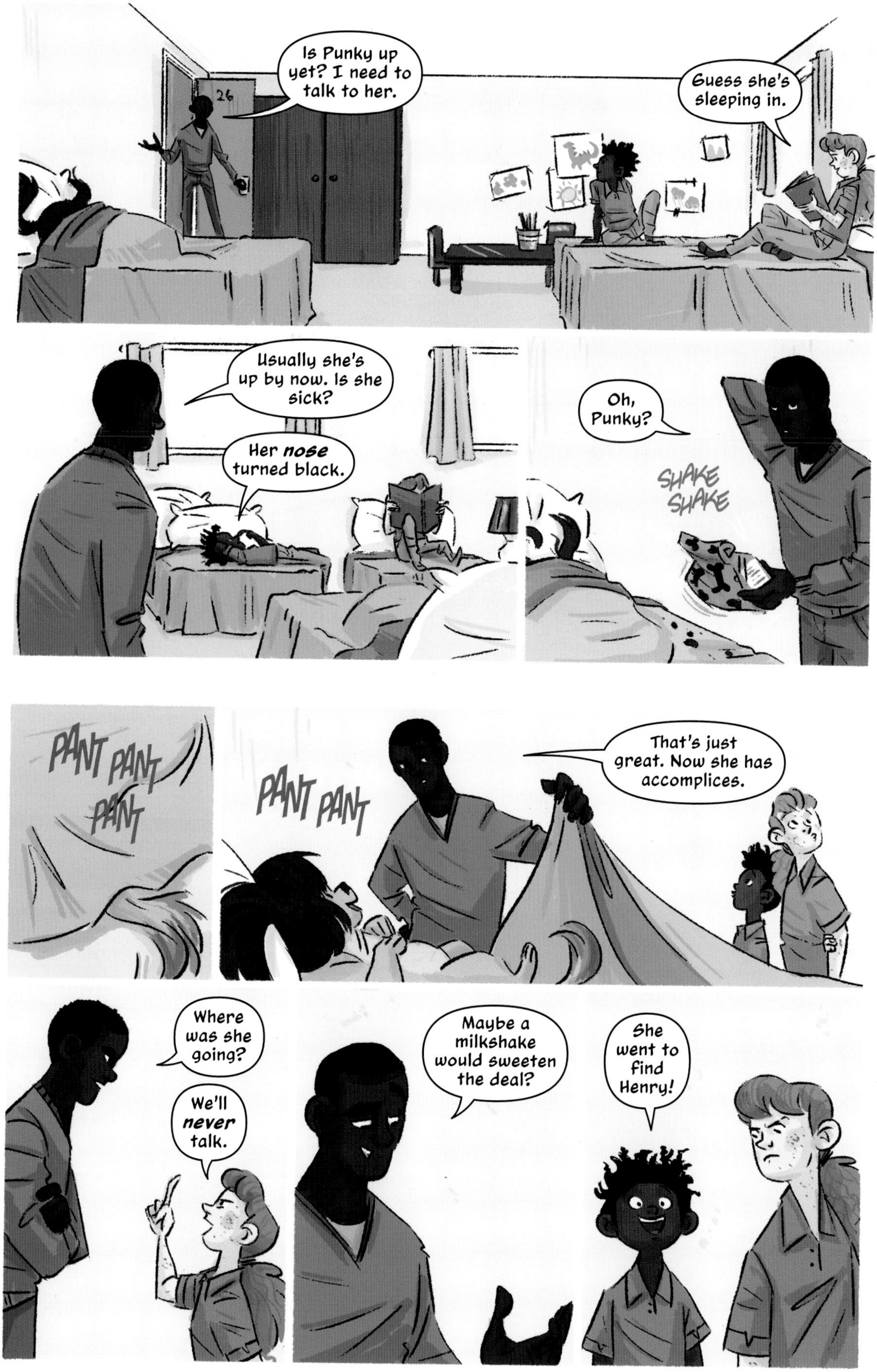
Is Punky up yet? I need to talk to her.
Guess she's sleeping in.
Usually she's up by now. Is she sick?
Her *nose* turned black.
Oh, Punky?
SHAKE SHAKE
PANT PANT PANT
PANT PANT
That's just great. Now she has accomplices.
Where was she going?
We'll *never* talk.
Maybe a milkshake would sweeten the deal?
She went to find Henry!

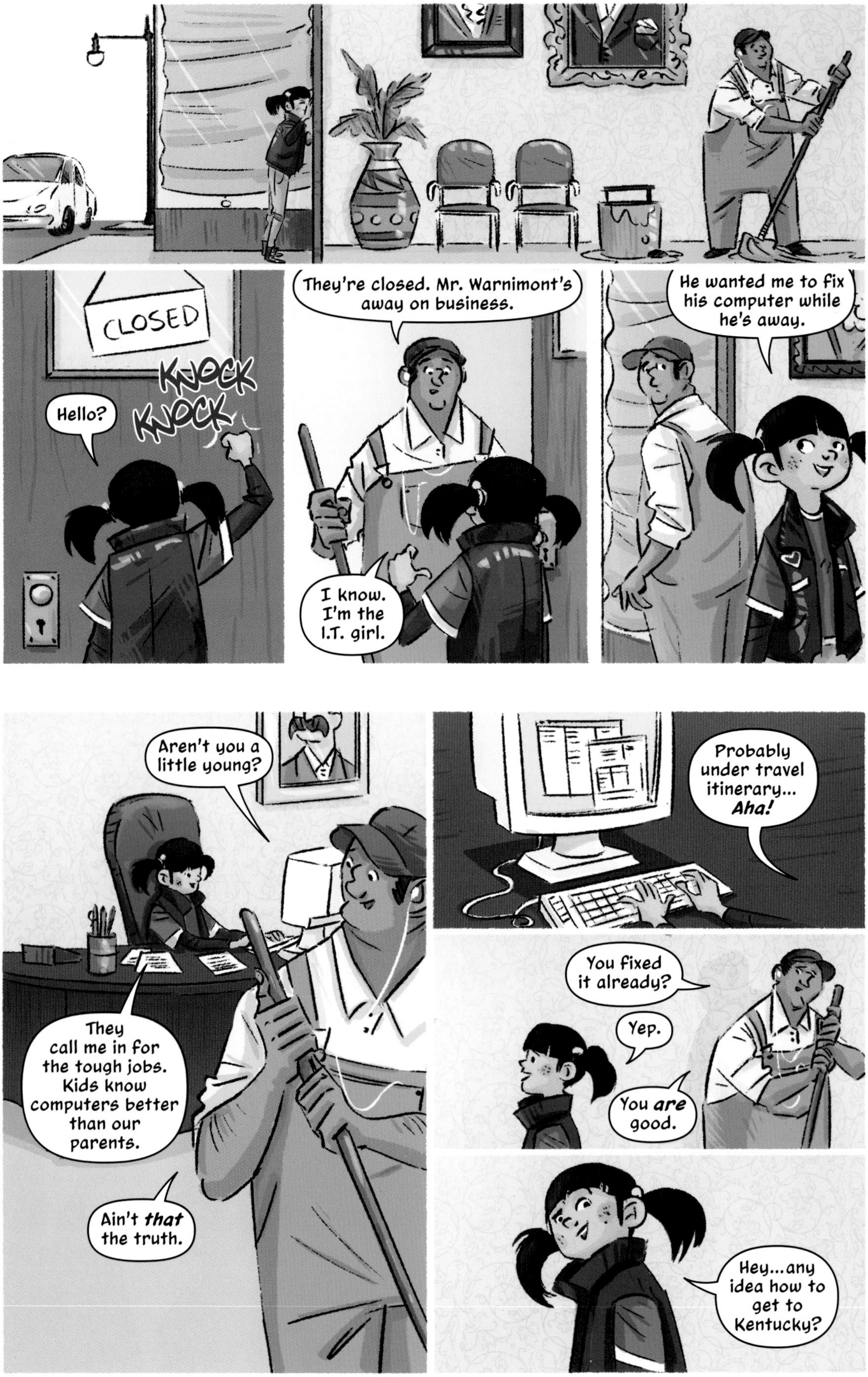
CLOSED
KNOCK
KNOCK
Hello?
They're closed. Mr. Warnimont's away on business.
I know. I'm the I.T. girl.
He wanted me to fix his computer while he's away.
Aren't you a little young?
They call me in for the tough jobs. Kids know computers better than our parents.
Ain't *that* the truth.
Probably under travel itinerary... ***Aha!***
You fixed it already?
Yep.
You *are* good.
Hey...any idea how to get to Kentucky?

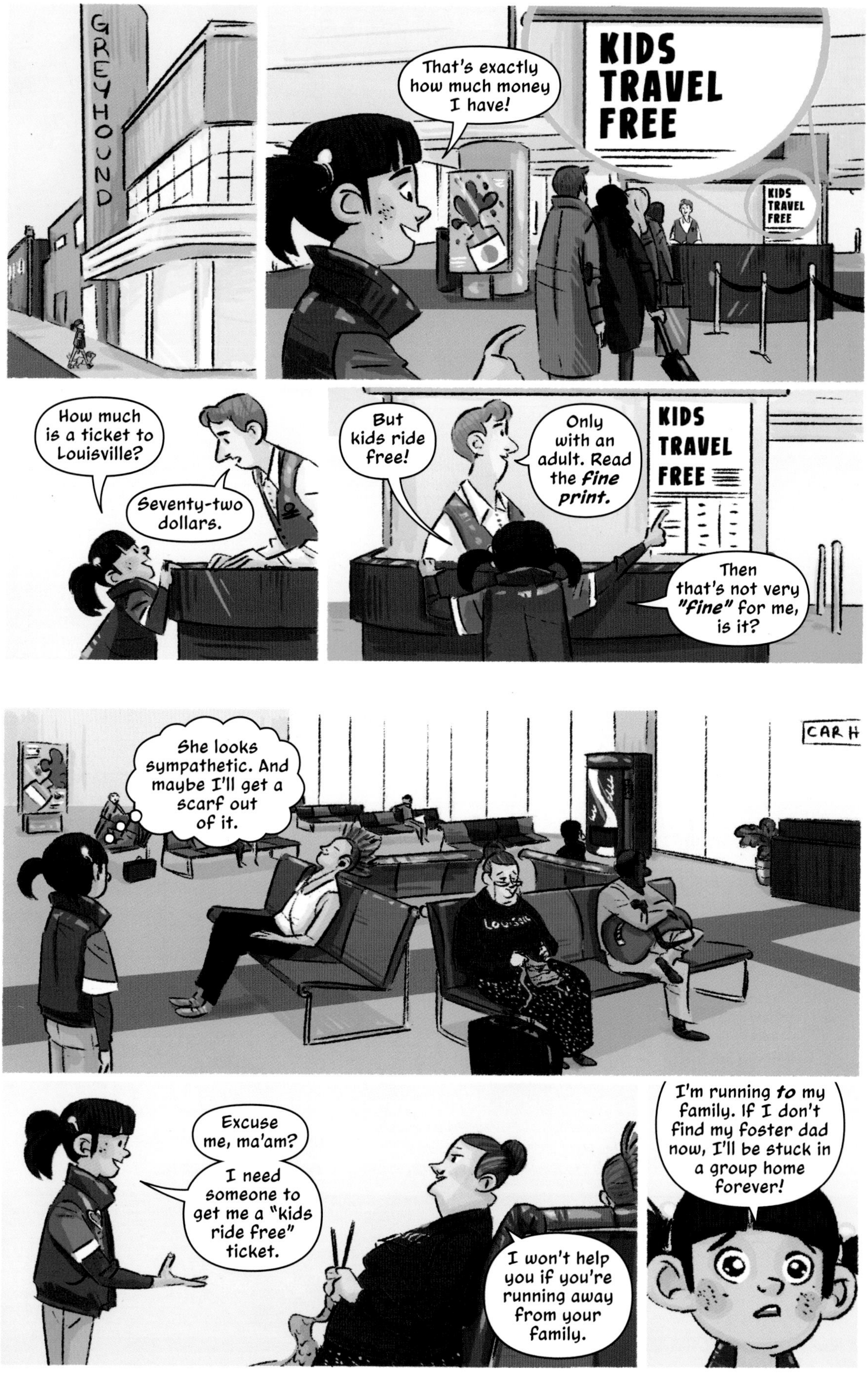
GREYHOUND
That's exactly how much money I have!
KIDS TRAVEL FREE
KIDS TRAVEL FREE
How much is a ticket to Louisville?
Seventy-two dollars.
But kids ride free!
Only with an adult. Read the *fine print.*
KIDS TRAVEL FREE
Then that's not very *"fine"* for me, is it?
CAR H
She looks sympathetic. And maybe I'll get a scarf out of it.
Excuse me, ma'am?
I need someone to get me a "kids ride free" ticket.
I won't help you if you're running away from your family.
I'm running *to* my family. If I don't find my foster dad now, I'll be stuck in a group home forever!

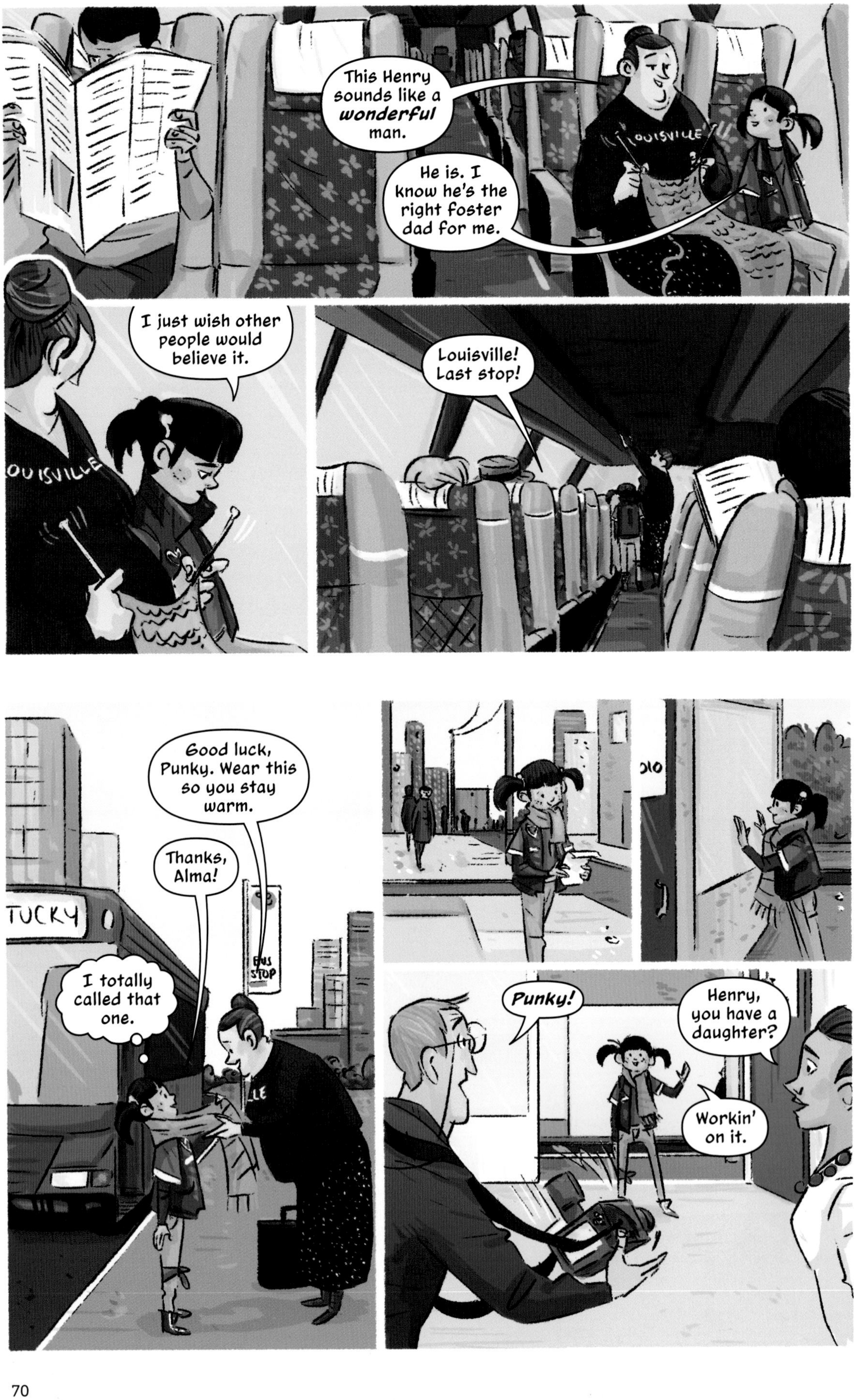
This Henry sounds like a *wonderful* man.
He is. I know he's the right foster dad for me.
LOUISVILLE
I just wish other people would believe it.
LOUISVILLE
Louisville! Last stop!
Good luck, Punky. Wear this so you stay warm.
Thanks, Alma!
TUCKY
BUS STOP
I totally called that one.
LLE
Punky!
Henry, you have a daughter?
Workin' on it.

CHAPTER 6

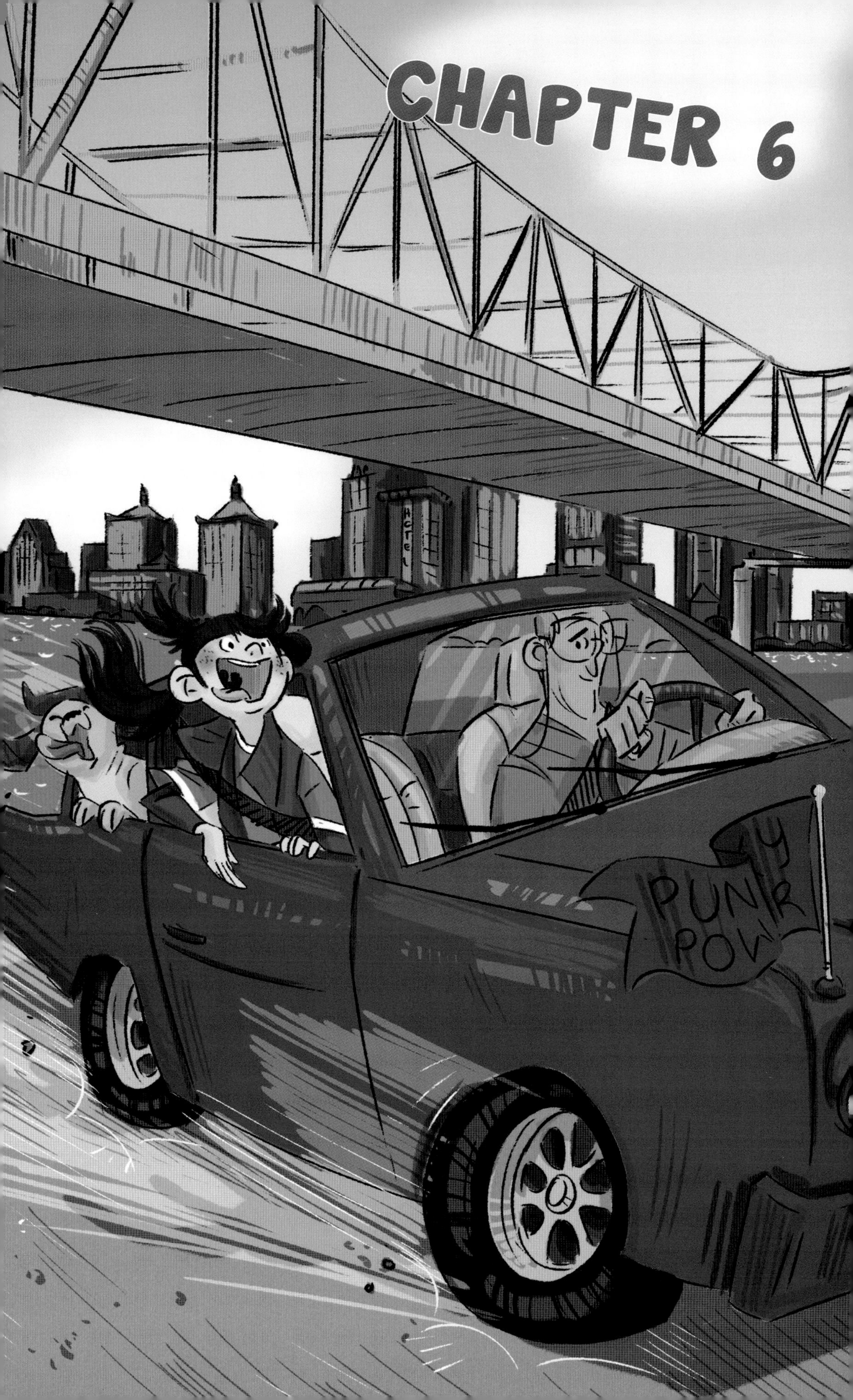

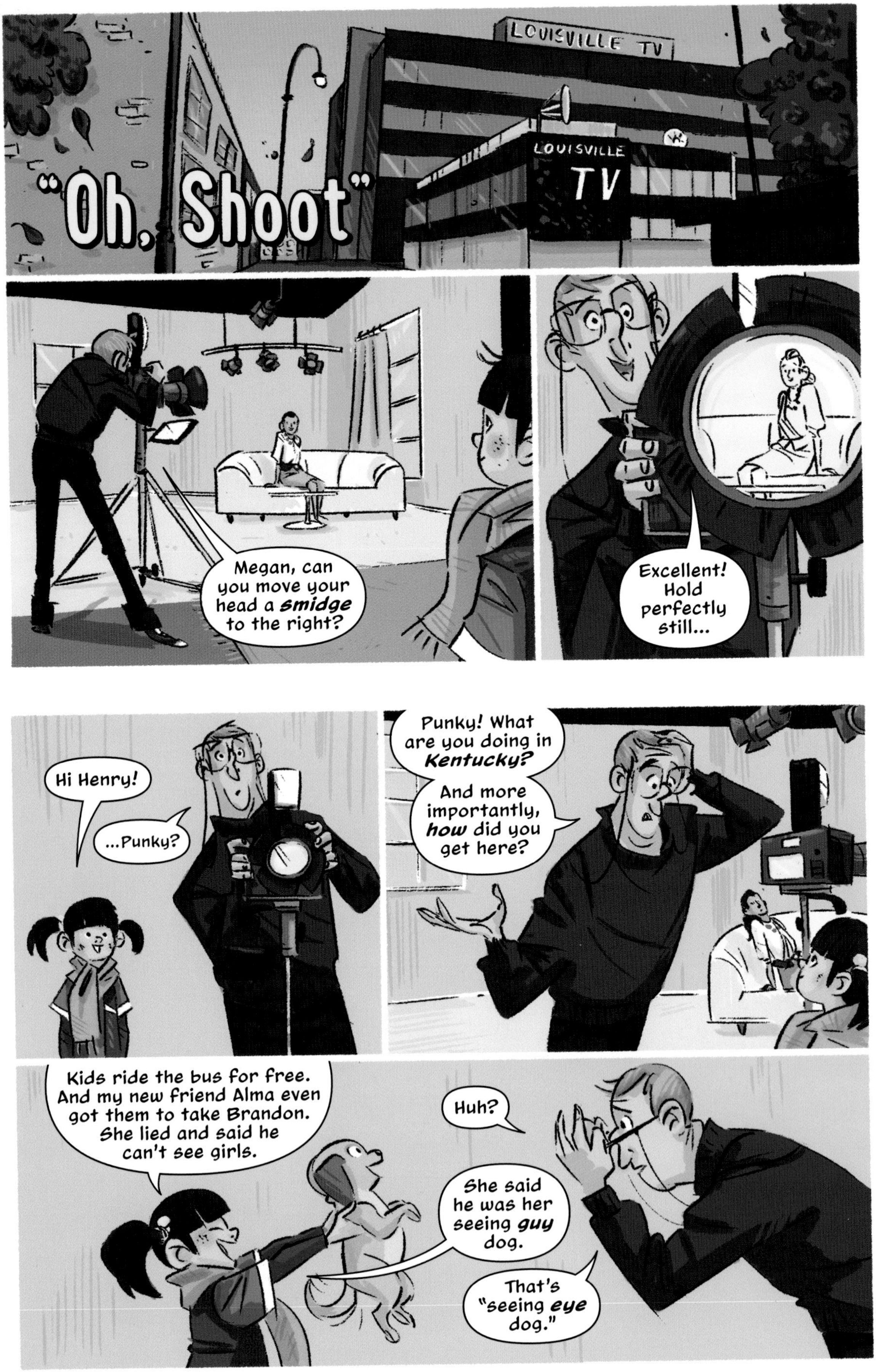
"Oh, Shoot"
LOUISVILLE TV
LOUISVILLE
TV
Megan, can you move your head a *smidge* to the right?
Excellent! Hold perfectly still...
Hi Henry!
...Punky?
Punky! What are you doing in *Kentucky?*
And more importantly, *how* did you get here?
Kids ride the bus for free. And my new friend Alma even got them to take Brandon. She lied and said he can't see girls.
Huh?
She said he was her seeing *guy* dog.
That's "seeing *eye* dog."

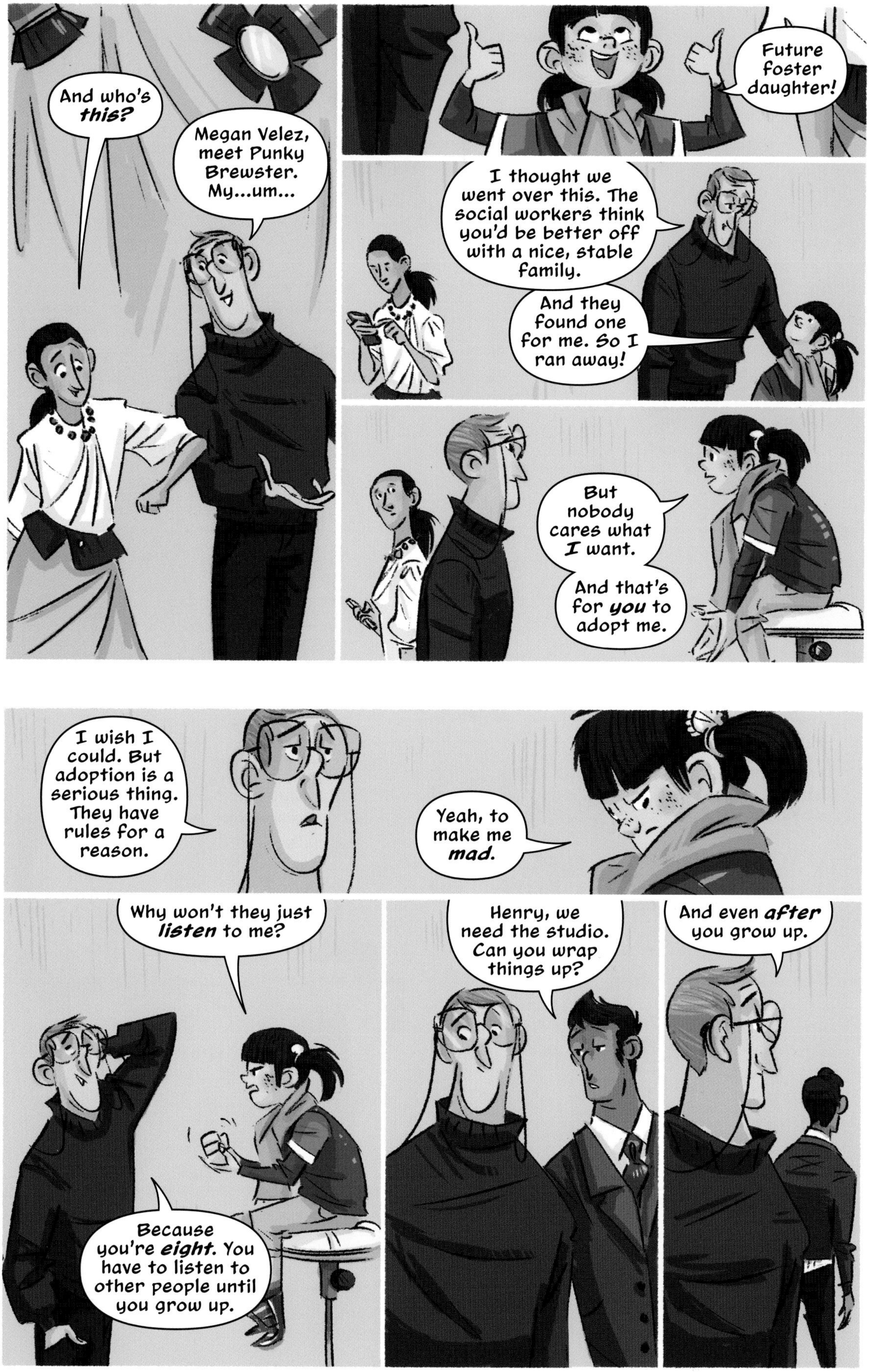
And who's **this?**
Megan Velez, meet Punky Brewster. My...um...
Future foster daughter!
I thought we went over this. The social workers think you'd be better off with a nice, stable family.
And they found one for me. So I ran away!
But nobody cares what **I** want.
And that's for **you** to adopt me.
I wish I could. But adoption is a serious thing. They have rules for a reason.
Yeah, to make me **mad**.
Why won't they just **listen** to me?
Because you're **eight**. You have to listen to other people until you grow up.
Henry, we need the studio. Can you wrap things up?
And even **after** you grow up.

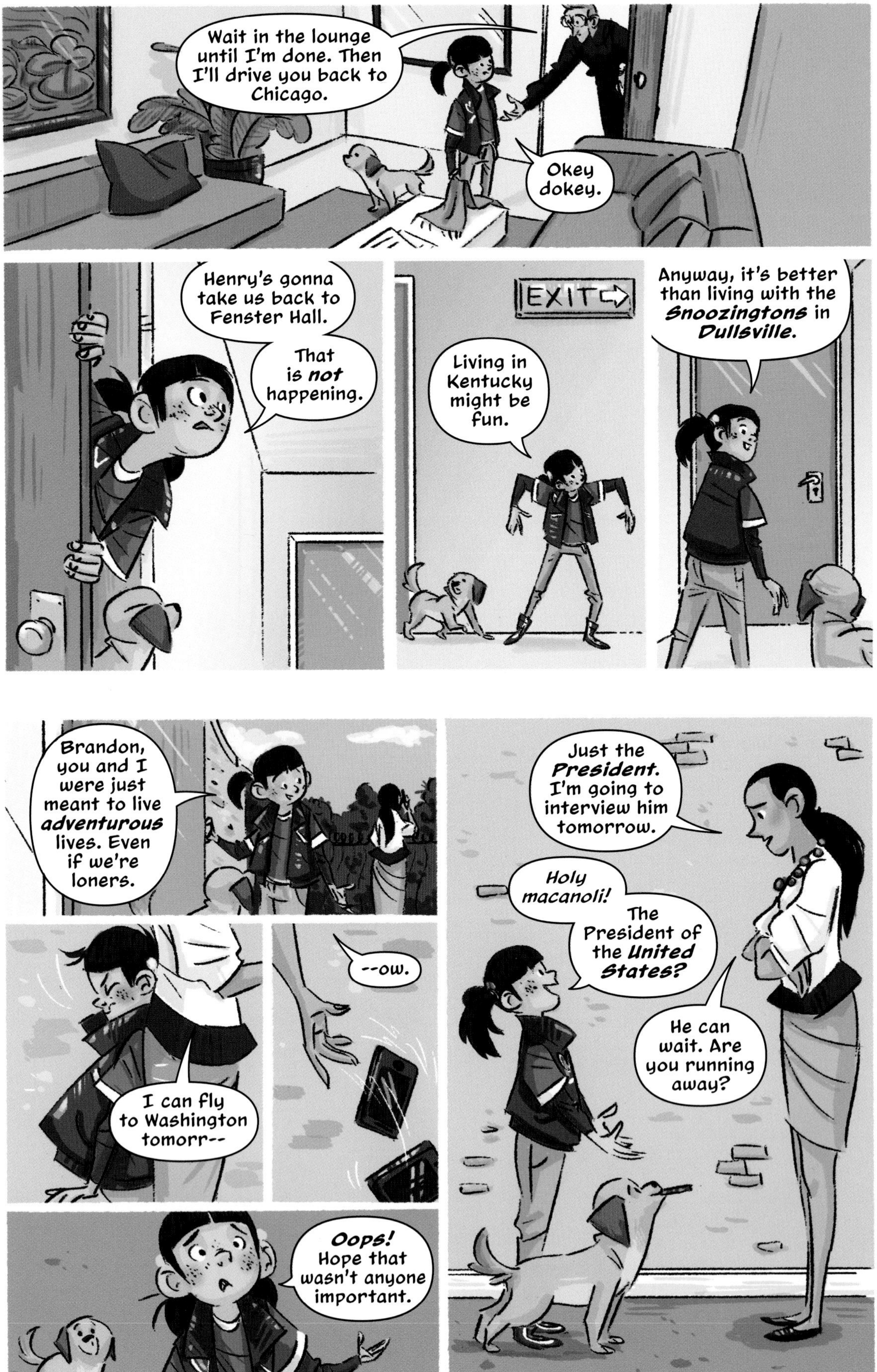

Wait in the lounge until I'm done. Then I'll drive you back to Chicago.
Okey dokey.
Henry's gonna take us back to Fenster Hall.
That is *not* happening.
EXIT
Living in Kentucky might be fun.
Anyway, it's better than living with the ***Snoozingtons*** in ***Dullsville***.
Brandon, you and I were just meant to live ***adventurous*** lives. Even if we're loners.
I can fly to Washington tomorr--
--ow.
Oops! Hope that wasn't anyone important.
Just the ***President***. I'm going to interview him tomorrow.
Holy macanoli!
The President of the ***United States?***
He can wait. Are you running away?

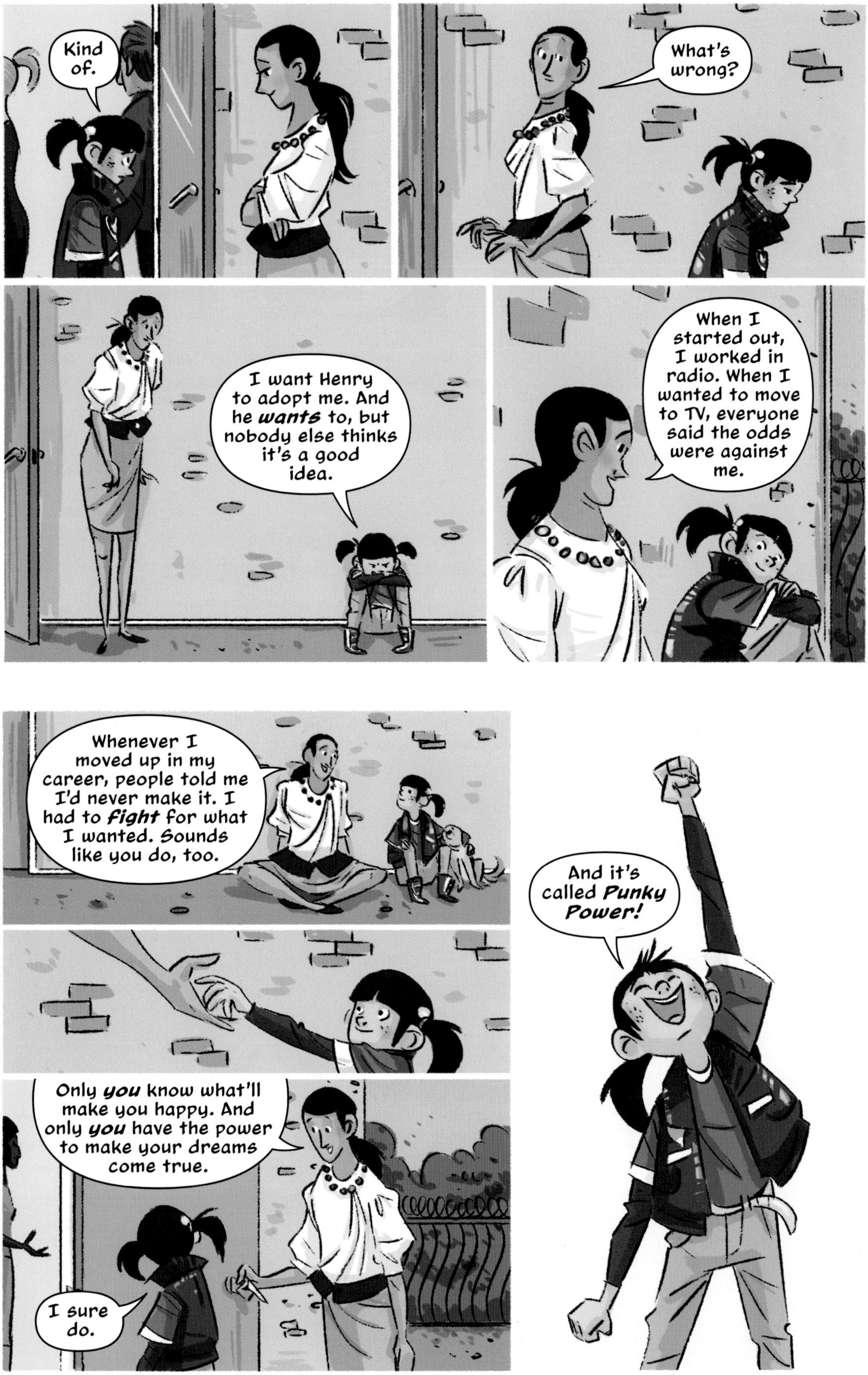
Kind of.
What's wrong?
I want Henry to adopt me. And he *wants* to, but nobody else thinks it's a good idea.
When I started out, I worked in radio. When I wanted to move to TV, everyone said the odds were against me.
Whenever I moved up in my career, people told me I'd never make it. I had to *fight* for what I wanted. Sounds like you do, too.
Only *you* know what'll make you happy. And only *you* have the power to make your dreams come true.
I sure do.
And it's called *Punky Power!*

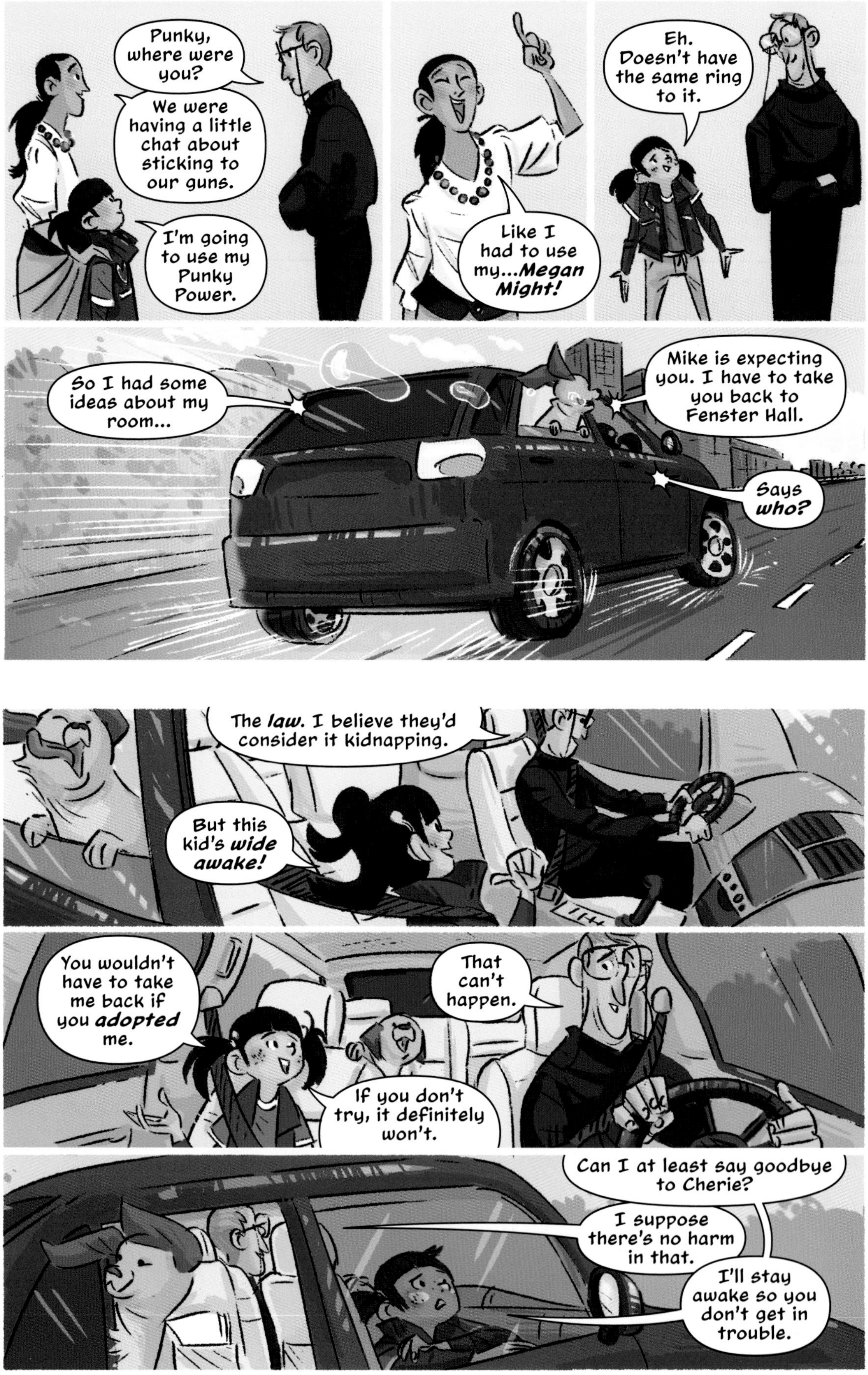
Punky, where were you?
We were having a little chat about sticking to our guns.
I'm going to use my Punky Power.
Like I had to use my...*Megan Might!*
Eh. Doesn't have the same ring to it.
So I had some ideas about my room...
Mike is expecting you. I have to take you back to Fenster Hall.
Says *who?*
The *law.* I believe they'd consider it kidnapping.
But this kid's *wide awake!*
You wouldn't have to take me back if you *adopted* me.
That can't happen.
If you don't try, it definitely won't.
Can I at least say goodbye to Cherie?
I suppose there's no harm in that.
I'll stay awake so you don't get in trouble.

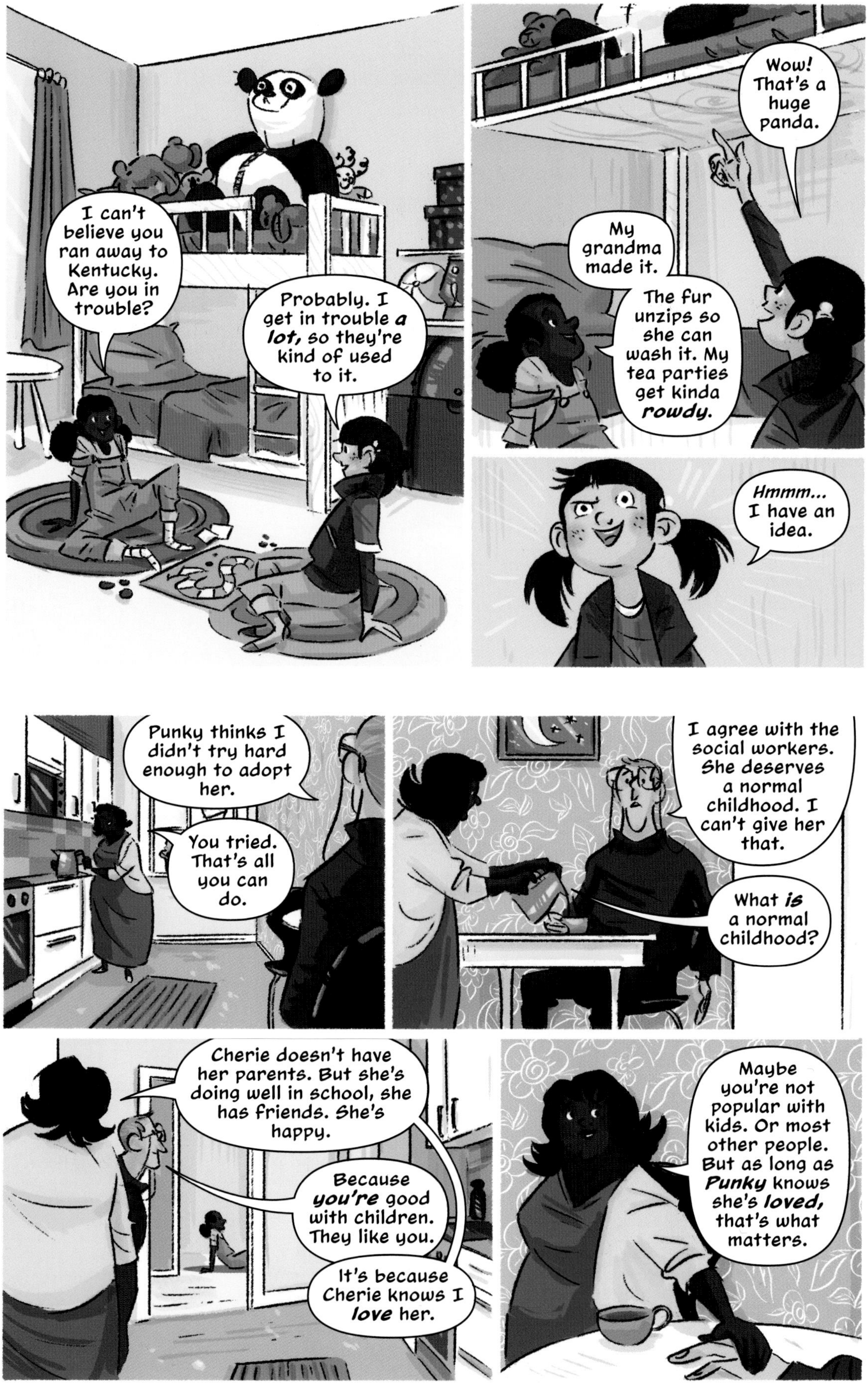

I can't believe you ran away to Kentucky. Are you in trouble?
Probably. I get in trouble *a lot,* so they're kind of used to it.
Wow! That's a huge panda.
My grandma made it.
The fur unzips so she can wash it. My tea parties get kinda *rowdy.*
Hmmm... I have an idea.
Punky thinks I didn't try hard enough to adopt her.
You tried. That's all you can do.
I agree with the social workers. She deserves a normal childhood. I can't give her that.
What *is* a normal childhood?
Cherie doesn't have her parents. But she's doing well in school, she has friends. She's happy.
Because *you're* good with children. They like you.
It's because Cherie knows I *love* her.
Maybe you're not popular with kids. Or most other people. But as long as *Punky* knows she's *loved,* that's what matters.

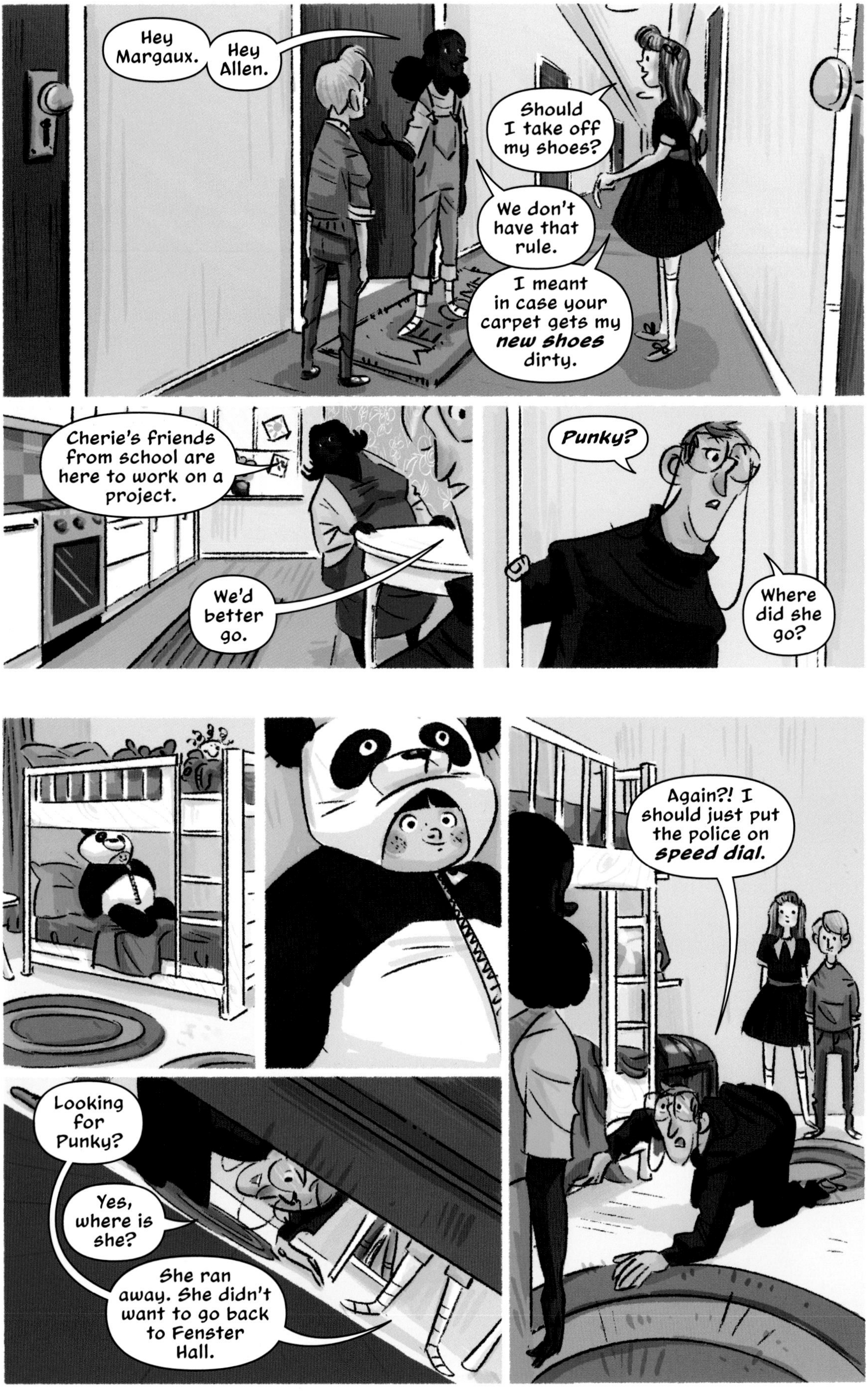
Hey Margaux.
Hey Allen.
Should I take off my shoes?
We don't have that rule.
I meant in case your carpet gets my *new shoes* dirty.
Cherie's friends from school are here to work on a project.
We'd better go.
Punky?
Where did she go?
Again?! I should just put the police on *speed dial.*
Looking for Punky?
Yes, where is she?
She ran away. She didn't want to go back to Fenster Hall.

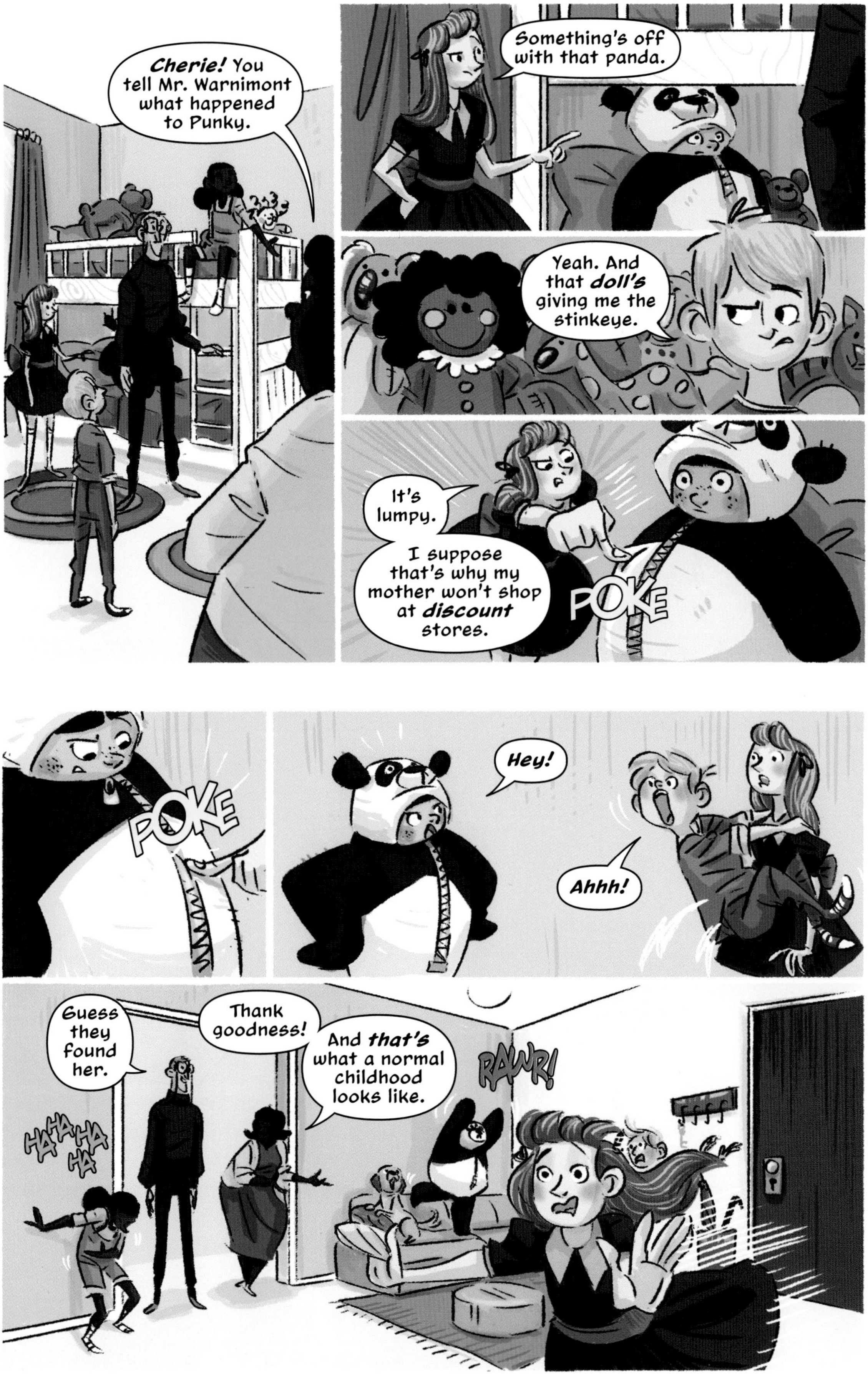

Cherie! You tell Mr. Warnimont what happened to Punky.
Something's off with that panda.
Yeah. And that doll's giving me the stinkeye.
It's lumpy.
I suppose that's why my mother won't shop at discount stores.
POKE
POKE
Hey!
Ahhh!
Guess they found her.
Thank goodness!
And that's what a normal childhood looks like.
RAWR!
HA HA HA HA HA

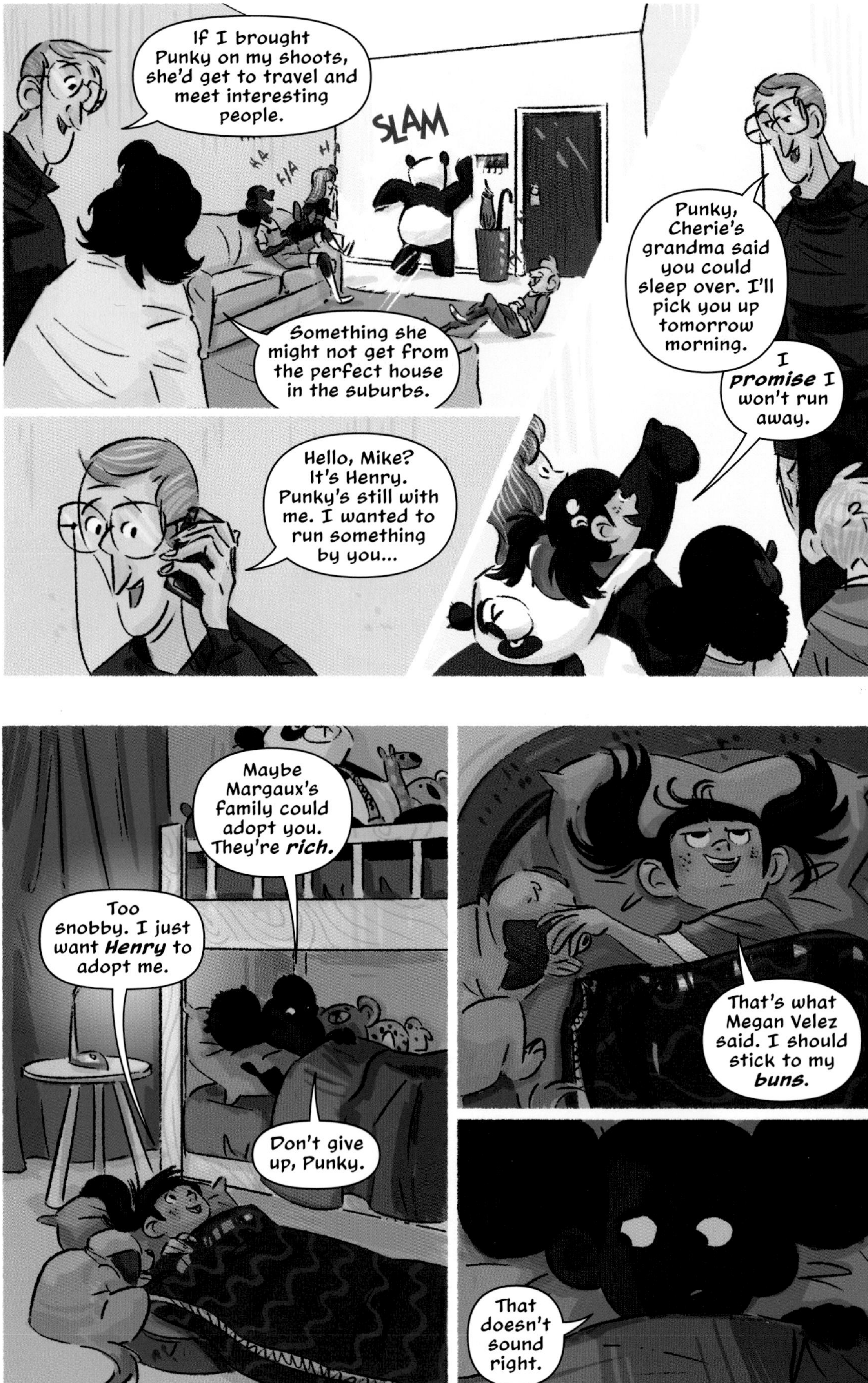
If I brought Punky on my shoots, she'd get to travel and meet interesting people.
HA HA HA HA
SLAM
Something she might not get from the perfect house in the suburbs.
Punky, Cherie's grandma said you could sleep over. I'll pick you up tomorrow morning.
I *promise* I won't run away.
Hello, Mike? It's Henry. Punky's still with me. I wanted to run something by you...
Maybe Margaux's family could adopt you. They're *rich.*
Too snobby. I just want *Henry* to adopt me.
Don't give up, Punky.
That's what Megan Velez said. I should stick to my *buns.*
That doesn't sound right.

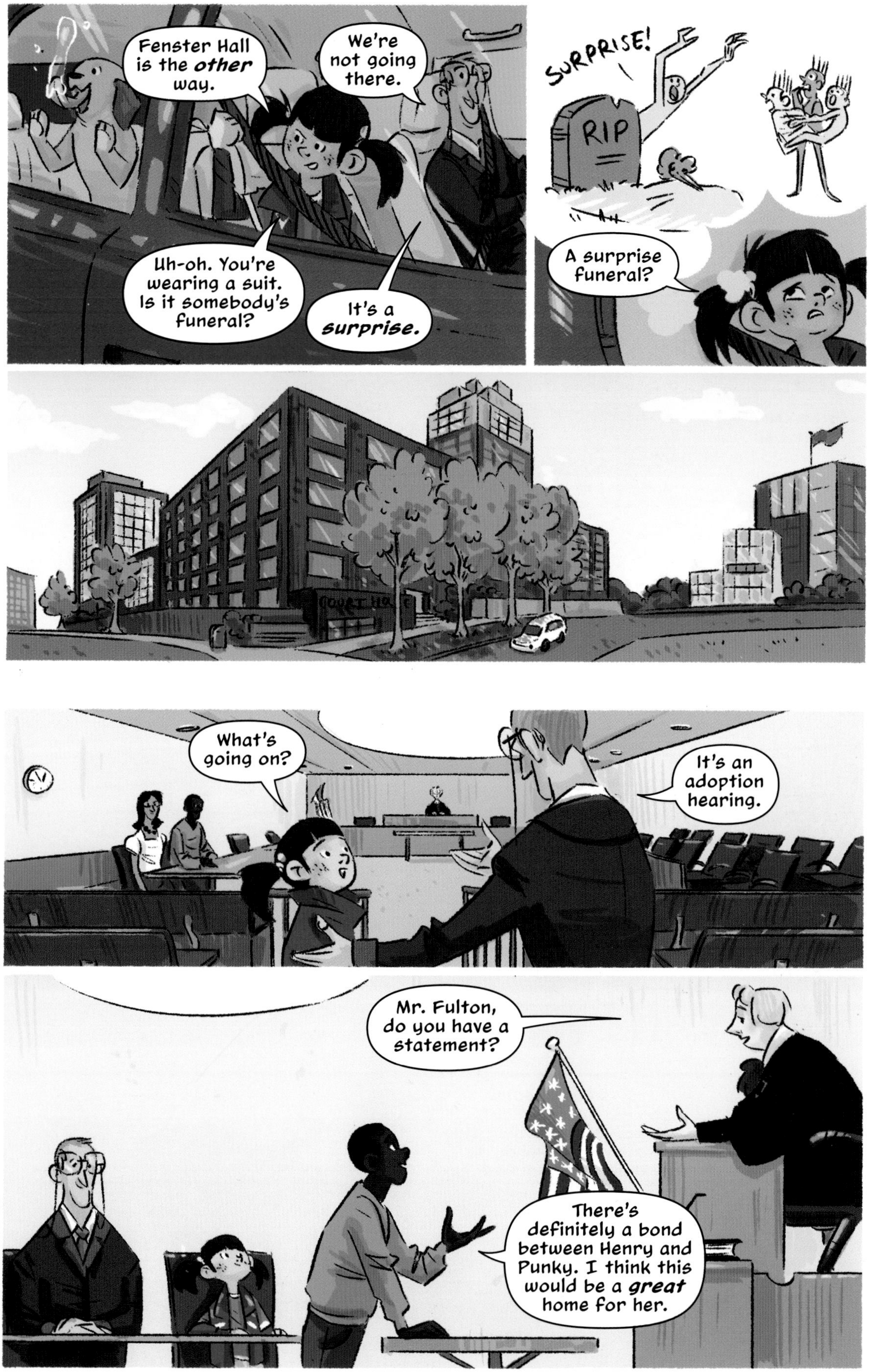

Fenster Hall is the *other* way.
We're not going there.
Uh-oh. You're wearing a suit. Is it somebody's funeral?
It's a *surprise.*
SURPRISE!
RIP
A surprise funeral?
What's going on?
It's an adoption hearing.
Mr. Fulton, do you have a statement?
There's definitely a bond between Henry and Punky. I think this would be a *great* home for her.

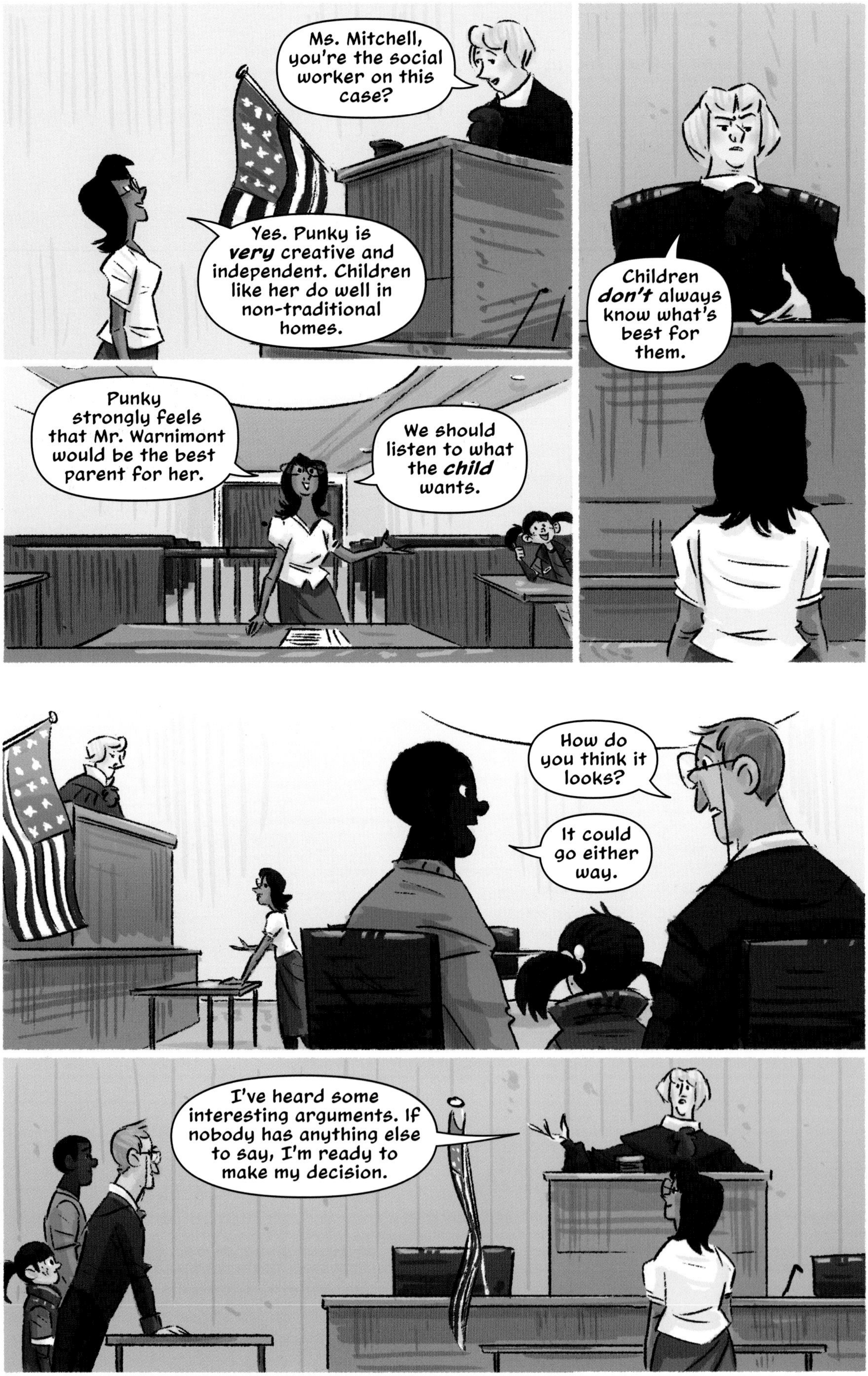
Ms. Mitchell, you're the social worker on this case?
Yes. Punky is *very* creative and independent. Children like her do well in non-traditional homes.
Children *don't* always know what's best for them.
Punky strongly feels that Mr. Warnimont would be the best parent for her.
We should listen to what the *child* wants.
How do you think it looks?
It could go either way.
I've heard some interesting arguments. If nobody has anything else to say, I'm ready to make my decision.

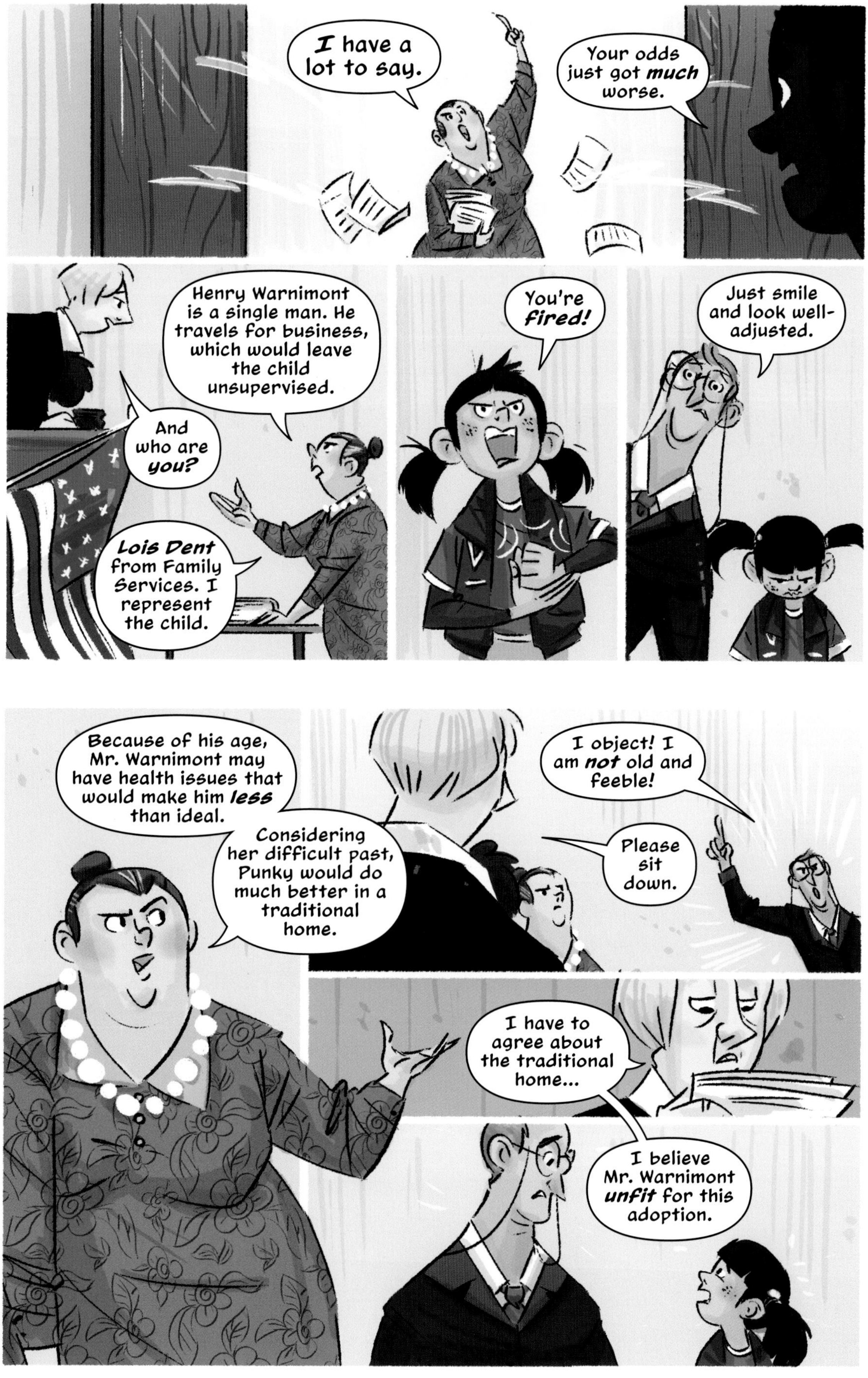

I have a lot to say.
Your odds just got *much* worse.
Henry Warnimont is a single man. He travels for business, which would leave the child unsupervised.
And who are *you?*
Lois Dent from Family Services. I represent the child.
You're *fired!*
Just smile and look well-adjusted.
Because of his age, Mr. Warnimont may have health issues that would make him *less* than ideal.
Considering her difficult past, Punky would do much better in a traditional home.
I object! I am *not* old and feeble!
Please sit down.
I have to agree about the traditional home...
I believe Mr. Warnimont *unfit* for this adoption.

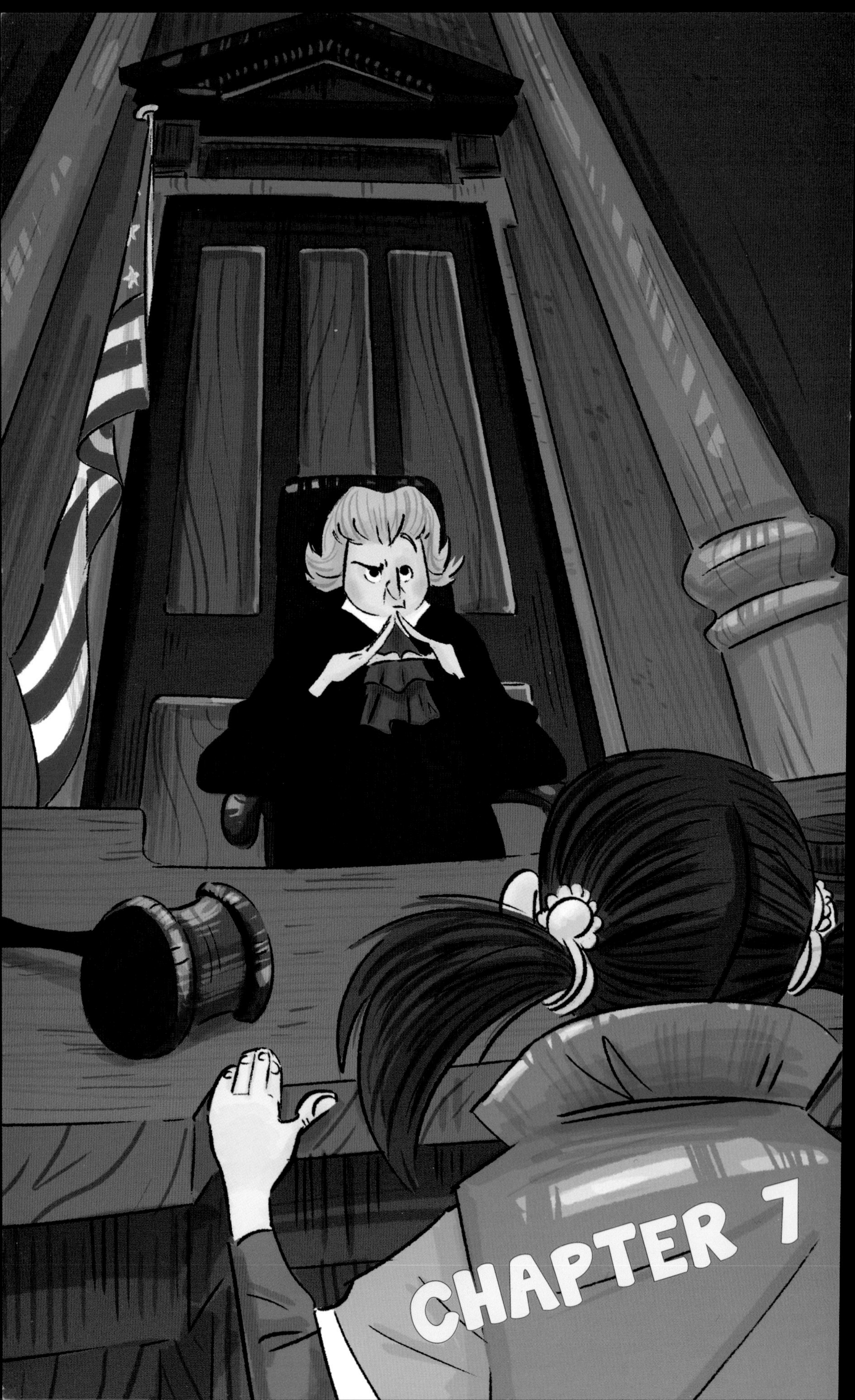
CHAPTER 7

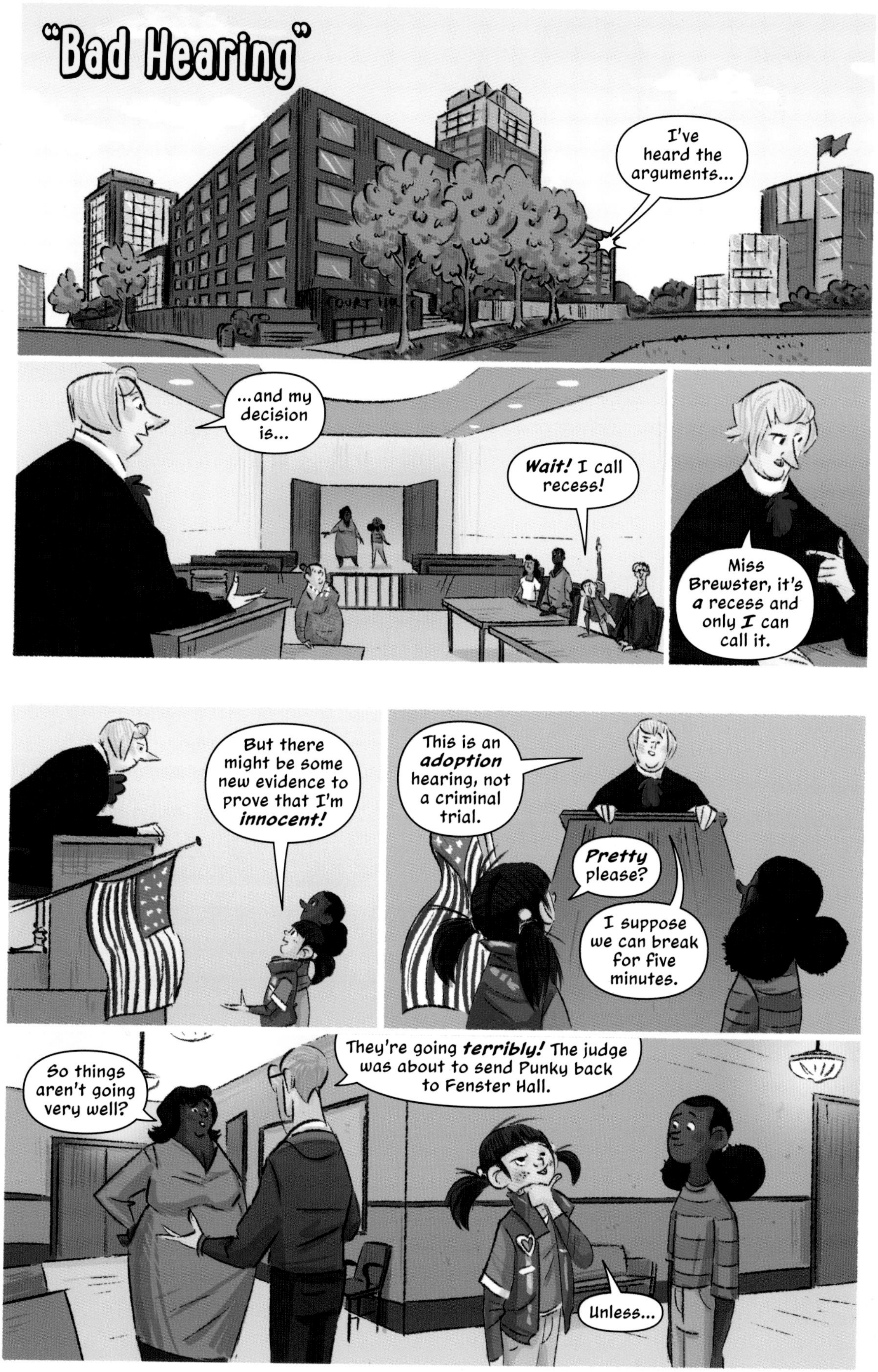
"Bad Hearing"
I've heard the arguments...
...and my decision is...
Wait! I call recess!
Miss Brewster, it's a recess and only I can call it.
But there might be some new evidence to prove that I'm innocent!
This is an adoption hearing, not a criminal trial.
Pretty please?
I suppose we can break for five minutes.
So things aren't going very well?
They're going terribly! The judge was about to send Punky back to Fenster Hall.
Unless...

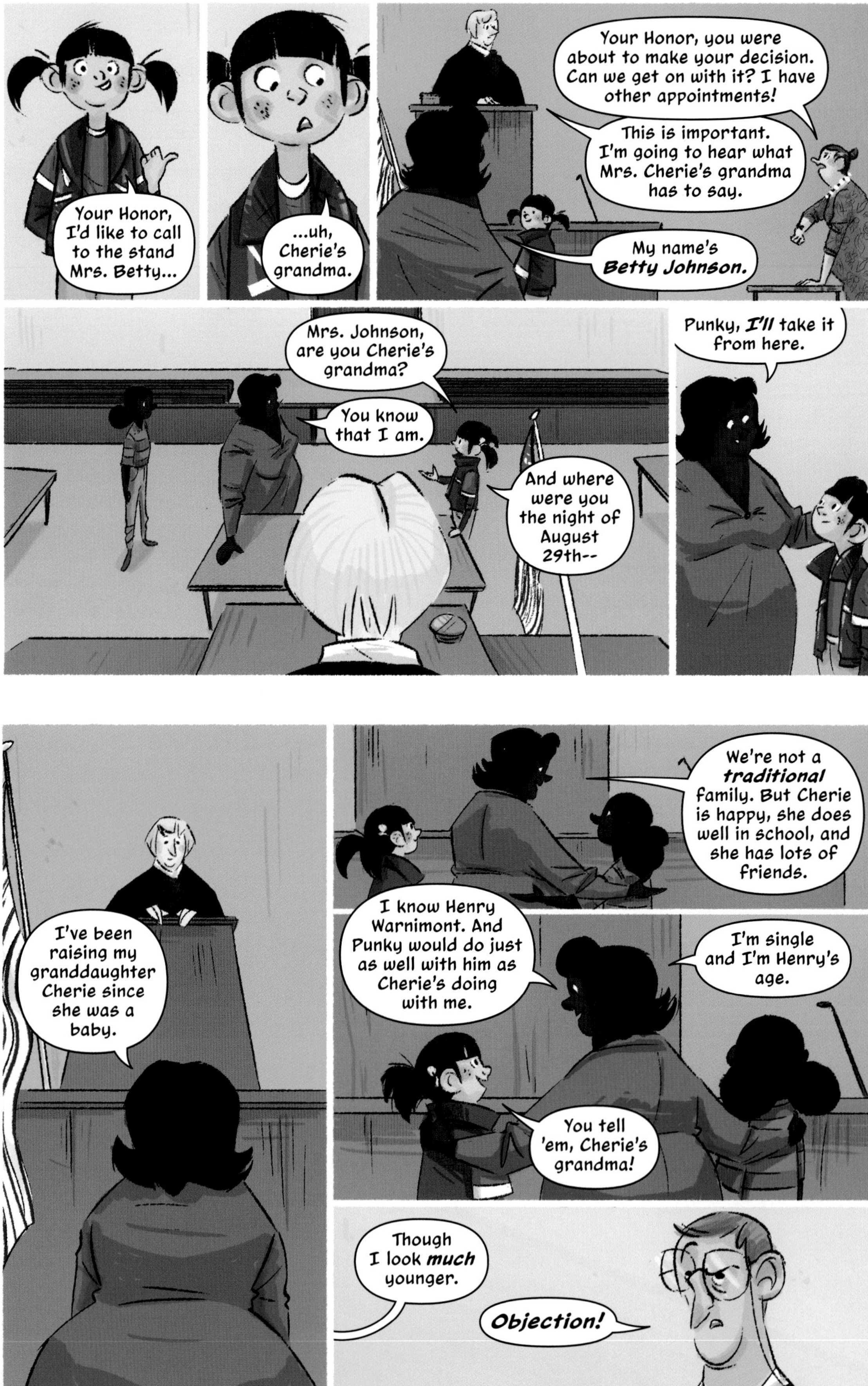
Your Honor, I'd like to call to the stand Mrs. Betty...
...uh, Cherie's grandma.
Your Honor, you were about to make your decision. Can we get on with it? I have other appointments!
This is important. I'm going to hear what Mrs. Cherie's grandma has to say.
My name's *Betty Johnson.*
Mrs. Johnson, are you Cherie's grandma?
You know that I am.
And where were you the night of August 29th--
Punky, *I'll* take it from here.
I've been raising my granddaughter Cherie since she was a baby.
We're not a *traditional* family. But Cherie is happy, she does well in school, and she has lots of friends.
I know Henry Warnimont. And Punky would do just as well with him as Cherie's doing with me.
I'm single and I'm Henry's age.
You tell 'em, Cherie's grandma!
Though I look *much* younger.
Objection!

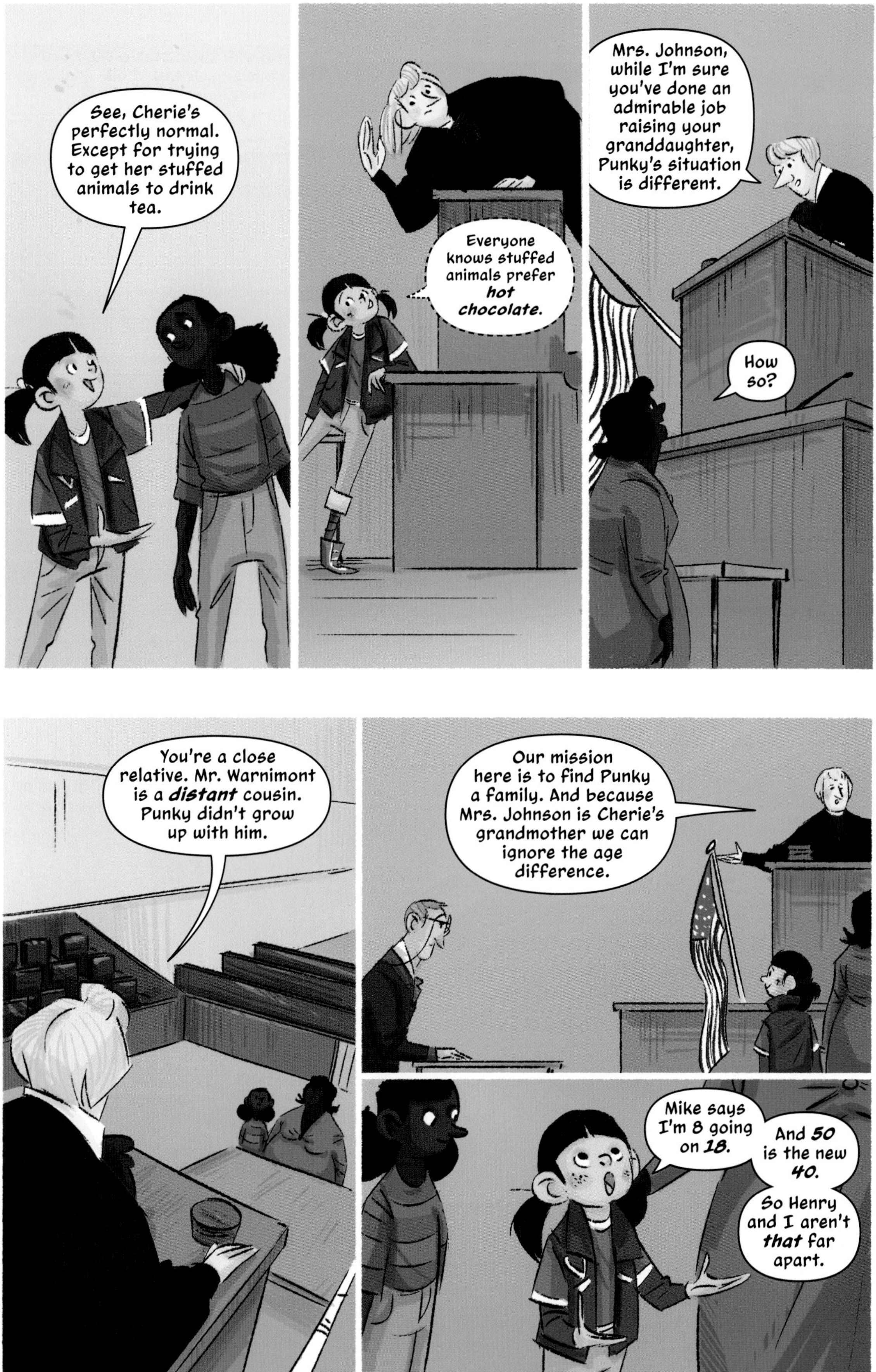
See, Cherie's perfectly normal. Except for trying to get her stuffed animals to drink tea.
Everyone knows stuffed animals prefer ***hot chocolate.***
Mrs. Johnson, while I'm sure you've done an admirable job raising your granddaughter, Punky's situation is different.
How so?
You're a close relative. Mr. Warnimont is a ***distant*** cousin. Punky didn't grow up with him.
Our mission here is to find Punky a family. And because Mrs. Johnson is Cherie's grandmother we can ignore the age difference.
Mike says I'm 8 going on ***18.***
And ***50*** is the new ***40.***
So Henry and I aren't ***that*** far apart.

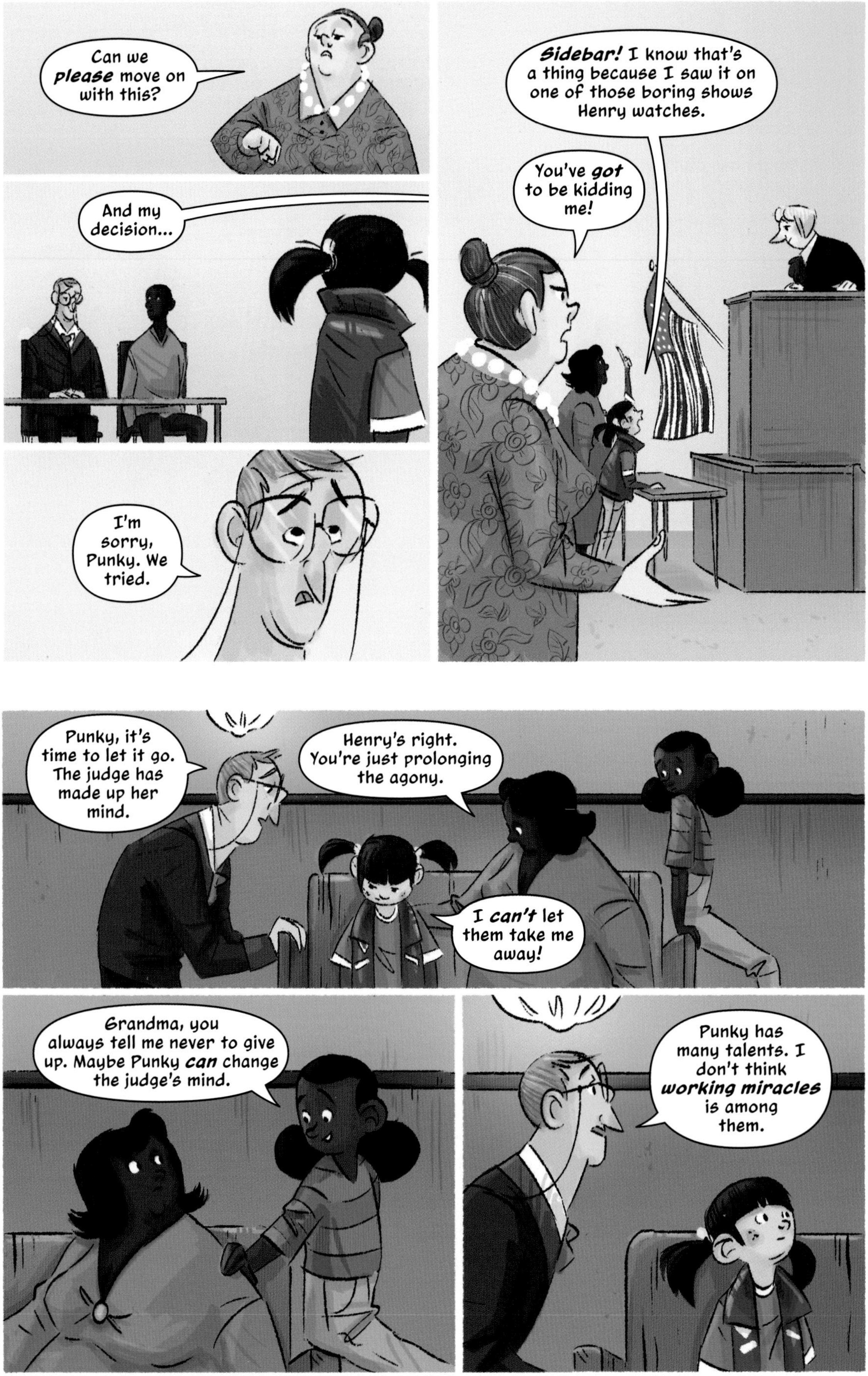
Can we *please* move on with this?
And my decision...
I'm sorry, Punky. We tried.
Sidebar! I know that's a thing because I saw it on one of those boring shows Henry watches.
You've *got* to be kidding me!
Punky, it's time to let it go. The judge has made up her mind.
Henry's right. You're just prolonging the agony.
I *can't* let them take me away!
Grandma, you always tell me never to give up. Maybe Punky *can* change the judge's mind.
Punky has many talents. I don't think *working miracles* is among them.

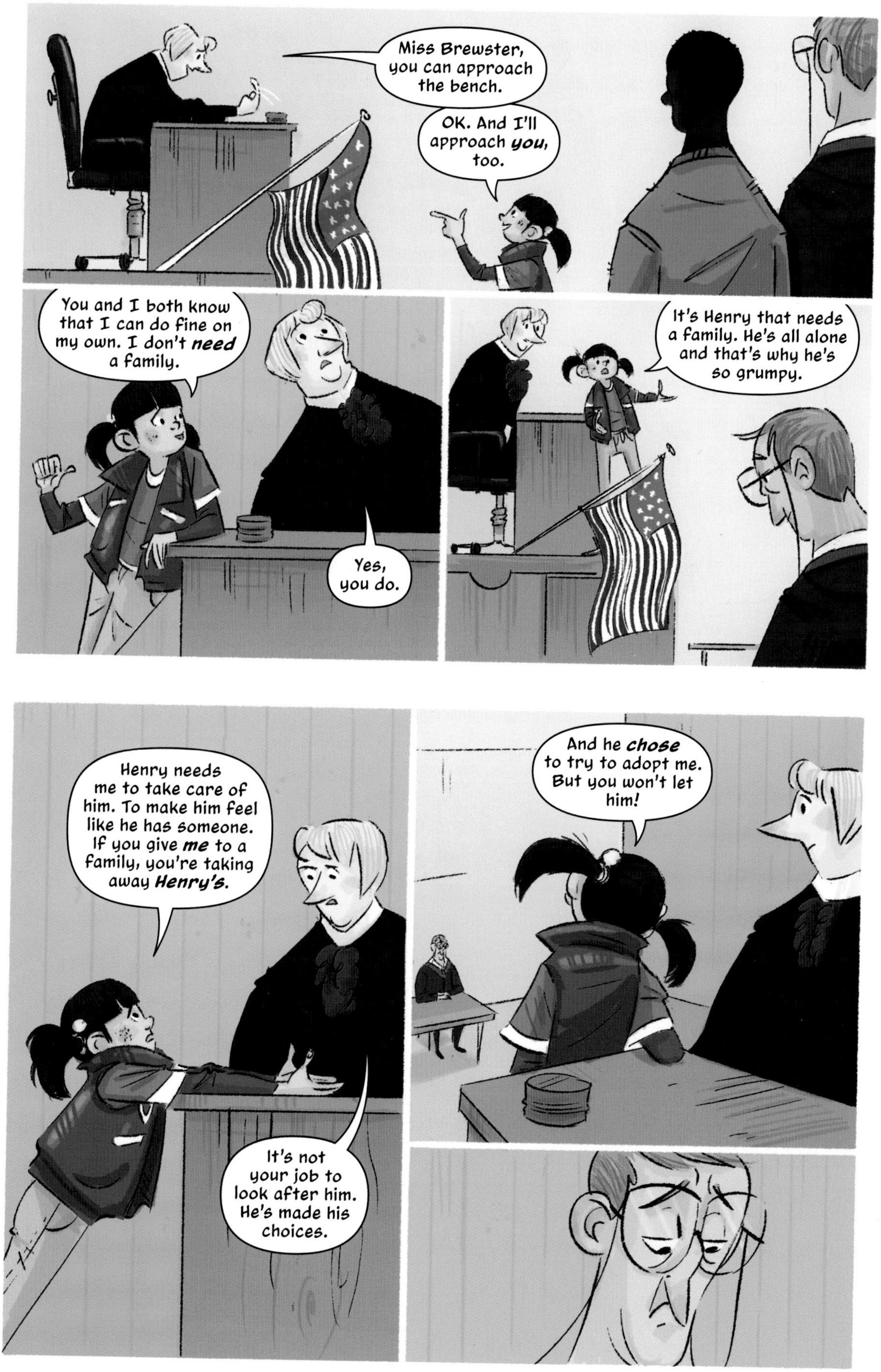
Miss Brewster, you can approach the bench.
OK. And I'll approach *you*, too.
You and I both know that I can do fine on my own. I don't *need* a family.
Yes, you do.
It's Henry that needs a family. He's all alone and that's why he's so grumpy.
Henry needs me to take care of him. To make him feel like he has someone. If you give *me* to a family, you're taking away *Henry's*.
It's not your job to look after him. He's made his choices.
And he *chose* to try to adopt me. But you won't let him!

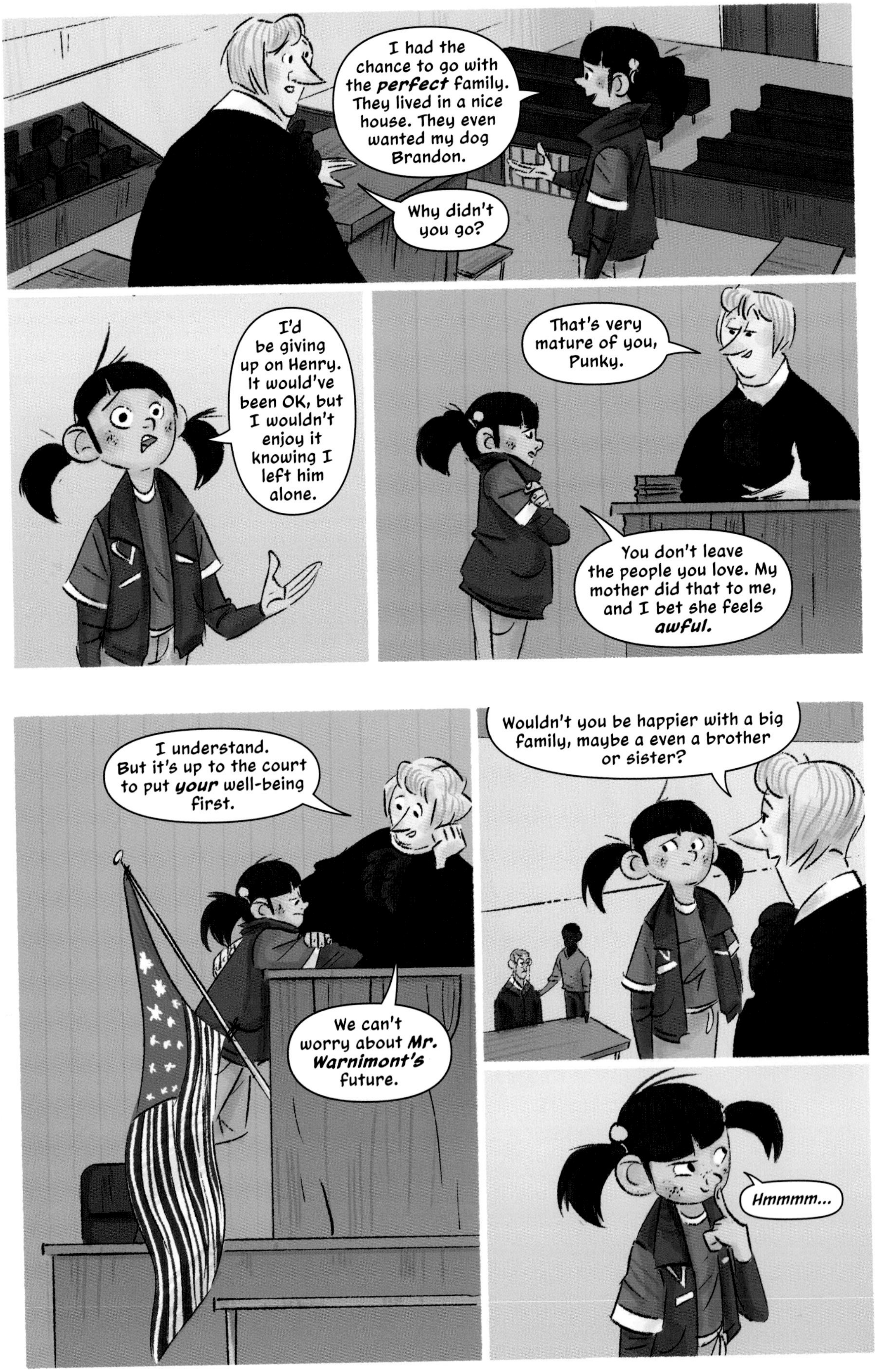
I had the chance to go with the *perfect* family. They lived in a nice house. They even wanted my dog Brandon.
Why didn't you go?
I'd be giving up on Henry. It would've been OK, but I wouldn't enjoy it knowing I left him alone.
That's very mature of you, Punky.
You don't leave the people you love. My mother did that to me, and I bet she feels ***awful.***
I understand. But it's up to the court to put ***your*** well-being first.
We can't worry about ***Mr. Warnimont's*** future.
Wouldn't you be happier with a big family, maybe a even a brother or sister?
Hmmmm...

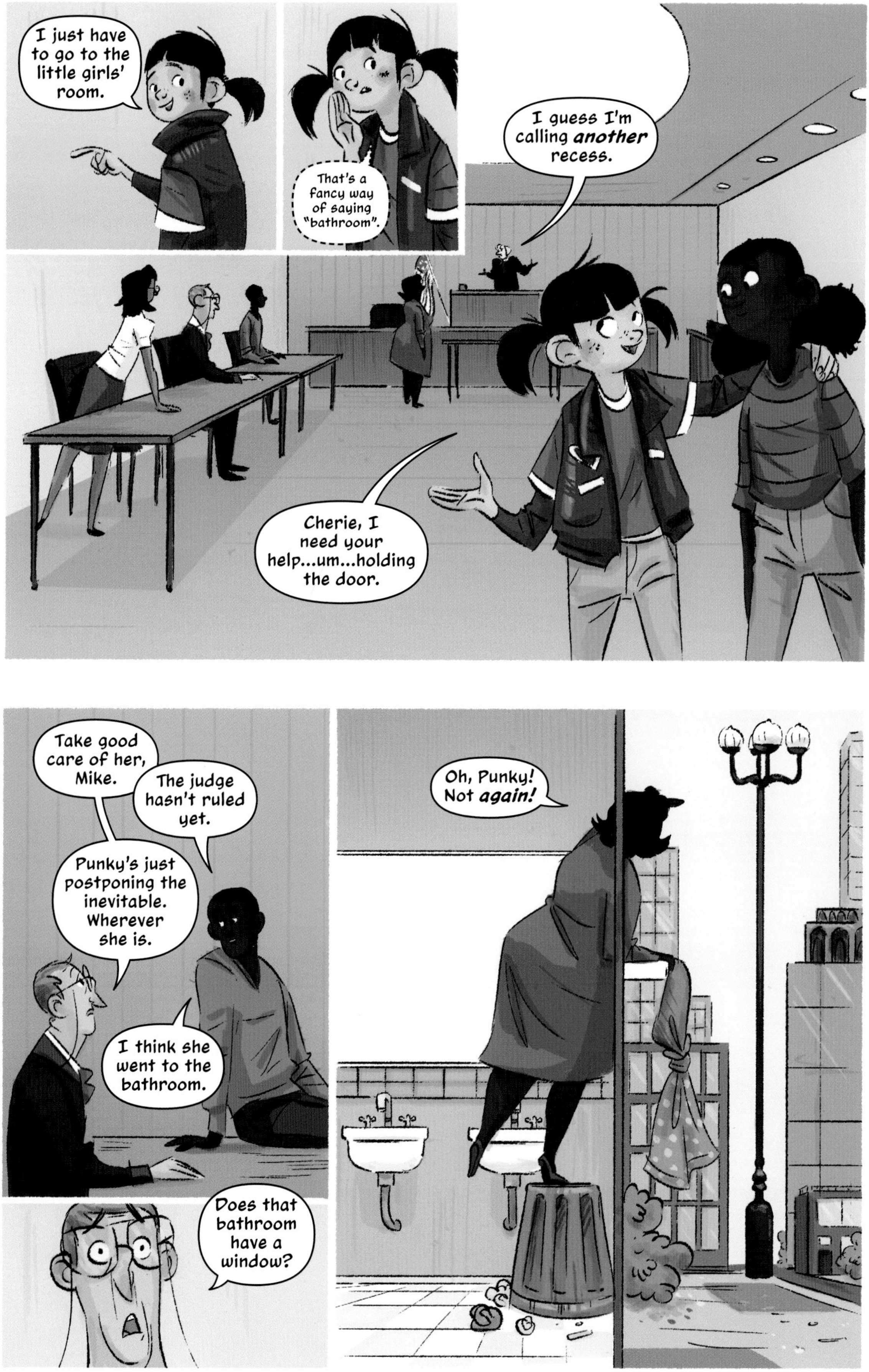

I just have to go to the little girls' room.
That's a fancy way of saying "bathroom".
I guess I'm calling **another** recess.
Cherie, I need your help...um...holding the door.
Take good care of her, Mike.
The judge hasn't ruled yet.
Punky's just postponing the inevitable. Wherever she is.
I think she went to the bathroom.
Does that bathroom have a window?
Oh, Punky! Not **again!**

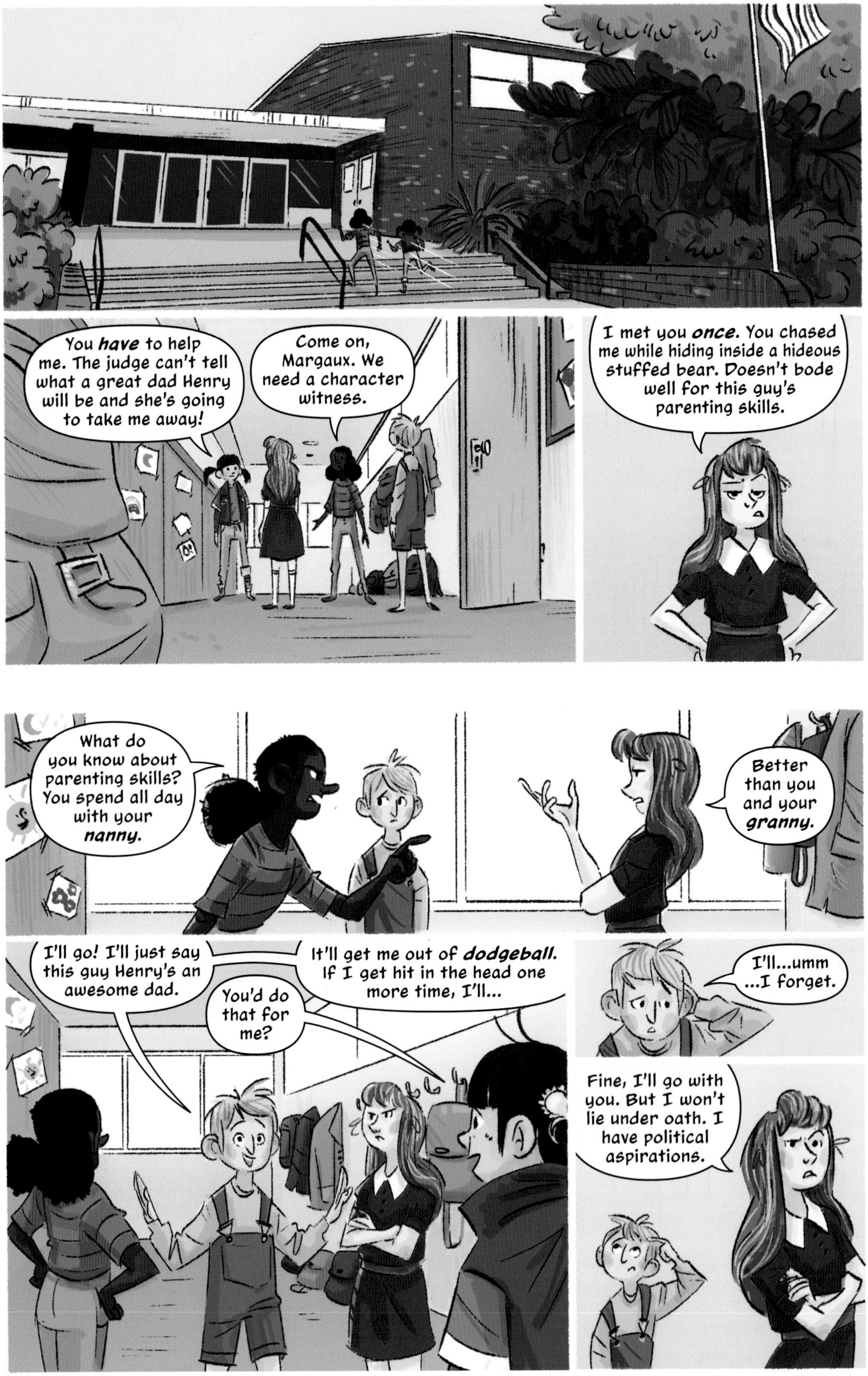
You *have* to help me. The judge can't tell what a great dad Henry will be and she's going to take me away!
Come on, Margaux. We need a character witness.
I met you *once*. You chased me while hiding inside a hideous stuffed bear. Doesn't bode well for this guy's parenting skills.
What do you know about parenting skills? You spend all day with your *nanny*.
Better than you and your *granny*.
I'll go! I'll just say this guy Henry's an awesome dad.
You'd do that for me?
It'll get me out of *dodgeball*. If I get hit in the head one more time, I'll...
I'll...umm ...I forget.
Fine, I'll go with you. But I won't lie under oath. I have political aspirations.

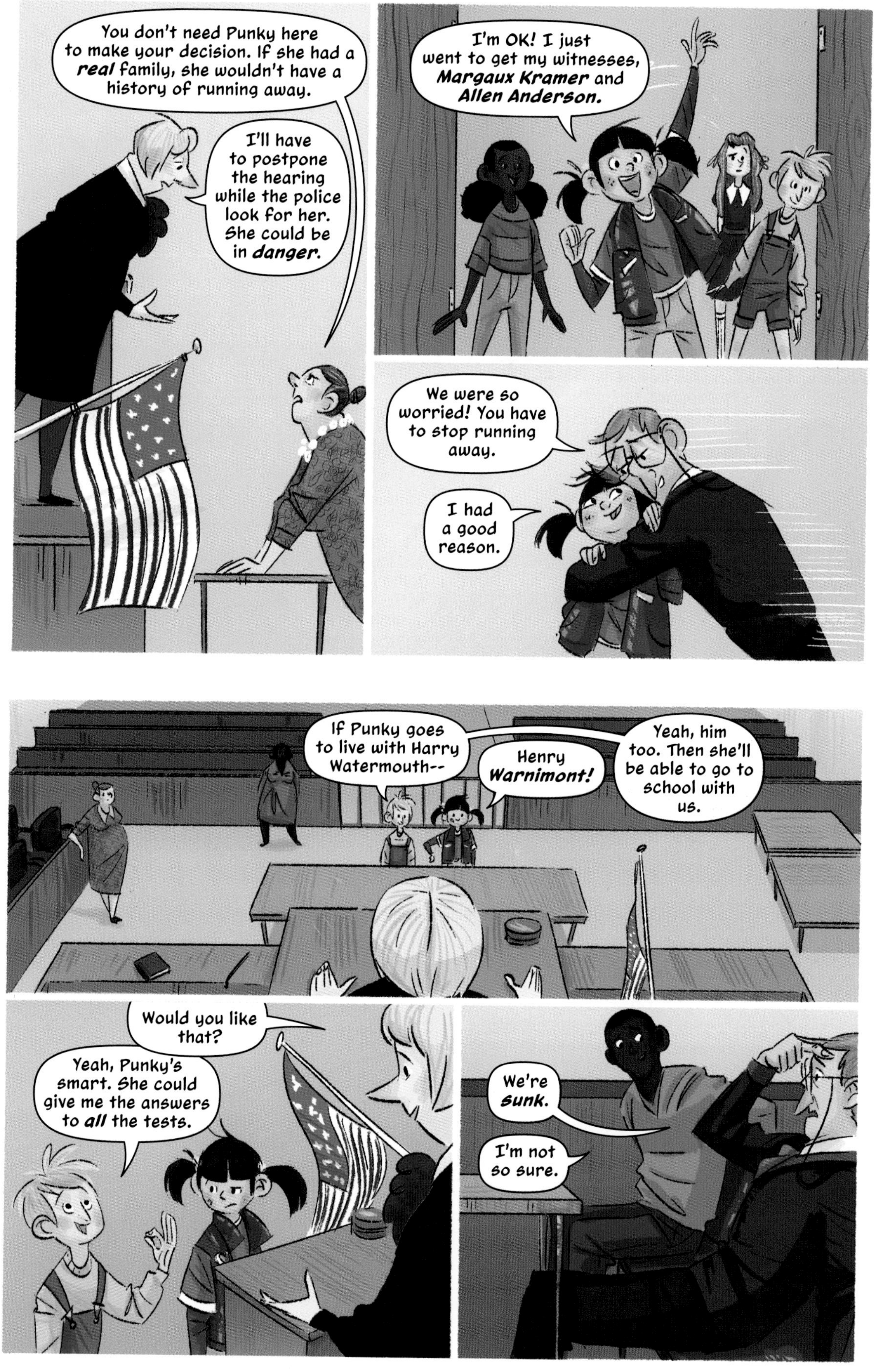
You don't need Punky here to make your decision. If she had a *real* family, she wouldn't have a history of running away.
I'll have to postpone the hearing while the police look for her. She could be in *danger*.
I'm OK! I just went to get my witnesses, *Margaux Kramer* and *Allen Anderson.*
We were so worried! You have to stop running away.
I had a good reason.
If Punky goes to live with Harry Watermouth--
Henry *Warnimont!*
Yeah, him too. Then she'll be able to go to school with us.
Would you like that?
Yeah, Punky's smart. She could give me the answers to *all* the tests.
We're *sunk*.
I'm not so sure.

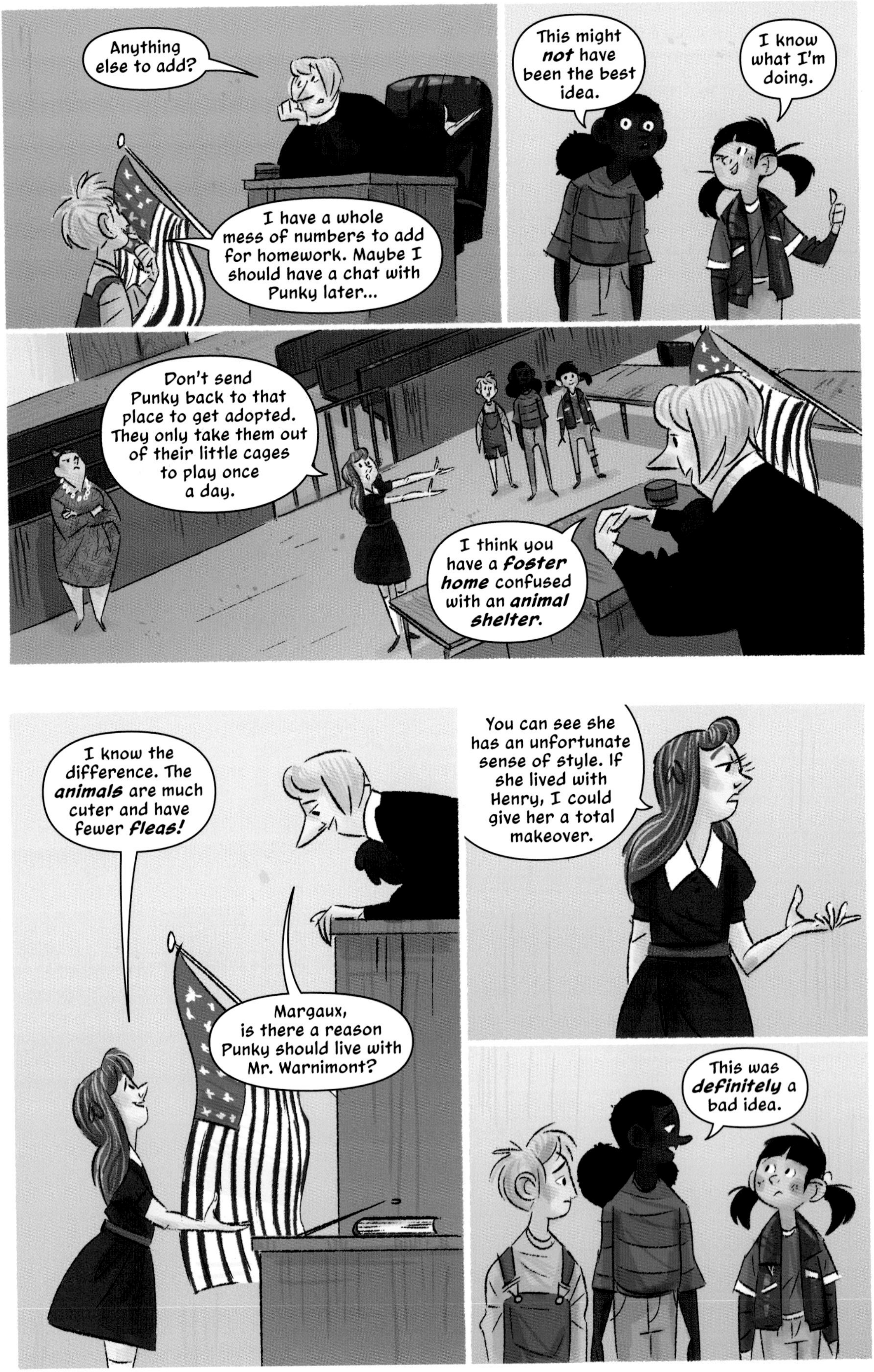
Anything else to add?
I have a whole mess of numbers to add for homework. Maybe I should have a chat with Punky later...
This might not have been the best idea.
I know what I'm doing.
Don't send Punky back to that place to get adopted. They only take them out of their little cages to play once a day.
I think you have a foster home confused with an animal shelter.
I know the difference. The animals are much cuter and have fewer fleas!
Margaux, is there a reason Punky should live with Mr. Warnimont?
You can see she has an unfortunate sense of style. If she lived with Henry, I could give her a total makeover.
This was definitely a bad idea.

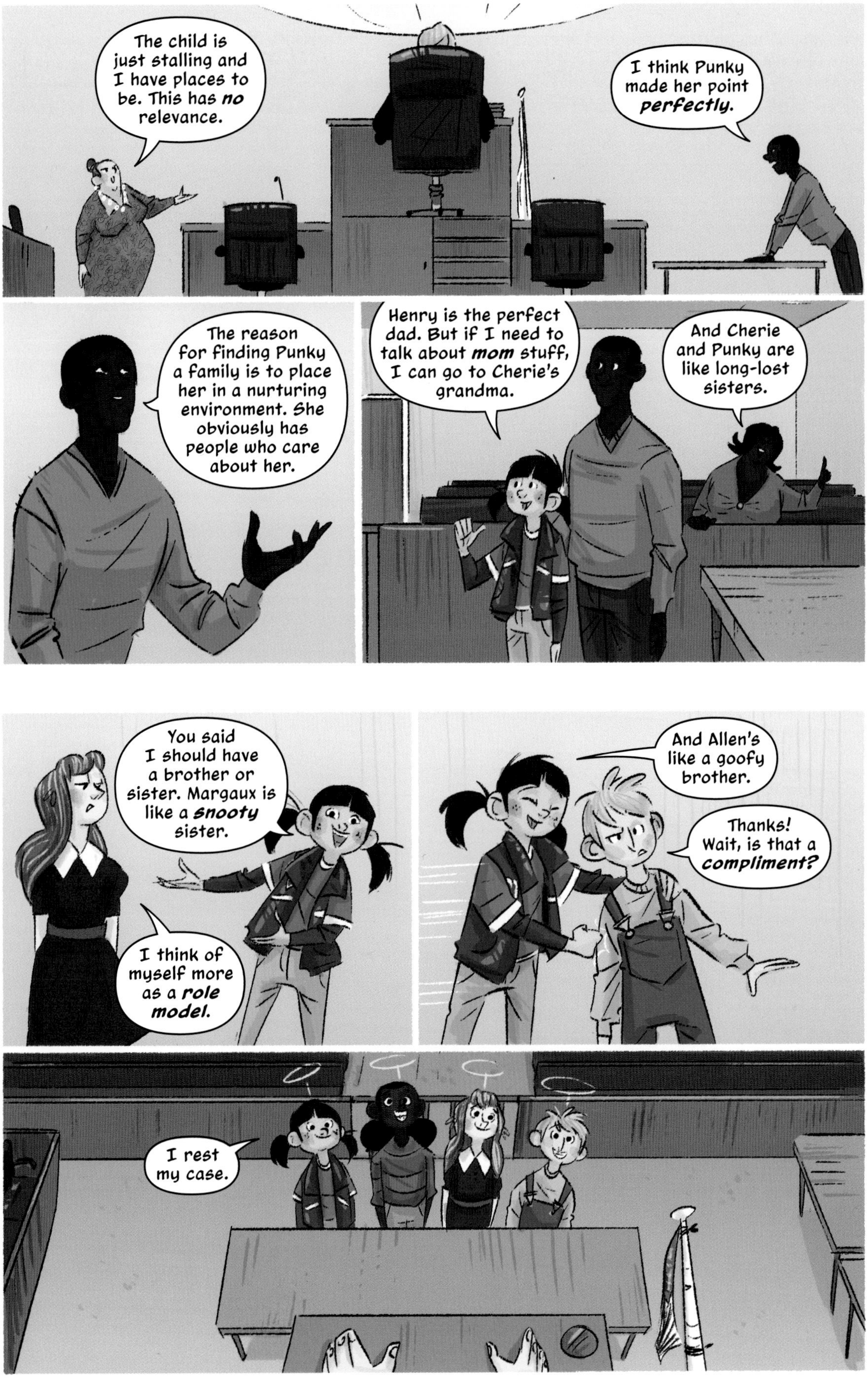
The child is just stalling and I have places to be. This has *no* relevance.
I think Punky made her point *perfectly*.
The reason for finding Punky a family is to place her in a nurturing environment. She obviously has people who care about her.
Henry is the perfect dad. But if I need to talk about *mom* stuff, I can go to Cherie's grandma.
And Cherie and Punky are like long-lost sisters.
You said I should have a brother or sister. Margaux is like a *snooty* sister.
I think of myself more as a *role model*.
And Allen's like a goofy brother.
Thanks! Wait, is that a *compliment?*
I rest my case.

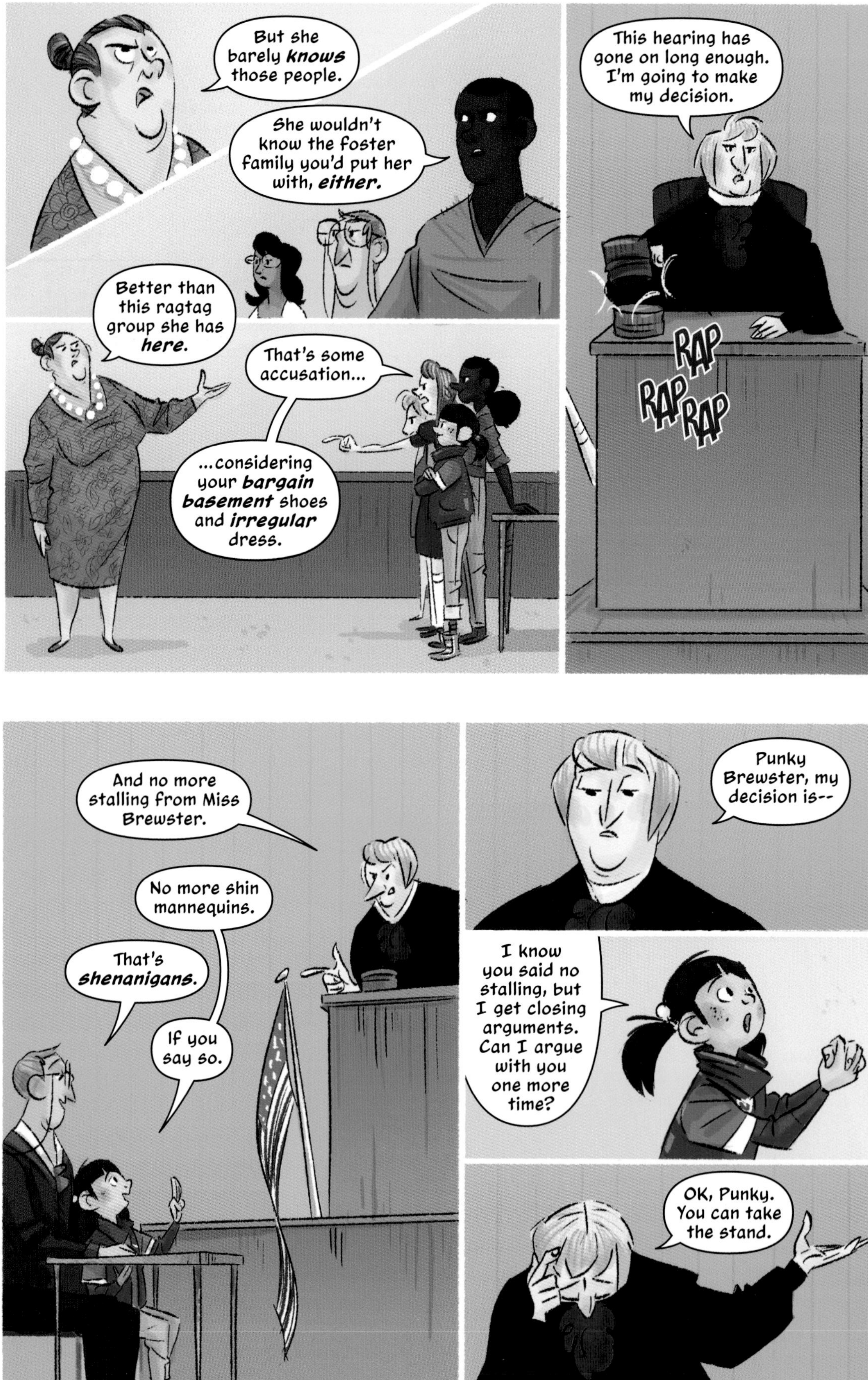
But she barely *knows* those people.
She wouldn't know the foster family you'd put her with, *either.*
This hearing has gone on long enough. I'm going to make my decision.
Better than this ragtag group she has *here.*
That's some accusation...
...considering your *bargain basement* shoes and *irregular* dress.
RAP
RAP
RAP
And no more stalling from Miss Brewster.
No more shin mannequins.
That's *shenanigans.*
If you say so.
Punky Brewster, my decision is--
I know you said no stalling, but I get closing arguments. Can I argue with you one more time?
OK, Punky. You can take the stand.

CHAPTER 8

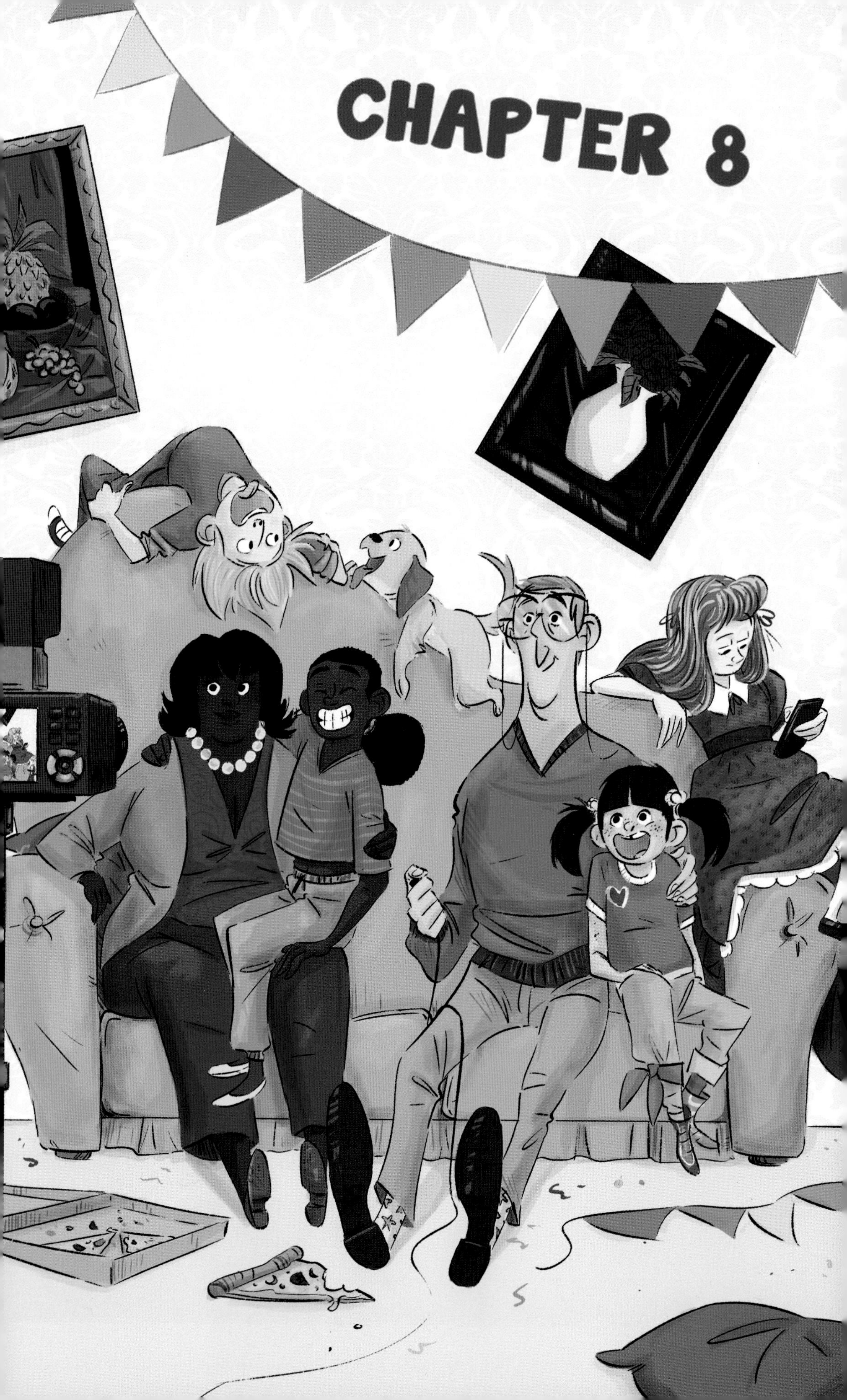

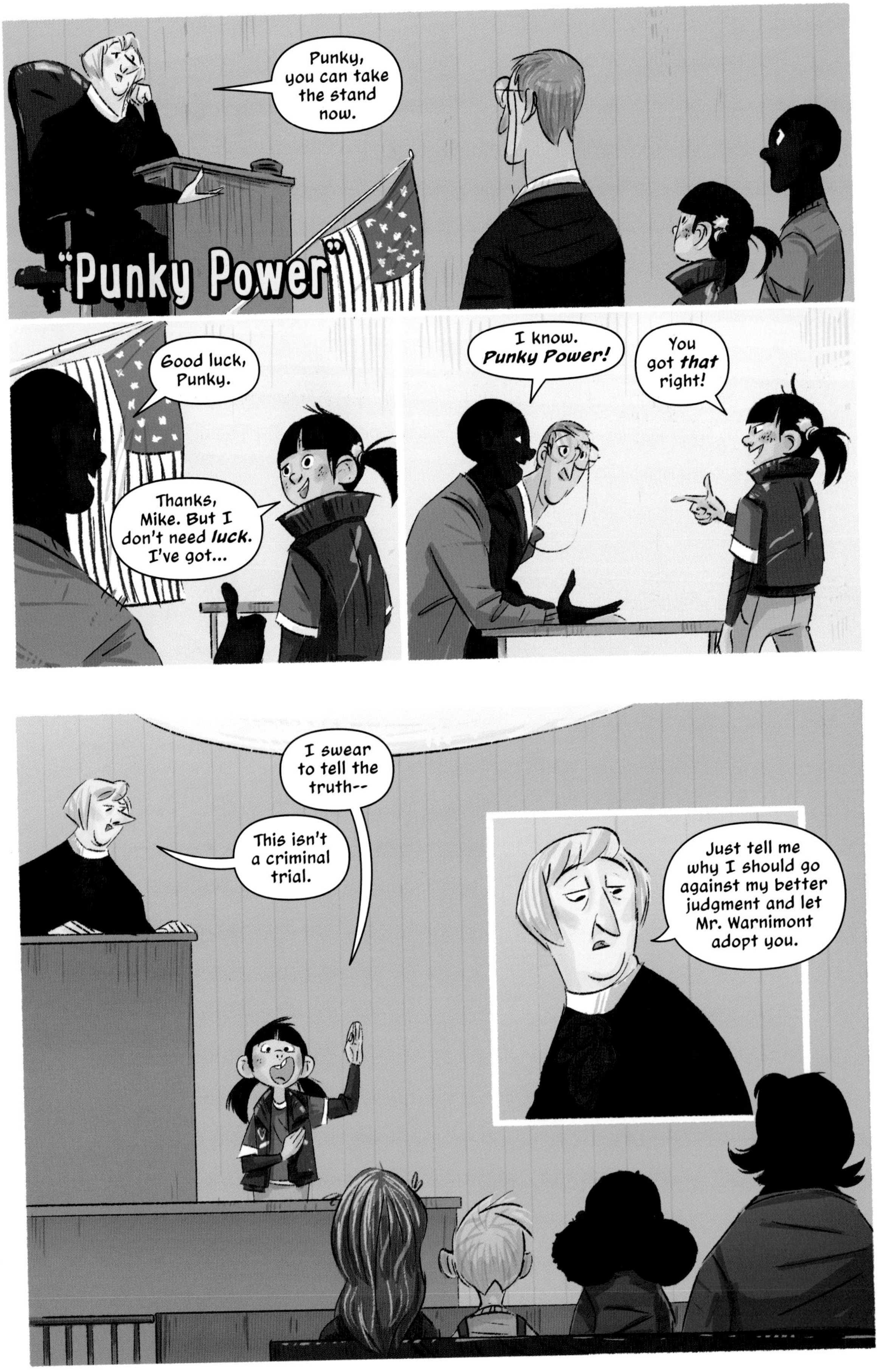
Punky, you can take the stand now.
"Punky Power"
Good luck, Punky.
Thanks, Mike. But I don't need *luck*. I've got...
I know. *Punky Power!*
You got *that* right!
I swear to tell the truth--
This isn't a criminal trial.
Just tell me why I should go against my better judgment and let Mr. Warnimont adopt you.

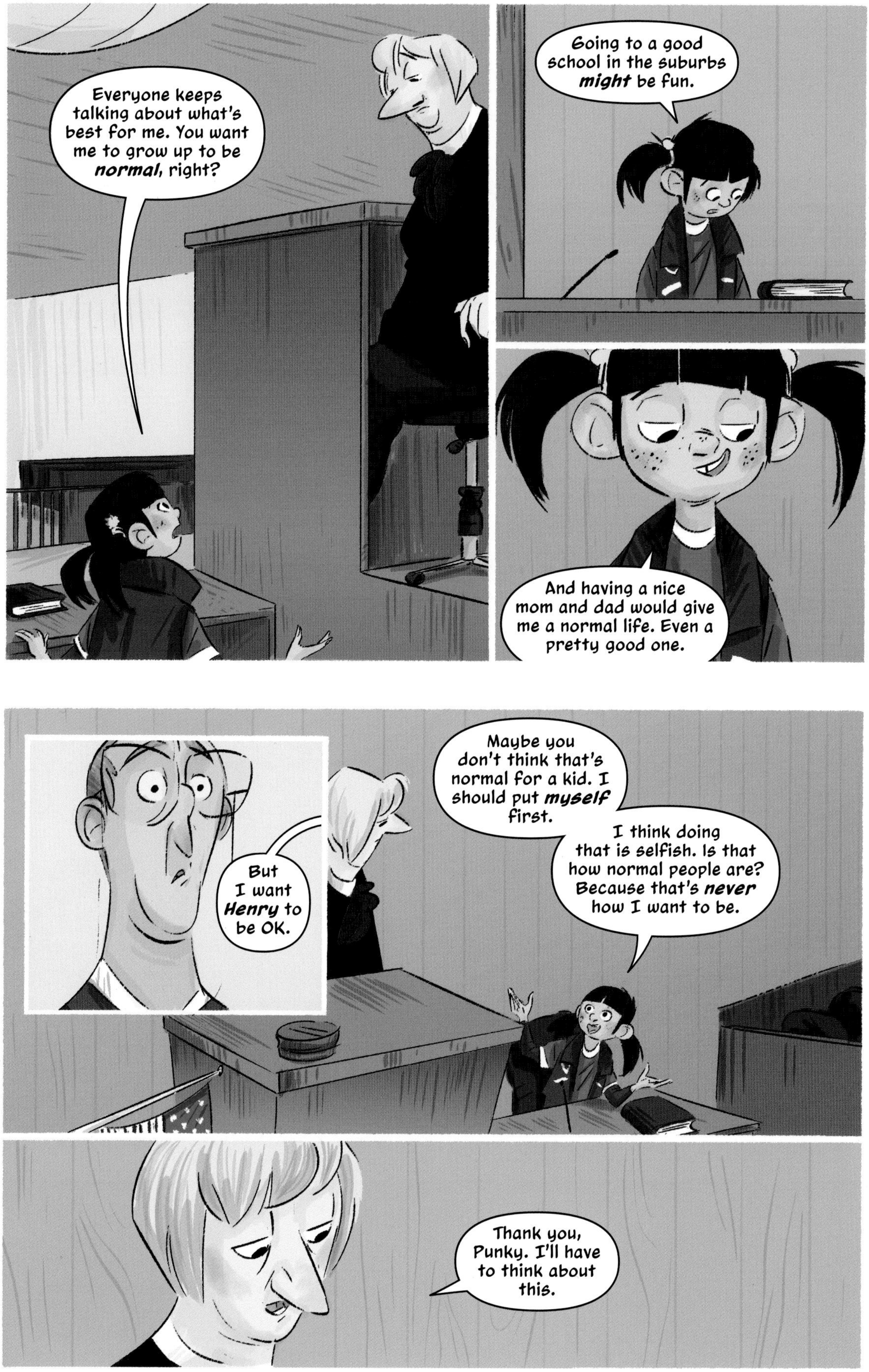
Everyone keeps talking about what's best for me. You want me to grow up to be *normal*, right?
Going to a good school in the suburbs *might* be fun.
And having a nice mom and dad would give me a normal life. Even a pretty good one.
Maybe you don't think that's normal for a kid. I should put *myself* first.
I think doing that is selfish. Is that how normal people are? Because that's *never* how I want to be.
But I want *Henry* to be OK.
Thank you, Punky. I'll have to think about this.

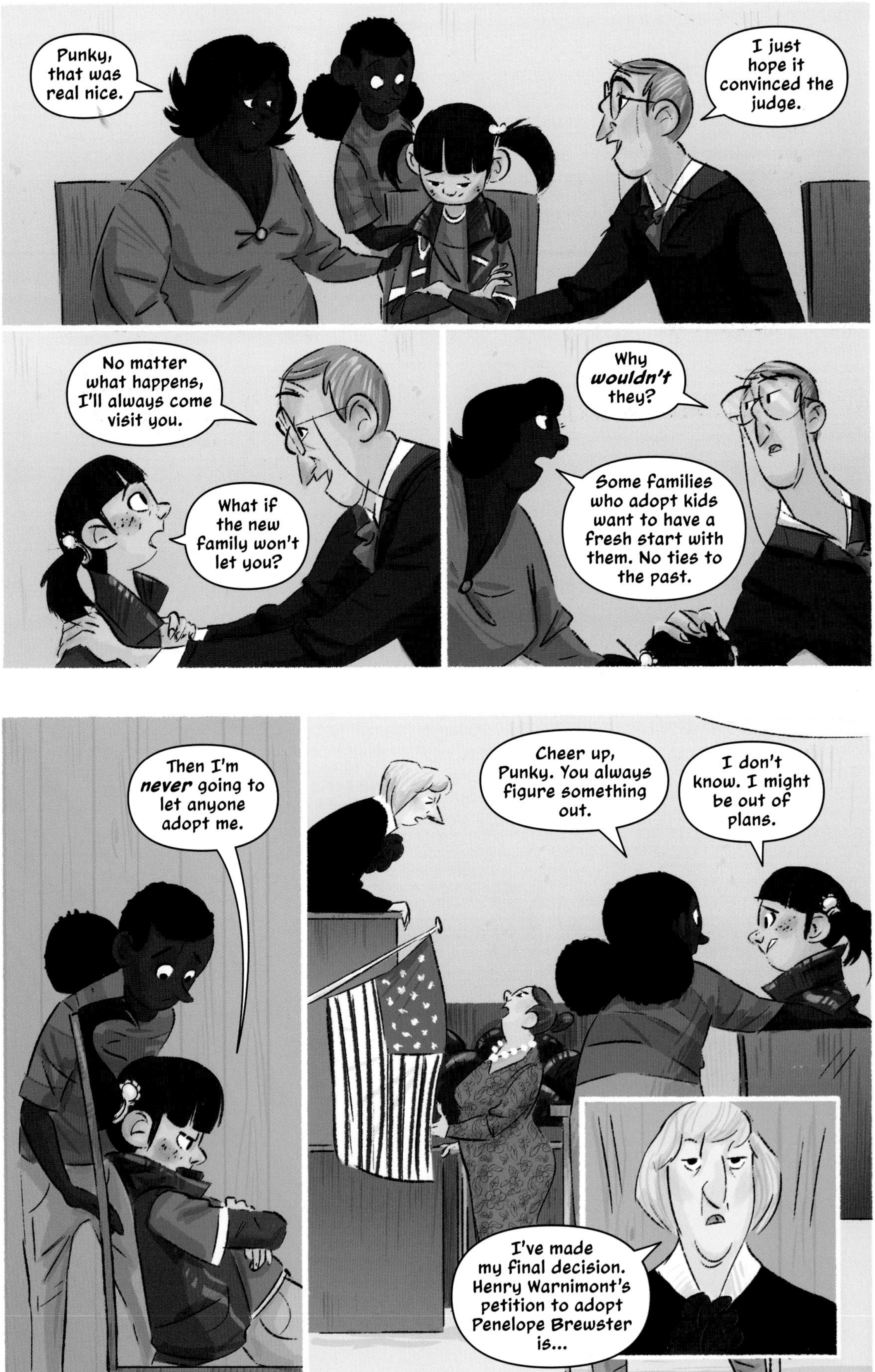
Punky, that was real nice.
I just hope it convinced the judge.
No matter what happens, I'll always come visit you.
What if the new family won't let you?
Why *wouldn't* they?
Some families who adopt kids want to have a fresh start with them. No ties to the past.
Then I'm *never* going to let anyone adopt me.
Cheer up, Punky. You always figure something out.
I don't know. I might be out of plans.
I've made my final decision. Henry Warnimont's petition to adopt Penelope Brewster is...

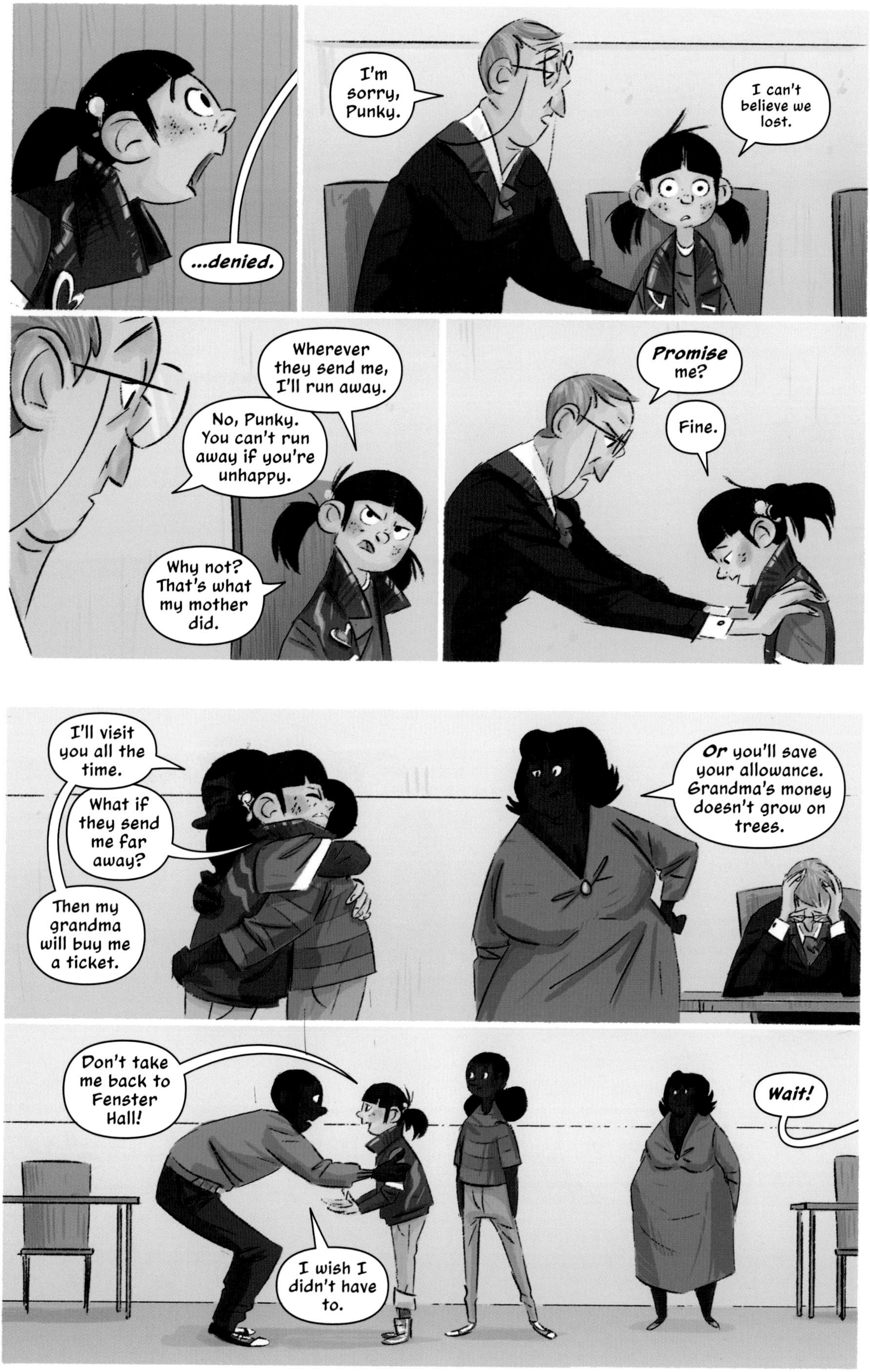
...denied.
I'm sorry, Punky.
I can't believe we lost.
Wherever they send me, I'll run away.
No, Punky. You can't run away if you're unhappy.
Why not? That's what my mother did.
Promise me?
Fine.
I'll visit you all the time.
What if they send me far away?
Then my grandma will buy me a ticket.
Or you'll save your allowance. Grandma's money doesn't grow on trees.
Don't take me back to Fenster Hall!
I wish I didn't have to.
Wait!

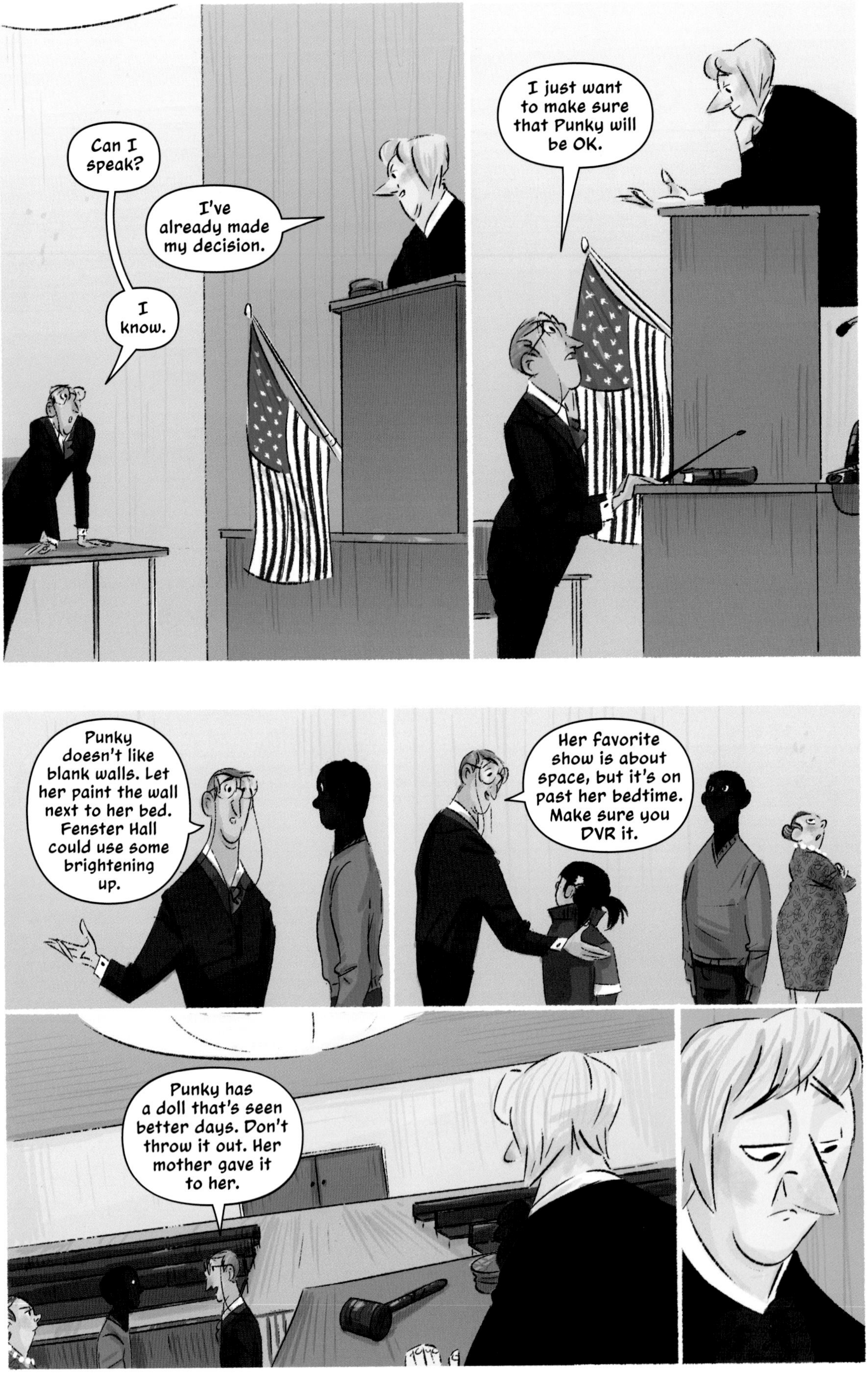
Can I speak?
I've already made my decision.
I know.
I just want to make sure that Punky will be OK.
Punky doesn't like blank walls. Let her paint the wall next to her bed. Fenster Hall could use some brightening up.
Her favorite show is about space, but it's on past her bedtime. Make sure you DVR it.
Punky has a doll that's seen better days. Don't throw it out. Her mother gave it to her.

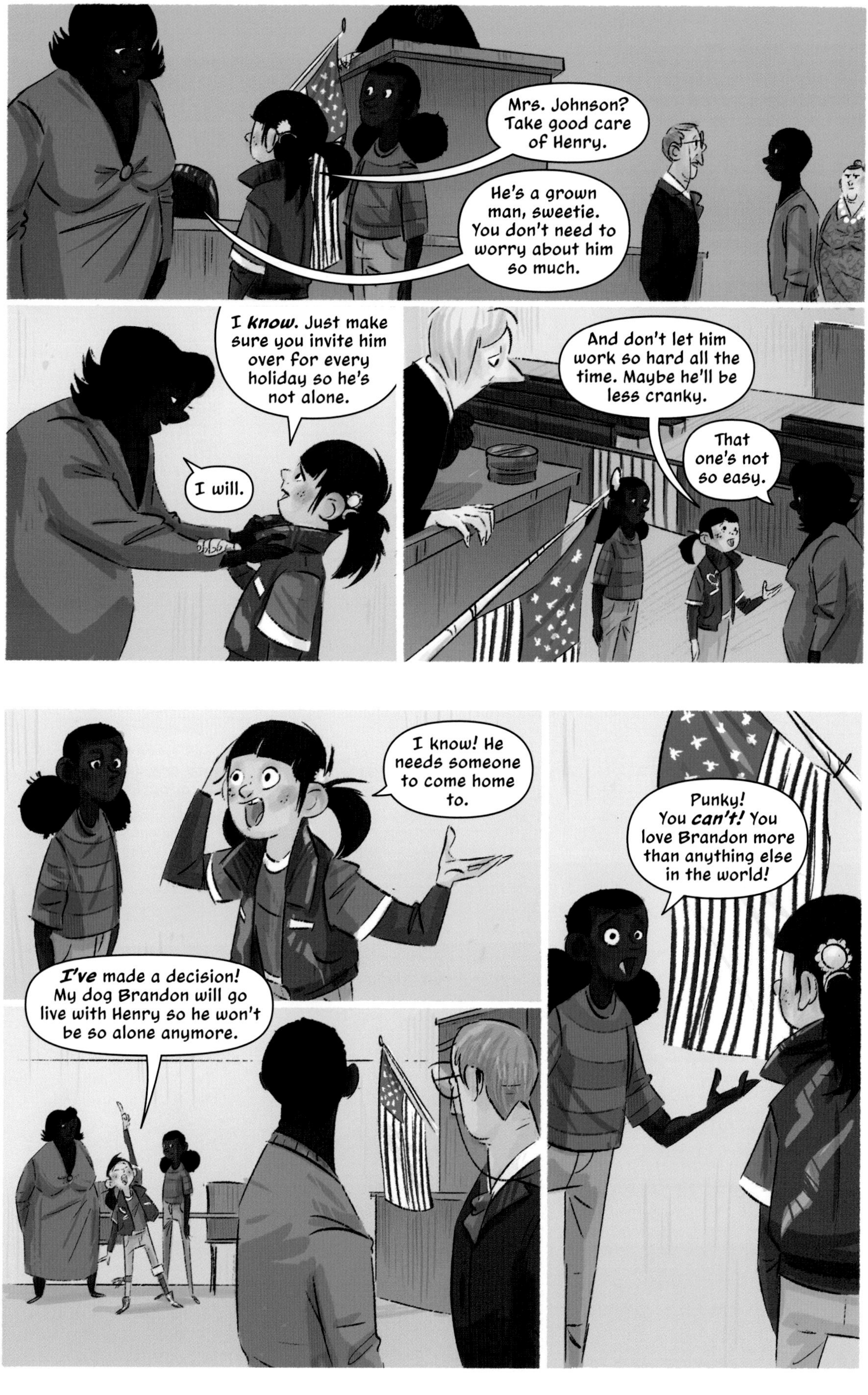
Mrs. Johnson? Take good care of Henry.
He's a grown man, sweetie. You don't need to worry about him so much.
I *know*. Just make sure you invite him over for every holiday so he's not alone.
I will.
And don't let him work so hard all the time. Maybe he'll be less cranky.
That one's not so easy.
I know! He needs someone to come home to.
I've made a decision! My dog Brandon will go live with Henry so he won't be so alone anymore.
Punky! You *can't!* You love Brandon more than anything else in the world!

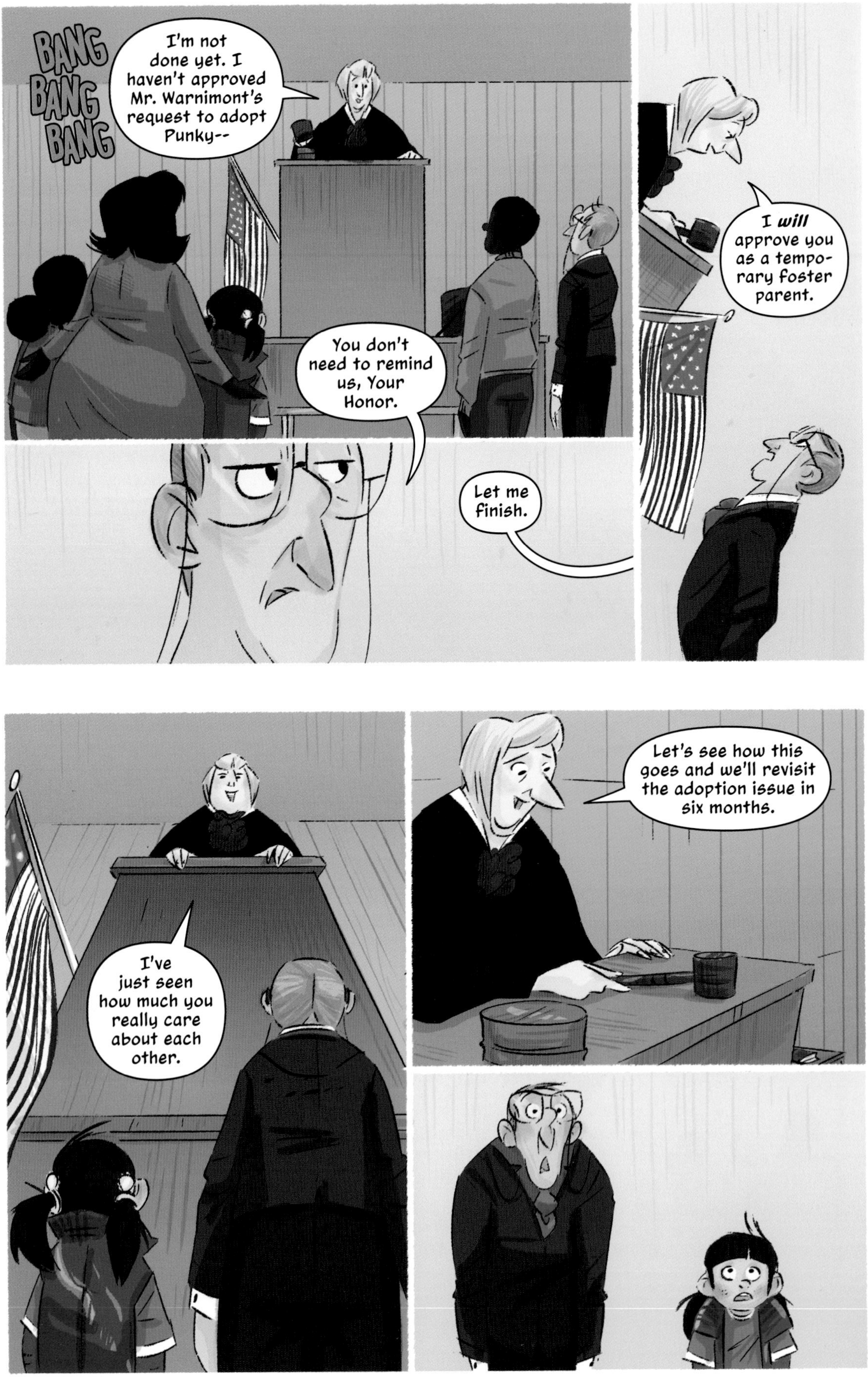
BANG BANG BANG
I'm not done yet. I haven't approved Mr. Warnimont's request to adopt Punky--
You don't need to remind us, Your Honor.
Let me finish.
I *will* approve you as a temporary foster parent.
I've just seen how much you really care about each other.
Let's see how this goes and we'll revisit the adoption issue in six months.

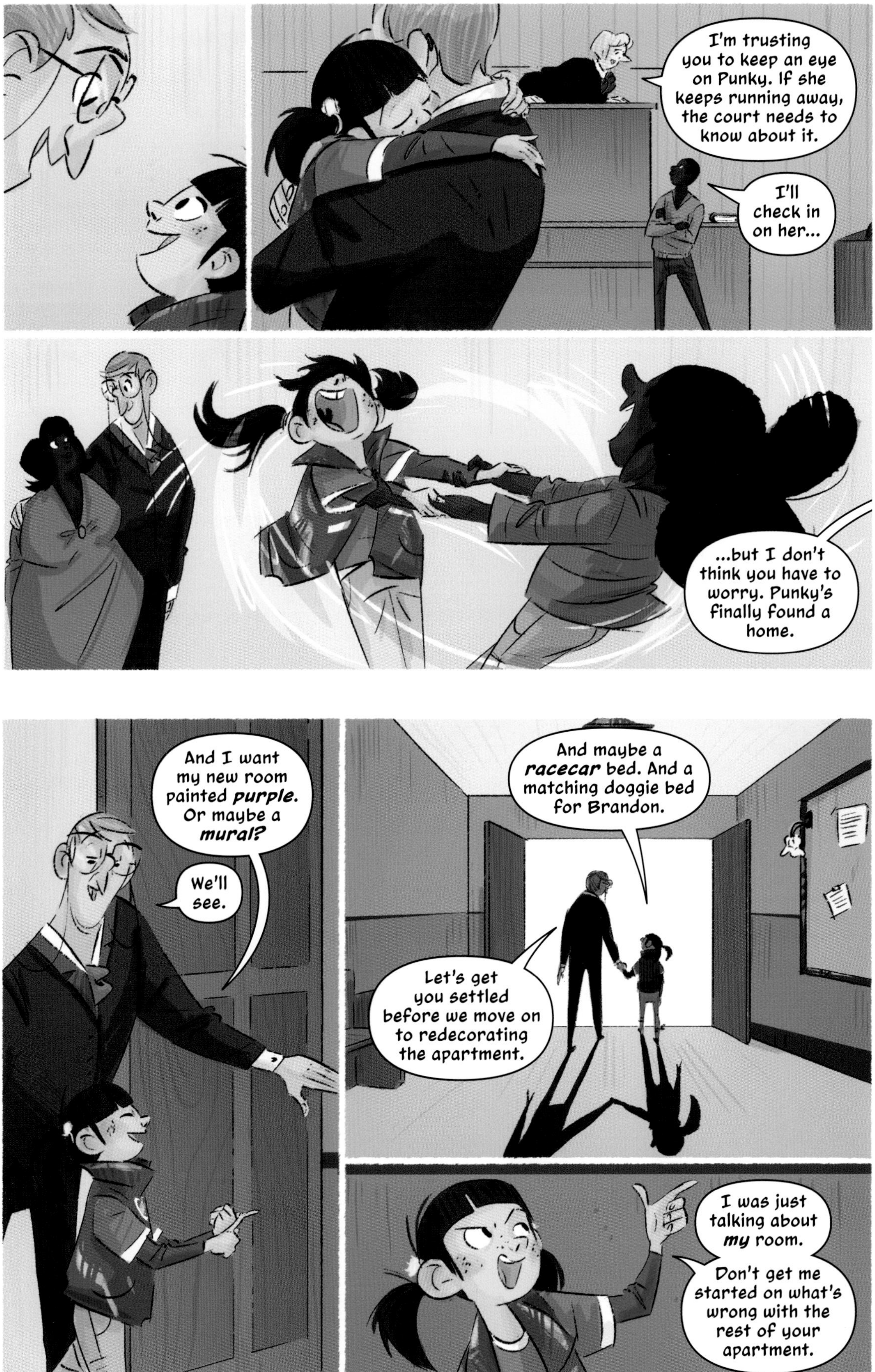
I'm trusting you to keep an eye on Punky. If she keeps running away, the court needs to know about it.
I'll check in on her...
...but I don't think you have to worry. Punky's finally found a home.
And I want my new room painted *purple*. Or maybe a *mural?*
We'll see.
And maybe a *racecar* bed. And a matching doggie bed for Brandon.
Let's get you settled before we move on to redecorating the apartment.
I was just talking about *my* room.
Don't get me started on what's wrong with the rest of your apartment.

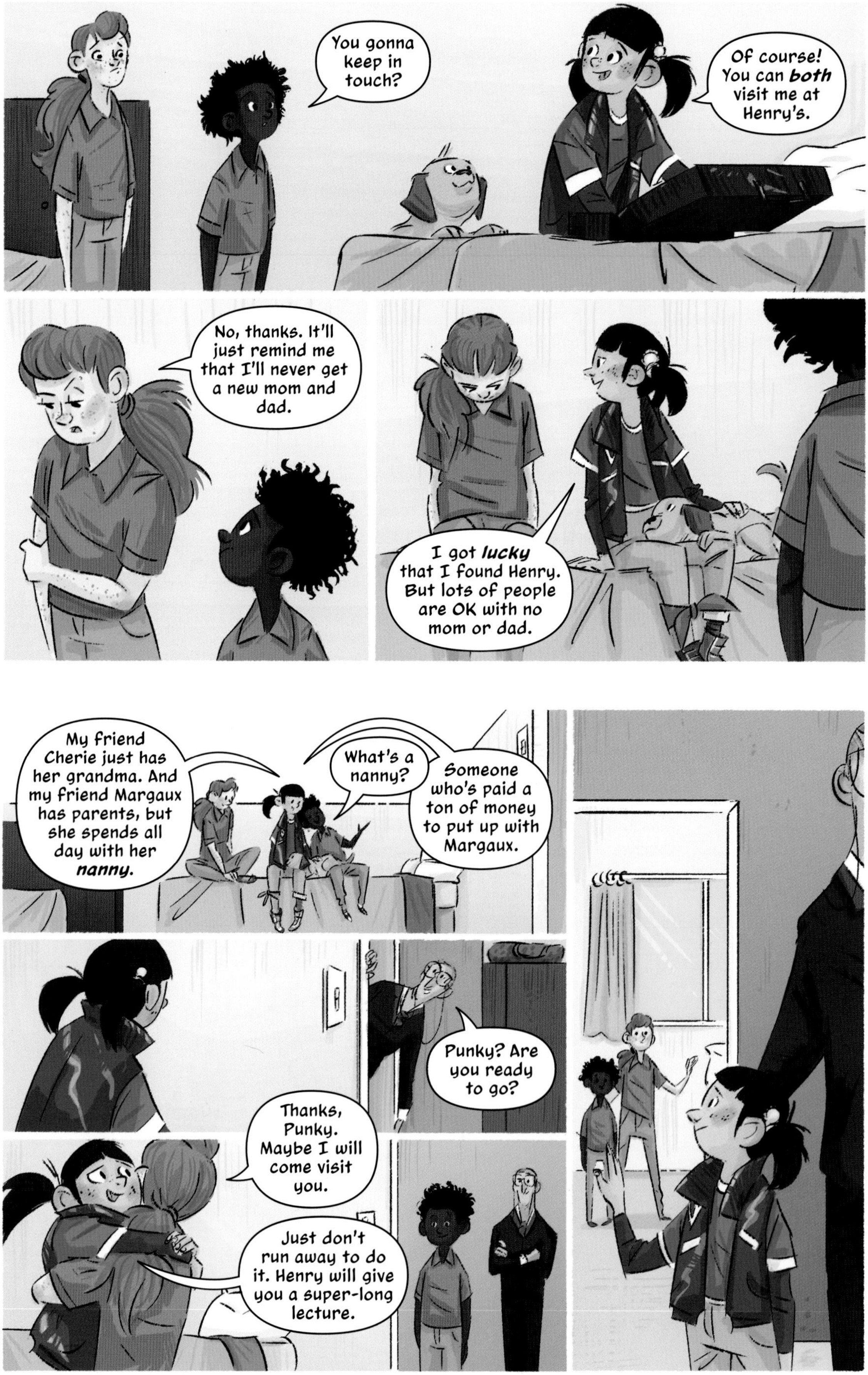

You gonna keep in touch?
Of course! You can *both* visit me at Henry's.
No, thanks. It'll just remind me that I'll never get a new mom and dad.
I got *lucky* that I found Henry. But lots of people are OK with no mom or dad.
My friend Cherie just has her grandma. And my friend Margaux has parents, but she spends all day with her *nanny*.
What's a nanny?
Someone who's paid a ton of money to put up with Margaux.
Punky? Are you ready to go?
Thanks, Punky. Maybe I will come visit you.
Just don't run away to do it. Henry will give you a super-long lecture.

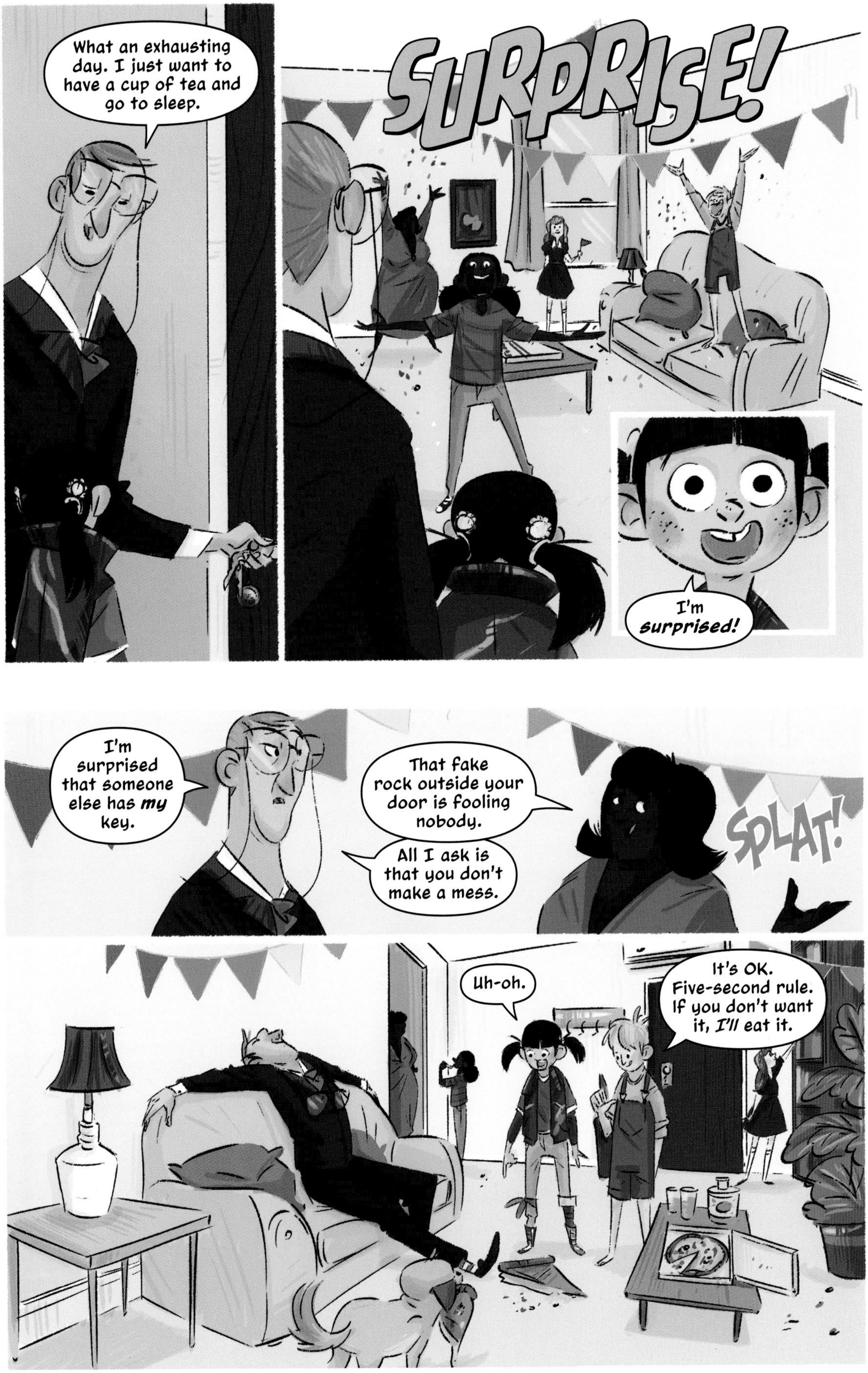
What an exhausting day. I just want to have a cup of tea and go to sleep.
SURPRISE!
I'm *surprised!*
I'm surprised that someone else has ***my*** key.
That fake rock outside your door is fooling nobody.
All I ask is that you don't make a mess.
SPLAT!
Uh-oh.
It's OK. Five-second rule. If you don't want it, *I'll* eat it.

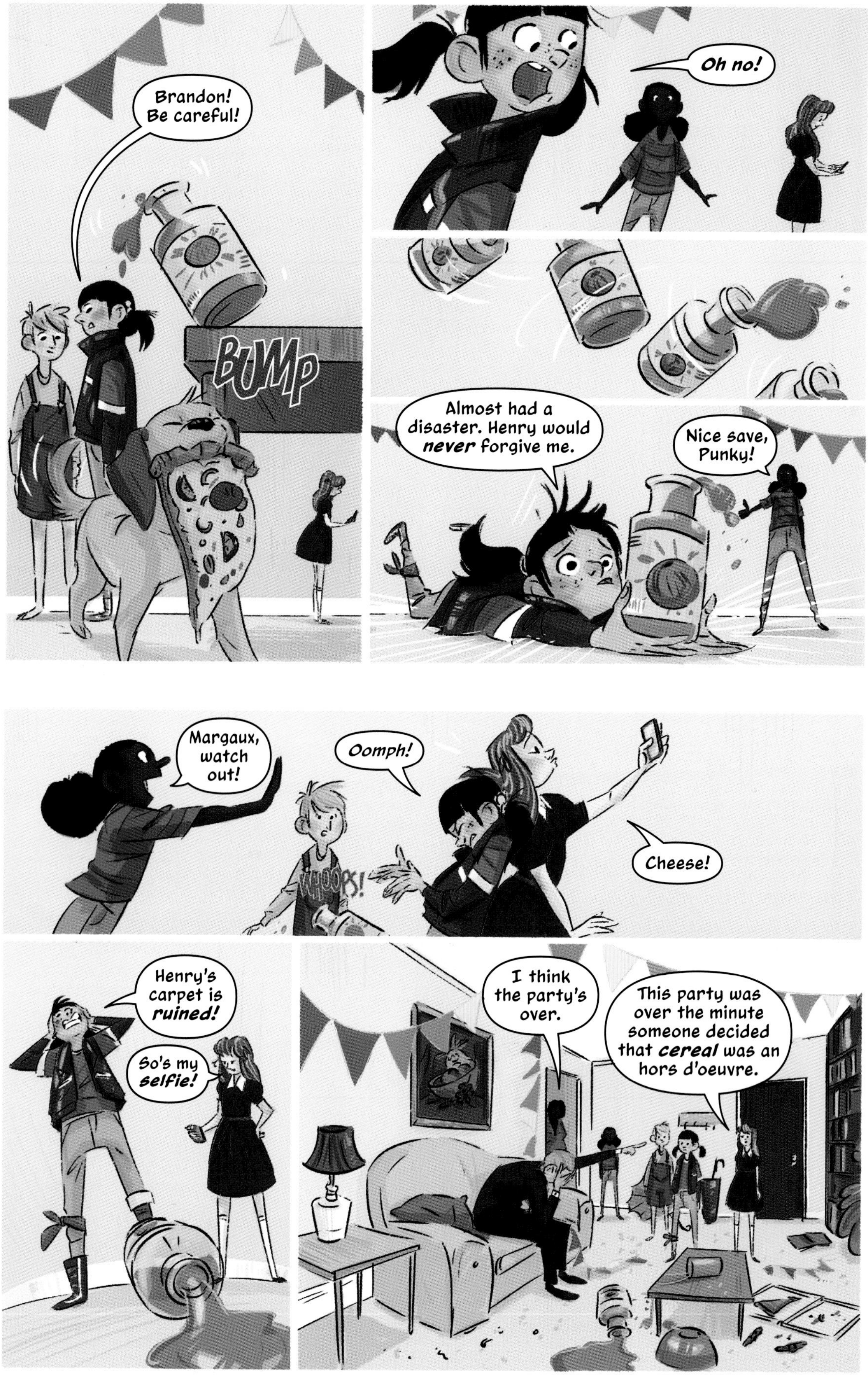
Brandon! Be careful!
BUMP
Oh no!
Almost had a disaster. Henry would never forgive me.
Nice save, Punky!
Margaux, watch out!
Oomph!
WHOOPS!
Cheese!
Henry's carpet is ruined!
So's my selfie!
I think the party's over.
This party was over the minute someone decided that cereal was an hors d'oeuvre.

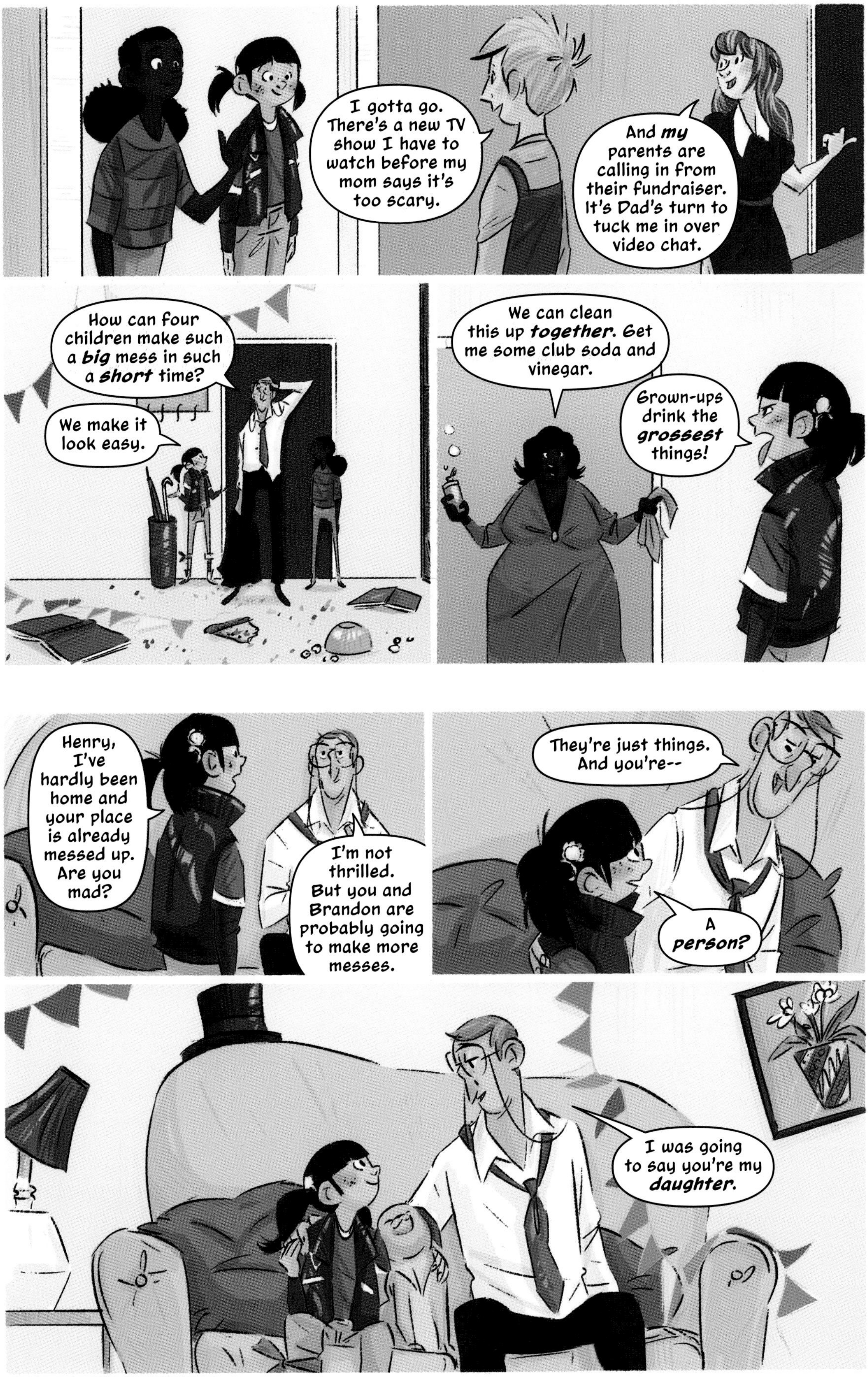

I gotta go. There's a new TV show I have to watch before my mom says it's too scary.
And *my* parents are calling in from their fundraiser. It's Dad's turn to tuck me in over video chat.
How can four children make such a *big* mess in such a *short* time?
We make it look easy.
We can clean this up *together*. Get me some club soda and vinegar.
Grown-ups drink the *grossest* things!
Henry, I've hardly been home and your place is already messed up. Are you mad?
I'm not thrilled. But you and Brandon are probably going to make more messes.
They're just things. And you're--
A *person?*
I was going to say you're my *daughter*.

BEHIND THE SCENES!

Original character designs from artist Lesley Vamos

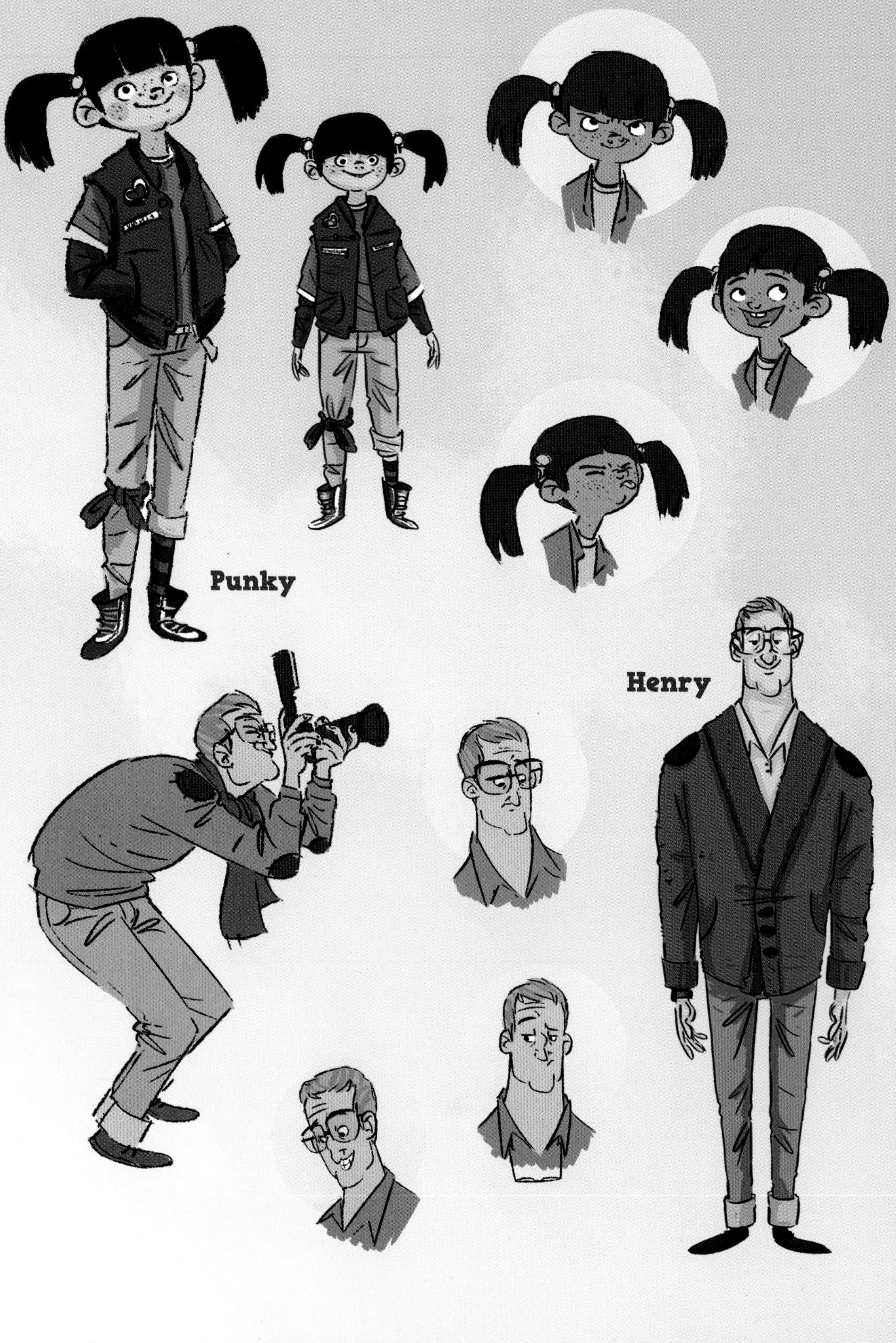
Punky
Henry

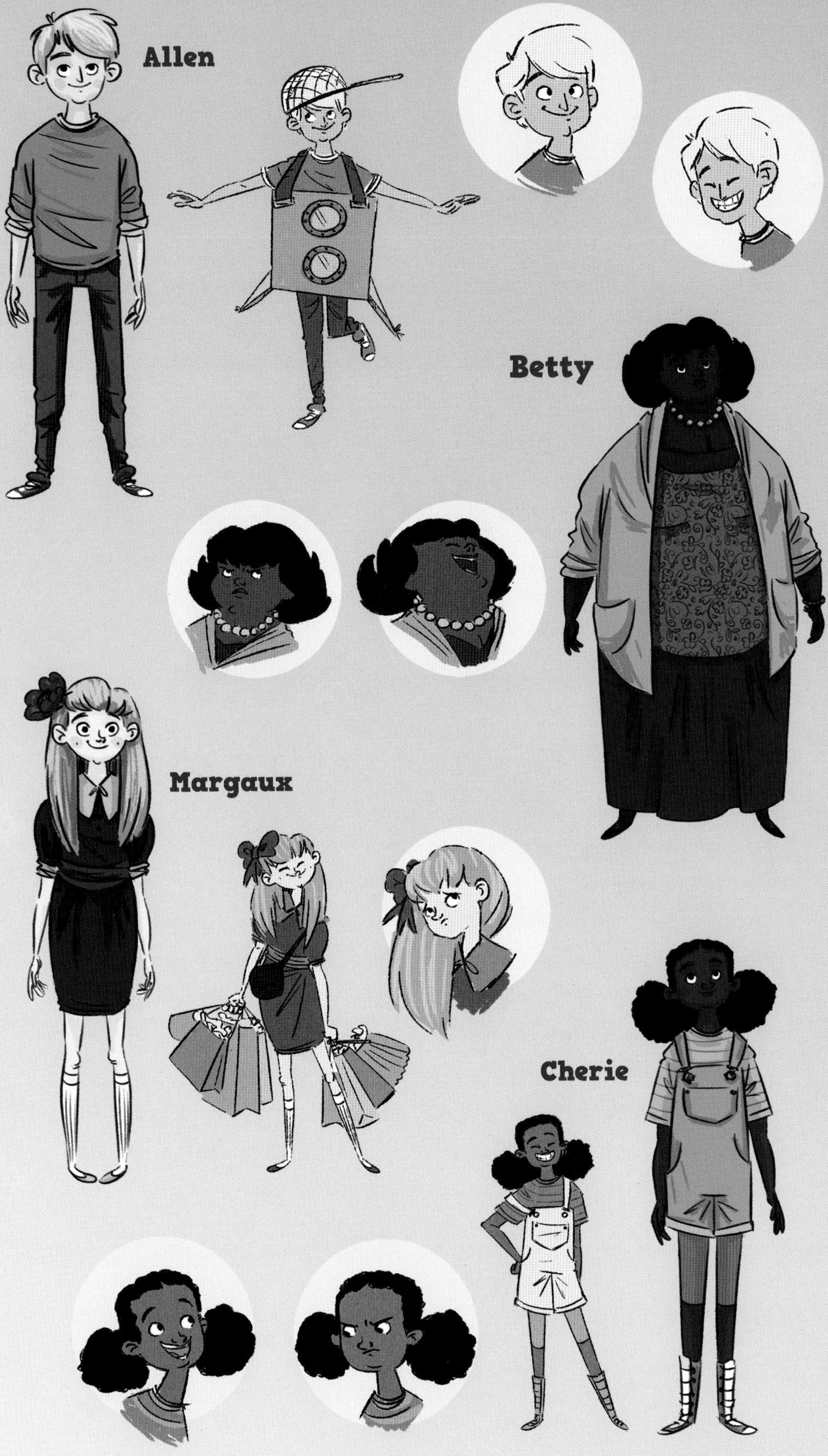
Allen
Betty
Margaux
Cherie

JOELLE SELLNER began her career as an advertising copywriter, writing award-winning print, radio, and television ads for clients such as Lexus Automobiles, In-N-Out Burger, Kleenex Tissues and Mattel. While working full-time, Joelle also began writing animation, starting with an animated series featuring the Olsen Twins: *Mary-Kate and Ashley in Action*. This led to writing assignments on *Teen Titans*, *Jackie Chan Adventures*, *Shin Chan*, *Secret Saturdays*, *Marvel's Avengers: Earth's Mightiest Heroes*, and *Ben 10*. Joelle has written comics for IDW, DC and Marvel in addition to her work on *Saved by the Bell*, *Punky Brewster*, *Wonderous*, and the upcoming YA title *MER* for Lion Forge Comics.

writtenbyjoelle.com

Having grown up in Australia, **LESLEY VAMOS** studied at the college of Fine Arts, receiving a Distinction and Animation Honor in a Bachelor of Digital media. Since learning how to hold a pencil (albeit incorrectly), the only time she puts it down is when she has to eat—and even then her food can be the victim of artistic subjection (camp mates will forever remember the time she attempted to carve the statue of David out of her mashed potatoes). Since graduating COFA Vamos has spent her time traveling, doodling, meeting friends with the same enthusiasm for creative expression and communication as well as getting to know and experience as many facets of the creative industry she can.

strippeddesigns.com